Readers lo...
by C...

Hell & High W...

"This book has it all, romance, action and mystery. It was a thrill ride from the first word until the very end."
—Love Bytes

Blood & Thunder

"The attention to detail, world building, and character development is some of the best that I've read in years."
—MM Good Book Reviews

Rack & Ruin

"A roller-coaster ride of epic proportions, *Rack & Ruin* is a breathtaking and emotional journey that you simply mustn't miss."
—Carly's Book Reviews

Rise & Fall

"…one of the best books I've read in a long time."
—It's About The Book

Against the Grain

"Every time I read a new THIRDS book I think it can't get any better… But it does!"
—Prism Book Alliance

Catch a Tiger by the Tail

"I love the THIRDS series. It's fun, action-packed, and hella sexy."

—Just Love: Romance Novel Reviews

Smoke & Mirrors

"If you aren't reading this series, well, you absolutely should be. And I, for one, have no qualms about recommending it to you."

Joyfully Jay

Thick & Thin

"This series has always amazed me and the amazement continued when reading this one…"

—Three Books Over the Rainbow

Darkest Hour Before Dawn

"The briskly paced novel is packed with exciting action, steamy sex scenes, melodramatic passion, and tender moments of romance."

—Foreword Reviews

Gummy Bears & Grenades

"*Gummy Bears & Grenades* was pure fun."

—Birdie Bookworm

By Charlie Cochet

Between the Devil and the Pacific Blue
Beware of Geeks Bearing Gifts
Healing Hunter's Heart
Love in Retrograde
A Rose by Any Other Name

THE AUSPICIOUS TROUBLES OF LOVE
The Auspicious Troubles of Chance
The Impetuous Afflictions of Jonathan Wolfe

DREAMSPUN DESIRES
#7 – Forgive and Forget
#41 – Finding Mr. Wrong

NORTH POLE CITY TALES
Mending Noel
The Heart of Frost
Vixen's Valor
Loving Blitz
Disarming Donner
The King's Courage
North Pole City Tales (Print Anthology)

SOLDATI HEARTS
The Soldati Prince
The Foxling Soldati

Published by Dreamspinner Press
www.dreamspinnerpress.com

By CHARLIE COCHET (Continued)

THIRDS
Hell & High Water
Blood & Thunder
Rack & Ruin
Rise & Fall
Against the Grain
Catch a Tiger by the Tail
Smoke & Mirrors
Thick & Thin
Darkest Hour Before Dawn
Gummy Bears & Grenades
Tried & True
THIRDS Beyond the Books Volume 1
THIRDS Beyond the Books Volume 2
Thick & Thin and Gummy Bears & Grenades
(Print Anthology)

Published by DREAMSPINNER PRESS
www.dreamspinnerpress.com

HELL &HIGH WATER

CHARLIE COCHET

Published by
DREAMSPINNER PRESS

5032 Capital Circle SW, Suite 2, PMB# 279,
Tallahassee, FL 32305-7886 USA
www.dreamspinnerpress.com

This is a work of fiction. Names, characters, places, and incidents either
are the product of author imagination or are used fictitiously, and any
resemblance to actual persons, living or dead, business establishments,
events, or locales is entirely coincidental.

Hell & High Water
© 2014, 2018 Charlie Cochet.

Cover Art
© 2014 L.C. Chase.
http://www.lcchase.com
Cover content is for illustrative purposes only and any person depicted on
the cover is a model.

Mass Market Paperback ISBN: 978-1-64108-081-1
Trade Paperback ISBN: 978-1-63216-011-9
Digital ISBN: 978-1-63216-012-6
Library of Congress Control Number: 2014939167
Mass Market Paperback published March 2018
v. 1.0

Printed in the United States of America
∞
This paper meets the requirements of
ANSI/NISO Z39.48-1992 (Permanence of Paper).

Acknowledgments

A BIG thank-you to Dreamspinner Press for believing in me and my stories, for all your hard work, your guidance, and for helping me stay sane by allowing me to get the stories out of my head and into the world. Thank you for giving me the chance to follow my dreams.

To my amazing beta readers for helping whip these bad boys into shape. The whip was optional, but I know how much you like to show these fellas you mean business. To Barb, Melanie, Nikyta, and Valerie, thank you.

To my wonderful readers who continue to pick up my books, show their love, and ask for more. Where would my stories and I be without you? Thank you.

And of course a big thanks to my family, friends, and fellow authors. You're always there with a kind word, comments that brighten my day, warm hugs, and amazing support.

Prologue

DURING THE Vietnam War, the use of lethal biological warfare led to the spread of the Melanoe virus, infecting millions worldwide and causing the deaths of hundreds of thousands. Although no country would take credit for releasing the virus, the world's top scientists came together to create a cure. The vaccine known as Eppione.8 used strains from animals found to be immune to the virus, but one year after distribution, the course of human history was forever changed. A dormant mutation within the virus was activated by the vaccine, resulting in the altering of human DNA, and giving birth to a new species: Therians.

When the first infected Humans began changing in the late seventies, some didn't survive. Their Human bodies were unprepared for the shift. Others died of cancer or infections due to weakened immune systems, while others vanished. Rumors ran rampant about governments trying to clean up their mess. When it was clear the "problem" wasn't going to go away, the US government tried to regain control of the masses, creating the Therian database and quickly passing new laws that would force all surviving Therians to register and get marked, supposedly for their own safety and that of their fellow Human citizens.

The government had been treating the first wave of Therians as a side effect of the war, one that would eventually die out. Then, in 1976, scientists discovered what was really happening. The first generation of purebred Therians had been born. The mutation had perfected itself. Solidified, inside these First Generations. Suddenly there was an advanced new species and along with it, a whole new set of fears.

In an attempt to restore social order, the US government quickly put new regulations and laws into place, along with a Therian branch of government. In 1999, Human and Therian legislators launched the Therian Human Intelligence Recon Defense Squadron, a.k.a. the THIRDS, an elite military-funded agency comprised of an equal number of Human and Therian agents and intended to uphold the law for all its citizens without prejudice.

As long as Humanity continued to repeat the mistakes of the past, organizations like the THIRDS would be needed to ensure Humanity had a future, even if they had to stumble along the way to get there.

Chapter 1

FUCK. MY. Life.

Dex closed his eyes, wishing this was nothing more than some freakishly vivid dream where any moment now he would wake up and everything would go back to the way it was. Of course, when he opened his eyes, nothing changed. He splashed more water on his face in an effort to ease the tension, but it didn't help. Not that he'd been expecting it to. After wiping the excess water from his face, he paused to glare at the man in the mirror. The guy staring back at him looked like shit, pale with reddish-brown circles under his eyes that made him look as if he'd either been crying or using crack. There were definitely a hell of a lot of sleepless nights involved. Dex didn't like the guy in the mirror. What an asshole.

"Are they out there?" His voice came out rough, as if waking from sleep—deep or otherwise—had been out of his reach for some time.

A hand landed on his shoulder, offering a sympathetic squeeze. "Yes. Remember what we talked about? As soon as you've had enough, you walk away."

Dex let out a snort. It was way too late to walk away. Had been about six months ago. He straightened and snatched a paper towel from the automated dispenser. It was like drying off with newspaper, the same newspapers that had his image plastered all over their pages. Images that had been run through some Photoshop douchebag filter to make him look like even more of a prick. He chucked the paper into the wastebasket and stood there, finding it difficult to face his lawyer.

"Hey, look at me." Littman stepped up to him and patted his cheek. "You did the right thing."

Dex looked up then, searching for something, anything that might help the pain go away, even for a little while. "Then why do I feel like shit?"

"Because he was your friend, Dex."

"Exactly. And I fucked him over. Some friend." He went back to leaning over the sink, his fingers gripping the porcelain so tightly his knuckles hurt. "Goddamn it!" That son of a bitch! What the hell had Walsh been thinking? Obviously he hadn't been, or neither of them would be in this mess. Or worse, maybe Walsh *had* thought it through. Maybe he'd been so certain Dex would have his back that he thought *fuck it*.

Dex closed his eyes, trying to get the man's face out of his mind, but he could still see it clearly. That face was going to haunt his dreams for a long time coming. The mixture of anger and pain when the verdict had been given—anger directed at Dex, and pain brought about by what he'd done—had been there for the world to see, especially Dex.

"No," Littman insisted. "He fucked himself over. All you did was tell the truth."

The truth. How could doing the right thing turn out so goddamn bad? Had it even been the right thing? It had seemed like it at the time. Now he wasn't so sure. Regardless, he couldn't hide out in the restroom all his life.

"Let's get this over with." A few deep breaths and he followed Littman out into the corridor. The moment he stepped foot out there, the locusts swarmed him, microphones buzzing, recorders and smartphones at the ready, flashes going off, cameras rolling, a litany of questions flying at him from every direction. It was as if he were underwater, hearing everyone outside the pool yelling and screaming as he sank to the bottom like a stone, no discernible words, only muffled sounds. Littman stepped up beside him, one hand behind Dex's back in assurance, the other held up to the crowd in a vain attempt to bring order to chaos.

"Detective Daley will do his best to answer your questions, but one at a time, please!"

A tall gray-haired man in an expensive suit pushed through his gathered comrades, ignoring their murmured grunts of displeasure, to place a microphone in front of Dex. A half a dozen more swiftly joined it.

"Detective Daley, what would you say to all the Humans who believe you betrayed your own kind?"

At least he'd been prepared for that one. Dex buttoned up his suit jacket, the gesture allowing him a few seconds to calm his nerves and collect his thoughts. Smoothing it down, he met the reporter's gaze. "I joined the Human Police Force to make a difference, and sometimes that requires making tough calls. I chose to tell the truth. No one is above the law, and my job is to enforce it."

A blonde woman in a tailored navy blue pantsuit swiftly jumped in. "Is it because your brother is Therian? Are you a LiberTherian sympathizer?"

It was hardly the first time he'd been accused of such. Having a Therian brother was the sole reason the Human Police Force had taken longer than necessary to consider him when he'd applied ten years ago. If his father hadn't been a respected detective on the force, Dex was certain he never would've been considered, much less hired. Knowing what they thought of his brother should have been enough to make him walk away, but it was those same close-minded individuals Dex had wanted to reach. That was why he'd joined the HPF, to continue making a difference from the inside, like his dad once had. It turned out to be a whole lot harder than he'd imagined, but that only succeeded in strengthening his resolve.

"My brother and I share the same beliefs when it comes to justice. Our fathers taught us to treat both Therians and Humans as equals. I may be liberal-minded, but my strong belief in justice for both species hardly makes me a sympathizer."

An auburn-haired man with a shit-eating grin shoved his smartphone in Dex's face, almost hitting him in the teeth. His expression told Dex he didn't much care if he had. Dex calmly pulled back, his jaw muscles tightening. "Detective Daley, why haven't you joined your father and brother over at the THIRDS? Is it because you didn't qualify?"

Dex returned the asshole's grin. "Whatever you're paying your sources, it's too much. I never applied to the THIRDS."

"But you did go through their training."

"I was offered the opportunity to take the three-week training course in the hopes I might reconsider becoming a candidate. I complied as a courtesy to my family, and I admit, a part of me wanted to know if I was up to the challenge." And damn, had it been one hell of a challenge! Three weeks of intense physical training and skill-building exercises, rappelling, fast roping, room entry procedures, building searches, close-quarter combat, and tactical weapons training. Dex had been pushed to his limits, and when he thought he couldn't give any more, he was forced to reach deep down and give an additional 10 percent. It had been the most grueling, demanding, psychologically stressful three weeks of his life. Nothing he'd ever done had come close to what he'd been put through in those three weeks, not even the HPF training academy.

The THIRDS were the toughest sons of bitches around, and Dex had wanted to prove to himself that he could hack it. But join them? That was something else altogether.

"Did you pass?"

Dex couldn't help his pride from showing. "Top of the class."

"Will you be applying now?" another journalist asked.

"I intend to continue offering my services to the HPF."

"What if they don't want you? Do you think they've lost their trust in you, knowing you helped send a good man, one of their own brothers, to prison?"

And there it was.

Dex turned his head to whisper Littman's name. His lawyer smiled broadly and held a hand up. "Thank you all for coming. I'm afraid that's all Detective Daley has time for. Please respect him and his family during this difficult time."

"What about Detective Walsh and his family? Have you spoken to them? How does his family feel about what you did?"

Dex waded through the toxic pool of newspersons, refusing to think about the hurtful and hateful phone calls, texts, and messages from Walsh's family. People he'd once had barbecues with, whose Little League games he'd attended. He'd never wanted to bring them so much pain, to take away their son, husband, father. Being on the receiving end of their anger was the least Dex deserved.

"Detective Daley! Detective!"

He ignored the onslaught of questions, from what his boyfriend thought about the whole thing to whether his career with the HPF was unofficially over, and everything in between. He wasn't going to think about any of that now. All he wanted was to get home to said boyfriend and maybe cry a little.

Dex walked as fast, but calmly, as he could, with Littman at his side, making a beeline for the north entrance of the Supreme Court Criminal Branch. Outside, the news teams tried to crowd him in, and officers did their best to control the growing mob. The railings on either side of the exit only proved to be a nuisance, corralling him as he tried to push his way through. The steps were blocked, so Dex grabbed Littman's elbow and hurried him down the makeshift ramp to the sidewalk. Thank God they had a car waiting for them.

Dex tried to be nice about getting the journalists to step back so he could get into the back seat. When a couple of jerks tried to cram in, Dex was left with no choice. He grabbed their smartphones and tossed them into the crowd behind them.

"You're going to pay for that!" one of them called out as he scrambled to retrieve his device.

"Bill me!" Dex climbed into the car and slammed the door behind him. The town car pulled away from the curb, and he slumped back against the pristine leather, letting out a long audible breath. Finally, it was over. For the time being anyway.

"You sure you don't want to be dropped off at home?" Littman looked nearly as haggard as Dex felt.

"Nah, the parking garage is fine. I need to drop off the rental anyway."

"You know I would've been happy to pick you up at your home and drop you off."

"I know." Dex stared out the window as they drove up Centre Street, made a left on White, and then drove down Lafayette. When they made a right onto Worth, the Starbucks on the corner had him pining for some frothy caffeine goodness. "I needed to drive around a while before court. Listen to some music, try to relax a little." He'd made sure to rent a car with the darkest tinted windows on the lot and a slamming sound system. Music was probably the only thing that had kept him from going crazy through this whole ordeal, what with his boyfriend's busy schedule. It would have been nice to have Lou there with him, but he understood the man couldn't drop everything for him. They both had demanding careers and sometimes sacrifices had to be made. Still….

"I understand. You should lay low for a while until this blows over. There's talk of that heiress—the one who's been having a not-so-secret affair with her Therian personal trainer—being pregnant, and Daddy's not taking it well. That should keep the vultures busy for a while. I suggest you take some vacation time, maybe surprise Lou with a nice little penthouse suite in the Bahamas or something."

In no time, the car pulled up to the curb in front of the deli next to the parking garage, and Dex mustered up a smile, holding his hand out to his father's old friend. "Thanks. I appreciate everything you've done for me."

"You know I'm always here if you need me." Littman took his hand in his and gave it a pat. "Dex?"

"Yeah?"

"He would have been proud of you."

The thought brought a lump to his throat. "You think so?"

Littman nodded, the conviction in his words going a long way to assure Dex. "I knew your dad a long time. Believe me. He would have been proud. And so is Tony. He's left me about ten messages asking about how you are. Your brother's probably worried sick as well."

Dex pulled his hand away to remove his smartphone from his pocket and chuckled at the fifteen missed calls from his family. He held it up. "You think?"

"Call your family before Tony hunts you down."

"I'll give them both a call soon as I get in. Thanks." After saying goodbye to Littman, Dex once again thanked him for helping him keep his sanity throughout all this and what was surely to come. Dex headed toward the rental in the parking garage. He wasn't stupid enough to drive his precious baby to the courthouse. It was hard to lose the media in an Orange Pearl Dodge Challenger. If they weren't in the city, he'd leave them eating his dust, but since he was in the city, it would make him a sitting duck.

As soon as he walked around to the rental's driver's side, he was doubly grateful he hadn't brought his car, though he was no less pissed. Someone had slashed his back tire.

"You've got to be fucking kidding me."

He kicked the tire, as if doing so might magically repair it. Goddamn it, he should have let Littman drive him home. All he wanted was to get indoors, get something to eat, and vegetate on the couch. Thank God for auto clubs. He reached into his pocket for his phone when someone across the lot called out.

"Detective Daley!"

Instinctively he looked up. A split second later, the air rushed out of his lungs when something solid struck him between his shoulder blades. He stumbled forward, a blow to his thigh forcing him onto his hands and knees with a painful growl. Around him, three large Humans in black ski masks and black gloves crowded him. Damn it, where had they come from? Dex moved, intent on pushing himself to his feet, when someone kicked him in the stomach, leaving him once again winded. He landed roughly on his side, holding on to his bruised ribs and stomach, his teeth gritted as he breathed heavily through his nose.

"You fucked up, Daley. You shouldn't have testified against your partner."

"Fuck you," Dex spat out. Another kick confirmed mouthing off wasn't appreciated. They obviously didn't know him. With a groan, he leaned slightly to take in the sight of their neat attire. Maybe they did know him. "Who sent you?" He didn't need to know. What's more, he didn't care. All he needed was enough time to figure out who he was up against.

"The Human race," one of them snarled.

Dex let out a laugh. What an ass. It hadn't taken him long to piece things together after noticing the gang's black dress slacks and shiny black shoes. With a curse, he rolled forward to press his forehead against the asphalt. The only surprising part of this whole encounter was the fact it hadn't come sooner. At least they weren't going to kill him, just make him bleed a little. "Well, I got the message, so you can all go home now. You did your duty." He received a blow to the arm with the shiny steel baton; most likely the same object they'd used to hit him in the back. Man, he was going to be sore tomorrow.

They dragged him to his feet, one holding on to each of his arms as the third came to stand before him. Dex closed his eyes and braced himself, his mind chastising him for being such a coward. The punch landed square across his jaw, snapping his head to one side and splitting his lip. *Fuuuck, that hurt.* He ran a tongue over his teeth to make sure nothing was loose. Nope, nothing there but the tangy taste of his own blood.

"Hey! HPF! Hands where I can see them!"

The Humans bolted and Dex's knees buckled beneath him. Strong hands caught him, helping him stay on his feet. His back stung, his arm, thigh, and face throbbed from the blows, and his stomach reeled at the knowledge he'd done nothing.

"Daley, you okay?"

Dex recognized that voice. He looked up, puzzled to find fellow Homicide Detective Isaac Pearce holding him up, concern etched on his face.

"Pearce?"

Pearce helped him to the rental and propped him up against it, performing a quick assessment. Seeming confident Dex could stand, he surveyed the parking garage, but the perpetrators were long gone. His attention landed back on Dex. "You all right?"

"Yeah. Wish I could say the same about my suit." Dex straightened, wincing at the sharp pain that shot through his body. "What are you doing here?"

"The usual summons, but my guy never showed. It was a nice day, so I figured I'd walk it. Glad I left when I did."

"Yeah, me too." Dex let out a small laugh, then winced at the sharp sting it brought his lip. Tony was going to lose his shit over this.

"Any idea who they were?" Pearce asked worriedly.

Yep. "Nope." Dex shook his head, wiping his hands on his slacks. "Just some pissed-off Humans." He had enough on his hands without bringing a whole new level of crap down on himself. "To be honest, right now I just want to get home."

"Don't blame you." Pearce motioned toward the slashed tire. "Need a lift?"

If he called the auto club now, Dex would have to wait for someone to come out—because he sure as hell didn't have the strength or will to change the tire himself, wait for them to swap it out, then drive the rental back to the lot. Or he could accept Pearce's offer and worry about the rental later.

"A lift would be greatly appreciated."

"Great." Pearce beamed at him. "I'm around the corner."

With a murmured "Thanks," Dex accompanied Pearce to his car, a silver Lexus that was more befitting a homicide detective. At least that's what his old partner, Walsh, would have thought. The guy never did approve of Dex's tastes. Come to think of it, Walsh was always making snide comments about what a "special snowflake" Dex was. He'd never paid much attention to the remarks, but in light of recent events, it was possible Walsh had always been a judgmental prick. Had Dex simply turned a blind eye to all of it? What if Dex had called him out on it sooner? Could they both have been spared all this?

"You okay?" Pearce asked again as soon as Dex was settled into the passenger seat beside him.

"Yeah, sorry. I'm still trying to wrap my head around all of this."

"Why don't you put on some music? Relax a bit. I'll even let you choose the station."

Dex gave a low whistle as he slipped on his seat belt. "You're going to regret giving me that kind of power." He turned on the radio and navigated through the touchscreen to *Retro Radio*. Dex grinned broadly at Pearce, wiggling his eyebrows when Billy Ocean's "Get Outta My Dreams, Get Into My Car" came blaring through the speakers. Pearce stared at him as if he'd lost his mind and Dex laughed. "I told you, you'd regret it."

With a chuckle, Pearce drove out of the parking garage. "Where to?"

"West Village, Barrow Street."

Despite Bobby McFerrin advising Dex a few minutes later not to worry and be happy, Dex was finding it difficult. *If it were only that easy, Bobby. If only.*

The ride down Sixth Avenue was quiet, filled mostly with power ballads and electro pop from the era of neon spandex, mullets, and shoulder pads with a wingspan to rival that of a Boeing 747. Dex appreciated Pearce letting him zone out instead of trying to make idle conversation. It was odd, being in Pearce's car with him. They'd never offered more than the usual office greetings, despite both working homicide from the HPF's Sixth Precinct. Then again, Pearce had retreated into himself after losing his brother over a year ago, and no one at the Sixth could blame him. Having a younger brother of his own, Dex could imagine how hard it must have been on the poor guy.

Traffic wasn't too bad this time of day, slowing down mainly near Tribeca Park and a few pockets down Sixth Avenue. Less than ten minutes later, they were driving onto busy Bleecker Street. Maybe he could convince Lou to pick him up a burger and fries from Five Guys on the corner. It was dangerous, having that place so close to his house. They pulled up in front of Dex's brownstone, and Pearce turned to him with a smile. "Well, here we are."

"Thanks for not kicking me out of your car," Dex said, shutting off the radio.

"I'll admit I came close when Jefferson Starship came on, but then I saw you tapping your hand in time to the music, and you had this sappy smile on your face… I didn't have the heart." Dex gave a snort and leaned back in his seat, smiling when Pearce started laughing. "You are one weird guy." Pearce's smile faded, and he suddenly looked a little embarrassed. "Want to get a coffee sometime?"

"Sure." Dex tried not to let the surprise show in his voice.

"I know we've never said more than a few words to each other, but you're a cool guy, Daley." His brows drew together in worry, making him appear older than he was. Dex wasn't more than a couple years younger than Pearce, but their job didn't exactly allow for aging gracefully. "Be careful. I'd hate—" Pearce's voice broke and he cleared his throat. "I'd hate for you to get hurt over all this. My brother, Gabe, believed in what he was doing, and look where it got him."

Dex frowned, trying to drum up what he remembered from the incident. He remembered it had been especially hard on Pearce, not having access to the case. But since Gabe had been a THIRDS agent, the HPF had no jurisdiction. "I thought the guy involved had been a Human informant?"

Pearce shook his head. "He was an HPF informant, but he wasn't Human. He was Therian. A kid."

Shit. Pearce's brother had been killed by a Therian informant and here he was, coming to rescue a guy who'd testified against his Human partner in favor of a young Therian punk. "So why aren't you kicking the shit out of me too?"

A deep frown came onto Pearce's face. "If your partner was stupid enough to let his personal prejudice affect his judgment, he deserves what he got. The truth is I admire you. Not everyone would've had the balls to do what you did. What happened to Gabe… was different." He sighed, his expression troubled. "I'm just saying to watch your back. There are a lot of zealots out there looking for any excuse to carry out their own justice, and things have been getting worse since that second HumaniTherian was found dead a few months ago. Some of these Humans are out for blood."

Pearce wasn't wrong on that. Two HumaniTherian activists had been murdered in the last six months, and the evidence was pointing toward a Therian perpetrator, which meant jurisdiction fell to the THIRDS. Although the organization was doing its best to reassure the public, a storm was brewing between Humans and Therians, especially if they didn't catch whoever was behind it soon. Dex's testimony against his partner couldn't have come at a worse time.

"Thanks for the warning, Pearce." Dex stepped out of the car and closed the door behind him, taking a step to the side to wave at Pearce as he drove off. As soon as the guy was gone, Dex let out a sigh of relief. He loved his quiet little tree-lined street. With a smile, he painfully climbed up the steps to his front door. Finally he was home. He stuck the key into the lock, turned it, and pushed the door open, baffled when it went *thump* halfway. Christ, now what? Something heavy was wedged up against it. With a frustrated grunt, he forced it open and carefully stuck his head in, frowning when he saw the large open cardboard box filled with DVDs, CDs, and a host of other things that should have been in his living room. His initial thought went to burglary, except he'd never run into thieves who stopped to bubble wrap their stolen merchandise.

"Lou?"

Dex locked the door behind him and wandered into the living room, his jaw all but hitting the floor at the near-empty state of it, along with the many cardboard boxes littered about in various stages of completeness. Something banged against the floor upstairs, and Dex took the stairs two at a time.

"Babe?" Dex found his boyfriend of four years upstairs in their bedroom, throwing shoes into empty boxes. "What's going on?"

"I'm moving out."

The words hit Dex like a punch to the gut, a feeling he was growing all too familiar with these days. "What?" He quickly maneuvered through the obstacle course of boxes and scattered manbags to take hold of his boyfriend's arms, turning him to face him. "Sweetheart, stop for a second. Please, talk to me." He went to cup Lou's cheek, only to have Lou move his face away. Ouch. Double sucker punch. Tucking the rejection away for later, he focused on getting to the bottom of this. "Lou, please."

"The nonstop phone calls, the reporters knocking on the door, the news reports on TV calling you a disgrace to your species. I can't take it anymore, Dex."

Guilt washed over him, and he released Lou. How many more casualties would there be as a result of his doing "the right thing"? "Give it some time. This will all blow over. What if we go somewhere far away from this, the two of us, huh?"

Lou shook his head and went back to packing. "I have a life to think about. I've already lost half a dozen clients. I can't afford to lose any more."

"This is New York, Lou. One thing you won't run out of is parties to cater. It's almost September; next thing you know it'll be Halloween and you'll be knee-deep in white chocolate ghosts and tombstone ice sculptures, telling your clients how throwing a party in a real graveyard is a bad idea." When his light-hearted approach failed, Dex knew this was serious. Of course, to most people, the packed boxes would have been a dead giveaway, but Dex wasn't most people. He refused to believe Lou would walk out on him when he needed him the most. "What about me? Aren't I a part of your life?" Dex was taken aback when Lou rounded on him, anger flashing in his hazel eyes.

"You sent your partner to prison, Dex!"

Unbelievable. It wasn't bad enough he was getting it from everyone else, now he was getting it at home too? Dex was growing mighty tired of being treated like a criminal. "*I* didn't send him to prison. The evidence against him did. He shot an unarmed kid in the back and killed him, for fuck's sake! How am I the asshole in this?" He searched Lou's eyes for any signs of the man who'd wake him up in the middle of the night simply to tell him how glad he was to be there with him.

"It wasn't like you'd be able to bring the kid back. Not to mention he was a delinquent *and* a Therian!"

Dex's anger turned into shock. "Whoa, what the hell, Lou? So that makes it okay? What about Cael?

He's a Therian. You've never had a problem with him." At least Lou had the decency to look ashamed.

"He's your family. I had no choice."

This was all news to him. Dex loved Cael. He would never push his brother out for anyone. He'd been upfront about his Therian brother when he and Lou had first started dating. If his date couldn't accept Cael, he couldn't accept Dex. "Where is all this coming from? Since when do you have a problem with Therians?"

"Since one ruined my fucking life!" Lou chucked a pair of sneakers at one of the boxes with such force the box toppled over.

"*Your* life?" This conversation grew more astounding by the minute. Dex thrust a finger at himself. "Have you seen my face? I got the shit kicked out of me in the parking garage, thanks for noticing. If a fellow detective hadn't come along, I'd probably be in the hospital right now. And you know what the most fucked-up part of that is? They weren't even street thugs. They were fucking cops!" Dex had known the moment he'd seen their attire and the telltale signs of an ankle holster on one of them. The bastards had probably been at the trial.

Lou threw his arms up in frustration. "Your own cop friends don't want to have anything to do with you, and you expect me to pretend like nothing's happened? To ignore everyone staring at me, saying, 'Oh, there goes that prick's boyfriend. He's probably a LiberTherian sympathizer too.' I don't want to get the shit kicked out me, Dex."

"Oh my God, seriously?" Humans loved throwing words like HumaniTherian and LiberTherian around as if they were insults. His strong belief that Therians and Humans deserved to be treated equally made him a HumaniTherian, even if he wasn't out picketing on the White House lawn, and he was fine with that. But that didn't make him a LiberTherian. He was hardly an anarchist, and considering he was in law enforcement, he'd never had a problem with authority, though he didn't follow it blindly either. He hated when someone tried to stick him in a little box with a label slapped on his ass. Like everything was black-and-white. Doing his best to summon patience despite his reservoir being nearly depleted, he took hold of Lou's hand and pulled him to their king-sized bed. Lou allowed himself to be led but refused to sit or even look him in the eye. "Do you care that much about what people think?"

No reply. Dex supposed he couldn't blame him. Things were so screwed up, he didn't know which way was up anymore.

"It's not just the trial."

Dex swallowed hard, wondering what new surprises Lou had for him. Sure, they argued sometimes, but no more than any other couple. They had fun together when their jobs allowed it, though now that he thought about it, it had been a while since they'd had a day off together. Lou had been as busy these days with his career as Dex had been with his own, but neither of them ever complained about not spending enough time together. Maybe that was the problem. He could fix that, though. He could take some time off work and take Lou somewhere nice, with sandy white beaches and cocktails. At least that's what he thought until he saw Lou's face.

It was over.

"I'm sorry. I can't do this anymore. I can't keep getting left behind; sitting here on my own until sunup while you throw yourself into the line of fire every chance you get." The hurt in Lou's eyes only added to Dex's guilt.

"It's my job," Dex replied quietly, exhausted from the day's events, and quite frankly, the whole of his life at the moment.

"Saving the world is not your job. It's your obsession. An unhealthy one that will get you killed. You told me you became an HPF officer so you could make a difference there, like your dad, but if you keep this up, you're going to end up like him."

Dex's chest tightened. "Don't."

"That's why they're the *Human* Police Force. They don't want to see things your way. Okay, so some of them might change their minds, some probably already feel the way you do, but not enough of them to change the way things are. Why do you think the government opened the THIRDS?"

"What do you want from me, Lou? Do you want me to change? Is that it?" Dex leaned toward him, pleading. "I can do that."

Lou shook his head. "You are the job, Dex. I couldn't ask you to change who you are. What I want is for you to take care of yourself, and please, don't call me or come to my job." Lou tugged at his hand, and Dex reluctantly let go. "I'll send the movers for the rest of my stuff tomorrow while you're at work."

"That's pretty much the entire house," Dex murmured, taking stock of the near-empty room. He was also pretty sure Lou was leaving some stuff behind for him, like the bedding.

"Why do you think that is, Dex? You were never here. I was the one who made this a home."

The words made Dex's heart ache and when he spoke, his voice was quiet. "Was I that bad?"

Lou stepped up to him and placed a gentle kiss on his cheek. "You're a great guy, Dex. We had fun, and you were good to me, but we weren't right for each other. If it hadn't happened now, it would have happened eventually." He ran his fingers through Dex's hair, the tender gesture bringing a lump to his throat. Shifting forward, Dex wrapped his arms around Lou's waist and squeezed, his cheek pressed against Lou's chest.

"Please don't go."

"I'm sorry," Lou replied hoarsely, pulling away. "I'll leave the key in the mailbox."

Dex nodded and fell back onto the bed, his body feeling heavy and in pain, inside and out. He was so exhausted he couldn't find the will to do anything but lie there and wish his bed would swallow him up.

"I'm sorry, Dex. I really am."

"Me too," Dex murmured softly. A few minutes later, he heard the front door close, making him cringe. He rubbed his stinging eyes for a moment before his hand flopped back down to the bed. He should get up and shower. Instead, he lay there staring up at the white ceiling. In his pocket, his cell phone went off. He ignored it and closed his eyes. The landline started shrilling, and he let out a low groan. It was probably his dad. The answering machine beeped and a saccharine voice that was definitely not his dad's chirped,

"Mr. Daley, this is a friendly reminder that your rental is due back at the lot before 6:00 p.m. Failure to do so will result in an additional day's charge being added to your credit card. We appreciate you using Aisa Rentals and hope you have a pleasant evening."

Dex checked his watch.

5:59 p.m.

Fuck. My. Life.

DEX WAS well on his way to having yet another spectacular clusterfuck of a week, despite feeling pretty confident things couldn't possibly get any worse than they'd been recently. After all, the last month had been pretty eple in the "screw you" department. It had been so bad, he'd actually been looking forward to the end of his two weeks' paid leave in order to get back to work. *Oh, Dex, you silly boy.*

Things can only get better.

Isn't that what Dex had been told this morning? Well, more like that's what the song on the radio had been harping about on his way to work. That's the last time he allowed himself to be reassured by an eighties song. *Retro Radio* was going to be deleted from his playlist first chance he got. That's if his head cleared up enough by the end of his shift to let him make sense of all the shiny glowing buttons on the dash of his car. *Nothing like a good old-fashioned shitkicking to start your morning on your first day back at work.*

It was true he'd been expecting some anger and hostility to come his way after what he'd done. The dirty looks and shoves into lockers or various similarly occupied spaces, his paperwork doubling as toilet paper in the restroom, his desk drawers filled with everything from doggie chew toys to rubber mice. All of it had been expected. Unpleasant, but expected. The friendly beatings? Not so much.

"Tissue?"

With a nod of thanks, Dex took the little paper hankie offered by Captain McGrier and dabbed his split lip. He resumed his slouch, tonguing the sore spot inside his mouth where he'd bitten himself after the first punch hit. His body was aching and his head was killing him, but at least he was pretty sure he wasn't concussed.

"Where'd they get you this time?" McGrier's bushy white brows drew together in an expression that could have meant anything from "I hope Anne's not making meatloaf again," to "I'm seriously considering punching you myself." For a man who only had one facial expression, he was sure tough to get a read on.

"Evidence," Dex replied. Knowing what McGrier was going to ask next, Dex didn't bother waiting. "And no, I didn't see who it was."

Peterson, Johnson, Malone, Rodriguez, and the IT guy with the mohawk and face full of shrapnel. What the hell was his name? Nick? Ned? Ned. Dick Ned.

Of course Dex had seen who it was. They both knew he'd seen who it was. Or more specifically, who *they* had been, but Dex wasn't about to rat out his own brethren, even if his brethren had happily worked him over moments ago in the isolated evidence locker. Damn. How had he become the most hated guy in the precinct? Even Bill—the guy who ate other people's lunches from the fridge—was less hated than him.

McGrier sighed heavily, his chair letting out a screeching protest as he leaned his heavy mass back.

"You're one hell of a detective, Daley, but the fact remains, this can't go on."

"No kidding," Dex grumbled. "My dry cleaning bill's tripled in the last month."

"You're the only detective I know who comes to work looking like he stepped out of a goddamn men's fashion magazine. What the fuck is that in your hair?"

Dex instinctively touched his tousled locks. "Forming cream."

McGrier leaned forward and sniffed. "And what's that smell?"

"Citrus mint," Dex muttered, leaning away from him. "FYI, that was kind of creepy."

"FYI, you realize you're a homicide detective, right?"

"What are you trying to say?" Just because he felt like crap didn't mean he had to look it. Judging by the state of his captain's office, it was a pretty safe bet McGrier didn't agree. It was as if the man had an aversion to tidiness. Whenever McGrier called him in, Dex always managed to hover by the door and not step foot inside the Den of Disorder. It was a clean freak's worst nightmare. *Dex's* worst nightmare.

The leaves of the fake potted fern on top of the beat-up filing cabinet were drooping from the thick layers of dust. There were stacks of files—crookedly stacked files—with sheets sticking out every which way on every available surface. On file boxes along the side of the room. On McGrier's desk underneath three coffee mugs—one of which deserved nothing short of incineration, though the tar-like remnants of what had once been a thin layer of coffee might cause it to explode. How did the man work in this? The whole place was in need of a hazmat team.

"You eat Cheesy Doodles at your desk," McGrier informed him.

How'd they go from hair gel to cheese snacks? "Hey, don't knock the crunchy cheesy goodness. You're always eating pistachios—which, by the way, are messier—and you don't hear me bitching about it." Dex nodded toward the war zone of tiny shells on the desk in front of McGrier.

"Kids eat Cheesy Doodles. Grown men eat nuts."

Dex arched an eyebrow and opened his mouth, only to have McGrier jab a finger at him. "Don't you even think about it, wiseass."

"I was only going to say that grown men eat Cheesy Doodles too. That's why they put *extreme* on the packaging. And explosions. What's manlier than explosions?" McGrier's lips pressed together in what Dex translated to be some form of disapproval, so Dex decided to be serious for a moment. "All right, sir, you didn't call me into your office to talk about my wardrobe, Cheesy Doodles, or my love of nuts." Well, he'd tried. Judging by McGrier's scowl, he'd failed. "Fine, I'm sorry. Tell me what this is about."

"I think you know what this is about."

Dex couldn't even come up with a smartass remark. "Yeah, I know. What was I supposed to have done?" No way McGrier would answer that, but Dex liked to play the "what if" game with himself every now and then.

"You did what you believed was right. You need to stop beating yourself up over it."

He would have thought McGrier was trying to be funny if he suspected for even a moment the man had a sense of humor. "Why would I beat myself up when I've got plenty of other people to do that for me?" McGrier was unsurprisingly not impressed with his reply.

"I know you feel like shit right now, and I'm afraid what I have to say isn't going to make things any better."

That got Dex's attention and he sat upright, getting a sick twisting feeling in his gut. In the back of his mind, he'd been waiting for it, but now that it was happening, he wasn't as prepared as he thought he'd be. "What?"

"The commissioner isn't happy about finding the HPF in the middle of this shitstorm, especially with those unsolved HumaniTherian murders. I've been informed to advise you that it's time for you to move on."

"Move on? Move on to what?" The suits were pushing him out? Dex propelled out of his chair so fast it toppled backward. "That's what this is about, isn't it? Votes? Ten years I've been busting my ass here, giving you blood, sweat, and tears, and they're going to push me out for doing my goddamn job?" He slammed his hands on the desk, turning the tiny pistachio shells into launched projectiles. "This is bullshit, Cap!"

"Daley," McGrier said with quiet emphasis, his brows set in a straight line as if he couldn't fathom the reason for Dex's hissy fit. Dex didn't give a damn what his captain thought this was. They were talking about his career, a career that was being dismissed without so much as batting an eyelash, all so a bunch of bureaucratic assholes could bullshit their way through another election.

"There's no way I'm taking this lying down. You hear me? I've seen some pretty fucked-up shit in my time, but this—"

"You're not being pushed out. You're being promoted. Sort of."

"I—what?" Dex blinked a few times as he tried to decipher the words that had come out of McGrier's wobbly mouth. "What do you mean I'm being promoted? *Sort of.*" Now he was really confused.

"What I said. So, why don't you sit back down and relax before you have a stroke or something."

After setting his chair back on its legs, Dex resumed his seat. Not because he had been told to do so, but because he was afraid if he didn't, he might just have that stroke. "I'm being promoted to…."

Fill in the blank.

"It's more like you've been recruited." McGrier studied him closely. What kind of response was his captain expecting from him other than *Huh?*

"Huh?"

"As of this afternoon, you are a Defense agent for the THIRDS." The man grew quiet, and Dex couldn't help but wait for him to throw his arms out and shout "Ta-da!" with a show of jazz hands.

What was happening here? If he'd been told he was getting transferred, he would've understood. If he'd been told he was getting demoted, he would've understood. Hell, he would've understood being let go, but being recruited by the THIRDS? Nope. He couldn't say he understood. Especially since he'd never applied for a position in the first place, as he'd recently found himself stating repeatedly.

"But… how? *Why?* Maybe you can, I don't know, explain? I'm feeling a little slow today. One too many kicks to the head."

McGrier stood and started pacing. "Daley, whatever you may think, I like you. You're an honest young man with a good head on your shoulders. You were a damned good cop and became an even better detective. Things may die down around here, they might not, but I think your skills would be better suited to an organization with a different way of doing things. We both know if they tried to push you out or demote you, they'd lose the Therian vote, but if they promoted you to an organization with a reputation for supporting both Humans and Therians, it'd be a win/win situation for everyone."

"Yeah, if I'd been trying to get in, which I hadn't been. Right now it's a win/what the hell situation."

McGrier continued as if Dex hadn't spoken. "I had a meeting with Lieutenant Sparks while you were on leave, and she happens to have a position open on her team. The fact that you scored top of your class during the training and have Sergeant Maddock to put in a good word for you has made you a key candidate. You know Maddock has always wanted you over there with him and your brother. The THIRDS is the only organization I know of that allows family members to work together, so why not take advantage?"

Dex's mouth moved but nothing came out, so he decided it was best to shut it. Maybe he *was* concussed. Maybe he was in a hospital somewhere hopped up on meds and dreaming about getting recruited by the Therian Human Intelligence Recon Defense Squadron. Jesus Christ, the government loved their acronyms. Somewhere some government suit had jizzed his pants coming up with that one.

The Sixth Precinct had been Dex's home for the last ten years. They were like family. Then again, his "family" had pretty much disowned him in the last few months. Should he fight to stick around where he wasn't wanted? He'd already been beat up twice. If that wasn't their way of flipping him off, he didn't know what was.

McGrier was right, things might die down, or they might get worse. As it was, his presence alone had everyone on edge, and those same dickbags who'd cast him out were forcing everyone else to pick sides. He could spare a lot of good people a whole lot of grief if he took this position, not that he was being given much of a choice.

It all came down to whether he left quietly. He should be grateful for the opportunity. There were officers out there who'd clean toilets if it meant getting their foot through the THIRDS' door. Plus, Dex would get to work with his real family. That didn't make leaving his job behind any easier. It was the only familiar thing he had left. He was—had been—one of the Sixth's top homicide detectives, and he'd worked damn hard to get there. Of course, sitting in McGrier's office with a tissue to his bleeding lip made it pretty obvious he didn't have much of a career left to get back to. With a resigned sigh, he nodded.

"Okay. When do I start?"

With a grim nod, his captain resumed his seat. "September 23. They're giving you a week to catch up on all the new policies and codes before your introduction."

A knock sounded on the door, and Dex tilted his head back to get a better look at the fair-haired detective hovering outside. Ah, Pearce, his knight in tarnished armor. One of the selective few who didn't feel the need to share his opinions about Dex's so-called betrayal. When Pearce noticed him sitting there, he smiled widely.

"Hey, Daley."

"Pearce." Dex returned his smile. It's a shame he was leaving. He could see himself hanging out with Pearce, shooting the breeze over a couple slices of pizza, sharing a few beers on a lazy Sunday afternoon.

"You wanted to see me, sir?"

"Yeah. Daley's leaving us. He's been recruited to the THIRDS."

The air was vacuum-sucked out of the room, and Dex looked from Pearce to the captain and back, hoping someone could shed a little light on the unscheduled loss of atmosphere.

"What team?" Pearce asked quietly.

McGrier actually squirmed in his seat before clearing his throat. "Destructive Delta."

Pearce went tense all over, his jaw clenched so tight, he looked as if he might crack something. Dex suddenly remembered Pearce's brother, and he prayed his luck wasn't that bad. The THIRDS was huge. What were the chances he'd end up on the same team Agent Gabe Pearce had been on? *Shit.* He was Gabe's replacement, wasn't he?

Dex looked up at Pearce. "Same team?"

Pearce merely nodded, his lips pressed together in a thin line.

This wasn't awkward at all. Just great. No one wanted to be the guy who came in after a dead partner. Dex hated baggage, and now he was about to walk into a partnership with enough to fill an airport terminal. His new partner probably had all sorts of expectations, and they hadn't even met yet. Howard Jones had lied to him. Things were not getting better. They were getting worse by the minute.

"Congratulations." The word just about managed to squeeze past Pearce's lips.

"Thanks," Dex muttered.

"Do you know who your partner is?" Pearce sounded a lot more casual than he was probably feeling. Dex couldn't knock the guy for trying.

"No, uh, it's all kind of caught me by surprise."

Pearce nodded and turned his attention back to the captain.

"Pearce, you're going to take Dex's place until we get people shuffled around here. Why don't you walk him to his car? Dex, we'll send your stuff to THIRDS Headquarters, along with any paperwork."

In other words, the cap didn't want Dex getting roughed up now that he was part of a shiny new elite force, and if Pearce was with him, Dex would make it out of the building in one piece. Good times.

Dex got up, removed his Glock from his holster and placed it on McGrier's desk, along with his badge. He exchanged the whole "it was a pleasure working with you" bull with the cap, knowing neither one of them had anything else to say. They didn't bother with the whole "keep in touch" thing because they both knew it wasn't going to happen unless it was in an official capacity.

Pearce walked silently beside him through the old precinct, shoulder to shoulder, lost in his own thoughts. Dex couldn't tell if the look on his face was due to grief or antipathy, but he felt for the guy. He wanted to apologize to Pearce for his loss, for the promotion that reminded him of his loss, for the actions that led to his promotion that in turn reminded him of his loss. Dex would have apologized for his whole damn existence if he thought it would make a difference, but it wouldn't, so he didn't.

Dex had opted for parking his baby in the private parking garage across the street instead of the precinct lot, just in case. The amount of money paid for parking would be far less than what he'd have to shell out for a new windshield or paint job.

When they reached his car, Dex turned to Pearce, figuring this was probably the last he'd see of him. No chance Pearce was going to want to share that coffee with him now.

"Nice car."

"Thanks." Dex patted the hood of his baby with a dopey grin. Sometimes he liked to pretend he was John McClane in a *Die Hard* movie, except with more speed limits, fewer explosions, and generally a lot less action going on. He really needed to start daydreaming a little bigger. As he suspected, Pearce gave him a curt nod and turned to walk away, but to Dex's surprise, stopped.

"Watch your back over there, Daley, and don't expect a warm welcome."

Well, that didn't bode well. "Why do you say that?"

Pearce seemed to mull it over before turning back, his hands shoved into his jacket pockets. "Destructive

Delta is in Unit Alpha, and those positions are the highest, most dangerous, most sought after in the THIRDS, yet Gabe's position is still open, has been on and off for over a year. What does that tell you?"

"I don't know, but I can imagine losing Gabe was probably tough for the team."

Pearce nodded, his lips pursed. "I'm sure it was, but the THIRDS don't mourn, they keep moving. They're not like the rest of us. Rumor is the team leader, Agent Brodie, has run off over half a dozen agents. I've met him, and believe me when I say he's the biggest asshole to walk this earth. As far as he's concerned, no one is good enough to replace Gabe. I would have found his loyalty admirable if he hadn't been the one to send Gabe to meet that Therian informant on his own the night he was killed."

"You think it was Agent Brodie's fault Gabe got killed?" Dex was concerned for Pearce. Maybe this team leader *was* an asshole, but if the THIRDS were as good as everyone claimed them to be, surely they wouldn't have sent in their own teammate knowing he couldn't handle himself. "You don't want to go down that path." Dex put a hand on Pearce's shoulder. "It doesn't lead anywhere good. I didn't know Gabe, but I get the feeling he wouldn't want you thinking like that either." Dex understood what it felt like to lose family at the hands of criminals. He also understood first-hand how dangerous it could be to fall into despair. Lucky for him, he'd had his adoptive dad—Anthony Maddock—at the time to pull him out before he'd lost himself.

"You're right." Pearce's scowl gave way to a sad smile. "Gabe wouldn't have wanted that. At least he died defending what he loved. Take care of yourself, Daley. I'll call you about that coffee."

With that, Pearce walked away, his footsteps resonating through the empty, cavernous garage until he disappeared into the shadows, leaving Dex standing by his lonesome facing an undiscernible future.

Damn you, Howard Jones!

Chapter 2

CONIUCTIS VIRIBUS: With United Powers

That's what the chiseled stone above the colossal gold-framed doors proudly stated.

Dex could count on one hand the number of times he'd been in front of this building and actually gone in. Its façade was as imposing as the organization it housed. Flanked by East Thirty-Eighth Street and East Forty-Second Street, The THIRDS Manhattan Headquarters on First Avenue was a monument to the realities of their ever-evolving world. It was amazing how the course of Human history could change in the blink of an eye, or rather the plunge of a needle.

Dex wasn't old enough to have been there when Eppione.8 threw the world into chaos, but he remembered being a little boy with his parents telling him stories, trying to make him understand why everything seemed to be burning and crumbling around them, why people were so angry all the time, breaking things, and being so scary. It was all so frightening to a five-year-old, and he didn't want to sleep in his bed alone. When his dad would leave for work, Dex would cry, afraid the bad men would get his dad. In the end, they did. His mom too.

No expense had been spared in creating the THIRDS' Manhattan Headquarters. It was grandiose in gray stone with gold accents enclosed in a huge expanse of well-manicured lawns and greenery, fortified by an impenetrable border of stone with gold-plated iron bars. A giant gold statue of some Greek goddess on a marble plinth stood in the center of a circular courtyard inside the expensive front gate with an array of fancy marble benches painstakingly arranged. It had been designed in an old Art Deco style to compete with the rest of New York City's classic structures. In truth, the building resembled the Waldorf Astoria more than it did any government building.

Dex didn't know a whole lot about how the THIRDS operated. He did know they were the guys you called when shit got real. After the May Day Massacre and the riots in the early eighties when violence erupted between Humans and Therians, citizens demanded a law enforcement agency that could not only handle Therian threats, but that could do so fairly.

The THIRDS was created and set up so every team had both a Human and Therian element, whether they were agents, secretaries, or bureaucrats. High-ranking officers were paired with other high-ranking officers, but not necessarily of their own rank; like Tony, who was a sergeant, was paired up with a Therian lieutenant. The THIRDS was also the first multicultural government organization promoting equality for all races, religions, genders, and sexualities. The intention was to show that despite varied cultures and beliefs, both Humans and Therians could come together under one common goal—justice for all. Of course, it wasn't as black-and-white as all that, but at least it was a step in the right direction considering the last forty-odd years.

Like any other military-funded government outfit, the THIRDS operated on a "need to know" and "what you don't know won't hurt you" basis. When you were a THIRDS agent, people got the hell out of your way. His dad and brother never discussed their jobs, not even with Dex. Now he wished he'd pushed them to know more. The THIRDS didn't trust anyone outside the family, *their* family.

"You gonna stare at it all day? Or you comin' in?"

The familiar baritone voice brought a big grin to his face, and Dex turned in time to receive a bone-crushing bear hug.

"Dad." Dex wheezed out the greeting as he was all but lifted off his feet.

Tony's chest rumbled with deep laughter, and he gave Dex one final squeeze before releasing him. "You don't know how happy I am." He held Dex at arm's length, a deep frown coming onto his stern face. "I was worried sick. What's the matter with you? You don't know how to pick up a damn phone to let me know you're alive?"

"I'm sorry. I meant to call, I did, but it's been a pretty shitty couple of weeks. I got home to Lou moving out, and then I had to return the rental but had to get the auto club to come out—"

"Slashed tire?"

Dex nodded. "And then—" He was cut off as his cheeks were caught between Tony's large hands and squeezed. Jesus, it was like he was thirteen all over again, grounded for fighting at school—he hadn't been the one to start it, of course—and Dex had the genius idea of climbing out his bedroom window to go to the park. Only his shoelace got caught on a nail in the windowsill, and he ended up falling headfirst into Mrs. Jones's rose bushes below.

"What happened to your face?"

"Um…." Dex tried to talk through his squeezed cheeks, mumbling until Tony finally released him. "I got jumped in the parking garage after the trial." Dex didn't bother trying to hide the truth, mostly because he'd never get away with it. "And then my first morning back, in the evidence locker."

"I see." Tony put his hands on his hips and rolled his big shoulders. With pursed lips, he ran a hand over his shaved head and down to his jaw where his salt-and-pepper stubble was growing in. *Shit.* "Tell me something, son."

Double shit.

"Dad…."

"Oh, you don't get to *Dad* me. Not while you're standing in front of me telling me you let a bunch of no-good sons of bitches beat the shit out of you."

"I didn't—"

Tony put a finger up to stop him. "We're not going to talk about this now because there is way too much shit to do, but you can bet your skinny ass we're going to sit down and talk about this. You work for me now, so if you think for one minute I'm not gonna take my frustrations out on you, you best think again. You hear me?"

"But—"

"Nope."

There was no point in even attempting to argue. "Yes, sir."

"Let's go." Tony motioned behind him and Dex straightened his shoulders, walking in tall like the agent he was, not the thirteen-year-old he felt like. Behind him, his dad cursed and mumbled under his breath. Maybe Dex had been a little too quick in his excitement to be working with his family. The minute he stepped foot inside, he heard his name being called.

"Dex!" Cael sprinted over and threw his arms around him, squeezing him tight. "I'm so glad you're one of us now."

"Well, not exactly. I don't purr and get the urge to play with giant balls of twine."

"You're such an asshat. I'm still excited you're here, but once the novelty wears off, I'll be sure to tell you to bite me."

Dex chuckled and gave his baby brother's cheek a pat. "I'm glad I'm here too."

"All right, break it up," Tony grunted, though Dex could tell he was holding back a smile. "Tender moment's over. Cael, get your ass back to Sparta."

"Yes, sir." With a wink at Dex, Cael sprinted off.

"What's Sparta, and please tell me there are guys in togas," Dex said, putting his hands together in prayer.

"No. It's the training facility. It's nicknamed Sparta, less for the guys in togas and more for kicking your ass until you're ready for battle." Tony walked off and

Dex quickly followed. Getting to work with his family almost made everything he'd endured worthwhile. *Almost*. "Did you go through your induction packet?"

"Yep." It was a good thing the files had been digital or they would have killed off a small forest printing the thing out. It had contained information on everything from Therian law to THIRDS policies on agent conduct. There had even been a section on stinky food at the workplace.

"There are several THIRDS field offices throughout Manhattan, including offices for specialized operations, but you'll be working out of the Manhattan Division's HQ. There are three main departments in this division—Intel, Recon, and Defense—with a total of eight thousand employees. Each department is broken up into four units—Alpha, Beta, Delta, and Omega. Units Alpha and Beta handle major crimes, with Alpha taking on the more violent crimes. Delta and Omega handle lesser crimes. Each unit is then broken up into squads, or teams. There are ten squads in your unit."

Tony led him through the pristine Art Deco main lobby, and for a moment Dex could have fooled himself into thinking they were at Grand Central Station during rush hour. Everyone walked and talked with purpose, as if whatever they were doing or saying was of the greatest importance. In the center of the lobby, high above the extensive marble reception desk, the THIRDS' shield hung proudly, the double helix shaped into a circle with an atom symbol in the center representing the connection between Humans and Therians. This was it. The big leagues.

They turned a corner toward a wide corridor filled with gleaming gold elevators, and Tony stopped at one situated at the end. Dex was pleasantly surprised when the gold doors opened on their own as soon as they stepped up to them. With a grin, Tony pointed at the floor.

"Motion sensors."

Inside, Dex watched Tony press his hand to a sleek black panel with a blue line outlining a handprint. When he removed it, his image flashed, along with his name and a whole load of other information, including clearance levels. Before Dex had a chance to work any of it out, Tony pressed the blue glowing A button on the gold panel and they were off. If the elevator was anything to go by, he couldn't wait to get his hands on the rest of the shiny gadgets the THIRDS had to offer.

"Uniform fits."

Dex looked down at himself. "Yeah. It's weird being back in uniform, though this one's much more badass than my old HPF one." He wore black military grade boots, heavy-duty tactical pants in a deep charcoal gray with tourniquets built into each upper leg, pockets for slip-in ballistic pads, and a padded adjustable waistband for added comfort. Secured from his utility belt were several pouches, along with a quick-release detachable thigh rig with a Drop & Offset kit containing two ballistic nylon tension straps fastened around his leg. It had a holster with a self-locking system to prevent anyone from removing the Glock 17 tucked away inside. On the same thigh rig was a tactical knife. Over his black undershirt, he wore a heavy-duty shirt matching his pants in color with two patches on one arm—one for the THIRDS NYC Division and one for Unit Alpha, Destructive Delta—and on his right arm, the THIRDS shield. Over his left breast pocket, THIRDS was stitched in white letters, and, similarly stitched over his right breast pocket, was D. Daley. Clipped to his belt was his shiny new badge, lucky 2108. Overall, it was pretty damn sexy.

"I'm sorry about Lou."

That was *not* sexy. "Me too," Dex grumbled. It had been nearly a month, and the sharp pain in his heart had downgraded to a dull ache, mostly because after a good deal of thought, he came to the conclusion Lou had been right. They'd been heading down that road a long time ago. Even so, when he thought of Lou being gone, he was hit with a sense of sadness, and in the beginning he'd really missed him. The morning after an exceptionally pathetic night of sitting on his couch in nothing but his boxers, drinking himself stupid, he thanked God he'd had the foresight to delete Lou's number from his phone. He knew himself too well, and the last thing he needed was to send his ex a bunch of whimpering drunken texts or, heaven forbid, voicemails. What did it say about their relationship that he'd never memorized his ex-boyfriend's number?

His dad's gruff voice interrupted his pitiful thoughts. "Can I be frank?"

"Sure. Can I be beans?" Without even having to look up, Dex knew what his dad was doing. "Stop. You know how I hate when you do that."

"Do what?" Tony grunted.

"Do that puckered-ass thing with your lips."

"And you know all about puckered asses."

Dex arched an eyebrow at his dad. "You know, at times I wonder who the grown-up is here."

The elevator pinged, and they exited into a long white hall with dark gray flooring. "And I wonder if you've lost more than a few marbles. Like the entire bag."

"Fine. Go for it."

"He wasn't the one."

Dex was at a loss for words. Tony had never mentioned anything before. Then again, he wasn't the sort to meddle in his kids' lives unless they did something that called for meddling; then he was a heavyweight champion. In their teens, Cael and Dex had created a superhero persona for him known as *The Meddler*.

Not sure he wanted to know the answer, but feeling the need to, Dex cleared his throat and asked, "What makes you say that?"

"Whose idea was it to be exclusive?" Tony came to a halt, his beefy arms folded over his broad chest as he faced Dex. Damn it. The stubborn set of his jaw and furrowed brow told Dex he couldn't joke his way out of this one.

"His, but I wouldn't have agreed if I wasn't ready."

"And whose idea was it for him to move in?"

"His, but again, I agreed because I was ready." Were they really going to have this conversation *now*?

"Or maybe you didn't care one way or the other and were only trying to make him happy."

Dex straightened, his voice going higher than it should. "Hey, I cared about him."

"I'm not saying you didn't, but I think maybe your relationship wasn't as perfect as you convinced yourself it was. Dex, I know you. Hell, I raised you. When you love something, you throw yourself into it, consequences be damned. Remember that police outfit I put together for you one Halloween when you were eight?"

A dopey grin found its way onto Dex's face. "Yeah, I loved that thing."

"You lived in it. You refused to wear anything else. You slept in it, ate in it, played in it, even went to school in it."

"I also got beat up in it," Dex added with a frown. "But then I suppose it didn't help that I kept trying to arrest my classmates." Hmmm. He was starting to sense a pattern.

Tony placed a gentle hand on Dex's shoulder. "My point is, when you're passionate about something, it shows in everything you do. With Lou, you were never bothered about anything."

"Not true. We fought about stuff."

"No, you fought about one thing, the one thing you truly loved. The job. You were willing to put your job before Lou every time. Boy, the excuses you came up with were something else. Worst part was you didn't even know you were doing it."

Dex took a step back and shoved his hands into his pockets, not liking where this conversation was heading or the fact that he could feel his anger rising. "So what? Now I'm a shitty boyfriend for caring about my career?"

"I'm saying if you weren't willing to risk everything for him, he wasn't the one for you." Tony gave him a gentle pat on the back before he strode off again.

They walked side by side in silence, and Dex wondered if Tony could be right. Had Dex been going along with the relationship just to make Lou happy? It didn't feel that way. Dex had been happy with Lou, and although it was true the only thing they ever argued about was Dex's job, it hardly meant he hadn't cared about anything else.

When Lou wanted his attention, Dex gave it. When Lou needed help to expand his catering business, Dex had supported him. When Lou had asked Dex how he felt about them living together, Dex said he was fine with it. Should he not have been? Lou had been the closest thing to a committed relationship Dex had ever had. There had been a lot of first-time moments.

No point in analyzing it now. His relationship, much like his career at the HPF, was over. All he could do now was what he did best, throw himself into his work. This was his last chance. He *had* to make this work.

Being a detective for the HPF meant he got shit from Humans, because that's where his jurisdiction started and ended. Being an agent for the THIRDS meant he'd be getting shit from Humans *and* Therians. Double the fun. He couldn't complain. It also meant he was getting double the pay and benefits, if he survived long enough to reap the rewards. Wait…. THIRDS, Therians, Alphas… *predators*.

"Oh my God," he gasped and abruptly clutched Tony's arm as reality set in. "I'm going to be shredded like string cheese!" He'd been stabbed, shot, received broken bones, fractures, sprains, beatings, bruising, cuts, but he'd never come up against someone who could kill him with one bite.

"What is it with you and cheese?" Tony pried Dex's fingers off his arm and continued to walk, ignoring Dex's near-panicked state. As an HPF detective, Dex had never faced any Therians in their Therian form, not even docile ones. After all, shifting in public was considered a misdemeanor, right up there with indecent exposure, and once they were in their Therian form, if they committed a crime, they were the THIRDS' responsibility. Now they were his responsibility, and he was going to be dealing with Therians who wiped their asses with the law.

The closest Dex had ever gotten to being mauled was when Cael hit puberty and his first shift happened. Therians could control their shift, but it was possible for an overly stressful moment to trigger a shift, which was why most first shifts happened when puberty hit and tended to happen spontaneously. Like every other young Therian going through the frightening ordeal for the first time, Cael went nuts. Despite having attended all the mandatory classes for Families with Therian Youth—which was meant to prepare them for that exact moment—they all panicked, and Cael managed to graze Dex's leg with his claws before Tony got his hands on the First Shift Response Kit containing the necessary sedatives.

As much as Dex understood it was still his little brother inside the cheetah Therian and that Cael hadn't meant to hurt him, Dex's blood all over the kitchen floor had left them all shaken. It was Tony who had then made certain his boys recovered, both physically and psychologically, from the aftereffects. The faint scars on Dex's leg no longer brought them the overwhelming guilt it once had—Tony for not preventing the near miss, Dex for being afraid of his own brother, and Cael for having hurt Dex.

"I'm not being a drama queen here. I am about to shit a brick."

Tony stopped to give him a pointed look. "You want to survive, Rookie, you listen to your partner."

"Rookie?" *What the hell?* "I've been on the force ten years!"

"The Human Police Force. In this world, you're a rookie. You'll be dealing with all the same nutjobs you were dealing with before, except now they have jaws and claws that will pull you apart like your favorite string cheese. Remember that. Jaws and claws. Repeat after me. Jaws."

He was serious. Dex took a deep breath and released it slowly, his anxiety giving way to irritation. "Jaws."

"And claws."

"And claws," Dex said, enunciating each word. He had a terrible urge to make claws with his hands, but he got the feeling Tony might kick his ass. Still, it was tempting. Clearly his face must have said as much, because Tony jabbed a finger in his direction.

"Don't fuck around with this, Dex. I'm serious."

"Yeah, I can tell by the way that vein on the side of your head is throbbing." He made to touch it only to have Tony smack his hand away.

"Boy, you must be out of your damn mind. Are you listening to me?"

"Yes, all right, I get it. Listen to my partner. Do you know who my partner is?"

They came across a huge door that looked as if it was made from bulletproof glass with the words

Authorized Personnel Only in large white letters displayed across it. Next to the door was another black screen like the one in the elevator. Was there anything on this floor besides walls and doors?

"Let me remind you of something else that seems to be slipping your precious little mind. I'm your sergeant. I know shit before you do. I also have the power to make your life miserable."

Dex peered at him. "But you already do that."

"Yeah, but now I get to do it around the clock." His evil grin had Dex taking a step back. *Note to self—think before opening big mouth*. "Also, if we're on the clock, you address me as Maddock, Sarge, Sergeant, or Sir. Also, you'll hear your brother referred to by his first name rather than surname. Less confusing."

"Got it, Sarge. So… would you care to elaborate on who my partner is?"

"You'll be meeting your team soon enough." Tony gave him a smug grin, and Dex cursed under his breath. That couldn't be good. How could Tony hold out on him? The man had been there for Dex when he'd hooked up with his first boyfriend and then proceeded to get dumped by his first boyfriend and now recent ex-boyfriend. Tony had been there to explain the importance of condoms and lube—now *that* had been an awkward conversation. Why wouldn't he tell him about his new partner? Was it that bad? Pearce's words echoed in his head. *Don't expect a warm welcome.*

At the end of the short corridor was a set of twelve-foot-high glass-paned double doors. In bold white letters high above, it read UNIT ALPHA. Well, here it was. Behind those doors lay a whole new life.

A life he was either going to excel at, or totally crash and burn.

Now that he stood with that title looming over him, he had a sudden bout of panic. What if he couldn't hack it as a THIRDS agent? Sure, he had shined during the training, but this wasn't training. He was part of a tactical team now, a team that included his family, his *real* family. If he failed, not only would he be letting them down, he could get them killed. Before those fears could burrow any deeper, a smooth male voice with a rich British accent called out from somewhere behind them. They turned to find a Therian male—whose markings on his neck stated he was a Canis Lupus—and a Human female in white lab coats quickly approaching.

"Sergeant Maddock, can we have a moment, please?"

"Hudson, Nina, great timing." Tony turned to introduce Dex. "This is our newest recruit, Agent Dexter J. Daley. Dex, this is Destructive Delta's medical examiner, Dr. Nina Bishop, and our chief medical examiner, Dr. Hudson Colbourn."

"Dr. Bishop, pleasure to meet you." Dex took the woman's hand with a smile. She was tall and slender with delicate features, deep brown eyes, and dark hair. She also had a sharp gaze that was currently sizing him up as she shook his hand. To Dex's relief, her pursed lips soon gave way to a warm smile, and Dex let out the breath he'd been holding.

"Pleasure's all mine, Agent Daley."

Next to her was the chief medical examiner, sporting trendy black-framed glasses. The Therian oozed elegance and confidence as he held out his hand. He was also pretty hot. "Nice to meet you, Dr. Colbourn." The way the doctor eyed Dex said he wouldn't mind giving Dex a personal examination. Shame they'd be working together. Dex never mixed business with pleasure. Even worse than relationship drama was workplace relationship drama. He'd never been mixed up in it himself, but he'd seen enough at the HPF to scare him straight—so to speak. It was also against THIRDS policy.

"It's a pleasure to meet you, Agent Daley."

Dex grinned widely at Dr. Colbourn and beside him, Tony rolled his eyes.

"Sergeant Maddock and Agent Cael talk about you so often, I feel like I already know you," Colbourn added.

"Lies, all lies," Dex teased. "Except for the good parts. Those are all true."

Dr. Colbourn gave him a wink. "Well, we look forward to working with you. And we apologize for interrupting your induction, but we need to borrow the sergeant. It concerns a case we're in the middle of."

Tony let out a heavy sigh, his brows furrowed with unease. "The HumaniTherians case. Cael and his partner Rosa Santiago have been working it for weeks."

"Any leads?" Judging by Tony's deepening scowl, Dex figured that was pretty much a no. Therian forensics was far more complicated than Human forensics, not to mention it was still in development, despite newer and more advanced Therian techniques coming to light all the time. Of course, that didn't help when you were trying to work a Therian homicide and your victim resembled ground beef.

"Nothing so far," Tony replied grimly. "We've got a briefing scheduled this afternoon, so I'll fill you in then. But it's not looking good. Why don't you find your way down to Sparta. I'll introduce you to the rest of the team and continue the tour as soon as I finish up here. Then we'll get you assigned a locker. Your details are already in the system, so use the identification pad in the elevator to go to level "B.""

"Sure thing."

"There's a lounge and a snack bar. Wait for me in either of those. Do *not* go wandering around." Tony gave him a warning look before motioning for him to get lost.

"Okay." He didn't know what Tony was so worried about. It wasn't like he was going to go running around like a crazy person. The last thing he needed was for his new team to think he was some kind of nut-job. He left Tony and the medical examiners to make his way back down the corridor, giving friendly smiles and greetings as he went. Those who weren't too busy saving the world from itself greeted him pleasantly enough. Most seemed more curious than anything.

It didn't take him long to get down to the basement and through a set of twelve-foot-high double doors with the word "Sparta" painted across them. Inside, the place was bigger than any gym he'd ever been to, bustling with agents in various stages of undress as they went from one part of the facility to another. Straight ahead of him in the center was an expansive open area filled with plenty of comfortable-looking couches and widescreen TVs, most likely the lounge. It was occupied with agents sitting around chatting, napping, or playing with their tablets. He wondered if any of these agents were part of his team. Tony said to wait in the lounge. He didn't say not to talk to anyone.

Dex scanned the room for any Therians who looked like they might be Alphas, and although he couldn't make out the marks on their necks telling him what classification of Therian they were, he could still discern them from the Human agents. Spotting Therians was pretty easy. All one had to do was look for the telltale sign—the clear presence of tapetum lucidum, the layer of tissue behind the retina that reflected visible light, released it back, and increased the light available to the photoreceptors. Or in other words, what helped animals see at night. When the light hit their eyes a certain way—boom, Therian.

Over on one of the large gray couches were three Therians, two male and one female, joking and laughing. They seemed approachable, in a "we can turn you into linguini but only if you piss us off" kind of way.

"Hey, sorry to interrupt, but I'm looking for Destructive Delta? I'm the new guy."

The three Therians regarded him before bursting into laughter. He wasn't really sure what they were laughing at, but he joined in on the fun, chuckling along with them, until it occurred to him they thought he was joking. "No really. I'm the new guy."

The laughter died.

Their mouths hung open, and the largest of the three agents stared at him wide-eyed. "Shit, you're not kidding. Sorry, bro, we thought you were messing around. You sure it's Destructive Delta?"

Dex tapped the patch on his sleeve that said so. "Yep. I'm guessing you guys aren't Destructive Delta."

"No, we're Intel for Unit Beta, Troop Gamma. Everyone comes down here because Unit Alpha has the best equipment."

The female Therian nodded in agreement. "And a bigger pool."

Unit Alpha had a pool? Sweet! Dex couldn't wait to use that.

"Also, it's fun to watch them kick each other's asses during training," the second male Therian added with an evil grin.

"Sounds like fun," Dex said cheerfully. "So, can you point me in their general direction?"

The female agent looked genuinely concerned. "You sure you don't want to wait for your commanding officer to be introduced? I think they're training right now. Agent Brodie gets pretty pissed when you interrupt his training."

"I'm not going to interrupt," Dex promised. "Just want a sneak peek." The last thing he wanted to do was get on his team leader's shit list from day one.

"Okay. It's your funeral." The largest of the agents pointed to a corridor behind Dex.

That was encouraging. "Thanks." He headed for the busy passageway, making sure to stay out of everyone's way and keep his head down. There were several enormous training areas filled with agents working the classy-looking treadmills, doing weights, push-ups, sit-ups, and everything else to keep their bodies in peak physical condition. The equipment was top-of-the-line, shiny and new. The floors were covered in dark rubber tiles that looked as if they had been installed only recently.

Some of the rooms were set up for martial arts, while others were set up for boxing. There was even a yoga studio that had as many male agents in it as it did female. No wonder so many agents crowded down here. There was no sign of a pool, though, so he figured it was on the other side of the facility. Who knew what else was down here. The place was huge.

"You son of a bitch!"

Dex straightened, listening to the litany of curses that followed the initial exclamation. Following the cursing, he found the room it was coming from. It was a large training bay at the end, but unlike the others filled with numerous agents, this one only had a handful of them. He made sure to keep himself discreetly tucked to one side of the open double doors as he carefully peeked inside. There were seven agents separated into little groups. He immediately spotted his brother on one side, sitting on the floor cross-legged with a tablet in his hand. What a nerd. Dex's phone buzzed, and he gave it a quick glance. *CaelMad liked your photo.*

"Seriously, dude?" Dex muttered under his breath, returning his phone to his pocket. There were hot, sweaty guys beating the crap out of each other in the same room, and Cael was playing around online. Dex was going to have a serious talk with his brother.

So these were the guys his brother spent so much time with. Cael never talked about them individually, always referring to them as his teammates, or if he was hanging with one in particular, his teammate. It didn't bother Dex that Cael kept his work life separate from his homelife, especially since the THIRDS loved to keep everything classified. With Dex having

been HPF, Cael was even less inclined to talk about
work. It was no secret the HPF and the THIRDS barely tolerated each other. Had he known he'd be ending
up here, he would have pushed his brother for more
information on the team.

Not far from Cael was a tall, slender Human female agent who was cursing up a storm in Spanish as
she sparred with another, more petite Human female
agent, who was also speaking Spanish. The petite
agent was giving as good as she got, though with a
bit less swearing. The fact that she was enjoying the
match far too much for her own good seemed to be the
source of her teammate's irritation.

A few feet from them were a blond Human agent
and his bigger Therian teammate, who was in the midst
of some major brooding. Dex couldn't hear what was
being said, but Mr. Broody didn't look pleased. He
shook his head and started to walk off when his blond
friend took hold of his arm. He kept his grip on his
larger partner, his head tilted to one side and back
as he was forced to look up to meet his teammate's
glower. Whatever he said made the large Therian nod,
and soon a small smile came onto his face. Well, at
least they'd worked out whatever it was that had been
bothering Mr. Broody. He didn't look like the kind
of Therian you wanted to piss off. Then Dex looked
over at the heavy mat in the center of the room and
changed his mind. Nope, *that* was the kind of Therian
you didn't want to piss off.

With his back to Dex stood a large Therian, over
six and a half feet tall, dressed in a black T-shirt and
matching sports pants. His knees were slightly bent,
and his muscular arms were up as he took a fighting

stance, waiting for the cursing Therian sprawled on his back to get up. It was pretty clear the guy on the floor was pissed as hell. The mark on his neck stated he was a lion Therian; he was also, strangely enough, wearing a blue T-shirt with a distressed image of Tony the Tiger on it. With a growl, Mr. Frosted Flakes— who had equally beefy arms and was actually bigger than black T-shirt guy—shot to his feet and charged.

Frosted Flakes drove into his opponent with such force, it should have sent them both crashing to the floor, but instead, Dex gaped as black T-shirt guy threw his arms around his attacker's waist, swiped his legs out from under him, lifted him, and slammed him down onto the mat with enough strength to momentarily stun the larger Therian. Clearly, black T-shirt guy was his new team leader, Agent Brodie. Dex remembered what Pearce had said about the Therian, but even so, Dex had to admire Agent Brodie. He exuded confidence, calm, and a quiet strength Dex hadn't been expecting.

"Watch your temper, Ash."

Ooh, Agent Brodie had a sexy, gravelly voice. Dex quickly pushed that thought out of his mind and watched as Agent Ash rolled over with a groan. "Fuck you, man. You're not supposed to be able to do that shit. I'm bigger and heavier than you!"

"How many times do I have to tell you, that doesn't mean anything if you're not focused."

"Fuck this shit." Ash got to his feet and took a swing at Agent Brodie, whose face Dex still hadn't managed to get a look at. Damn it, why couldn't they swap places or something? Not that Ash was bad to look at, but it was lost underneath all the snarling. Oh

God, what if this Agent Ash Whatever was his new partner? Well, he wasn't exactly spoiled for choice. Being Human, his only options were Ash, Mr. Broody, or Agent Brodie sexy-voice supposed-asshole.

Awesome.

Agent Brodie had neat black hair, and when he turned his head just enough, Dex could see scruffy stubble, which, despite his age—Dex estimated maybe late thirties—was sprinkled with gray. He was also fit. The muscles under his black T-shirt flexed and shifted as he moved, his biceps causing the sleeves to stretch. He had powerful legs and a mighty fine ass. Dex hoped Agent Brodie kicked the tar out of Agent Ash. He didn't know why, but the bigger Therian rubbed him the wrong way.

Dex was expecting a few punches to fly between them, not the epic, Bourne-like close-quarter combat that ensued. The two Therians didn't look like they were playing around, except for the lack of broken bones, which Dex was pretty certain they could have easily provided had they wanted to. Ash was bigger, fiercer, and meaner, but Agent Brodie was calm, focused, and fast as hell. Dex tried to keep track of the moves, looking for vulnerabilities and signs of predictability. The way Agent Brodie blocked Ash's punches was impressive, because it was clear the larger Therian was a pro at fighting up close and personal.

Ash twisted his body to get out of Agent Brodie's choke hold. Ash landed beside Brodie and threw an arm around Brodie's neck, forcing Brodie to bend over before delivering a blow to the ribs, or at least attempting to. Ash's fist was smacked away, and Agent Brodie quickly retaliated by throwing his elbow up, making contact with Ash's face, sending him reeling back with a bloodied nose. Ash wiped at his nose with the back of his hand.

"Fuck! Come on, Sloane. I got a date tonight."

Agent Sloane Brodie finally turned around, and all Dex could think was *Well, hello there*.

Shit, his team leader was *hot*. What was the likelihood that he was as big of an asshole as Pearce said he was? Dex made it a rule never to judge anyone based on someone else's opinion of him, especially someone he had yet to meet. So far, there didn't seem to be any signs of it, but then again, he was sure the agent hadn't been promoted to team leader at the THIRDS because he gave the best hugs.

Sloane caught a towel the petite female agent tossed to him. "Thanks, Letty. Ash, tell her what you tell all your dates. That you got hurt saving some kittens from a burning building."

"Surrounded by ninjas," Cael added suddenly, a dopey grin stretched across his face. So his brother *was* paying attention.

Ash thrust a finger at Cael. "Don't encourage him."

Everyone laughed as Ash cursed them all out. The camaraderie among the team was evident in the way they ribbed each other and cursed at each other. Even when they were angry or annoyed, it was clear there was nothing spiteful or malicious behind it. They were a family, and Dex was about to intrude on that sanctity.

It wasn't only the whole family-unit thing Dex was worried about. As he quietly turned and headed back toward the lounge, he couldn't stop thinking about Sloane Brodie and Ash. The level of skill they showed during their sparring session spoke volumes.

Ash's form had been better than Sloane's, denoting close-quarter combat as one of his proficiencies. He hadn't had to think about the moves, he simply reacted, no doubt from years of practice. It was his temper that let him down, whereas Sloane had experience in determining what was coming his way. His level of concentration in considering the surrounding variables had been impressive. He observed, adapted, and applied himself without hesitation.

Dex dropped down onto one of the empty couches in the lounge. He was *so* out of his league. After a few minutes of wallowing in his own misery, he mentally shook himself off and stood up. Okay, so maybe he was out of his league at this particular junction of his career, but it was only his first day.

You can do this, Dex. His team had been training and working out in the field for years. As much as he hated to admit it, Tony was right. He was a rookie. If he wanted to be up to par, he'd have to work damn hard. Of course, working damn hard would be a whole lot easier after something to eat. He joined a number of the other agents in the large snack bar lined with wall-to-wall vending machines providing everything from energy bars to gummy bears. Spotting one of his favorite snacks, he stepped up to the shiny machine and tapped the digital screen, watching as the last packet of Cheesy Doodles flopped down into the tray.

"Mm, cheesy goodness." Dex had just picked up the orange-and-black foil packet when a shadow loomed over him.

"Hey."

Turning, Dex's greeting died on his lips when instead of being met with an average-sized individual,

he was met with a Therian who made Ash look like
a hobbit. "Um, hey." He peeked at the mark on the
Therian's tree-trunk of a neck. Ursus arctos. *Fuuuck.*
"How's it going?" Dex smiled brightly and took a
small step to his right. Near-black eyes pinned him
with a glare, and a hefty finger pointed at the Cheesy
Doodles in Dex's hands.

"That's the last pack."

"Yeah. Sorry, man." Dex moved away a little
more, aware of how the other agents in the room were
either staring at him wide-eyed or snickering quietly.
He appreciated the way they were doing *nothing* to
help him, bunch of pricks. *Okay, Dex, time to grow
a pair.*

"Hand it over," the Therian growled.

Or not. Dex blinked up at him. "I'm sorry, what
now?"

"Everyone knows those are mine."

Therian or not, Yogi Bear needed to learn some
manners. "Considering I paid for them, I don't see
how that's possible."

"All of them are."

"Seriously? You're calling dibs on a vending machine's worth of Cheesy Doodles?" Dex looked from
the sneering Therian to the Cheesy Doodles in his
hands and back. He arched an eyebrow at Yogi before
reaching into the packet, plucking one, and popping
it into his mouth, followed by a wide grin. The room
erupted into laughter and catcalls.

Yogi made a swipe at him with one massive hand,
but Dex dropped to the floor before he could get clobbered. He scrambled to his feet, shoved the packet into

his roomy back pocket, and bolted from the room, yelling out behind him, "Bastards!"

Yogi was fast on his heels as Dex sped through the lounge, down the busy corridor, and past the training bays. "Excuse me! Coming through!" *Shit, shit, shit!* Who'd have thought Yogi would like Cheesy Doodles as much as he did?

"Give them here!" Yogi growled.

"Go find your own pic-a-nic basket!" The deep feral growl he received in response was most likely a no.

Dex ran into the training bay hoping to get help from his little brother, or at least use him as a shield, when he slammed into something hard, bounced back, and hit Yogi, who shoved him harshly into the first hard body Dex had hit. An arm came around him as the three of them crashed into a large martial arts display. As he fell, Dex braced himself.

This was going to hurt.

Chapter 3

A BOOMING crash echoed through the room as Sloane hit the floor along with the ten-foot display, everything from wooden bokkens to bo staffs landing on him and clattering around him. When the Human agent collided with him, Sloane's instinct had been to throw his arm around the man in the hopes of regaining his equilibrium, but instead, the man's flailing sent them both toppling over. With a groan, Sloane rolled over and smacked his head against someone else's.

"Son of a bitch!" Sloane spat out at the idiot on the floor next to him rubbing his own forehead. "What the hell?"

The man's eyes opened wide, and for a moment Sloane was speechless. They were the palest crystal blue he'd ever seen, a sharp contrast against tan skin, dark brows, and dirty-blond hair. The agent, however, was unfamiliar to him. Must be new, or Sloane would have remembered him.

"Shit," Blondie exclaimed, his face going bright red. The guy was embarrassed, but Sloane didn't have time to ask questions as Blondie let out a yelp and was hung upside down from his ankles by a pissed-off-looking Therian agent.

"Give it here!"

Blondie twisted and pulled at his legs. "Fuck you, Baloo!"

Sloane quickly got to his feet, the rest of the team running up to join them, their expressions of stunned disbelief mirroring Sloane's.

"What the hell is going on?" Ash asked.

"Good question." Sloane crossed his arms over his chest, his eyes narrowing at the seven-foot agent. "What are you doing, Agent Zachary? Put him down."

Zach's bottom lip jutted out pathetically as he motioned to the agent dangling from his grip. "He stole my Cheesy Doodles."

Sloane's jaw dropped. Behind him, his team snorted and giggled like schoolchildren. "Are you telling me all this"—he snapped, thrusting a finger at the mess of equipment on the floor—"is over a pack of *cheese snacks*?"

Blondie pulled himself up by his legs and attempted to loosen one of Zach's hands with no luck. "In my defense, I was eating, minding my own business, when Yogi Bear over here tries to kill me!"

"Why did you steal his snack?" Sloane asked, mystified. Was the guy crazy or stupid?

"I didn't!" Blondie cried indignantly. "I *bought* them, but apparently he called dibs on a whole fucking vending machine!"

"Fine. Why didn't you give them to him, then?"

With a groan, Blondie stopped struggling and went back to hanging upside down, his arms folded over his chest and his chin set stubbornly. "Because they're mine."

"Everyone knows they're mine," Zach growled.

"Oh for the love of…." Sloane pinched the bridge of his nose and summoned patience. "Where are they?"

Blondie reached into his back pocket, pulled out the cause of this ridiculous event, and held it out. Sloane snatched the packet from the Human agent and stuffed it into Zach's front breast pocket. "There, now put him down." Before he could tell Zach to do so gently, Blondie was released. They all cringed as the agent hit the floor with a painful thud.

"Ow! Motherfucking piss buckets!"

"Thank you," Zach said with a wide grin.

"Share next time, okay?" Sloane patted Zach's arm and sent him on his way. He looked down at the mess of an agent on the floor. God help the team this guy was on.

"Dex!"

Sloane glanced up sharply. Oh fuck no. "You?" He gaped at the blond man bitching and cursing as he got up.

"You don't have to look so happy about it," Dex muttered, brushing himself off.

It couldn't be. "This has to be a mistake."

"Try using your inside voice. Less awkward."

Cael ran over and grabbed Dex's arms. "Are you okay? I was in the bathroom when I heard what happened. The minute they said 'crazy guy,' I knew it was you."

"Gee, thanks."

"You're Detective Daley?" Sloane still couldn't believe it. This couldn't be the same guy Maddock was always talking about. Impossible.

"*Agent* Dexter J. Daley. You can call me Dex." Dex put his hands on his hips and looked around the stupefied team with a broad grin. "So which one of you is my new partner?" Everyone turned to Sloane, and the smile fell off Dex's face. "This day just gets better and better."

"Absolutely not." Sloane shook his head, as if doing so would make the whole disturbing problem disappear. This was not acceptable. He understood he was going to be dealing with a rookie, but this, this…. No.

Dex turned to him, his expression sincere. "Look, I'm sorry about earlier. That was stupid, I know. I didn't mean to panic. I've never had a Therian threaten my life over cheese snacks before. Well, except for Cael, but we're family. Give me a chance."

Damn it. It's not like he had a choice in the matter. He'd already been warned by Lieutenant Sparks. He *had* to have a partner, and she was frustrated with him as it was for the half-dozen or so agents he'd scared off. In his defense, they had been absolute fuckwits. Okay, they hadn't been. In fact, they'd been perfectly capable, but none of them had been a good fit for his team, and in the end, that was as important as competence. "You're not what I expected."

"Surpassed your expectations?" Dex asked with a hopeful smile.

Jesus, it was worse than he thought. Sloane narrowed his eyes. "No."

"Right. So um, this is the team, huh?"

He was going to have a serious talk with Maddock about this. In the meantime, he turned to the rest of the team to make the introductions, starting with Ash—who Sloane refused to so much as make eye contact with. The only reason Ash wasn't having a total shit fit about their newest recruit was out of respect for Cael. Thank God for small miracles. As soon as Cael was out of earshot, he was going to have to listen to Ash bitch. The thought alone exhausted him. "This is Ash Keeler, our entry tactics and CQC expert, and his partner, Julietta Guerrera, our weapons expert."

"Letty," the petite agent corrected with a serious nod.

Sloane motioned to the youngest agent on their team. "You know Cael. That's his partner, Rosa Santiago, our crisis negotiator and medic."

"Rosa, nice to meet you," Dex said, smiling pleasantly.

Rosa pursed her lips, her arms crossing over her chest. This was going to be fun. Sloane could feel it already. Turning to the next two members of their team, Sloane braced himself.

"This is Calvin Summers, our sniper, and his partner, Ethan Hobbs, our demolitions expert."

Dex pressed his lips together, and Sloane knew what was coming next. Dex's gaze went from the tall brooding Therian to his smaller, equally brooding, blond, spiky-haired partner and back.

"So...." Dex began, looking up at Hobbs whose Therian form was clearly marked as being a tiger. "Do they call you Ethan or...."

"They call him Hobbs," Calvin said with a roll of his eyes. "Get it out of your system."

Dex was biting his bottom lip, trying his hardest not to laugh, but in the end gave in. "I'm sorry, I am. So they call you two Calvin and Hobbs? It's just… that's… so awesome."

"It is awesome," Calvin drawled as he turned to Hobbs. "Isn't that what I was telling you this morning? How awesome it is? The cartoon jokes never get old, do they?" Dex's gaze went to Ash's Frosted Flakes T-shirt, and Calvin let out a snort of disgust. "Christ. You and your fucking T-shirts, Ash."

"What?" Ash shrugged innocently. "I happen to be a fan. Hey, how come you never wear that red-and-black striped T-shirt I got you for your birthday last year?"

Hobbs let out a low growl, and Calvin gestured rudely. "Blow me, Ash."

"Grow a pair of tits and I'll think about it." Ash returned the lewd gesture and added his tongue into the mix.

Sloane didn't need this right now. "Guys," he pleaded. "Come on."

"Don't pay any attention to them," Rosa told Dex. "They're busting your balls because you're the new guy."

An evil grin came onto Ash's face. "Speaking of balls, Rosa show you hers yet?"

Rosa gave Ash a rough push, which only made him laugh. "Pendejo, vete pa'l carajo. Puta."

"I love it when you talk dirty to me." Ash laughed, dodging her blows as she went after him. "I keep telling you, baby. One night with me, and I promise you, I'll get you back onto beef. You can invite your girlfriend."

"Fuck you, Ash. You—"

"All right, that's enough!" Sloane hissed, getting everyone's attention. "Ash, go clean that shit up." He jutted his thumb over his shoulder, and as expected, Ash turned a menacing glare on Dex before storming off, cursing under his breath. "Rosa, go help him."

Rosa's hand went to her hip, her other arm coming up as she flipped Ash off. Sloane didn't even want to know what Ash was doing behind his back. The less he saw, the better. "Why do I have to go help that *puta*?"

"Because you two drive me fucking batshit crazy," Sloane ground out before motioning toward Dex, "and if you haven't noticed, I have enough to deal with." With nostrils flaring, Rosa went off after Ash. "Calvin, you and Hobbit continuing your romp. Lefty, go get Dex a locker assignment. Cael, take five." Everyone dispersed and Sloane was left with his new partner, who should have been accompanied by their sergeant, not left to wander around on his own, especially since he couldn't seem to do so without creating chaos. "Where's Maddock?"

"With Dr. Colbourn and Dr. Bishop. They needed to discuss something with him about the HumaniTherians case. You know, you didn't introduce yourself." Dex smiled and held a hand out to him.

With a pleasant smile, Sloane took his hand and shook it. "I apologize. Hi, I'm Agent Sloane Brodie, your team leader. I enjoy reading, cozy nights in, and the soothing sounds of classic rock. I also like to browse the internet for funny cat videos, but deep down, I think I'm more of a dog person."

Dex eyed him, uncertain. "You're being sarcastic."

"Yes, Rookie, I'm being sarcastic." Sloane pulled his hand away. "All you have to know about me is that

I expect you to do what I say. Got it?" He received a curt nod.

"Got it."

"Good. Now we're going to get on that mat, and you're going to show me what I've got to work with."

A startled look came onto Dex's face. "You want me to fight you?"

"Judging from the bruise on your lip and the scratches on your face, I'd say it's not exactly a foreign concept to you." Dex opened his mouth, and Sloane quickly held a hand up to stop him. "I don't care. You're at work now, and when you're at work, your ass belongs to me. You got a problem with that?"

"No. I just wasn't expecting to get my cherry popped on the first day."

"I'm sure that sounded better in your head. Whatever expectations you had about the job and the THIRDS, I suggest you forget all of them. Now get your ass out there. Shoes and shirt off. You can hand your rig to Cael. Oh, and Rookie?"

"Yeah?"

"Now!"

Dex quickly removed his boots, revealing bright orange socks and drawing a sneer from Sloane. Standard issue was black, but Dex clearly thought himself to be special. There was gel in his hair and from here, Sloane could smell some fruity, citrusy concoction. The uniform shirt was removed next, and Sloane did his best to dismiss the stir in his abdomen as he took in the rookie's semiundressed state. Muscular arms and an equally muscular chest beneath a snug black T-shirt flexed attractively. He wasn't as tall, bulky, or wide as Sloane, more sinewy and athletic, but he was well-built.

Sloane wasn't above admitting when he found someone physically attractive, and the agent before him was. Now that he'd gotten that out of the way, he could focus on the job, a job that had suddenly become a lot more difficult. Dex removed his rig from around his leg, and after whistling to his brother, tossed it over. Cael caught it and placed it on the floor beside him before going back to his tablet. Did that kid ever put that thing down?

Sloane observed Dex as he made his way to the center of the mat. The guy had a nice ass too. On that note, maybe it was time for Sloane to get laid. It had been way too long since he'd picked anyone up, but then, the only thing that seemed to interest him these days was the job. Why the hell was he thinking about sex now? He followed Dex onto the blue mat and stopped a few feet away from him, pushing any and all sexual thoughts out of his mind. He had work to do. *A lot* of work to do.

Dex readied himself, stretching his neck and back. Despite his disastrous introduction, the guy actually had excellent poise. He balanced perfectly on one leg while he pulled the opposite knee up to stretch, then swapped and did the same with the other. He bent over and grabbed his ankles with ease, then slowly rolled his back to stand upright again. Rotating his shoulders, he shook himself off and hopped on his toes for a few seconds to warm up. His movements revealed he was lithe and flexible, yet Sloane couldn't understand how this was the same guy who had scored top of his class during the training run. It was true he didn't know much about Dex, but he'd read the file the moment he'd been informed of the decision.

Both parents had been killed during the riots when he was five years old. He'd been adopted by his father's friend and work partner, Anthony Maddock. A year later, his baby Therian brother was rescued and adopted. Went to Berkeley at eighteen for four years, earned a bachelor of science degree in Justice Studies, and joined the HPF a year later. Four years after that, he was promoted to homicide detective. Dexter J. Daley, thirty-three years old, unmarried, and recently testified against his Human partner in a murder trial. Sloane was still figuring out what to think about that last part.

Dex took his stance, bending his knees, his left leg a little farther up than the right, and his fists up near his face.

"Your stance is good," Sloane murmured, ignoring Dex's surprised look. Taking up his own fighting stance, Sloane motioned for Dex to advance. "Okay. Come at me."

Dex shook his head. "No."

Sloane paused. Was the rookie messing with him? "What do you mean 'no'?"

"How about *you* come at *me*."

"That's not how this works."

"I've seen what attacking you head-on does. You want to see what I can do? You'll have to work for it."

Sloane arched an eyebrow. Well, if nothing else, the guy had balls. "Okay. Remember, you asked for it." He advanced, faked with his right to land a left hook to Dex's ribs. A swipe to his left foot brought Dex crashing down to the mat.

"Fuck," Dex moaned, rolling out of the way. He jumped to his feet and rounded his shoulders. "Okay." Bouncing on his toes, he circled Sloane. "Let's try this again."

This match was over. Rookie just didn't know it yet. Sloane was good at exposing weaknesses, and he was already working on discovering his new partner's.

They slowly circled each other, and Sloane got closer to Dex with each step until he was close enough to throw a punch. Dex blocked it, his concentration focused on keeping Sloane from landing a hit. He was studying Sloane, trying to get a handle on his technique so he could formulate a plan of attack. Rookie was using his head—that was good—but he was taking too long to decide on his course of action, and that was bad. Hesitation was something his Human partner couldn't afford out in the field, not when dealing with Therians. As a species, Therians were faster, stronger, healed quicker, and had a higher level of tolerance when it came to pain.

Dex blocked a left hook to the ribs with his right elbow tucked up against his body, but in anticipation of Sloane faking a right, he tucked his left elbow in as well, leaving his head exposed. Sloane took advantage and clipped Dex under his chin. His head came up, once again leaving himself exposed long enough for Sloane to give his cheek a smack. Dex shuffled back, eyes wide.

"What the fuck was that?"

"I'm sorry. Did I smear your makeup?" Sloane held back a smile at Dex's glare. This was too easy. Forgetting all about keeping his distance, Dex charged him.

A fierce combination of hooks, jabs, and an attempt at an uppercut were nicely executed, but still not enough to catch Sloane off guard. He blocked Dex's advances, ducked under a right hook, and grabbed Dex's leg. With a forceful pull, Dex was once again sprawled on his back.

"I haven't spent this much time on my back since college."

Sloane laughed. "It's a good look for you, Rookie."

"You asking me out on a date? Because I don't date assholes," Dex grumbled, sitting up.

"I may be an asshole, but even I've got standards."

With a smirk, Dex hung his head and held an arm out.

"Giving up already? How disappointing." Sloane reached out and took Dex's hand, ready to pull him up when Dex twisted his torso and kicked a leg out, catching Sloane on the side of his knee and sending him down onto it. He was jerked forward and Dex's legs wrapped around his waist. He twisted his lower body to throw Sloane onto his back. Dex landed on him, his hands pinning Sloane's wrists to the mat beneath them, their faces inches away from each other.

"So, about that date," Dex said, laughing breathlessly. His eyes shifted to Sloane's lips before moving back up, and his smile grew wider. The little shit was taunting him.

Sloane didn't know what pissed him off more, that he'd been caught by surprise, or that he was enjoying it. His anger started bubbling up inside him, and that pissed him off even more. He didn't get angry. Anger meant the rookie was getting to him.

With a pleasant smile, Sloane jerked his left wrist free to snatch Dex's in a tight grip. He looped his arm around Dex's neck, forcing Dex's arm to come up and around as well. With a swift yank, Dex spun off him and onto the mat.

That was better. Sloane casually got to his feet with a satisfied grin. He took a deep breath to regain his calm and turned, frowning at the sight of Dex on his stomach, his back arching as he let out a frustrated groan. He ignored the curve of the rookie's spine and the way he looked when he got onto his hands and knees. Jesus, what was wrong with him? It was time to put a stop to this… distraction.

"Come on," Sloane snarled. "Get up. I'm not here to be your Xbox buddy."

"Come on, Dex!" Cael sat on the floor a few feet away, and Sloane tilted his head, his bottom lip jutting out in a pout as he teased Dex.

"Aw, isn't that cute? Baby brother is cheering for you."

Dex lunged at him, throwing his arms around Sloane's waist in an inane attempt to knock him over. Sloane didn't go down. He was bigger, stronger, and heavier than Dex, but to the rookie's credit, he managed to get in a nice jab to the ribs. With a well-maneuvered twist of his body, Sloane was out of Dex's grip and holding him in a headlock. Instead of punching him, he delivered another slap to his cheek. Dex let out a frustrated growl and tried to push away from him.

"Stop doing that!"

"Ooh, Rookie's got a bit of a temper." Sloane ruffled Dex's hair, pissing him off further.

"Aw, isn't he cute," Ash teased from the end of the mat.

"Fuck you, Simba!"

Rosa burst into laughter, and Ash glared at her. "Are you fucking serious?" He turned back to Sloane with a scowl. "You better kick his ass."

Dex struggled in Sloane's grip. "Come on, Rookie. Is this the best you got?"

"This isn't fighting," Dex spat out. "This is you being a prick."

Sloane shrugged. "Either way, I've seen what you can do and I gotta say, it's pretty uninspiring."

"Uninspiring, huh?" Dex pulled back a fist and Sloane released him, jumping back and narrowly missing Dex's fist, his knuckles brushing Sloane's crotch. Sloane gaped at Dex.

"You were going to punch me in the nuts?"

"You said it yourself. This isn't a fight, so yeah. And I would have enjoyed it too."

"Hey, watch it." Sloane stormed up to Dex, who held his ground, his chin lifted defiantly. Rookie had nerve, but he needed to learn his place. Sloane grabbed him, hauled him off his feet, and slammed him into the mat. "Stay the fuck down, if you know what's good for you."

Dex ignored him, his breath coming out heavy as he got back on his feet and threw a punch. Stupid little bastard didn't know when to quit. Sloane ducked, grabbed Dex around the waist, and once again slammed him back down on the mat. With a low groan, Dex rolled onto his side and pushed himself onto his hands and knees. Sloane wiped the sweat off his brow with the back of his hand as he circled Dex. He'd lost count of how many times he'd dropped Dex, yet the guy kept getting back up. Granted, each time took a little longer than the last, but he pushed himself to his feet regardless. Sloane didn't know whether to be impressed or aggravated.

"You're not cut out for this, Rookie."

Dex didn't reply, simply glared at him. He charged Sloane with a growl, ducking under Sloane's right hook and landing a jab to Sloane's exposed ribs. Gritting his teeth against the pain, Sloane used the adrenaline pumping through his veins to keep going and bring his fists down onto Dex's back. Dex hit the mat painfully, his head smacking against it.

Fuck. Sloane touched his ribs and winced. Damn, the rookie had gotten him pretty good. "Why don't you stay down? It's only going to get worse."

With a humorless laugh, Dex rolled onto his back, his chest rising and falling rapidly. "Let me guess. This is the part where I'm supposed to go crying home to Daddy. 'Ooh, my new partner hates me. Boo-hoo.'" Sloane could see the strain on the rookie's face as he struggled to stand, sucking in a sharp breath when he straightened. "Well, fuck you. Here's a little FYI for you. I would rather fucking *bleed* to death than give you the satisfaction, you prick."

Sloane arched an eyebrow at him. "Charming."

"I *am* fucking charming!" Dex shouted, his entire face going beet red. "I am the most charming motherfucker you will ever know, so kiss my perfectly perky ass!"

After some consideration, Sloane cocked his head to one side and shrugged. "I've seen better."

"Oh, now you're insulting my ass?"

Sloane opened his mouth when a booming voice came over the speaker system.

"Destructive Delta, please report to briefing room A in one hour as per Sergeant Maddock's orders."

"Looks like you were saved by Daddy after all." Sloane turned to his team and clapped his hands together. "Okay, hit the showers. See you upstairs." Everyone headed out, and Sloane made his way to the towel rack. He grabbed himself one to wipe his face, and when he turned, he almost ran into Dex, his rig hanging from one hand.

"Well, let's see it."

Sloane threw his towel over his shoulder. "See what?"

"You know."

"Are you asking me to go feral or whip out my dick?"

Dex looked like he was actually considering it. "Come on. I want to see the alpha beneath the asshole. We've got lions, and tigers, and…." Dex shifted his gaze to Sloane's neck, a strange little smile coming onto his face as he looked back up at Sloane. "Jaguar. Oh my."

Holy shit, the guy was serious.

Dex shrugged. "I don't see what the big deal is. You're my partner, we're in a wide-open space, and there are vending machines down the hall for postshift. We've got time before we need to get to the briefing room. It's my turn to see what I'm dealing with."

Sloane mulled it over. "Okay."

"Yeah?"

"Sure." Sloane circled Dex and crowded him, making him retreat until his back hit the wall. With his arms to the sides of Dex's head, he watched Dex's Adam's apple bob as his new partner swallowed hard. Just as Sloane suspected, Dex was clearly having second thoughts about seeing the "big bad alpha." He leaned in close, his lips inches away from Dex's jaw as he inhaled deeply. "Do you know why jaguar Therians are the most lethal of the Felids?"

"Um...."

"My Therian bite has twice the strength of a lion's. I can use a deep-throat, bite-and-suffocation technique where my fangs pierce through the temporal bones of your skull, right between your ears, and pierce your brain." Sloane gave a little demonstration with his fingers on Dex's scalp, earning him a scowl. Sloane laughed, then whispered in Dex's ear. "I bet the only words you heard from all that were *deep-throat*."

Dex lifted his chin, his eyes dropping once again to Sloane's mouth before moving back up to meet his gaze. He licked his lips, his eyes clouding over. "Your pupils are dilated. Does that mean you want to fuck me or eat me? Because I might have a problem with one of those."

Sloane congratulated himself on not letting his surprise show. Rookie definitely had some balls. He curled a hand around Dex's neck and gave it a gentle squeeze, fully aware of the stirring in his groin. He chose to ignore it. "Next time a stupid idea occurs to you, keep it to yourself. I'm not here to perform tricks for you, and I sure as fuck am not your pet. You got me?"

"Got it." Dex gave him a curt nod then held a finger up. "Question."

"No." Sloane pulled back and strode out of the training room with Dex on his heels. He did his best to ignore the guy, but he didn't know what he found more disturbing—when the rookie wouldn't shut up or when he actually did. Sloane glanced over, releasing

a groan when he saw the wide grin on Dex's face.
"What?"

Dex gave a lazy shrug. "Nothing."

"Why are you following me?"

"Because I prefer not to reek of stank during my
first briefing, and I don't know where the showers are."

Sloane eyed him suspiciously. Minutes ago the
guy had been about to hurt something cursing him out,
and now he was acting like they were best buddies.
"You are a very strange man."

Dex beamed up at him. "I prefer the term
'unique.'"

"Let's agree to disagree." With a shake of his
head, Sloane continued across the lounge, murmuring
the occasional acknowledgment to fellow agents who
greeted him. On the other end of the facility were the
locker rooms, and he was relieved to see Letty outside
the males' locker room waiting for him. She handed
him the confirmation paperwork. Good, he could get
Dex off his back for a few minutes until he finished
showering.

"Here you go. Dex's locker assignment."

Sloane frowned at the number on the sheet of paper. "Seriously, Letty?"

Right next to his. Perfect.

Letty shrugged, though her eyes lit up with
amusement. "What? It was the only one available."

"Are you sure?" Maybe he could convince someone to swap with Dex. If all else failed, he could always *make* someone swap.

"Well, there is one." Her troubled expression
twisted his gut. "But I didn't think you'd want me to
give him that one."

"Why?" Dex peered around Sloane's shoulder at the paperwork. "What's wrong with the other locker?"

"Nothing's wrong with it," Sloane snapped.

Dex threw his hands up and took a step back. "All right. Geez, you don't need to bite my head off."

"Keep acting like a jackass and next time I go feral, I might." Sloane shoved the paperwork at Dex and stormed into the locker room. He shouldn't have snapped, but he couldn't help it. He didn't like Dex being here. Maybe if the guy had been assigned to another team, things would have been different. They might have even gotten along. But Dex wasn't on another team. He was on Sloane's team, trying to replace Gabe. No one could replace Gabe.

In a foul mood, he got undressed and wrapped a towel around his waist, doing his best not to think about his partner. Of course, that went about as well as all the other times he tried not to think about Gabe.

Beside him, Dex quietly went about opening his new locker, his brows drawn together thoughtfully as he put his boots in. "I'm sorry about the locker. I didn't know it was his."

Sloane didn't reply, grabbed his toiletry bag, and slammed his locker shut. When he turned to face Dex, the compassion in the rookie's eyes sent a pang of remorse and sorrow through Sloane.

"I'm sorry about Gabe," Dex added.

"If you crack one smartass joke about him, so help me…." The warning was a low, menacing growl, but he was relieved when Dex shook his head, his expression one of sincerity.

"I know what it's like to lose someone you care about. I'm not that much of a jackass."

Sloane nodded, feeling somewhat guilty for making the assumption, but then he was aware how defensive he was about Gabe regardless of who was talking about him. With nothing left to say, he left Dex to get undressed and headed for the showers. The rest of his team was already in there, laughing and joking as they washed the day's workout off. Ash knew him too well by now, and his smile faded before he tilted his head in question. Sloane appreciated his friend's concern and gave him a reassuring smile. Ash Keeler might be an unbearable prick at times, but he was Sloane's best friend and the only one who knew what he'd suffered.

Turning on the cold water, Sloane stood under it, letting it wash his tension away. His muscles welcomed the tiny spikes of cold liquid, and he brushed his hair away from his eyes, telling himself he needed a trim. He rotated his muscles, feeling himself relax until he heard *him*.

"Aw, private stalls? Where's the fun in that?"

"Some of us'd rather not have our junk stared at," Ash replied with a growl.

Sloane stepped out from under the showerhead and grabbed his shower gel, catching Dex's eyes on him as Dex said, "Not staring, appreciating," before turning his attention back to Ash. "And who doesn't partake in a good gander every so often? If you're gonna stand there and tell me you ain't never sneaked a peek at another dude's love truncheon, I'm calling bull-poopie."

Calvin leaned his arms on the frosted glass divider, shaking his head at Dex. "I don't know what I find more disturbing, your choice of vocabulary, or you in general."

Dex laughed as he stepped into the empty stall between Cael and Sloane. Cael hadn't batted an eyelash at his brother's antics. Ash, on the other hand, turned to Cael in exasperation.

"Seriously, man, does your brother ever shut the fuck up?"

Cael paused, as if thinking. "No. Wait, when he's asleep. Most of the time."

"Great."

"I love you, bro." Dex reached out and pulled his brother over to plant a big kiss on Cael's head, earning him a noise of disgust and a shove.

"Gross! We're in the showers."

Dex laughed off his brother's horrified expression, turning on the shower and testing the temperature. "It's not like we're sharing one. That was when we were kids. You should have seen him. He was so cute. He had this teeny little—"

"Dex!"

"What?" Dex blinked at his brother innocently. "I was only going to say penis."

Sloane let out a choking noise and quickly turned away, putting a hand to his mouth to keep himself from laughing. That idiot. Calvin had no such luck, and he burst out laughing.

Cael obviously wasn't as amused as the rest of them. He gave his brother a murderous glare. "I hate you so bad right now."

"I'm sure you're not alone in that," Ash pitched in.

"I'm messing with you. I'm sure your penis has grown way more since then." Dex wriggled his eyebrows as he started lathering himself up, and Sloane forced himself to look away. Dex was not amusing, and he sure as hell was not cute.

"What's wrong with you?" Ash shut off his shower and grabbed his towel to wrap around himself.

"Relax. We're brothers. It's what we do."

Ash's expression said he was underwhelmed. "I feel sorry for you, Cael, I do."

"Hey," Dex jutted his citrus shower gel at Ash. "You might have fallen for that I'm-so-adorable-I-should-be-in-a-boy-band look, but I grew up with him. I know the evil that lurks inside him. Did he tell you about the time he drugged me, shaved my head, and dyed the fuzz neon green? I went to the prom with my head looking like a giant tennis ball."

"Oh yeah," Cael chortled. "That was pretty funny."

"Go Cael." Ash and Cael bumped fists; Dex didn't look pleased.

Is this what it was going to be like all the time? Usually it was Ash who was always getting on everyone's last nerve. Looked like his best friend had some fierce competition in that department, and they all knew how much Ash *loved* competition. Fun-fucking-tastic.

"Sure, laugh it up. It's all fun and games until you end up with tennis ball head."

Cael shut off his shower, wrapped himself up, and snatched his toiletry bag before turning to his brother with a deadpan expression. "Remember when I said I was glad you were here?"

"Yeah?"

"The novelty has totally worn off."

Dex threw his head back and laughed. After rinsing himself off, he shut off the shower and gave Sloane a big grin. "I think I'm gonna like it here."

God help them all.

Chapter 4

"YOU COULDN'T stay put, could you?"

Dex followed Tony out of the elevator, eager to finally get a look at his workspace. He was far less anxious now than he had been before he met his team, though he had plenty of other concerns.

"I think it went well."

"*Well?* It was a disaster! Your new team leader beat the shit out of you, which, by the way, is starting to become a disturbing habit." Tony stepped to one side, that vein pulsing in his head, the same one that had been pulsing when he found Dex getting dressed in the locker room and not in the lounge as he'd instructed. After a few choice words, and after he'd sent the rest of the team to the briefing room to wait, Tony had looked at Dex, opened his mouth, then closed it before marching off and barking for him to follow. "Do you think this is a joke? I stuck my neck out for you, and you couldn't even wait for me to make the proper introductions?"

Dex frowned. "You act like you don't know me. I like to do things my way because my way works. I'm not going to change who I am because I'm on the demolition squad. I appreciate what you've done for me, you know I do, and I'm grateful to be here, but you need to trust me. I know what I'm doing."

"And what's that?"

Dex met his hardass father's gaze. "Trying to save your team from itself."

"What are you talking about?"

With a discreet glimpse to make sure no one was within hearing distance, Dex explained. "Your team hasn't healed, and your team leader is hanging by a thread." Tony appeared to be momentarily stunned. Seeming to shake himself out of it, he motioned for Dex to continue. In the short time since he'd met his team, Dex had managed to pick up on a lot, and it concerned him, greatly. His new partner especially.

"You think Agent Brodie beat the shit out of me because he doesn't like me? He beat the shit out of me because something about me got under his skin, and that pissed him off. He doesn't want me here. If I stay, it means he has to leave Gabe behind, and he's not ready to do that. It's not about my being good enough. It was never about that. You can't tell me the last six or so agents he's run off didn't know what they were doing. The guy practically punched my lights out for talking about Gabe's locker, for fuck's sake."

"What else?"

"Ash is a certified prick. He's channeling his pain into anger that he takes out on whoever tries to step into Gabe's shoes. Cael is in his own little world because he doesn't want to face what happened. Calvin and Hobbs—I haven't even heard Hobbs talk. Does he talk?"

"He's a Therian of few words. Come to think of it, I think I've only heard him talk maybe a handful of times since I've known him," Tony murmured. "Anyway, get on with it."

"Calvin and Hobbs are seriously codependent on each other. We both know how dangerous that can be. We have protocols and right now, I'm not sure they'd adhere to them. Letty, she's trying to keep her head down. Rosa—despite her demeanor—is coping a lot better than the rest of them. She's learned how to deal."

"And you managed to pick up on all that while being hung upside down by a fellow agent, getting yourself beat to shit by your new team leader, and tormenting your baby brother in the showers?"

"Yes. I would have had more, but you know, I was momentarily distracted by all the soapy six-packs."

"Fraternizing with your teammates is not permitted."

Dex gave him a sly grin. "Who said I wanted to fraternize? I was thinking more along the lines of having hot, sweaty man sex."

Tony rolled his eyes. "Same thing."

"No. If you don't want your employees having sex with each other, you should say 'Don't have sex with each other,' or 'intercourse,' or 'consummation,' or whatever ridiculous alternative you can come up with that initially means sexy-time."

"Dex."

"I'm *joking*. I'm not going to have sex with any of my teammates, and since one of them is my brother, that only leaves the one who dislikes me, the one who really dislikes me, and the one who wants to push me in front of a moving bus." Dex gave Tony a pat on the back. "I think we're good."

"Let's get on with this. We have a briefing to get to." They soon arrived at their previously waylaid destination. Unit Alpha. "Here we are."

Dex guessed they were done talking about the team. He wanted to know what Tony was going to do—if anything—with the information he'd given him. Dex wasn't trying to rat out his teammates; he was genuinely concerned. As the one with the least experience, he was the most vulnerable. As good as his teammates supposedly were, if the shit hit the fan, he needed to know they'd have his back.

Sloane Brodie was his biggest concern. The guy was capable, but it didn't take a PhD to know Sloane had been hit the hardest by Gabe's death, as was expected. Sloane and Gabe had been partners, working on and off the field, in each other's hair day in and day out. They'd become close, probably even good friends. It wasn't as if Gabe had been transferred—in Walsh's case, transferred to prison for doing something stupid—he was killed on the job. Dex was going to have to figure out how to handle Sloane. For now, he'd focus on Tony's tour and making sure his new partner didn't push him in front of a moving bus.

Unit Alpha took up the whole of the twenty-first floor and was as impressive as the rest of the building. On the other side of the thick glass doors sat an expansive marble reception desk with half a dozen

receptionists consisting of three males and three fe-
males, an even number of Humans and Therians. With
a friendly greeting exchanged between them, Tony
led Dex past the desk to make a right down a wide
hall with numerous closed doors on each side. After
another right turn, they came to stand before a set of
thick glass doors. They read Defense Department in
bold white letters. Through there, Dex wasn't surprised when he saw yet another set of glass doors, and
on the other side, he could just about make out what
appeared to be a bullpen, except unlike the Sixth Precinct's bullpen, this wasn't made up of desks but rows
of classy, thick glass-partitioned offices that stretched
from floor to ceiling with a wide path down the center.
Before they went into the Defense Department, Tony
paused to point to the large hallway on the left.

"Down that way is Unit Alpha's Intelligence Department, made up of eight hundred employees, all of
which are divided up among Unit Alpha's squads. Intel agents are responsible for gathering, analyzing, and
monitoring information using our Themis system."
He turned and pointed to the equally large hallway on
the right. "Down that way is the Recon Department
and its four hundred employees, who are also divided
among the squads. Recon handles all investigations.
They're also the only agents who work with both Intel
and Defense. You'll only be dealing with Recon."

Tony put his hand to the panel, and the doors
to the Defense Department opened. Inside, soothing
music played. To their right, the reception area was
manned by two Humans and two Therians. Tony
greeted them and introduced Dex. They were friendly, though a couple eyed him warily. Dex was on his

best behavior, giving them a friendly smile and hello. Then, like busy little bees, they went back to work. To the left was a waiting area with seating, coffee tables, reading material, a flat-screen TV playing some news station on mute with subtitles, and a refreshment area with coffee, tea, water, and accompaniments.

In the center of the floor, the THIRDS logo was once again proudly displayed. Tony came to a stop a few feet away from the second set of doors.

"There are a total of one hundred Defense agents broken down into fifty teams of two agents, which are then grouped into the ten squads. Your squad is Destructive Delta. Each squad works with its own Intel and Recon teams. Your squad has been assigned sixty Intel and twenty Recon agents. Defense agents are the trackers and muscle. They provide backup for Recon out in the field, aiding investigations and taking the necessary action to neutralize any threats. They're our sharpest and toughest. If there aren't any immediate large-scale threats, you and Sloane will accompany Cael and his partner on their high-risk cases. In between, you'll be asked to handle everything from high-risk warrants to barricaded subjects and extractions. Every quarter, you have to qualify in weapons and physical proficiency. When you're not out in the field, you'll be training or filling out reports."

The double glass doors slid open as they approached. Inside, a wide path cut straight through the expansive bullpen. It wasn't as busy as Dex thought it would be. The teams—except for his, which was in the briefing room—were most likely out in the field or training. There were rows upon rows of extraordinarily spacious offices to each side of the carpeted path, all of them made up of transparent and frosted glass panels. They walked to the end of the path, and a few turns later, they stopped at one of the offices, but before going in, Tony pointed to a black door on the right.

"That's briefing room A. You'll be spending a good deal of time there. There are three more to the right of it, a kitchen and lunchroom, followed by the male locker room, female locker room. At the end of the hall, make a right and you get to the sleeping bays. To the left of the briefing room is the Archives Room. Make a left at the end of that hall, and there are more sleeping bays. Canteen is on the fifteenth floor, you already know where Sparta and the main locker rooms are." With that said, Tony walked into the office.

Inside, it was twice as big as his old captain's office and much, much nicer. In the center of the room, two large black desks were pressed together facing each other, each one with a shiny, sleek black surface. There didn't seem to be a computer in sight.

"Where are the computers?" Dex was momentarily distracted by the lack of machinery. He'd eavesdrop on Sloane's side of the office later.

Tony gave him a cheeky smile, and Dex almost wet himself in anticipation. "We'll get to that. Now, we use a system called Themis. It runs a series of highly advanced algorithms to scan surveillance submitted by our Recon agents. It also looks for psychological and behavioral anomalies in order to identify potential threats. Our Intel guys gather information through whatever means necessary, be it cooperating with other agencies, or interception. Any questions so far?"

"There is one. Stop me if I'm wrong, but wouldn't it have made more sense to put the homicide detective on Recon rather than with the demolition squad? You've seen me, right? I mean, I'm in shape, but I can't bench-press a bus."

"None of our guys can bench-press a bus." Tony considered his words for a moment. "Maybe a Mini Cooper, but definitely not a bus."

"Not helping."

"Dex, Defense isn't made up of no-brained muscle. These guys have to make split-second decisions. Decisions which will mean the difference between saving someone's life and watching them get torn to shreds. It's one of the most physically and mentally demanding roles at the THIRDS. The reason you're Defense is because your physical endurance score was as impressive as your mental endurance score. You also did everything within your power to preserve life during your simulations exercises. And that's your objective, Dex. Preserve life."

"And when a three-hundred-pound Felid is trying to use me for a scratching post, how am I supposed to preserve life? Namely mine."

"You train. Also, that's where your partner comes in. You'll find working with a Therian partner to be unlike any partnership you've ever had. If one of you lets the other down, it could have dire consequences for the both of you and the team."

"You're referring to something in particular?"

"Post Shift Trauma Care."

Dex had experience from growing up with Cael how Therians needed care after their shift. The change in body mass took its toll on their Human side once a

Therian shifted back. Years ago, scientists claimed the effects of Therian Post Shift Trauma weren't all that different from the aftereffects of an epileptic seizure, only on a smaller scale, including muscle soreness, bruising, brief disorientation, and hunger. Eating after a shift was extremely important, as not eating could lead to the Therian collapsing and a host of other health issues if they didn't. It was scientifically proven that Humanity remained neurologically present while Therians were in their Therian form. It meant they could remain in that state for extended periods of time. However, research confirmed remaining in Therian form for more than a year could mess with the mind, and the Human side might slip beyond retrieval.

"What about it?"

"It's your responsibility to make sure Sloane receives PSTC, which means being ready with his PSTC kit if you're away from the BearCat and taking care of his gear while he's in his Therian form when necessary."

Dex's eyes widened. That could be anywhere from 120 to 160 pounds worth of gear. "Are you serious?"

"Better get started on those bench presses." Tony looked too happy for his own good.

"Thanks. So, besides being responsible for carrying my gear and possibly his, what's in a PSTC kit, and please tell me it doesn't weigh much."

"Energy bars, snacks, bottle of Gatorade, disposable set of clothes—couple of T-shirts, pants, underwear, socks, blanket, and a pair of sneakers."

"Damn it, sneakers too?"

"Well, we supply disposable booties, but as you can imagine, the agents aren't too fond of them, so they often bring their own shoes." Tony shrugged. "It's not against the rules. They lose 'em, they gotta pay to replace them. Sloane prefers sneakers."

Dex looked down at his own size tens. He'd been somewhat preoccupied during their little sparring match to notice the size of Sloane's feet. "Don't suppose they're average-sized sneakers?"

"Sloane weighs in at 240 pounds and is over six foot six."

"Pissbunnies. Maybe I can convince him to switch." Or swap them out and pretend he had no idea how it happened.

"Yeah, good luck with that. Now are you going to bitch all day, or do you want to get to the toys?"

Finally they were getting to the exciting part. "Sex toys?"

"I'm going to have to set boundaries, aren't I?"

"No. I'm sorry. I'll behave." Dex made a cross over his heart with his finger. "I'd like to see the toys, please."

Tony stepped up to the desk on the left and motioned Dex over. "See this box here?"

There was a thin blue-lined rectangle on the bottom left-hand corner of the desk's shiny surface. "Yeah."

"Put your hand there."

Wiping his left hand on his pants, Dex placed it where Tony instructed, squealing like a schoolgirl when the desk's surface flickered to life. "Now that's what I'm talking about! This is some *Star Trek* shit right here." He was so excited he could barely contain it. He loved getting shiny new toys.

"Yeah, all right. Easy there, Solo."

"I'm going to pretend you didn't say that. Seriously, man. You raised two kids, and you still can't tell the difference between *Star Wars* and *Star Trek*?"

"They both take place in space with weirdly dressed dudes. That's all I gotta know about it."

Dex hung his head in shame. "I weep for you."

"Be quiet and pay attention. Themis uses handprint recognition for log-in. More secure than a password. Essentially, your desk is like a big tablet. When you're both logged in, you can share information by sliding files from one surface to the other. You can keep your old cell phone number, but you'll be given a new portable communication device that will allow you access to the desktop's interface. The passkey on the portable device will be made up of a combination of your choosing using your fingerprints." He pointed to the glowing blue symbols in the shape of a keypad on the right side of the desktop. "These control everything else in the room. Tap the rectangle with the checker box pattern."

Dex was all but bouncing. The second he tapped the button, the top half of the frosted cubicle wall to his left lit up.

"That's your board."

"I get my own board?" Dex gasped in awe.

"Don't come in your pants yet. Yes, you get your own board. It's also a touch screen, so it allows you to easily open multiple files, shuffle things around, add notes to it, and then update the information on your system. When you're not using it, it goes into stealth mode like the rest of your desk, or you can press the Sleep button. To wake it up, press your hand to the panel again." He pointed to a set of large black filing cabinets in the corner of the office. "Any information that can't be digitally scanned in is kept in those locked cabinets. Everything else is kept in the Archive Room. Now open the top right-hand drawer of your desk."

Dex did, pulling out something that resembled one of those small wireless headset earpiece things Wall Street douchebags used to communicate with other Wall Street douchebags.

"It's a wireless headset with links to the switchboard and your team. It also takes voice command. While you're on duty, you wear it." Tony pointed to his own secured around his ear. "The tiny A will glow blue if you're connected, red if you're disconnected, and orange if you're incapacitated, sending a signal to the rest of your team and headquarters. If you have a call coming through, pressing down on the A will activate the microphone. The tiny button above the A dims the light, so it doesn't give away your position. The emergency signal can be activated verbally or by holding down this button up here." He reached over and pointed to a tiny red button on the side.

"After the briefing, Letty will take you to the armory, show you to your locker and your personal gear. Your arms locker also requires your handprint to unlock. After that, we'll break for lunch. Okay so far?"

"Yep." Lunch. He could do with some lunch. Especially since that bastard Sloane gave his Cheesy Doodles away. What kind of guy does that? A bastard, that's who. Did he not respect the male code of honor—thou shalt not steal another dude's snacks?

"What now?" Tony groused.

Dex pouted miserably. "Sloane gave my Cheesy Doodles to Grizzly Adams."

"I don't know what you're talking about and I don't want to know. Put your earpiece in and get your ass moving." Tony ushered him out, and Dex followed with a pout, securing his earpiece into place. It was going to take a while to get used to. Then again, there was a good deal to get used to. When they reached briefing room A, Dex took a deep, steady breath before going in.

A large table in the shape of a semicircle with about two dozen chairs occupied the center of the spacious room. Seven of those chairs were currently seating his teammates, most of whom didn't appear particularly happy to see him, except for Cael, who smiled at him, but that was a given. Across the semicircular table at the head of the room was a low stage with a black podium, and high above it a massive flat-screen TV. To each side of it were slightly smaller flat-screen TVs. Beneath the outside TVs sat two medium-sized tables with chairs, the chairs on the right currently occupied by Dr. Colbourn and Dr. Bishop, who sat facing the team, each with a tablet in their hands.

"Sit down," Tony told him, motioning at the empty seats between Sloane and Ash before he made his way to the podium.

Crap. Where should he sit? If he sat next to Ash, Sloane might think he was trying to avoid him, but if he sat next to Sloane, Ash might think he was flipping him off. Or he could be a complete douche and sit across from his team. Yeah, that would go down well. Okay, he was overanalyzing this. He walked to Sloane, but before he could sit down, Sloane stood and moved over so he was next to Ash, leaving the seat in front, *right at the front*, the only one available to him. Dex sat down and swiveled his chair to face the front. Great. It was high school all over again. Front of the class with the asshole captain of the football team sitting behind him, waiting for the teacher to face the board so he could torment Dex and then pretend it was all in good fun so he could copy his homework.

"All right, team. As you all may know, the THIRDS were handed jurisdiction on the HumaniTherians case months ago, after the HPF concluded the evidence was pointing toward a Therian perpetrator. It was originally assigned to Unit Beta, until further evidence suggested it was the same perp. Now it's our case. So far, there have been two victims." Tony tapped the surface of the podium in front of him, and an image of a fair-haired man in his mid- to late thirties popped up on the large screen. "Mr. Dan Bennett." He tapped the podium again, and this time an image of a dark-haired woman, also in her mid- to late thirties, popped up on the screen beside the first victim. "And Ms. Paula Chambers. Both victims received severe lacerations to the throat, hitting the main artery and causing the victims to quickly bleed to death. Hudson and Nina have been working hard to find a tear they can analyze, but the cuts are inconsistent. We do know these were violent acts. I'll let Cael and Rosa fill you in on what they've got. Agents."

Cael and Rosa made their way to the podium. Tony stepped to one side, his hands placed against his lower back as he watched his agents. Cael cleared his throat and tapped away at the podium.

"Like the sergeant said, definitely a lot of anger involved in these murders. Intel has run both victims through Themis looking for connections between the two, but so far nothing has come up. Although both were HumaniTherians, they worked for separate organizations, and neither crossed paths professionally or personally. There are no records of any communication between the two. No emails, phone calls, nothing. Mr. Bennett was found dead in his apartment late in the evening after the HPF became notified by Mr. Bennett's employer when he didn't show up to work after three days. Mr. Bennett never so much as took a sick day before then. The apartment building's tenants were questioned, and no one saw anyone come in or out of the apartment. The building has no surveillance inside or out, no security either. It's badly maintained, if at all, so plenty of places for the perpetrator to hide." Cael stepped aside, and Rosa took the podium.

"The second victim, Ms. Chambers, had argued with her Therian girlfriend, a Ms. Ruiz, the evening before. Neighbors say it was common. We interviewed Ms. Ruiz and according to her, she slept in her own apartment after they argued. She took some sedatives to calm her nerves and help her sleep. Toxicology confirms this, as do her neighbors, who saw her black Ford Fiesta parked in front of her house all evening. We can also confirm Ms. Ruiz's Therian form is a Canidae. These tears were made by large claws, not teeth. We believe our suspect is a large Felid."

Dex heard Sloane's quiet curse behind him, but he didn't turn around. Considering Destructive Delta was made up of large Felids, he could understand their frustration. Also, Felid Therians had a pretty bum rap. Statistically, Felid Therians made up a smaller portion of the criminal population, but since the homicides committed by criminal Felids were usually so violent, they overshadowed the more numerous crimes committed by Therians of other classifications, which of course made them a media target.

"Any questions?" Rosa asked.

Dex held up a hand, ignoring the groan he heard come from his partner.

"Yes?"

"The HPF receives hundreds of reports every day from Human Therians who've received violent threats. Only a tiny fraction of those are actually investigated, and by then they've usually escalated. Can Intel get their hands on those reports and run them through Themis for potential suspects? I'm guessing the right algorithms should whittle down the list, especially once you start cross-referencing Felids with priors or histories of violence."

Rosa blinked at him, the room silent before she snapped out of it and spoke. "That's a very good question." Dex gave her a wink, and although she shook her head, she smiled before turning to Tony. "Sergeant?"

"Glad you brought that up. Lieutenant Sparks has spoken with the HPF Commissioner, and they'll be granting us temporary access to the files. It'll take a few days while they gripe about it, but we should have it soon. I'll have Intel notify Cael and Rosa as soon as we know something."

A strange low alarm resonated through the room, giving Dex a start. "What is that?"

"Shit." Sloane was immediately on his feet along with the rest of the team. A wide red bar with flashing white letters scrolled across all the screens: *Alert! DB Hector Ortiz HHMA. Requesting OS: Unit Alpha— Destructive Delta: DDME, DDRA, DDDA.*

Dex read through all the abbreviations, recalling them from his training material, the first half of which he was familiar with since the HPF used the same codes. Dead body, Hector Ortiz, Human, Hispanic, Male, Adult. The rest were THIRDS specific codes, the "DD" in front pertained to his team: Destructive Delta, the ME: Medical examiners, the RA: Recon agents, and the DA: Defense agents. Fuck, another homicide. Looks like they were being called in to backup Recon, which meant this was a bad one.

"Okay, team, let's roll out. Everyone knows what to do. Letty, give Dex a brief rundown of his gear downstairs. Aside from the modified tranq guns, it won't be anything he hasn't handled before. Dex, you stick close to your partner, got it?"

"Yes, sir." Dex gave a curt nod, falling into line behind Sloane as the team left the briefing room in a neat little row like a military drill. The few agents who were around the department stayed out of their way, and ahead of them, a receptionist waited by the glass doors. When the team neared, the receptionist accessed the panel, the doors swishing open. They soon reached the elevators and Tony pressed his palm to the screen. In no time, they were all heading to the sub-basement where the armory and garage were located.

As soon as the elevator doors opened, everyone headed out. The armory was as extensive as he'd expected, with wall-to-wall secured metal cages and lockers. Letty quickly showed him to one wall of cages. The sign fixed above it read: Destructive Delta. She stopped beside Sloane, who already had his locker open and was slipping into his tactical vest.

"This one's yours. A lot of this is standard issue with a few new toys."

Dex put his hand to the screen situated where a lock would normally be, and the cage went *click*. She pointed down at the large shield carefully propped up to one side.

"That's your level IIIA ballistic shield with high-intensity dual lighting system, including strobe capability." She grabbed a vest and held it up to him. "Your level IIIA tac vest with side protection, front opening system for easy on/off, front pocket with pull-down groin protection—"

Dex opened his mouth, and Letty cut him off. "If you make any dick jokes I will blow yours off."

"Got it."

"It's also got a retractable ballistic nape, ballistic throat and shoulder protection, with integrated collar system. This sucker is heavy as balls before you add all your shit to it, so have fun with that." She shoved it at Dex and pointed to one of the shelves. "Those are your level IV armored plates, and that there is your ballistic helmet with retractable visor."

Dex nodded as he strapped himself into his vest, leaving the throat and nape protection unfastened for the time being, and Letty started quickly handing him attachments.

"Gloves are flame-resistant, cut-resistant, and thermal-resistant, with removable molded knuckle protection. Taser, which I will use on you if you break any of this shit. Zip ties." She kept handing him things and he tried his best to keep up, finding pockets, hooks, and places for everything. As soon as each piece was tucked somewhere, she shoved a black backpack at him. Unfastening the Velcro flap at the front, she swept her hand across the various tools a la Vanna White.

"Hooligan Kit includes bolt cutters, Thunder-maul, and breacher. Det cord for blowing shit up, sledgehammer, ax, crowbar. In the BearCat, we've got a battering ram for breaching—performed by the rookie, i.e., you. Chains and hooks for burglar bars." She then unfastened the straps at the top and opened it for him. "Inside you have your nonlethals—flash-bangs, smoke bombs, pepper-spray canisters, sting-er grenades, and tear gas. In the BearCat you'll find beanbag rounds, shotguns, and 40mm grenade launch-ers." With an evil grin, she handed him the backpack and he slipped into it, attaching the straps in their ap-propriate places. Then he noticed the straps with clips on his shoulders.

"Crap." He'd been so busy working out where all his accessories went, he forgot all about the key pieces of his equipment. The guns.

"Okay, now that we've gotten that out of the way, we get to the hard-core stuff." She swatted the side of his thigh and he gave a jump, his eyes widening at her evil grin. "You've already got your Glock 17. Now behind me is your Remington 870 12 gauge, your double-aught buck with steel bearings, MP5 sub-machine gun, the AR15—your primary entry weapon, and this baby here...." She grabbed one of the rifles and handed it to him. "It looks like your AR15, but it's actually your new best friend—a modified tranq gun. The tranqs in this use a combination of ketamine and xylazine. The BearCat is equipped with M99 and M5050 tranquilizers, but only Rosa handles that shit. She'll be giving you a step-by-step on how to use it properly without killing yourself dead."

Sounded like something he would say. He liked her already. Dex clipped the tranq rifle to his vest straps. "You scare me."

"Good." She gave him a smack on his ass as she walked off. Letty was small, barely reaching his shoulders, but he had no doubts she could kick some serious ass. She'd have to, being in Unit Alpha. It couldn't be easy for her and Rosa with all the testosterone flying around, a hefty portion of it coming from Ash alone. Yet she had a sweet smile and very soft features. If Dex had seen her walking down the street in civilian attire, he never would have guessed she packed enough heat to take on a small army.

By the time Dex was finished strapping everything into place, he felt winded. He'd completed the THIRDS training while wearing the same equipment, but a good deal of what got him through it was knowing that once he got to the other side, he wouldn't have to worry about it again. But this was it. Every time that screen flashed, he'd be going out to face Therians in their most dangerous form. Taking a deep breath, he grabbed his helmet and nearly jumped out of his skin when he received a firm pat on the shoulder.

"No time for daydreams, Rookie. Move your ass." Sloane gave him a gentle shove forward and Dex bit his tongue. Now would not be a good time to tell his partner to go screw himself. He slammed the cage door shut, the lock clicking into place. Sloane brushed past him and Dex hastily put his helmet on—visor up—and fastened the chinstrap before putting on his gloves. He held on to his rifle and followed Sloane along with the rest of the team out of the armory.

The THIRDS tactical vehicles were parked in the HQ garage attached to the rear of the building and accessed through a short tunnel. There was no time for Dex to browse the pretty black service cars, one of which he would be riding in with Sloane when they weren't in the BearCat. The team didn't stop until it reached a massive armored truck, and Dex couldn't help but gaze at it in awe.

It was shiny and black with large white letters on the sides displaying THIRDS and below in smaller letters NYC Unit Alpha. It was much longer in length than the typical ballistic vehicle, and on the outside, it was equipped with the works. It had blue lights on the roof and on the winch at the front. On the side, two narrow ballistic glass panels up high, three gun ports beneath the panels, and an additional gun port on the passenger-side door. The roof contained a rotating hatch, a CS gas deployment nozzle, and a Common Remotely Operated Weapons Station program with a mounted M240 machine gun that Dex hoped they didn't need to use.

Hobbs ran around to the driver's side while Calvin climbed into the passenger side. The rest of the team stood to one side behind the vehicle as Calvin opened the back doors. Dex followed the rest of his team inside, taking in everything around him.

It was unlike any armored vehicle Dex had ever seen. Along one side were cages filled with an armory of weapons, locked cabinets, and drawers. Across from the cages was a long black bench with straps and beside it, a small wall of surveillance equipment, including a sleek console, chair, several touch screens, slim computer keyboard, and plenty of glowing, flashing buttons hc would be sure to stay away from. Toward the front of the truck was a medical station that resembled the inside of an ambulance, including a defibrillator, syringe driver, suction unit, ventilator, immobilization equipment, and a stretcher. There were refrigerated units, more locked cabinets, and a small restroom. Toward the rear of the truck, there was a wide-open rectangular space, and Dex noted the grooves and panels tucked into the floor. The iron panels came up if they had a Therian who refused to shift back to his or her Human form. The idea disturbed him. How did his Therian teammates feel about sticking their own kind in a big iron cage?

Above the cage, stretching across the width of the truck, was another groove with a looped strap sticking out of each end. It appeared to be some kind of pulldown screen, and Dex realized it was for privacy. It had completely slipped his mind that his teammates would most likely shift inside the truck, and seeing as how they had to get naked to do it, it made sense there would be some designated space for them to do it in.

Everyone took a seat on the bench and strapped in. There was a singular space across from them, tucked next to the cages, where Tony strapped himself in to face them. The rumble of the BearCat roaring to life sent a small shiver up Dex's spine. This was it. The truck drove through the garage and out into the street, the sun filtering in through the ballistic windows. They hit a pothole and Dex closed his eyes at the unexpected jolt. He had to relax. *It's going to take a little getting used to, that's all, so chill.*

Ash gave a snort from the end of the bench. "What's the matter, Rookie? I thought you'd be used to having something big and hard under your ass."

Dex leaned forward to grin at the burly agent. "That an invitation, Ash?"

"Fuck you."

The guy was too easy. "Not without dinner and a movie first, big boy." Ash's growl made Dex chuckle. The rough-around-the-edges agent was used to getting his own way, and if someone challenged him, Ash would simply throw his weight around or use aggressive tactics to make his opponent back down. There was no way in hell Dex was going to back down.

"I'm going to kick the shit out of you if you don't shut the fuck up."

"One night with me, baby, and I promise you, I'll get you onto beef," Dex said, echoing Ash's words.

Rosa let out a snort before she started laughing. "Oh shit."

"What the hell, Ro?" Ash scowled at her, but Rosa simply laughed it off.

"What? You can dish it but you can't take it, *cabrón*?"

The rest of the team, with the exception of Sloane, joined in the laughter. "You know what, screw you all." Ash sat back with a miserable pout.

"Ooh, kinky." Dex wriggled his eyebrows.

"That's enough." Sloane put his hand to Dex's chest and pushed him firmly back against the truck's wall. "You're supposed to be paying attention."

"To what, the inside of the truck? I wasn't the one who started it," Dex replied, frustrated he was the one getting told off and knowing Ash was enjoying every second of it.

"Are you questioning me? Because I'm pretty sure I made myself clear on how this worked."

"Yes, but—"

"Stop. Talking," Sloane demanded harshly. "Your job is to listen and learn, not provide comic relief."

Dex sat back with jaw clamped shut. Mostly because he didn't even know where to start with everything that pissed him off right now. He glanced over at Tony, whose lips were pressed in a thin line. Great, so not only was Sloane making him look like an asshole in front of his team, but in front of his father too. The truck headed toward its destination and Dex kept his gaze forward, ignoring the fact that the rest of the team carried on as if nothing had happened. Apparently talking and ribbing was allowed as long as it wasn't coming from him. Okay, if that's the way his partner wanted to play it, Dex could play.

When the truck came to a halt, Tony was the first to unfasten his harness. He stood and addressed the rest of them, including Calvin and Hobbs, who came through the large metal door protecting the front cabin.

"Hudson and Nina are already inside examining the body. Cael, Rosa, you know what to do. Sloane, you and Dex keep them company while they do it. Ash, Letty, and I will scout the perimeter. Calvin, you and Hobbs stay in the BearCat and keep your eyes peeled."

Dex unfastened his belt and stood, almost running into Sloane, who loomed over him. The rest of the team hopped to it, with Calvin and Hobbs taking seats on the bench, pretending Sloane and Dex weren't there.

"What?" Dex finally asked, bracing himself. Sloane looked pissed, though Dex had no idea what he could possibly have done now other than exist.

"You stay close, keep your mouth shut unless it's relevant to the case, and try not to make an ass out of the both of us. I don't care who your daddy is. You fuck up, you ignore direct orders, and I will charge you with insubordination. Understood?"

Dex worried his bottom lip, his insides twisting, and his head screaming for him not to take this bullshit. Instead, he looked Sloane right in the eye and gave him a curt nod. "Perfectly."

As suspected, Dex's compliance and lack of insolence only proved to aggravate Sloane further. The guy had been expecting a fight, *hoping* for a fight, maybe so he could do exactly what he said he would. With his threat backfiring, Sloane thundered out of the BearCat, and Dex let out a deep breath.

"Give him time."

Dex turned to Calvin, a look of concern etched across his boyish face. Beside him, Hobbs sat quietly, his expression guarded.

"Time for what? For him to find an excuse to push me out, like he did with all the others?" Dex could feel his anger growing. It wasn't as if he'd been expecting a ticker-tape parade, but a little effort on Sloane's part wouldn't have gone amiss. "How long should I keep my mouth shut, worried I'm going to get disciplined for fucking breathing? As much as I feel for him, it's not my fault he refuses to go to therapy and cry out his feelings. What happened to Gabe was tragic, and I would happily give up my post if it meant you got him back. But Gabe is gone, and I shouldn't have to pay for that."

Calvin and Hobbs both straightened, their eyes going wide at something behind Dex. A sense of impending doom washed over him. *Shit.* He must have broken a house of mirrors in his former life to justify having this much bad luck. Closing his eyes, Dex shook his head. Well, this was going to be fun. He braced himself and turned, expecting the end of his very short career at the THIRDS. Instead, he was met with a crushed expression, and it hit Dex like a punch to the gut. Dex stood motionless, watching Sloane struggle with something within himself before he inhaled deeply. As if waking up from a trance, Sloane shifted his gaze to Dex, his voice quiet when he spoke.

"Let's go. Cael and Rosa are waiting." With that, he disappeared around the truck.

What just happened? Something he'd said must have struck a chord with Sloane, and a part of Dex felt guilty for his words. Maybe he needed to cut the guy some slack and not expect miracles so soon into their partnership. Dex jumped down, rifle in hand, and with renewed determination jogged to catch up to Sloane, who was waiting silently for him in front of the French Gothic-style mansion. They were on a street lined with pretty trees, spotless sidewalks, multimillion-dollar homes, and luxurious apartments, just around the corner from the Metropolitan Museum of Art.

The Ortiz mansion was impressive, from its limestone façade to its intricate iron gates protecting the heavy wooden front doors, but more impressive than the multimillion dollar mansion was Sloane opening one side of the iron gates for him.

With a nod of thanks, Dex stepped inside, telling himself he was going to try harder. Patience wasn't one of his virtues, but he was going to have to learn. It was time for a different approach. One he hoped would lead to them getting along better and hopefully not to Dex being used as a scratching post.

Chapter 5

SLOANE DISLIKED Dex. Really disliked him.

The rookie's words were still ringing in his ears as they made their way through the grand foyer of the mansion. As much as he hated to admit it, Dex was right. Another reason to dislike him. The list was growing by the minute. Despite what Dex believed, Sloane had seen a therapist, a THIRDS-appointed one, the same one the rest of his team had been forced to see after the incident. It had been a slippery slope, but Sloane managed to say all the right things to get himself cleared for duty. Afterward, he did his best to avoid facing the painful truth—that Gabe was gone.

His chest ached and the back of his eyes stung, but he quickly pulled himself together. For a long time, he'd managed to avoid the harsh reality. It had been easy while Gabe's position remained open. Every time a new partner was assigned, reality threatened to chip away at the tremulous delusion he had created for himself. Of course Gabe was gone. He'd simply put off accepting it for as long as he could, until the thought no longer threatened to cripple him. He'd been terrified about facing his grief, of what it would do to him if he allowed himself to give in to it. Only Ash knew his fears, what it could mean for Sloane. When Sloane had finally given in, it had been frightening, but he'd pulled through. By no means had he completely healed, but at least it no longer felt like an open festering wound.

Beside him, his new partner was pensive, and Sloane felt a pang of guilt. Dex had been right about Sloane placing blame on him, punishing him for being placed in Gabe's position. Under different circumstances, it would have been one hell of a promotion for the ex-HPF officer.

Sloane told himself he would have to make more of an effort to make this partnership work, no matter how much he disliked it. The sooner he accepted things could no longer be as they once were, the better it would be for all of them. The two of them would be spending a lot of time together. Did he really want to spend that time arguing with the guy? Their job was difficult enough as it was without him making it more difficult.

They made their way through the opulent home decorated in hues of blues, reds, and gold, everything designed in a neo-French Renaissance style, from the walls adorned with large oil paintings in antique gold frames to the molded and sculpted staircase. Beneath their boots, the extravagant carpet swallowed their footsteps, and the silk curtains hanging from the expansive archways brushed against the rough cotton fabric of their uniforms. In each room, a crystal chandelier glittered above their heads. No one looked more out of place than they did.

The home was crawling with their squad's Recon agents, all twenty by the looks of it. The agents were busy taking statements from the guests, some of whom were in tears, while others looked affronted that they were even being questioned. Considering how many rooms the place had, this was going to take a while. In his helmet, Sloane received the confirmation he'd been awaiting from Ash.

"House and perimeter are clear."

"Copy that." Sloane removed his helmet and clipped the straps to the back of his vest, Dex doing the same.

Dex whispered at him. "I didn't know charities paid so well."

"They don't. Ortiz was already wealthy before he took over HumaniTherians United." They went up two flights of stairs to Ortiz's office, where Hudson and Nina were crouched over the body. The office was as opulent as the rest of the house, rich mahogany and glass-cased shelving units around the room, with a fancy drink cart in one corner and a couple of leather wingback chairs. Everything looked pristine and in its place, except for Ortiz lying in a pool of his own blood. Sloane received a nod in greeting from Hudson and Nina as they approached; all around them, CS agents were busy sweeping the place.

"What have we got?"

Hudson got to his feet. "Mr. Hector Ortiz, Chairman of HumaniTherians United. His body was

discovered by his wife around noon. According to her
statement, he'd been mingling with guests all morning, but when she went to make introductions to newly
arrived guests, she couldn't find him. She figured he
had snuck off to do some work, as he had a habit of
doing. Came up here and found him dead."

"And you're sure we're dealing with the same
perp?" Sloane studied the corpse. Ortiz lay with his
throat torn, like the previous victims.

"We're certain it's the same killer, but there's
something bothering us about this one."

"Oh?"

Nina pointed down to the victim's neck, and
Sloane crouched down for a better look, Dex following
his lead. "See here? There's a small tear where the claw
hooked the victim's neck and pulled, but the movement wasn't carried through. It's as if he was quickly
released. Like maybe the victim moved unexpectedly."

Dex cocked his head to one side, studying the
tears. "That makes sense. If someone was trying to
slash his throat, wouldn't he try to get away?"

"Not if he didn't know he was going to be at-
tacked. The movement suggests he was turning when
he was struck. Something might have spooked the attacker, who quickly regained his objective and struck
again, only the second swipe was successful, tearing
the throat and allowing the victim to bleed to death."

"What's the strange part?" Sloane's concern regarding this case was steadily increasing. Something
wasn't adding up. He stood to face Hudson, whose
troubled expression mirrored his own feelings on this.

"The depth of the tears and the direction of blood
spatter indicate the strength behind the swipe was far

weaker than that of your average Felid, unlike with the previous victims."

Sloane considered that. "Is it possible the victim fought back and injured his attacker?" It was a long shot. Hudson dashed his hopes with a shake of his head.

"There are no traces of fur or skin under his fingernails, no hairs on his clothing, and the evidence suggests it's likely that all the blood is his, but we need to get it all back to the lab to confirm. So far, CS agents are having trouble finding any evidence the attacker was even here other than poor Mr. Ortiz. My theory—and this is only a theory until we can properly examine him—is that the last two victims were smaller than the attacker, whereas Ortiz was bigger."

Sloane frowned. "I don't see how that would make a difference."

"Exactly," Hudson replied. "I hate to say this, lads, but there's an awful lot not making sense here."

"Like the fact that the attacker only attacks with his right."

The three of them turned to Dex, who was still crouched down beside the victim. He pointed at the victim's neck. "All three victims had their throats slashed from left to right. Plus, according to the case file, none of the victims had any other scratches on them, which is pretty implausible."

"How so?" Hudson asked curiously. Nina brought up the forensic reports of the previous victims, studied them, and nodded her agreement.

Dex continued, "All three victims had been standing at the time. For a Felid to have reached their necks, especially with someone as tall as Ortiz, he would've had to get on his hind legs. How did he manage to strike each victim with his right, yet not leave any scratches at all anywhere with his left? Even if he'd knocked them over, he would've had to have left some mark on at least one of them. Do you know how many times Cael clobbered me with his left paw during play when we were growing up? Nearly every time. And even with his nails clipped, he left a hell of a lot of scratches."

"He's right," Sloane agreed, aware of Dex staring at him, complete surprise on his face. "It's pretty damn strange that our attacker left no other serious wounds or even scratches. It's too clean. What else do we know?"

Nina scrolled through the notes on her tablet, her grim expression not boding well. "Recon's interviewing the guests, but so far no one witnessed any suspicious activity or saw the chairman arguing with anyone. There was live music going on at the time, and despite a supposed attack from a Felid this size, no one heard a sound. There's a long list of enemies, but it's to be expected from a man like Ortiz. Intel's running them through Themis now. His wife says nothing was stolen from the office. His wallet and keys were still in his pockets."

"At this point, we can probably rule out theft gone wrong," Dex pitched in.

Sloane carefully mulled over everything he'd learned so far, but he was no closer to piecing anything together now than he had been when this mess started. The only reason they knew their perp was a Therian was due to the slash marks consistent with a Felid attack. Sloane surveyed the room, taking note of all the guards and HPF officers lingering about. "How'd he get past all the security?"

"Good question. Do you think it could be an employee?" Dex offered. "Or someone dressed like an employee?"

"Dex might be right."

Cael approached them with Rosa at his side, and as soon as she was close, she motioned for Sloane and Dex to join them. "Thanks. Let me know as soon as you get anything new."

"Absolutely," Hudson replied, his blue eyes observing Dex keenly. "Dex, nice to see you again."

Wait, what was that? Was Hudson flirting with Dex? Sloane glanced over at his partner and the dopey grin on his face. Well, if he was, Dex was enjoying it. Not that Sloane cared. If Dex wanted to risk his job by hopping into bed with Hudson, that was his problem, though Sloane should at least make an attempt to steer his partner away from danger. He grabbed Dex's arm, hauled him to his feet, and led him to Cael and Rosa. Dex didn't say a word, but his arched eyebrow indicated his humorous surprise. What Dex found so amusing was beyond him. What's more, he didn't care. They walked off to one side, away from all the other agents and hired security.

"What have you got?" Sloane grunted, ignoring his partner's stupid grin.

Cael tapped away at his tablet before handing it to Sloane. It was a list of everyone who had been in attendance at the time, from guests to employees, including which were Therians and their confirmed classifications. "The guest list is small. We're lucky it was a brunch and not an evening event. There were only twenty-five guests, with three times the number of employees. Mrs. Ortiz has used the same security firm for the last ten years, plus a few HPF officers working overtime. So far, no one's seen or heard anything out of the ordinary. Only three of the fifty guards employed by Mrs. Ortiz are Felids, and they were in Mrs. Ortiz's company the whole time, confirmed by several guests. She did hire an offsite, high-end catering company—Thalia's Kitchen Events & Catering on Fifth and West Thirty-Third. The staff is still being interviewed at the moment, but so far no Felids. They're also all present and accounted for. I doubt whoever killed Ortiz would stick around."

Sloane nodded, going through the list before handing it back to Cael. "In other words, we've got nothing. Has Intel run Ortiz through Themis?"

"They're working on it now," Rosa replied.

A Recon agent came rushing toward them. "Agent Cael, Agent Santiago, one of the staff says he has some information that might help."

Cael gave the agent a nod. "Thanks, Russo."

Finally they might have something. Tracking Therian perpetrators was difficult, but there was always something—a hair, a fiber, saliva, a tooth—something left behind during a violent encounter when a Therian's instinct was at its most animalistic, despite the Human inside. It took a great deal of control to strike the right balance. These attacks were too controlled.

They followed Agent Russo out of the office and down the stairs, through the drawing room into the dining room. A dark-haired waiter sat in one of the dining room chairs. When he saw them approach, he jumped to his feet and made his way over, stopping abruptly when he saw Sloane. A sneer came onto his face, his sharp eyes scrutinizing. At the end, he turned to Dex.

"I'll talk to you," he said with a haughty sniff, looking Dex over.

Dex's eyebrows shot up in surprise. His partner obviously hadn't been expecting such a blatant display of discrimination so early in the game. He'd better get used to it. Dex opened his mouth when Cael discreetly shook his head. With pursed lips, Dex addressed the waiter.

"Sir, you stated you had some information involving the victim?"

"Yeah, I know who killed him," the waiter replied with confidence.

"You saw what happened?"

"No, not exactly. There was this Therian freak—" The waiter cut himself off when he saw the disapproving look on Dex's face. Sloane had to admit, the rookie had a pretty intimidating perhaps-you'd-like-to-re-phrase-that-before-I-beat-you look. "Uh, I mean, this Therian. He was a bartender with the catering company, and he was acting all weird and nervous. He was Unregistered."

"How do you know?" Dex asked.

"He was wearing a turtleneck and kept fussing with it. It wouldn't be the first time Mrs. Ortiz used a company that hired Unregistered Therians. She thought she was doing good. So much for that."

Dex looked thoughtful. "So you didn't actually see or hear this Therian attack Ortiz?"

"No." The waiter grew less certain. "But he was up to something. So I confronted him, told him I was going to call you guys to pick him up. The prick kept on working like I hadn't said anything. So I called it in. Of course, when I went back, he was gone."

"What time was this?"

"It was before eleven when I confronted him," the man replied.

"Could you describe this Therian for us?"

"Yeah, he was tall, pretty big, over six feet. Amber eyes," His gaze darted to Sloane before moving away. "Um, dark hair. If I had to guess, I'd say a Felid."

"What makes you say that?"

"A lot of the time you can tell, you know? The way he moved. Like he was stalking."

"Can you tell us anything else?" The waiter shook his head, and Dex looked over at Rosa, who'd been recording everything and converting it to text. "Okay. Agent Santiago will go over your statement with you. She'll also need a signature from you. Thank you so much for your time." He motioned to Rosa, who ushered the waiter to the table. Dex met Cael's gaze and motioned to the doorway. Sloane followed.

"What was that?"

"What?" Cael looked confused.

"You let that racist prick shut you out of your own investigation."

Cael merely shrugged. "If talking to you meant he was going to cooperate, then I don't care."

"You should care, damn it. If you don't, how can you expect assholes like that to care?"

"They don't care, Dex, and they're not going to. That's why they're assholes." Cael leaned into Dex and poked him in the vest. "This isn't the HPF. You're in our world now, and it's scary, and ugly, and fucked-up. They won't pat you on the head and tell you how special you are because you have a black daddy and a Therian brother who proudly waves his rainbow flags with you. Here you're a freak like the rest of us, so don't tell me how to do my job." Cael stalked off, and Dex stood speechless. The silence didn't last long.

"What just happened?"

Sloane let out a low whistle. "Wow. I didn't even know he could get that mad. Guess I was wrong. Nice going, Rookie."

Dex blinked at him. "What did I do?"

The hurt expression on Dex's face was too much for Sloane to bear, and he took pity on his partner, guiding him toward the front door. "Look, I understand what you were trying to do, but it's not that easy. I know you're proud of your baby brother, and believe me, he's proud of who he is too, but what you need to understand is that being a THIRDS agent means facing a whole new level of stupid." They stepped outside into the crisp late-September air, the sun shining and the neighborhood peacefully quiet. The only indication anything was amiss were the scores of agent vehicles blocking off both ends of the street and the numerous agents securing the area.

"As an HPF agent, you only had to worry about dealing with other Humans, getting shit for being a cop. Here, everyone hates you for one reason or another, and sometimes it feels like you can't win no matter what you say or do." Sloane let out a heavy sigh. "Some of us have learned how to deal, but Cael's a sweet guy, grew up in a loving home with Humans who accepted him from the start. It's harder for him. You need to let him cope in whichever way is best for him." Sloane chose his words carefully, knowing in the end it wouldn't matter. Dex would come face-to-face with harsh reality sooner or later. "I'm more worried about how you're going to deal."

"Me?" Dex gave him a smirk. "Maybe you haven't noticed, but I'm a big boy. I know the world's not all sunshine and unicorns."

"What I mean is, how are you going to deal when someone decides to be a little more proactive with their hate than that prick of a waiter? You're going to come to his rescue? Because I can tell you right now how well that's going to go down."

"So I'm supposed to stand there and do nothing?" Dex let out a frustrated breath. "I can't do that."

"No, you let your brother do his job, handle things his way, and if he needs you, he'll let you know. Your job is to back him up and protect him from any physical threat that puts his life in danger. It is not your job to come riding in on your white horse to slay all the dragons because they insulted him. Or threw bricks."

Dex's eyes clouded with anger, and when he spoke, it was through his teeth. "Someone threw bricks at him?"

"Don't worry. Ash threw them back." Sloane gave Dex a smile. He wasn't sure why he was going out of his way to reassure Dex. He told himself he was doing it for Cael. "You're not the only one looking out for him, Rookie. Okay?"

Dex nodded, though there was no telling if any of what Sloane said had actually found its way into that thick skull. They headed to the BearCat, a deep frown on Dex's face. "Sometimes the amount of stupid in this world confounds me. I swear some of these citizens are evolving backwards."

"We've come a long way," Sloane offered, though he had to admit, sometimes he found it a little difficult to believe it himself.

"Not enough, if you ask me."

"You sound like a grumpy old man."

Dex cast him a sideways glance as they rounded the back of the BearCat. "Shut up and get off my lawn."

"I'm not on your lawn. I think the Alzheimer's setting in." That earned him a chuckle, and Sloane held back a smile. When he wasn't fighting it, Sloane could fall into an easy banter with Dex, something he hadn't had since Gabe. The thought that he might actually have found a partner he could get along with should have made him feel relieved, but instead, it made him feel guilty. Before his thoughts could delve any deeper, he told himself now was not the time to be thinking about this.

Cael was already in the truck when they climbed in, and the young agent scooted to the end of the bench. With a subtle prod to Dex's arm, Sloane motioned toward Cael. Dex slid up to his brother, bumping his leg playfully. When Cael's frown only deepened, Dex leaned in to talk quietly. Sloane couldn't make out exactly what was being said, but he did hear the sincerity in Dex's low voice. He also heard something that sounded like an apology.

As Sloane took a seat and watched Dex, he felt a hint of sadness wash over him. How different might things have turned out if he'd grown up in a family like Maddock's, a loving home rather than padded white walls, siblings and parents instead of doctors and nurses. Cael's laugh snapped him out of his dark thoughts, and he found himself smiling at the brothers. Dex's arm was around Cael's neck as he teased him, Cael's words filled with affection despite his cursing.

"You're such a dork," Cael laughed softly, shaking his head at his brother.

"All right, team. We're heading to the catering company," Maddock declared, joining them along with the rest of the team. Dex removed his arm from around Cael as everyone took their place on the bench and buckled up. Rosa waved her tablet from beside Ash to get their attention.

"We've got a possible lead from a witness who stated there was an Unregistered Therian employee—a bartender and possible Felid, working with the catering company. According to guests, they were served drinks by him at his station until just after noon, when he left—the guy was pretty hard to miss. To be honest, I don't think he's our guy. He would have had to slip away long enough to undress, shift, kill Ortiz without leaving anything behind, shift back, and even if he managed to dress himself afterward, he would have needed PSTC. No one claims to have seen anyone with PST symptoms. Still, he's the closest thing to a lead we've got right now. We need to interview him."

Next to Rosa, Letty spoke up. "Even if the catering company hired an Unregistered, you really think they're going to admit it?"

"They don't have to," Dex pitched in. "They'll have records."

Sloane regarded him. "You sound pretty certain."

"My ex owns a catering company. He's dealt with Unregistered Therians in his business before and there's always a trail. Invoices, receipts, schedules, something."

"A cop's boyfriend hiring Unregistered Therians?" Ash sneered. "How'd that work out?"

"It didn't, because he didn't hire them." Dex pinned Ash with a glare before turning his attention to Maddock. "Lou might not have hired Unregistered Therians, but he worked with vendors who did. They usually handled backend duties like making deliveries or working storerooms. The vendors always kept some kind of record to cover their asses."

Maddock gave a nod. "Okay. Cael, you and Rosa go in and see about those records. Sloane, you and Dex go in as backup. Ash, Letty, stake out the perimeter. Calvin and Hobbs will handle surveillance. Cael, bring up everything you've got on the catering company." He stood and made his way to the surveillance console, Cael joining him. Next to Sloane, Rosa and Letty chatted when Ash leaned over Sloane to sneer at Dex.

"Ex, huh? What's the matter? He couldn't handle all that Daley charm?"

Dex's jaw muscles tightened, but he remained silent.

"Shit, Rookie's got no comment? Must have been bad, then. Means he dumped your ass."

"Ash," Sloane warned, frowning at his friend. It was starting, just as it had with the other agents.

Candidates who passed their training and made it to the final round of the application process were interviewed by the team, and although all the other agents who had slipped in and out of Gabe's position had been approved, it hadn't been because the team believed they'd fit in, but because they knew they wouldn't, making it seem like it was the rookie who couldn't hack it once he was in. It was fucked-up, Sloane was aware of that. And if their superiors found out he'd not only known about what was going on but had allowed it, he'd be in deep shit. The simple truth was, his team hadn't been ready for anyone new, but the higher-ups didn't care. They were a man down. Sloane didn't hold it against them. They didn't know what Gabe had meant to his team, to him. With anyone else, Sloane would've let Ash do his thing, but now… he wasn't so sure.

"What? We're a team. If Daley really wants to be a part of it, he needs to share with us."

Sloane was about to advise his friend to mind his own business when Dex leaned over him, his intense pale gaze focused on Ash. The anger and pain in those blue eyes caught Sloane by surprise. He didn't know what it was about Dex, but the guy had a way of getting to him.

"Yes, he did dump my ass, because apparently I'm an asshole for believing an unarmed kid, Therian punk or otherwise, didn't deserve to be shot in cold blood in the back. Because the guy was already dead, right, so why be a dick and turn my partner in? Why turn my whole fucking life upside down for a silly little thing like the truth? My ass got dumped because the whole thing became such a fucking inconvenience for someone who was supposed to have given enough of a shit about me to be there for me, who promised me he would stick by me, but at the first sign of real trouble, bailed. And why wouldn't he when the fucking Titanic was sinking around him? Is that enough sharing for you, Ash? Because if not, I've got some great stories of me when I was a kid and found out my parents had been killed by a bunch of street punks. Would you like to hear about that? No? Then shut the fuck up and keep your dick comments to yourself, you self-absorbed prick."

The truck fell into thick silence before Maddock's gruff voice cut through it. "Dex, come here a minute."

"Coming, sir." Dex unfastened his belt and stood, pinning Ash with another glare before leaving them to join Maddock.

"What the hell was that?" Ash said with a laugh.

"That was your being a dick." Sloane shifted in his seat to put some distance between him and his friend. As expected, Ash's grin faded, and he glared at Sloane.

"Wait, so you're on his side now?"

"I'm not on anyone's side, but if you pull a shitty move, I'm going to call you out on it, and you know it." Their friendship had never been easy, but it was honest, no minced words between them.

"Yeah, but not with him," Ash hissed. His eyes went wide and he ran a gloved hand over his hair before leaning into Sloane. "Please don't tell me you actually like him."

Sloane closed his eyes and let his head fall back against the truck's padded panel, momentarily forgetting how nauseated it made him feel. Damn it. His mind had put it all behind him. Why couldn't his body do the same? Inhaling slowly, then releasing through his mouth, he sat forward again, his elbows coming to rest on his legs as the sick rolling in his stomach eased.

"I don't have to like him to get the job done. That's something you should consider."

"So he's staying?" Ash stared at him, stunned.

Why were they having this conversation? Ash unfastened his belt and walked to the end of the truck and waited. Great. Just what he needed. With a sigh, Sloane unhooked his own belt and joined his friend, knowing he could be as stubborn as Ash if he wanted to be. Ash put his hands to his hips and shrugged.

"What, Ash? Get it out of your system now so we can get back to this case."

"He can't stay."

Sloane arched an eyebrow at him. "Is that so?"

"Get rid of him." Ash gave him a poke in the vest and Sloane frowned. Why did his friend have to make everything so damn difficult?

"First of all"—Sloane batted his hand away—"I have no intention of getting my ass handed to me by Lieutenant Sparks for running off another partner. She's made it clear. This is my last chance to play nice. We don't have a choice. Considering all the other agents we've had, Dex is the best fit."

"That jackass?" Ash shook his head in disbelief. "Look, I know he's Maddock's kid and Cael's brother, but that doesn't mean he's a good fit."

"And who is, Ash? Who's going to be good enough to take Gabe's place, huh?"

Ash swallowed hard, his gaze dropping to his boots.

"That's right. This isn't easy for me either, okay? So cut me a fucking break. Please, I'm asking you, as your best friend, don't make this any harder than it has to be." He held his breath, waiting. If Ash didn't want to do something, there was nothing on God's green earth that could make him do it. Ash could be a stubborn, hardassed, unbearable prick, but he would come through for Sloane no matter what. He always had and always would. After a silent moment, Ash nodded.

"Okay, but I hope you're not asking me to be nice to him, because there's a fucking limit."

"Heaven forbid," Sloane muttered. "Just leave his personal life out of it. Got it?"

"Yeah, fine. You fucking gay boys are so sensitive."

Sloane rolled his eyes and started to walk off when Ash grabbed his arm. "Hey, wait. This is serious. I want to get him something to make it up to him. What do you think he'll like better, a knitted sweater or a couple of tickets to *Mamma Mia*? You can go as his date." He slapped Sloane's arm. "I can knit you one too. Then you can match."

"You know what, man." Sloane jabbed a finger at Ash. "Fuck you." He marched off to the sound of Ash's cackling. Well, at least order had been restored. For now.

"What, you don't think I'm capable of picking up a knitting needle?" Ash called out after him.

"Not unless you were going to stab someone with it. Now sit down and shut up." Sloane dropped down onto the bench, Letty and Rosa both watching him in amusement. "What?"

Rosa shrugged. "Nothing."

Ash stayed where he was, holding on to one of the ceiling straps as the truck drove through Manhattan, a shit-eating grin on his face. When Ash turned his head to the ceiling, seeming to lose himself in his own thoughts, Rosa slid up to Sloane, bumping into him playfully.

"Hey."

Sloane glanced over at her with a small smile. He felt weary, but he didn't want to take it out on his team, and Rosa—as brash as she could be—was always fussing over him and somehow getting away with it. "What can I do for you, Rosita Bonita?"

She pretended to be put off by the tender nickname. "You can hear me out."

With a discreet peek to see if Dex was still busy with Maddock and Cael, Sloane leaned toward her. "Okay, but if it's to tell me to get rid of him, I—"

"Shouldn't," she cut in, a determined expression coming onto her face. She leaned in to Sloane, speaking quietly. "I know you don't like to talk about it, so I won't. All I'm going to say is, he's not like the other ones. You should give him a chance. If you need someone to kick Ash in the nuts, you know where to find me."

Sloane didn't know what to say. He sat speechless as Rosa went back to her side of the bench and resumed chatting with Letty. Now that he thought about it, the only protests concerning Dex he'd heard so far had all come from Ash. In fact, Sloane had spotted more ogling coming from his teammates toward Dex than dirty looks, and he'd yet to hear any snide comments. Had his team accepted Dex without either of them realizing it, and in such a short span of time?

It took them a little over twenty minutes to get to Fifth and West Thirty-Third Street. As soon as the truck pulled up to the building, Sloane and Dex jumped out, Cael and Rosa close behind. The catering company was across the three-lane street and the second-to-last shop on the skyscraper's storefront. There were various delivery trucks parked up and down both sides of the road, with the sunlight reflecting off windows but mostly blocked by the large skyscrapers. As they approached the catering company, Sloane caught sight of a loading dock one store over, and he remembered what Dex had said regarding hiring Unregistered Therians. He caught Dex's elbow.

"You go ahead. Call if there's an emergency. I'll be there in a minute."

"Where are you going?"

"To check something out." He didn't bother to wait around to see if Dex had listened to his orders. Using a parked truck to shield him, he swiftly crossed behind it and onto the sidewalk to the building, edging his way closer to the loading dock. Inside there was a van displaying fancy scripted lettering. It belonged to Thalia's Kitchen Events & Catering, and it was parked with the rear toward the loading dock's raised cement platform. Three large males were removing boxes from the van, all of them wearing turtlenecks. Sloane crept toward them, his tranq rifle in his hand at the ready. One of the males turned, his eyes confirming Sloane's suspicion. When the Therian spotted him, he gave a start.

"Easy now. I know you're thinking about running, but we both know how that's going to end."

The three males reluctantly put their hands in the air. Sloane stopped a few feet away and gave them a curt nod. "Let's see those necks." He eyed them cautiously as they each pulled down their turtlenecks, revealing nothing but skin. Sloane tapped the side of his earpiece. "Ash, I've got three Unregistered males in the loading dock two doors down from Thalia's. Bring the TIK." Hopefully the Therian Identification Kit would tell him what he needed to know.

Within minutes Ash and Letty were at his side. Ash approached the Therians with a growl. "Turn around. Hands behind your backs."

"We didn't do anything," one of them protested as Ash hooked a Therian-strength zip tie around each Therian's set of wrists and gave the ends a tug, securing them tightly.

"Besides maybe break a law or two," Ash replied, stepping back as they turned around.

Sloane motioned toward the bay doors. "There a back way into your employer's shop?"

One of the men gave a nod. "Yeah, second door. There's a hallway that leads to the back entrance."

"Okay, let's go. We'll have a chat inside." The last thing they needed was the news stations showing up, and curious bystanders were already starting to gather. They led the three males inside, down a stone passage with several metal doors. Their subjects came to a halt before one of the doors, and the tallest of the three tilted his head toward it.

"You need a security code to get in."

Ash stepped up to the keypad and grinned. "You can trust us."

With a muttered curse under his breath, the Therian relayed the security code that Ash typed into the pad. A little green light flashed and Ash opened the door, stopping the males before they could go in.

"Learn some manners."

Letty gave them a salute before walking in, rifle in hand.

"That's rather chauvinistic," one of them huffed.

Ash let out an amused laugh. "I didn't let her in first because she's female, you jackass. I let her in first because she likes to shoot things, and I'm very considerate that way."

"All clear," Letty called out.

"I suggest you boys behave, or I'll let her use you for target practice. Now get in there." Ash pushed the first of their subjects through the doorway, the two behind quickly following.

Inside, they found a large pantry filled with all manner of catering supplies and equipment, folded tables, chairs, and along the wall, several industrial-sized freezers. Ash ordered the Therians to line up before he removed the TIK from one of the pouches in his utility belt. Luckily the kit was nice and slim, so there was no need to untie the Therians in order to use it. "I won't lie. This is going to hurt like a bitch." Ash grabbed one of the Therian's arms, pushed up his sleeve, and clamped the black digital band around the guy's arm under the elbow. The small screen flickered to life, and Ash pressed his thumb against it to log in. A few taps later, the Therian subject flinched as the identification kit accessed and analyzed his DNA.

While he waited for Ash to perform the necessary scans, Sloane touched his earpiece. "Dex, what's your position?"

"Reception area. Ms. Thalia's assistant is trying to give us the runaround, insisting her boss isn't in, but a courier on his way out was carrying paperwork with her signature. Rosa's doing her thing."

"Okay, I'll be there in two." Sloane tapped his ear-piece again and turned to Ash. "What's the verdict?"

"Three confirmed Unregistered Therians, none of them Felids," Ash replied, handing Sloane the TIK with the completed analysis report. Damn. Okay, he could still work with this.

"Ash, read them their rights and begin registration. They've got a week."

Ash gave him a nod and addressed the three solemn Therians. They'd have one week to report to their nearest CDC clinic, complete their registrations, and get marked, otherwise warrants for their arrest would be issued. Leaving his teammates to handle the bound Therians, Sloane left the pantry, walking out into a cream-colored hallway with lots of fancy gold frames, gilded tables, and crystal vases filled with fresh flowers. A young woman came out of one of the rooms and gave a start, her hand flying to her chest.

"It's okay," Sloane assured her. "Can you tell me how to get to the reception area?"

She shakily pointed to the end of the hall and a set of white double doors. With a thank-you, he made his way into what appeared to be some kind of small lobby. From there he could see the reception area where Dex, Cael, and Rosa were standing. A tall, slender woman sporting a painfully tight bun stood with her hands clasped in front of her as she looked down her nose at the agents, their stark dark uniforms and heavy artillery a sharp contrast to the ostentatious surroundings. When she spoke, it was in a clipped tone.

"Allow me to reiterate, Agent Santiago. I am in the middle of a very important meeting with a client and have no time to waste on nonsense, nor do

I appreciate the accusations. I have not, nor would I ever hire Unregistered Therians. So unless you have something more official to present me with other than your ghastly presence, I suggest you stop wasting my taxes and go catch some criminals."

"Ms. Thalia."

Everyone's attention turned to him, including the irate owner's, her gasp audible through the deathly silent reception area. A couple sitting by the door quickly got up and left, while the remaining customers looked on in interest. Sloane was aware of how intimidating he was and could be. It made the job much easier when dealing with citizens like Ms. Thalia. He ḥ꜕ᴜᴍ ᴅ ꜱ꜖ᴀ꜉ꜱ ꜱ ᴀ ꜱ, ꜰ꜉꜉꜉ꜱ ꜱ ꜱꜱᴜᴀᴀꜱ꜖ꜱꜱꜱ ᴀᴀ ꜱ꜉ꜱ

"Now, we can either speak somewhere private, or we can continue this discussion here. Either way, it's in your best interest to cooperate."

The woman lifted her chin, her eyes darting from Sloane to the customers who remained.

"Very well, Agent…."

"Brodie," Sloane offered with a smile.

"Very well, Agent Brodie. We'll discuss this in my office." She spun on her very high heels and marched toward a door to the left of the reception area, opposite of where Sloane had come in. Cael and Rosa trailed after her, with Sloane and Dex close behind.

"Where were you?" Dex asked quietly, holding the door open for their team.

"You're about to find out." Sloane walked past Dex into the short hallway leading to an extravagantly decorated office lined with elegant white-and-silver wallpaper sporting several black frames of various shapes with event photographs. The silver glass-topped desk looked exceptionally pricey, as did the two white wingback chairs with silver stripes that were angled toward it. He hated being in a room with that much white.

Sloane positioned himself next to Rosa in front of Ms. Thalia's desk. The woman made a great big show of sitting down, straightening objects, closing her personal diary, and adjusting the angle of her tablet before finally clasping her hands together and smiling up at him.

"What can I do for you, Agent Brodie?" She swept her gaze over him in approval, the look in her eyes turning sinful. And they called *him* a predator.

"Ms. Thalia, you were recently hired to cater a brunch held by the Ortiz family for HumaniTherians United. Is that correct?"

"Yes. Why?"

"Ortiz was found dead earlier today." He watched her intently as his words sank in. The smile fell off her now-pale face, her delicate hand going to her pink lips as she let out a gasp.

"Oh my God. I spoke with him this morning. How… what happened?"

To her credit, she looked genuinely stricken. "We're going to need a list of Therian employees who worked the charity event."

"Yes, of course, but you don't believe one of them had anything to do with it, do you?" She tapped away at her tablet, the slim document printer beside it churning to life and spitting out several sheets. As soon as it was done, she handed them to Sloane.

"Right now, we're following all possible leads," Rosa stated, taking the documents from him after he gave it a cursory glance.

"Thank you. Now I'm going to need the list of all your Unregistered employees."

Ms. Thalia's gray eyes went wide, and she shot to her feet. "Now see here. I don't—"

"Enough." Sloane brought her protest to an abrupt halt. "I have three Unregistered Therians detained in your pantry. I caught them unloading *your* company van. Now, you can cooperate and get me that list, or I will arrest you for the hiring of Unregistered Therians, shut you down, confiscate everything, and find the list myself."

With an anxious nod, she quickly went about printing another list. This one was much shorter. Removing a pen from his front breast pocket, Sloane scratched out the three names he recognized from the TIK analysis. That left seven. "Is there anyone on this list who was scheduled to work at the brunch?"

Ms. Thalia resumed her seat. "Yes. I don't normally send Unregistered employees offsite unless they're making deliveries, but one of my bartenders called in sick at the last minute, and Lloyd had bartending experience, so I sent him. I told Mrs. Ortiz he was in the process of registering."

"Full name?"

"Lloyd Everton."

Cael tapped the information into his tablet. "We're going to need everything you have on file for him."

Ms. Thalia clasped her hands tightly in front of her. "I'm afraid that's all I have. He came recommended by one of my vendors. They wanted to keep him on but had to make cutbacks. Look, these guys are grateful to get any work they can. They don't make demands and neither do I. It's all cash under the table.

Lloyd's been working for me for months. He would never hurt anyone."

Unlike a lot of other employers Sloane came across, Ms. Thalia hadn't jumped at the chance to hurl blame upon her Unregistered Therian employees. Still, that didn't mean she didn't take advantage of them. Sloane had to consider all possibilities. "Well, someone isn't hurt, Ms. Thalia, they're dead, and so are two other victims. We need to find Mr. Everton and bring him in for questioning. He's the only one unaccounted for."

"I'm sorry." She rushed around her desk and put her hands on his arm. "I swear, if I had any more information, I would give it to you, but that's all I have."

It was amazing how quickly the haughtiness disappeared when faced with the possibility of prison time. Sloane pretended to give the matter some thought. "Okay, here's what I'm going to do. I'm going to leave you with a warning. Either get your employees to register or call them in. No more hiring illegal help. Got it?"

"Yes." She nodded vigorously before releasing his arm. "I'll do that."

Reaching into his front breast pocket, he pulled out one of his contact cards and handed it to her. "If you hear from or see Mr. Everton, you call me immediately."

"Of course. Thank you, Agent Brodie." She motioned toward the door and they headed out, stopping in the reception area. Ms. Thalia caught his arm again and went on about how sorry she was about her tone, how she would do everything within her power to help, and whether there was anything she could do

to make it up to him. The last part had been a loaded question, and Sloane passed her on to Rosa with
a pleasant smile. Leaving Cael and Rosa to get Ms.
Thalia's contact details, Sloane turned to find himself
short one partner. He strode out into the lobby filled
with several white loveseats, dark coffee tables with
elaborate centerpieces, and more framed photos of
classy events lining the walls. No smartass agents in
sight.

Sloane cursed under his breath. He could easily
call Dex on his communicator, but he didn't want anyone else overhearing how he'd let his partner give him
the slip already. He couldn't wait for this day to be

Chapter 6

DAMN IT. His partner couldn't have gotten far. How Dex had managed to slip away without Sloane noticing was something he was still trying to figure out. Maybe he wasn't giving the guy enough credit. He'd have to be extra vigilant around the rookie from now on.

A petite woman appeared before Sloane. "Agent?"

"Yes, ma'am?" He expected her to start asking all kinds of questions regarding their presence and what was going on. Instead, she gave him a knowing smile and pointed to a set of doors tucked into the corner of the room.

"I believe you'll find what you're looking for in the kitchen."

Teeth gritted, Sloane gave her a nod in thanks before taking off in search of Dex, telling himself that shooting his partner would most likely be frowned upon. Maybe he could get away with a small flesh wound? Accidents in the workplace were, after all, very common occurrences. He stepped through the swinging doors into a huge kitchen filled with wall-to-wall stainless steel appliances, storage units, and fridges. Down the center of the room was a row of wide stainless steel tables, and toward the end, Sloane spotted what he was looking for.

What the hell? Sloane gave a slow, disbelieving shake of his head at the sight before him. In the middle of the kitchen, a pretty, young Therian stood on his toes popping something into Dex's open mouth.

"Mmm," Dex hummed as he chewed, his eyes closed and the look of sheer pleasure on his face unsettling. After swallowing, Dex opened his eyes, his tongue poking out to lick at his bottom lip. "Now that was really good. What was in that one?"

The young Therian chef batted his lashes and leaned in to wipe something nonexistent from the corner of Dex's mouth, his big brown eyes all but devouring the agent. "Hazelnut praline with dark chocolate."

Dex beamed at him. "That was good. I really liked that one. It was even better than the strawberry and white chocolate thingy with the little chocolate shavings."

The young Therian placed his hands on the stainless steel table behind him and arched his back, his eyes on Dex's lips. "Tell me, Agent Daley. Do you like café con leche?"

Dex's face lit up. "I *love* café con leche."

"Agent Daley," Sloane barked, causing the two to jump.

"Crap." Dex cleared his throat and gave the young chef an apologetic smile. "Sorry, Jordan, duty calls. Thanks so much for the free samples."

"Any time, Agent Daley." The Therian was practically purring.

Sloane waited, his jaw clenched as Dex hurried over. As soon as they were outside the kitchen, Sloane turned to Dex in disbelief. "We're in the middle of a case, and you're flirting?"

"I wasn't flirting, I was eating. I'm starving. Which is your fault."

"My fault?" Clearly he'd had a momentary lapse of judgment by thinking the two of them could get along. The urge to punch the guy was steadily rising. "How is this my fault?"

"You gave my Cheesy Doodles away!"

"Jesus Christ, again with that?" Sloane tried to summon patience, but instead he kept seeing Dex's stupid tongue poking out to lick his bottom lip. He pushed that thought away, grabbed Dex's arm, and hauled him toward the exit. "That back there had nothing to do with food, unless we count you being a part of the menu. The guy was two seconds away from pouncing on you."

"What? No way. We were talking about chocolate and café con leche."

Sloane stopped in his tracks. "You're not serious, are you? You can't be that oblivious."

"To what?" Dex's wide eyes told Sloane he most probably was. How could a guy like Dex be so clueless? The way Hudson kept trying to have eye sex with him, the Therian in the kitchen undressing him with his eyes? Hell, Sloane had even caught Letty eyeing Dex's ass on more than one occasion. Yet Dex never seemed to notice.

"To the fact that he wasn't talking about drinks, you idiot. He wanted *you* to be the leche in *his* café."

Dex frowned when it dawned on him. "Ohhh. I misread that."

"I don't…." Sloane shook his head. He didn't even have words. "Get in the damn truck before I shoot you." He pushed Dex from behind, guiding him into the lobby, grunting every time Dex paused to talk at him over his shoulder.

"You know, you should try yoga. Find a way to channel all that aggression."

Sloane gave him another push. "I have found a way. It's called shoving my foot up your ass."

"That doesn't sound very relaxing."

Push. "I'm sure I'll feel plenty relaxed afterward."

"You got a problem." Dex grimaced at him, and Sloane gave another push to get him moving again.

"Yeah, and I'm looking right at it." This situation was a heart attack waiting to happen. He just knew it. The stress of the job, now this. Yep, he was going to keel over. He could see the writing on his tombstone now: *Sloane Brodie departed this world at age 37 due to massive coronary trauma as a result of idiot partner Dexter J. Daley.*

"Ouch, man. That's harsh."

Sloane had just about reached the front door when Calvin's voice came over his earpiece.

"Sloane, we got a problem."

"What is it?"

"Press is outside."

"Shit." Sloane crept up to the large glass front, grateful for the wall-to-ceiling venetian blinds. Careful not to jostle the thin wooden slats, he peeked outside. Damn it, there were at least three news vans that he could see. He pulled back and tapped his earpiece. "What about Cael and Rosa?"

Rosa's concerned voice came over his earpiece. "We're in the truck. We didn't see you guys so figured you'd already headed out."

Sloane cast Dex an accusing glare. "We got momentarily held up. Dex had to take a shit."

Dex's jaw dropped. He made to touch his earpiece when Sloane caught his wrist and twisted his arm behind him, making him double over.

"Ow, ow, ow," Dex moaned, glaring up at him.

"Thank you for the disturbing visual," Rosa grunted. "What now?"

"We're going out the back. Have the BearCat ready to go as soon as we get there." He released Dex's arm, pulled him up, and grinned at the sour expression on Dex's face.

"That was not cool, man."

"Maybe next time you'll think twice about wandering off. Now let's go."

They rushed through the lobby and reception area to the double doors on the right. Behind him, Dex mimicked him, lowering his voice as he repeated Sloane's words, adding an unintelligible rambling of grunts and growls at the end.

"There's something seriously wrong with you." Sloane followed the hallway he'd come in through earlier to the pantry and out into the hall leading to the loading dock.

"Must be the company I've been keeping," Dex quipped. Sloane turned and grabbed Dex by the shoulders.

"Okay, shut up for a minute. Let's pretend you're a normal agent for a sec, and that you weren't sent to drive me out of my freaking mind. Can you do that?"

Dex pursed his lips. "I'll have to reach really deep for that one, but I think I can manage."

"Good. Soon as we get out there, make a beeline for the truck, and try not to shoot anyone."

"No promises," Dex muttered.

Sloane unclipped his helmet from where it hung at the back of his vest and put it on before lowering his visor. He motioned for Dex to do the same. It wouldn't deter the press, but at least their helmets would keep the cameras out of their faces and offer a little more anonymity. He grabbed the heavy metal door and pulled. With a quick glimpse to make sure the coast was clear, they hurried through and jumped down the concrete platform, making a dash for the sidewalk.

"There!"

One of the journalists saw them and the rest descended, shrouding them like a thick fog. Sloane held on to Dex's vest so as not to lose him. The BearCat was only a few feet away. Questions flew at them from every direction, and Sloane tried his hardest not to put anyone's lights out as they carefully pushed their way through the crowd.

"Agent Brodie, when is the THIRDS going to catch this murderer?"

As soon as you get the hell out of our way. "We're following up on all possible leads. Excuse us, please."

"How do the THIRDS justify sending killers to catch a killer?"

The question had Sloane gritting his teeth, but it wasn't anything he hadn't heard a hundred times over. As if Therians were the only ones capable of killing. Homicides had existed long before his kind. Dex made to stop but Sloane gave his vest a tug, keeping him walking. He leaned over so his partner could hear over the buzz of reporters and equipment. "Don't stop." The last thing they needed was to give the vultures any more ammunition, and after everything Dex had been through during the trial of his partner, Sloane had no idea how the guy would react to any of the callous questions thrown at them. When one of the reporters shoved a recording device under Sloane's visor from somewhere over his shoulder, Dex became the least of his worries.

"Agent Brodie, you don't seem to have much luck when it comes to partners. What do you think are the chances of this one ending up like Agent Pearce?"

Sloane came to an abrupt halt, the reporters around him stumbling and running into each other so as not to bump into him. He turned, his fists curled at his sides. With a growl, he took a step forward, ready to plant one into the son of a bitch when Dex materialized before him.

"Hey, partner." Dex maneuvered him into the nearest open shop doorway, closing it on the swarming reporters and locking it. To Sloane's surprise, Dex lifted both their visors before gently taking hold of Sloane's face and pulling him close. He was ready to snap at Dex, but having those pale blue eyes staring intently into his own stopped him cold. He didn't know why, but he found himself unable to look away. More disturbing was the knowledge a part of him didn't want to. He stood, focusing on the pools of crystal blue. When Dex spoke, his voice was soothing.

"Come on. Focus. Focus on me. Not them. Me."

Sloane gritted his teeth, his anger fluctuating. He wanted to stay outraged, but the more he looked into Dex's eyes, the harder he found it.

"Look at me. Breathe. That's it. Just breathe. They don't know you."

"You don't know me either," Sloane replied roughly.

"I know enough. I also know the job. It's easy for them to talk shit when they're not the ones out there, putting their lives on the line, making the tough decisions. They don't see the faces when they close their eyes. They don't have to live with the guilt. All they want is to see you as some dangerous animal, to watch you fail and prove them right. Don't give them the satisfaction. You're better than those assholes and you know it."

Dex was right. Sloane was playing into their hands. It was a cheap shot, using his dead partner to stir a reaction out of him, but it wasn't the first time they'd stooped that low over the last year. He breathed in deeply and released it slowly. Maddock's voice came in over their earpieces.

"Where are you two?"

Dex looked around them. "We're in a café. Vultures got too close. They're swarming outside. We're going to need a distraction."

"How long?" Maddock asked.

Dex craned his neck, and Sloane turned, not surprised to see the large glass display filled with all kinds of baked goods. When he turned back to Dex, his partner was looking up at him with big puppy eyes. No. Absolutely not. He was not going to….

"Okay, fine," Sloane muttered. "But hurry up."

Dex tapped his earpiece. "Ten minutes, Sarge."

"Fine."

With an excited bounce, Dex rushed to the counter, and Sloane stared after him. He'd never met anyone who got as excited about food as Dex. From the grin he had on his face, you'd think the guy had hit the lottery or something. Lucky for them, there were only a couple of customers inside, one wearing headphones and so engrossed in whatever was on his tablet that he hadn't even noticed them come in, and a tiny wisp of a girl who smiled at him, turned in her seat, held up her phone, and snapped a picture of Dex bending over to point at something behind the display. When she turned around, Sloane arched an eyebrow at her.

She gave him a shrug. "Your boy's got a fine ass."

Seriously? She tapped away at her phone, and Sloane wondered if he should tell his partner his ass was about to get its fifteen minutes. Nah. It *was* a pretty fine ass.

Dex turned to Sloane, a look of sheer joy on his face. "You want anything?"

Why the hell not. "A bear claw."

"Nice choice, partner." Dex turned back to the counter and put in his order with the startled-looking barista. From the sounds of it, Dex was ordering for the whole team.

"Don't get anything with nuts for Ash. He's allergic," Sloane called out.

Dex gave a snort. "Of course he is."

With two plastic bags full of cakes and drinks, Dex walked up to Sloane and motioned toward the door. "Looks like Sarge has cleared the way. Ready to make a break for it?"

"Yeah." Dex made for the door when Sloane took hold of his arm. "Listen, about earlier…."

Dex tilted his head to one side, his expression softening. "Don't mention it. You need me, just… you know. Now let's get going."

Sloane opened the door for him and, with a quick glance to see the flock of reporters down at the end of the block surrounding Maddock, they made a run for the BearCat sitting idle in the street. The back doors opened, and Sloane helped Dex up before climbing in after him.

"You guys okay?" Cael asked before sniffing the air, his eyes going huge. "Oh my God, did you get food?"

Dex held the bags up. "Bear claw is Sloane's and the cinnamon bun is mine. Anyone touches it and I swear I will bust your shit up." He started handing out little white paper bags along with drinks.

"Oh my God, this is sooo good," Rosa moaned. "Dex, if you didn't have a penis, I would totally sex you up right now."

Dex gave her a wink. "And if you had a penis, I would totally let you."

Sloane couldn't help but chuckle. "Idiot."

"What?" Dex warbled through a mouthful of cin-namon bun.

"What the hell is going on in here? Sounds like a goddamn orgy."

Everyone froze, cakes and breads half-stuffed into mouths. Dex swallowed what he'd been chewing before holding a hand up. "My fault, Sarge. We were in the café, I was starving, so I thought why not have a quick bite on the way to wherever we're going next?"

"So you got sugar."

"And carbs," Dex added. He rummaged in the bag and held up a white paper bag, waving it at Maddock. "Chocolate croissant."

Maddock marched over and snatched the croissant from him. "You think that's going to cut it, Agent Daley?" Dex held up a Diet Pepsi, which Maddock promptly swiped as well. "Thought so." He went to his seat and got busy eating his croissant. "Calvin, Hobbs, finish up your damn donuts so we can get moving. We're heading back to HQ."

Calvin murmured an acknowledgment around a mouthful of donut, and Hobbs merely continued eating. As Sloane quietly ate his bear claw, he observed his team all smiling and laughing. Each of them had learned to cope with Gabe's death in their own way. It had been only recently that his team had regained some of its lightheartedness, something needed to keep them sane on the job. There had been a lot of anger, anger that had manifested itself in different ways. Sloane had been aware, but his own grieving had made it difficult to address. How could he help them move on when he couldn't find the strength to do it himself?

Now there was a dirty-blond enigma making his team laugh so hard they were in tears, and it was only his first day on the job. None of the others had lasted, not with Sloane, and not with his team. The only reason they'd given Dex a chance was because of Cael and Maddock, but the more Sloane watched the team interact with Dex, the more he started to believe maybe the rookie would be good for them. He *was* charming, in his own weird way. He talked a hell of a lot, always had a stupid smile on his face, and Sloane had caught him a couple of times humming some cheesy ballad. But the light in Dex's blue eyes seemed to be spreading to the rest of his team. Sloane didn't know what that meant, other than it was scaring the shit out of him. His team needed this, so he would suck it up and ride it out as long as he could.

SLOANE AND his team returned to HQ, shed all their gear, and headed for their respective offices. Re- ⸻ leads until they came up with something, while Hudson and Nina worked with the lab to get every tiny piece of evidence analyzed. The moment they got a hit, Sloane and the rest of Destructive Delta would suit up and head out again, but until then, they'd go about their usual duties.

After lunch, where Dex nearly came in his pants from the sight of the canteen and all the vendors offering an assortment of free food, Sloane had spent a good deal of the afternoon training his partner on Themis, how it worked, how to create, access, and amend files, helpful shortcuts that would make the process more streamlined, and how to send information to their fellow teammates.

"Shit, I broke it." Dex pushed himself away from his desk and threw his hands up.

Sloane chuckled and rose to his feet, walking around to Dex and wheeling him back to his desk. "You didn't break it. Themis won't let you do anything

you shouldn't." He hovered over Dex's shoulder to
see what he'd done now. It was the fifth time the rookie had supposedly broken their intelligence network.
Sloane slid a finger down near the edge of the desk,
and three files popped up. "There they are. You only
minimized them. When you tap the same spot twice
inside the file, it brings them to the bottom, and the
screen flashes once to let you know they're still open,
just out of sight."

"Awesome. Now how do I access Google?"

Was he serious? "Why do you need Google?"

"When *don't* you need Google?"

He was serious. There were moments Sloane
wondered how Dex had made it this far. Either the
guy was deceptively clever or extremely talented at
pretending he was. "How about when you have a powerful, multimillion-dollar government interface linked
to numerous intelligence agencies across the globe
right in front of you."

Dex squinted at him, his lips pursed thoughtfully.
"So… is that a no on Google?"

"Are you on medication?" Sloane asked, eyeing
him. "Because that's the kind of thing I need to know
if you're going to be handling anything more dangerous than a smoke bomb."

Dex let out a bark of laughter. "I knew you had a
sense of humor."

"I'm not trying to be funny. I'm very concerned."
He pointed to his face. "This is my concerned face."
He could tell Dex was trying very hard not to laugh.
Sloane was a lot better at pulling it off.

"It looks a lot like your pissed-off face."

Sloane shook his head. "The two are very different."

"Really?" Dex's eyes lit up with amusement. He sat back, stretched his legs out in front of him, and laced his fingers over his flat stomach. "Because the two look the same to me."

Sloane walked around him to take a seat on the edge of Dex's desk beside him, one arm resting on his leg as he leaned forward. "I'll make it easy for you. This face means you've done something that concerns me. While this face, accompanied by physical pain upon your person, means you've done something to piss me off. Face and no pain equals concern. Face and pain equals pissed off. Easy as that."

"I really appreciate this. Is this part of the training?"

"Yep. You'll find I can be a very nurturing partner if you do exactly as I say without question."

Dex let out a snicker before sitting up and leaning forward, his grin wide. "Is that also your sex face?"

"I'm not touching that." Sloane narrowed his eyes as Dex invaded his personal space. He was onto Dex, and there was no way Sloane was about to break first. There was nothing Dex could do to get under his skin.

"Will you at least poke it?"

Damn it. Sloane found himself laughing. "You're an idiot."

"Actually, I'm pretty smart." Dex wheeled his chair an inch closer. "I like to lull my victims into a false sense of security."

"And what exactly am I a victim of?"

Dex wriggled his eyebrows and Sloane braced himself. He clearly would never know what was going to happen with Dex. That thought was either very frightening or strangely entertaining. He still hadn't figured out which.

"There's one thing I need you to clarify," Dex said.

"You didn't answer my question."

His partner gave a slow nod, his expression growing somber before he started rambling on about someone putting out Sloane's fire. It sounded oddly like an old Eagles song. Wait…

"Are those song lyrics?" Sloane let out a groan and sat back. "That's a song, isn't it?"

Dex jumped to his feet as he sang and played invisible instruments around Sloane.

"Oh dear God, it gets worse." Sloane let his head fall into his hand.

Dex's earpiece flashed blue, and Sloane watched in amusement as Dex tapped it. "You've reached the voicemail of Agent Dexter J. Daley. I'm away from my desk at the moment having hot monkey sex in the archive room with my partner, Agent Sloane Brodie. Please leave a message after the snarl."

"You son of a bitch." Sloane jumped to his feet and made a swipe for him. Dex laughed and darted around to Sloane's desk.

"Relax, it's only the sarge."

"What?" Sloane squawked.

Dex doubled over laughing. "Oh shit! You should see your face!"

"I'm going to kill you," Sloane ground out through his teeth.

"I'm kidding, man. It's my brother, and he's on a private line." Dex tapped his earpiece again. "What up, nerd?"

Sloane stormed over to his desk, pushing Dex out of his way so he could sit down. Dex laughed as he ambled to his own chair and dropped into it.

"Yep, I'm still alive," Dex glanced over at Sloane with a grin. "But if looks could kill, it'd be a different story. I don't know." He checked his watch, then glanced up at Sloane. "Depends on whether our team leader has some more training—"

"Get out."

"Well, what do you know, looks like it's quittin' time. I'll meet you at Reception." Dex got to his feet, his usual big dopey grin on his face. "Want to come? We're going to grab some dinner."

"In case you missed my subtle gesture, I'm trying to get rid of you."

"Gotcha." With a wink, Dex headed for the office door. "See you tomorrow, partner."

"Get lost." Sloane tapped his desk's surface and pulled up Dex's report on his observations from the last crime scene. The door swished quietly and Sloane glanced up, letting out a sigh of relief. Finally a little peace and quiet. It was hard to believe today had been Dex's first day. It felt like a lot longer. To say the guy was unlike any partner Sloane had ever had would be the understatement of the century, but there was also an easy way about him, something that made those around him comfortable. Sloane could easily fool himself into believing he'd known the guy much longer.

Everything about today should have been routine. A routine introduction, routine callout, routine ride in the BearCat, yet nothing about today had felt routine. Dex wasn't intimidated by him, but he wasn't challenging Sloane's authority at every turn in order to prove his mettle either. He went with the flow, and although his inability to shut his trap grated on Sloane's nerves at times, there were also times when the guy seemed to know exactly what to say. The whole thing was somewhat confusing.

"You okay?"

Sloane's head snapped up at the unexpected intrusion, and he felt embarrassed at being caught with his head in the clouds by his sergeant. "Hey, boss. Yeah, I'm fine. Why?"

Maddock gave a lazy shrug before he walked into the room and made himself comfortable in Dex's chair. "Nothing. Just, you were smiling."

"Oh." Sloane cleared his throat, unaware he'd been doing that. "Just thinking about something stupid. Don't worry about it."

"Something Dex did?"

That alone had Sloane trying to hold back a smile. There was no point lying to his sergeant. The guy could smell bullshit from two towns over. The thought had him chuckling. "Yeah, he was singing some cheesy song and playing air guitar or drums, I don't know, something ridiculous like that."

"Get used to it. He does that a lot. He also doesn't know any songs after 1989."

Sloane peered at him. "You're kidding me, right?"

"Nope." Maddock shook his head, his usual stern expression unmoving.

Inexplicably, Sloane broke into laughter, and when Maddock joined in, Sloane was laughing so hard, he had tears in his eyes. A few moments later, he finally managed to get ahold of himself. He gave a sniff and wiped his eyes. "No disrespect, Maddock, but your kid is fucking weird."

Maddock chuckled, his grin wide. "Yeah, he is." He sobered up and leaned forward, meeting Sloane's gaze. "But maybe he's precisely the kind of weird the team needs."

Sloane mirrored his sergeant's pose. "You think so?"

"I do, and I know you've had the same thought."

Sloane arched an eyebrow at his sergeant, not in the least bit surprised the guy had figured out as much. There was no hiding anything from Maddock. Growing up in the Maddock household must have been interesting, to say the least. He didn't know who to feel sorrier for: Maddock having to keep Dex and Cael out of trouble, or Dex and Cael for undoubtedly being caught before any of their boyhood shenanigans had a chance to take off. "Okay," Sloane admitted, "yes, maybe the thought crossed my mind."

"Good. How was his first day?"

Sloane mentally recapped their day, from the moment Dex had run into him in the training bay to their sparring session where the guy wouldn't stay down, the showers and the carefree way he ribbed his baby brother, the briefing room and mansion where he'd shown insight, their encounter with the media and how Dex had managed to calm Sloane with his sincerity and compassion, to moments ago where Dex had made him laugh like he hadn't laughed since… since Gabe. Sloane met Maddock's steady gaze.

"He's going to do fine here. If he doesn't drive us all crazy first."

Maddock smiled and stood. "That's all I wanted to know." He headed for the door and paused. When he turned, his softened expression was unexpected. "It's good to hear you laugh again, son."

Sloane swallowed hard, his voice rough when he spoke. "Thanks, Sarge."

With that, Maddock was gone, leaving Sloane in the empty silence of his office, a silence he had grown accustomed to. Not that it ever bothered him. In fact, in his line of work, moments of solitude were slim to nonexistent, and he often found himself needing those moments to gather himself and his thoughts. He focused his attention on the open reports, deciding he was better off losing himself in his work rather than the minefield in his head. He started reading through everything to make sure Dex hadn't left anything out, doing his best not to feel the lingering effects of Maddock's words and the reminder of how hard the last year and few months had been for him. Shaking himself out of it, he told himself not to go down that route again. He scanned the report, his sight landing on the digital sticky note with his name neatly scribbled across it. How was it the guy freaked out when he minimized his own documents, but he had no trouble adding a personal note to his report, which was a multistep process?

Their desk interface allowed for secure communication between them, away from the prying eyes of other agents if marked as such. Sloane eyed the yellow rectangle, wondering why he hadn't opened it yet. There was absolutely no reason not to. Tapping it, it expanded. There was nothing on it except for a Play symbol. It was an audio file.

"Don't do it, Sloane." He stared at the little triangle, a sense of foreboding washing over him. "Nothing good can come from pressing Play." His finger hovered over the note. What if it was important? Sloane grimaced. If it were important, Dex would have told him. He cringed and tapped the button, knowing he was going to regret it.

The melody of a harmonica blared from his desk, and he gave a start. A few seconds in, a woman's voice started singing away, telling him to keep on smiling. Several more artists joined the cheesy eighties ballad with saccharine lyrics about shining and friendship, with the wailing harmonica not missing a beat. Sloane had never heard anything more terrifying.

"Oh dear God." He hit the Mute button on his desk, confused when nothing happened. He tapped it repeatedly before bringing up the speaker settings on his desk. Nothing seemed to work. This couldn't be happening. With every cheesy word, the song got louder. "You've got to be kidding me." No matter what he did, he couldn't get the damn thing to stop playing. "Oh God, please make it stop."

"What the fuck are you doing?"

Sloane's head shot up to find Ash standing by the door, gaping at him. All Sloane could offer was a helpless shrug and a panicked cry. "I can't get it to stop!"

Ash came running over, hovering at his side. He tapped the Mute button to no avail, moved the sliders, tried removing and deleting the audio file, but nothing worked. It only seemed to make the damn thing louder. Calvin and Hobbs came into the office, along with the rest of the agents on the floor wandering over to see what was going on.

"Call IT," Ash said over the wailing of the harmonica.

"Are you crazy? I'm not getting IT up here. They'll think I'm fucking nuts!"

Ash thrust a hand in the direction of their fellow agents, all laughing and sniggering as they crowded by the door. "It's a little late for that. Besides, at this rate you won't have to call them because they'll be able to fucking hear it from there!"

An idea came to him, and he frantically tapped a sequence into the panel at the side of his desk. "Come on." A beep later, the sound cut off, and his desk went black. Blue letters scrolled across the surface. *Rebooting... please wait.*

He gritted his teeth and pinned his fellow Defense agents with a glower. "Laugh it up. Just remember this. If he can get to me, he can get to you. You won't know when, you won't know how, but when it happens, it will be loud, horrifying, and involve awful pop music. I will also be there to enjoy every second of it. Now get the hell out of my office." The agents all scrambled away with the exception of Ash, Calvin, and Hobbs.

Calvin cleared his throat, doing his best not to crack a smile. He was failing miserably. "I'm going to go out on a limb here and say that you're not a fan of that particular song."

"What gave me away," Sloane grunted, waiting for his desk's interface to finish loading.

"I'd told Dex as much."

Sloane peered at him. "Elaborate."

"Well, at lunch he asked me if I thought you'd like it. I had no idea what song he was talking about, so he explained it and sang the first chorus. I said there was a good chance you'd want to hurt him afterwards."

A smug grin appeared on Ash's face. "Still want him to stay?"

"Shut up. I hope he gets you next," Sloane grumbled.

Ash shook his head. "Not going to happen. I would hurt him. Physically. Not in your sorryass, hurt feelings kind of way, but really inflict some bodily damage."

"Go away." Sloane dropped his head onto his desk's surface and closed his eyes. "I have to plan my revenge."

Ash appeared beside him. "Can I help?"

"No."

"Why?"

"Because I want to make him suffer, not maim him."

"You're no fun." Ash headed for the door, Calvin snickering behind him, and Hobbs leaving no evidence he was ever there. His door swished closed, and Sloane quickly got out his smartphone, texting Dex.

I don't know how you did it, but you're going to regret it.

Seconds later, his phone buzzed.

I'm sorry. It's a… Hard Habit to Break.

"Fuck me." Sloane stared at his phone in disbelief. He quickly texted back *Don't you dare.*

His phone buzzed again. *I hope this doesn't mean we have to go our… Separate Ways.*

Sloane groaned before replying *Stop.*

You're right. I need to learn some… Self Control.

I'm serious. The guy just never quit.

Would I Lie to You?

"Jesus Christ." *I hate you so much.*

:D

Sloane stared at the little happy face before tossing his phone on his desk. *That's it.* There was no way he could win against someone who was clearly unstable. *Great. Just great.* The scariest part? He might actually like the guy.

With another groan, he hung his head. "I'm so screwed."

Chapter 7

DEX WAS falling asleep when he heard his name, scaring the hell out of him. He would have toppled back out of his chair if he hadn't thrown his arms out and clung to the edge of his desk for dear life. He frantically looked around the room.

"What? What happened? Who died?"

"No one died," Sloane said with a laugh. His partner leaned back in his chair and shook his head in amusement. "Sorry, I didn't mean to scare you. I wanted to tell you to go home."

Dex squinted at his watch. "It's not quitting time yet."

"Rookie, quitting time doesn't exist here. It's okay, you've earned it. It's been one hell of a week. Recon is searching for Lloyd Everton's whereabouts, but the guy's covered his tracks pretty good. We're still waiting on the lab to get back to us, but they're having trouble finding anything that would give us a lead. I'll finish up the reports. You go home, get some sleep. If we get anything, I'll call you."

Dex eyed him warily. Was this a trick? Sloane had yet to make his move after Dex had coerced his innocent brother into hacking Sloane's desk, disabling all the audio tools except for the speakers once Sloane hit Play on Dex's little love note. The next day, Dex had walked into the Defense Department to a standing ovation, much to Sloane's annoyance. Dex was officially one of them. His sense of victory, however, had been short-lived when he sat down at his desk and was promptly informed by his partner of his imminent demise. Either Sloane had forgotten all about it, or he was biding his time. Dex didn't like it one bit.

"You're volunteering to do reports? Are you going to write something really offensive and then sign my name? Is that what's going to happen? Or draw penises all over the page?" That's what he would do.

Sloane gave a very attractive snort. "Right. Because I'm going to risk disciplinary measures for a prank. No ulterior motives, Dex. I hate reports, but I can deal for one night. Go on, get lost."

Dex didn't have to wait around to be told again. He jumped to his feet and stretched. "Okay. Thanks, man." With a yawn, he headed for the male locker room, greeting his fellow Defense agents as he walked by.

Man, he was dead tired. Every day this week they'd been rushed off their feet, driving from one end of the city to the other, catching their meals in the BearCat and napping in shifts. Recon had put their informants to work, but for every helpful lead, there were dozens of false alarms. The media was tearing them apart, showing up at several locations, provoking the already riled public. Every time a reporter recognized Dex, he or she brought up Walsh's trial. It was exhausting.

In between the callouts, Dex still had training, including sparring sessions with all his teammates except for Ash, thankfully. Sloane seemed reluctant to send them onto the mat together. Dex couldn't say he was disappointed. Then there were hours of lifting weights, cardio, running, swimming, boxing, and yoga, followed by hours of filing reports. He was surprised they didn't make him fill out a report every time he had to take a dump. If his team got one more call from a nutjob claiming he was the HumaniTherians killer, Dex was going to…. He didn't even know what he'd do other than wish a thousand fiery deaths upon him. His brain was too tired to function. All he wanted was to get home and crash.

The showers and locker room were empty, with everyone still busy working out in the field or their offices. Sloane was right about one thing—it had certainly been one hell of a first week. It had started out rough, but when he thought about the last few days, he found himself smiling. He liked his new team. They were far from perfect, but they were a good bunch, and he was slowly starting to earn their trust, helping them understand it was okay to keep on living without their fallen comrade. Ash was still being a dick, but he hadn't brought up Dex's relationship or anything personal that hit a sore spot. He figured Sloane had something to do with that. The problem was, they were waiting for permission, permission that should have come from their team leader.

Dex opened his locker, got out his toiletry bag, and tossed it on the steel bench behind him. Maybe one of these days he'd try to have a talk with Sloane. It was still too early in their partnership for him to not get flung out a window for broaching the subject. It had only been a week, but they were definitely getting along better, and Dex had even managed to make the guy laugh on more than one occasion. Smiling suited Sloane. It was a shame he didn't do it more often. There was a pretty wicked sense of humor and who knew what else buried underneath all the pain and anguish. Dex wondered, if he dug deep enough, if he might be able to find the guy Sloane used to be. His phone rang, snapping him from his thoughts. Picking it up, he frowned at the unfamiliar number.

"Hello?"

"Daley?"

"Speaking," he murmured, trying to place the familiar voice.

"It's Isaac Pearce."

"Oh, hey, man. Sorry, I'm a little out of it at the moment." He began to undress as he spoke, his muscles protesting every movement.

"Rough day?"

"Rough week," Dex replied with a groan, wrapping a towel around his waist and taking a seat on the bench, his bare feet chilled against the rubber-tiled floor. "How've you been?"

"Good. I hope you don't mind that I got your number from the captain. I realized I forgot to ask you on your last day. I was calling about that coffee."

Dex blinked. "Oh."

"If you're busy, I understand."

"No, sorry. I thought maybe you changed your mind."

"Why?"

That was a good question. Why had he assumed Pearce wouldn't want to have anything to do with him? "I guess I figured you might not want to now that I'm a THIRDS agent."

There was a pause before Pearce answered, the smile evident in his voice. "You thought I wouldn't want to hang with you because you're one of the cool kids now?"

Dex let out a soft laugh, embarrassed for having dismissed Pearce so quickly. "Something like that. I'm going to take a shower, maybe catch a nap when I get home so I don't fall asleep on you. How about meeting up for a beer instead?"

"Even better. How about we meet at Poena over on Second around eight? That's only about five minutes from you, so you don't have to rush."

"Thanks, man. I appreciate that. See you then." With a smile he hung up, left his phone in his locker, and headed for the showers. A little nap and he'd be good as new. The thought of inviting Sloane for a few drinks crossed his mind, and then he remembered why that wouldn't be a good idea. Something told him having Pearce and Sloane in the same room might be more than a little awkward.

Turning on the shower, he adjusted the temperature, making it nice and hot before stepping under it. He moaned with contentment, lingering a little longer than he should have, but his muscles were finally starting to relax for the first time that day. When his eyes started drifting shut, it was time to get out.

After dressing in his jeans, a comfy, long-sleeved tee, his Chucks, and his favorite black leather jacket, he grabbed his stuff, closed his locker, and realized there was no way he could drive in the state he was in. He was practically falling asleep standing up. He remembered the sleeping bays and silently thanked the THIRDS.

The sleep bay was basically a long hallway with rows of doors on both sides. If a room was unoccupied, the door was open, which most of them were at the moment. He picked a room and closed the door behind him. Talk about a sweet setup. The last time he'd slept at the office, it had been at his desk at the HPF. He'd woken up with a stiff neck and half his paperwork stuck to his face.

The room had a double bed and beside it, a desk with a chair. There was a lamp, outlets for several gadgets, a small safe on one of the shelves underneath the desk, and even a minifridge. There was a communicator attached to the wall beside the headboard, and the wall across had stylish cubbyholes with everything from extra linen to coffee mugs. With a grin, Dex removed his jacket and chucked it on the chair before flopping down onto the bed. He could get used to this. The moment his head hit the pillow, he drifted off into a heavy sleep.

Dex gasped, his back arching at the feel of strong hands kneading his asscheeks, pushing them apart as the head of his lover's slick cock aligned itself, then pushed in slowly, the pressure both painful and exhilarating. God, it had been too long. Dex palmed his erection as he was entered, his lover burying deep inside him inch by inch. Hard muscles pressed up against his back, lowering Dex onto the mattress, his breath coming out ragged as his lover buried himself to the root and started rotating his hips, drawing out, then pushing back in painfully slow. Dex moaned, his stomach filled with butterflies, the anticipation building like nothing he'd ever felt before. His whole body was on fire, and he writhed with need beneath the deliciously heavy weight. He couldn't remember Lou feeling like this. Had it always felt this damn good?

Dex moaned when lips pressed against his skin beneath his ear.

"Easy there, Rookie."

Dex's eyes flew open and he bolted upright, his fists grabbing handfuls of the unfamiliar bedding as he tried to get his bearings. *Shit. Oh fuck.* He shook his head and quickly got to his feet. No, this couldn't be happening. He did not just dream of getting fucked by his team leader. If Tony got so much as a hint that Dex was dreaming about sleeping with his partner, a brand-new level of shitstorm would rain upon him, and Dex had enough on his plate at the moment.

With a frustrated groan, he dropped onto the edge of the bed and ran his hands through his hair. He was still painfully hard, the images of his very vivid, very hot dream replaying in his mind. Checking his watch, he let out another groan. It was quarter to ten. So much for a quick nap. *Shit.* He was supposed to have been at the bar almost two hours ago.

He quickly put on his jacket and rushed from the room, turning the lights off on his way out when he slammed straight into something hard. Strong hands grabbed his arms to keep him from losing his balance, and he found himself staring up into deep amber eyes.

"Whoa, where's the fire, McClane?"

"Uh." Dex opened his mouth, then closed it, the heat rising to his face as very inappropriate images of the guy before him flashed through his mind. It didn't help that Sloane was looking pretty damn hot, showered and shaved, a clean-cut look in jeans, a black V-neck T-shirt under a preppy gray cardigan, and biker boots. His hair was wet and combed back, his full lips slightly parted, and his head cocked to one side in question.

"You okay? Your face is all red. You coming down with something?" Sloane put his hand to Dex's forehead, and Dex let out a choked noise that startled the both of them. "Okay. You're weirding me out."

"Sorry." Dex snapped himself out of it and took a step back, trying to act normal and not like a complete basket case. "I was supposed to meet a friend after a short nap, and that was two hours ago."

"Oh." Sloane gave him a broad smile, which went straight to Dex's groin, and stepped aside. "Well, don't let me hold you up. I'll see you tomorrow morning."

"Thanks." Dex motioned to the bays around them, hoping he didn't sound as nervous as he felt. "You heading for a nap yourself?"

"No, getting my backpack." Sloane shoved his hands into his pockets and shrugged. "If you spend as much time in one of these as some of us do, it's easier to get reception to assign you a room. You get a personal keycard and can leave your stuff in there. It's better than having to go home for clothes or supplies."

"Kind of like a dorm, without the keg parties and orgies," Dex snorted, then realized what he'd said. He really needed to learn to think before he spoke.

Sloane arched an eyebrow at him. "Wow, wild times at Berkeley, huh?"

"Not really, I—Wait, how'd you know I went to Berkeley?" Dex's eyes widened. "You read my file?"

Sloane scoffed. "Of course I did. It's your personnel file, Dex, not your secret diary. What? You thought I was going to take on a new partner without knowing anything about him?" He leaned into Dex with a smirk. "Wake up, Rookie. This isn't a buddy-cop movie. We're part of a military organization operating as law enforcement under the eye of the Secretary of Defense. No one cares that someone stole your juice box or didn't invite you to their *Star Wars* birthday party."

"Are you done? Or have you got some more bad metaphors you want to throw my way? No? Good, because I've got somewhere to be, with big-boy drinks and company void of passive-aggressive jerks."

Sloane's jaw muscles tightened as he pulled back, his expression denoting he was less than pleased. It was best to walk away. Why was it that whenever Dex thought he was finally getting along with his partner, the guy did something to confirm he was as big an asshole as Pearce claimed him to be?

Walking off, Dex called out over his shoulder. "Go home, partner, get some sleep. Or better yet, get laid. Might help relieve some of that tension." Dex smiled to himself. That ought to learn him.

"Or maybe I'll take a long nap and *dream* of getting laid."

Dex kept moving despite the butterflies in his stomach. "Screw you, Brodie."

"Actually, it sounded more like screw you, Daley. Maybe in your next dream."

Keep walking, Dex, just keep walking. He could hear Sloane's laughter getting farther away until it was lost behind a closed door. Okay, so somehow he must have said something in his sleep and Sloane had heard. The bastard knew Dex'd had a sex dream about him. No big deal, right? It wasn't like Sloane was going to tell anyone about it. Would he? Dex stopped in his tracks. Swallowing his pride, he spun on his heels and walked back down the hall to the only other closed door. His fist hovered over the white door before he bit the bullet and knocked. Sloane opened the door, a smug smile on his face. He was cursed. He had to be.

"What can I do for you, Agent Daley?" Sloane leaned an arm against the doorframe. "Are you here to discuss the sex dream you had about me?" He licked his bottom lip, his pupils dilating as he leaned into Dex. "So, how was I?" he asked, his voice low and raspy.

Dex lifted his chin, his gaze never wavering. "I've had better."

"I doubt it." He leaned in, his warm breath tickling Dex's ears. "You're still hard."

Two could play this game. Dex turned his head so his lips brushed against Sloane's cheek. "Maybe, but unless you're prepared to do something about it, get the fuck off my back."

Sloane pulled away, his eyes dark and filled with something dangerous. Dex licked his lips and waited. They both knew there was an attraction between them, but they also knew what a mistake it would be to give in to it. Sloane wasn't merely some guy Dex had picked up at a bar, a fun but brief night of getting off before they each went their separate ways. Maybe that's what made Dex feel so bold, knowing nothing would come of it.

Sloane gave him a pat on the cheek. "Not going to happen, Rookie, but don't worry. I won't tell the rest of the team about my being cast as the porn star in your sex dream. Maybe."

"I see." Dex smiled sweetly. Sloane still had the upper hand, and Dex couldn't allow that. Removing his smartphone from his pocket, he stepped back and snapped a picture.

"What are you doing?"

Dex waved his phone at him. "You really are a nurturing partner letting me have this. It'll do nicely."

Sloane's eyes widened. "For what?"

"What do you think? For jacking off, silly."

"You son of a bitch! Give me that!" Sloane lunged at him, and Dex barely slipped out of his grip, making a break for it. As Dex sprinted through the bullpen, he admitted that perhaps he might have been a wee bit rash with this decision. He hit the button on his communicator as he zigzagged between offices. The lilt of the friendly Therian receptionist on their floor came through.

"Yes, Agent Daley?"

"Lisa! Open the doors." Dex dodged a swipe from Sloane as he rounded a corner. "Fuck!"

"Come here, you little shit!"

"Sir, is everything all right?" the receptionist asked worriedly.

"Yep, peachy. Open the doors. All the way to the elevator, please." He rounded another corner, slipping out of Sloane's reach by a hair.

"Are you sure—?"

"Yes, yes, yes!" The doors opened and Dex sped down the path straight through, calling out behind him. "I owe you a Coke, Lisa!" He tore down the hall toward the elevator at full speed.

"You know you're going to have to stop when you get there. Then I'm going to kick your ass!" Sloane hollered.

Damn, he was right. Considering all his options, Dex made a split-second decision, faking his trajectory toward the elevator before making a sharp turn, slipping past Sloane, and heading to the stairwell instead. He grinned as he threw the doors open, Sloane cursing up a storm from somewhere in the distance. Dex took the stairs two at a time, jumped the railing, and landed on the set of stairs below. He heard the door slam open above him and he didn't wait around, jerking open the door to the twentieth floor and dashing to the elevator. The doors pinged and slid open. He put his hand to the panel, cursing at the elevator, urging it to hurry the hell up. The doors closed as Sloane reached him. With a breathless laugh, Dex leaned back against the wall feeling victorious. That had been a close call. Too close.

Removing his phone from his pocket, he tapped the screen and found the image. Sloane's pouty face filled his screen. Damn, he was hot. For a complete psycho. The elevator doors to the parking garage opened, and he slipped his phone back into his pocket. With a quick scan of his surroundings, Dex hurried up the incline to his car, reaching for his keys when he was slammed against the trunk from behind, one arm pulled up over his back, making him cry out.

"Give me the damn phone," Sloane growled.

"Jesus Christ, you scared the shit out of me!"

"Good. Did you really think I was going to let you off that easy?"

"Don't you mean let me *get off* that easy?" Dex said with a snicker.

"Give. Me. The. Phone."

"Nope. You want it, you're going to have to go in there and get it."

Sloane leaned into him and Dex winced, but he refused to give in. "What is your problem, Daley?"

"I don't have a problem. I'm a carefree kind of guy. You, on the other hand…. You got a lot of pent-up sexual frustration, and it's not really conducive to our partnership. You should think of doing something about it."

Sloane leaned closer, the bulge in his jeans pressing against Dex's ass and making him groan. Oh God, the guy was as hard as he was.

"Is this what you want?" Sloane's voice was low and harsh. He rutted against Dex, one hand on his shoulder holding him, the other still pinning Dex's arm to his back. Sloane's weight on top of him was making his arm ache, but he didn't care. He arched his back, pushing his ass back against Sloane. He was asking for trouble, but they had to do something to move on from this little game they were playing.

"Fuck," Sloane breathed. He dragged Dex around to the side of the car, pushing him against it. The huge black SUV parked next to him provided enough shadow to conceal them. Before Dex could ask what Sloane was doing, their mouths were crushed together in an ardent kiss.

Sloane kissed him hungrily, and Dex returned the fervor, sucking Sloane's bottom lip between his teeth before slipping his tongue inside. Sloane's hands were on Dex's belt, and Dex inhaled sharply at the feel of Sloane's hand closing around his dick, his thumb brushing across the head to wipe at the precome. Dex didn't say a word, afraid if he did, Sloane would stop. Instead he thrust into Sloane's hand, their breathing coming out ragged as they kissed. Dex fumbled with Sloane's jeans, unfastening his belt and pushing his pants down enough to pull out Sloane's thick, hard cock. Sloane pressed against Dex, his large hand palming both of their erections and jerking them off.

"Oh God," Dex gasped against Sloane's lips, his fingers digging into the hard muscle of his chest. Sloane moved his lips from Dex's mouth onto his neck, biting down, then licking the sore spot and kissing his way up his neck. "Sloane," Dex warned. There was no way he was going to last long, not with the images of his dream lingering and the very real, very excruciating heat building up inside him.

"Come in my hand," Sloane murmured softly, taking Dex's earlobe between his teeth and sending a shiver through him. He grabbed Sloane and thrust, his movements fast and erratic. He could feel his abdomen tightening, the heat spreading through his whole body as his orgasm slammed through him, his body tensing as he came. "Fuck, oh fuck…." he gasped, hearing Sloane's low groan as he gritted his teeth, his head pressed to Dex's and his free hand grabbing a fistful of Dex's hair, gripping it painfully as Sloane's orgasm hit. Sloane gave them a few more gentle tugs, drawing out their release until Dex sucked in a sharp breath. Sloane released him, tucking Dex back into his boxer briefs. Their heads were still pressed together as their pulses slowed and their breaths steadied.

Dex opened his eyes, meeting Sloane's, the pain in them not at all what he'd expected. Then again, what just happened was far away from anything he'd imagined would happen as a result of his attempt to drive Sloane crazy. Sloane used the end of his T-shirt to wipe his hand before giving Dex a hard look.

"There. I did something about it."

"But—" Dex's words were cut off when Sloane loomed over him, his tone clipped when he spoke.

"This can't happen. You understand?" He reached into Dex's pocket and pulled out his phone, tapping the screen until he appeared to have found the image. He paused for a moment, looking at it. He tapped the screen once more, his finger then hovering over what Dex knew was the tiny trashcan symbol. Closing his eyes, he inhaled deeply, and with a shake of his head, tapped the screen again. Then he shoved the phone at Dex and stormed off.

Dex quickly got his keys out and slipped behind the steering wheel, slamming the door behind him. He swallowed hard, a mixture of feelings running through him, none of which he could decide on. Exhilaration, fear, disbelief, panic, joy... disappointment. He started the engine and looked down at his phone. When he tapped the screen, Sloane's picture was still there. He hadn't deleted it. With a frustrated groan, he let his head fall against the steering wheel.

"Dex, what are you doing?"

His job suddenly got a lot more complicated.

Music. He needed music. He tapped his radio and scrolled down his list of albums until he reached the one he was looking for. Ah, a little Eagles was just what he needed. He was about to reverse when a tap to his window scared the hell out of him. Sloane stood on the other side of his door, his expression guarded. Hitting the button for his window, Dex patiently waited for it to lower despite his head advising him to drive off and not look back.

Once the window was down, Dex calmly looked up at Sloane and spoke with a deceptively cool voice. "Yes?"

"Hey," Sloane cleared his throat, his voice thick and unsteady. "I know you're running late, but could I uh," he pointed to the passenger seat, "for a minute?"

Dex nodded and unlocked the car, waiting with his heart in his throat as Sloane slid into the passenger seat beside him. There was an awkward silence as they both sat there looking forward. Why had the guy come back? It didn't take a genius to figure out Sloane was regretting what happened, but what Dex couldn't figure out was why he cared enough to come back.

"I'm sorry," Sloane finally said, his determined gaze meeting Dex's uncertain one. "I should never have taken things that far. I got carried away, and it was stupid, and I understand if you want to report me."

"What?" This night was full of surprises.

"I stepped over the line, Dex."

"Yeah, well, I did a pretty good job of shoving you toward it. This is on both of us, not just you, and quite frankly, fuck you." Sloane's adorable pout frustrated Dex.

"For what?"

"For thinking I would go running to Daddy. I don't need my dad to fix my problems for me, so you can stop with that bullshit right now." He studied

Sloane, for the first time seeing a whole other side to
the tough alpha, a vulnerable side Dex hadn't known
existed. There was something going on, something
underlying the gruff attitude. It was true, this was on
both of them, but there was something eating away at
Sloane, something that made him come back when he
probably would have gone on as if nothing had happened, expecting Dex to suck it up. Whatever it was, it
made Dex feel shitty for having pushed back so hard.

"Look, sometimes shit happens. It's been a rough
week, we were both a little… tense, and pushing each
other's buttons didn't help any. I'll admit, there's an
attraction here, but it's not something we can pursue
for a list of reasons. Now that we've gotten it out of
our system, we can move on. Who knows, we might
even start getting along. What do you say?"

Sloane blinked at him. "You… you're cool with
that?"

"Yeah." Dex shrugged and smiled at him, leaning
in with a wink. "I mean, I know this is hard to resist."
He swept a hand over his chest.

Sloane pressed his lips together in an obvious attempt not to laugh, but in the end he gave in. "You're
such an ass."

"What?" Dex asked innocently. "It's dangerous
having this much game."

Sloane bit his bottom lip. "Stop it."

"Okay," Dex sighed, "but only because I don't
want you getting swept up in the gravitational pull of
my awesomeness."

With a chuckle, Sloane got out of the car, closed
the door before he walked back around to the driver's
side, and held his hand out to Dex. "Thanks."

Dex took Sloane's hand, ignoring the warmth that spread through him. "That's what partners are for, right? See you tomorrow."

Sloane stepped back and shoved his hands into his jacket pockets. "Drive safe." He gave him a nod before turning and walking off, up the incline. Dex watched him go, a strange feeling he couldn't explain going through him when Sloane was out of sight. Telling himself he'd done the right thing, he backed out of the parking space and headed out.

Reaching into his jacket pocket, he pulled out his phone, his eyes on the road as he tapped the bottom of his screen, then the top right. "Call Isaac Pearce," he told his phone, tapping the center, knowing it's where the speaker button was. Pearce answered on the second ring.

"Daley, you do realize that fashionably late still requires you to show up."

"I'm so sorry, man. My nap went into overtime." *And then some.* "You still up for that drink?"

"Yeah. I figured that might be the case, so I hung around and grabbed a bite to eat. If you hurry, there might still be some wings left."

"Sweet. Be there soon as."

Dex found a parking space around the corner from Poena. At this time of night on a weekday, the pub would be busy, but not overly, especially since it was small and cozy, consisting of mostly scuffed wood and old vinyl with two copper beer stations. The walls were lined with faded black-and-white photos from the 1940s. It was one of those old bars that had been around for ages, the world around it changing while inside it stayed the same. Dex was a little surprised

Pearce had picked this place. Once inside the dimly lit pub, he searched Pearce out, finding him at a small table in the corner.

"Sorry," Dex said when he arrived, removing his jacket and placing it on the back of his chair before he took a seat.

"Stop apologizing, Daley. Just buy me the next round."

"You got it." Dex motioned for one of the waitresses, and a pretty brunette came over, removing a pen and small white pad from her short apron. He ordered two beers. At least he was no longer falling asleep, though he was pretty hungry. He added a burger and basket of fries to his order. Sloane would probably kill him, but what the hell. It wasn't as if the guy wasn't going to make him work it off in their next training session anyway. Sloane wasn't a health nut, but he definitely frowned upon Dex's junk-food habit.

The waitress promptly returned with their beers, popping the caps off and placing the bottles on the table before going off to continue her rounds.

"I thought maybe you got called out on an emergency." Pearce grabbed his beer and made a toast with Dex in thanks.

"Don't jinx it, man. We've been called out every day this week. It's a bad one." He took a sip of his cold beer and let out a contented sigh. Damn, that felt good. "I'm not used to sitting in the passenger seat while my baby brother does all the driving." Looking Pearce over, Dex wondered if maybe the guy didn't have a bad case of his own going on. He looked like he could do with a long nap himself, or several.

Pearce's expression turned sympathetic. "The HumaniTherians case?"

"Yeah." Dex's food arrived and he thanked the waitress before offering Pearce some fries. When Pearce declined, Dex dug in. The pub wasn't much to look at, but it sure made a damn good burger.

Pearce leaned forward, resting his elbows on the table. "That sucks about the case." His gaze shifted down, his body subtly trembling. Dex sat back, wiping his mouth with his napkin as he discreetly took in Pearce's bouncing leg.

"You okay?"

"Yeah. No." Pearce let out a humorless laugh. He shook his head, looking as if he was trying to think of what to say or how to say it. Concerned at Pearce's sudden rattled state, Dex leaned forward, his hand coming to rest reassuringly on Pearce's arm. Something was definitely up. Maybe he hadn't known Pearce long, but it didn't take a genius to know something was bothering the guy.

"Hey, you can talk to me."

"Okay. I didn't just ask you here to have a drink. I wanted to talk to you because I'm worried. I saw the news footage of you outside that catering company last week. You were being dragged along by Agent Brodie, and well, I couldn't…." He frowned and rubbed at his jaw. "I couldn't keep it quiet any longer. You gotta be careful, Dex. Watch your back."

"I know, it's a tough case—"

"I'm not talking about the case," Pearce said quietly, shifting in his seat. "I'm talking about your partner. There's a lot you don't know about him. The guy has secrets. Things he doesn't want getting out in the open. Things the THIRDS don't want getting out in the open."

Dex sat up, wondering what could possibly have Pearce so worked up. "What are you talking about?"

"Have you read his file?"

"No." Technically Sloane had been in the right, checking out Dex's file. He had every reason to know who his new partner was going to be, especially someone recruited from the outside. It stung a little, but Dex understood. Of course, that didn't mean he would go running out to do the same. "Anything I need to know, I'll find out on my own."

"You think he hasn't read yours?"

Dex's expression must have said it all, because Pearce gave him a nod.

"He already has. Nice. Well, I've read his."

"How?" There was no way the THIRDS would give the HPF access to their agents' personnel files unless there was a damn good reason, and he was sure the information available would be limited once permission was granted. What reason could Pearce possibly have given to receive access to a THIRDS team leader file?

"I pulled in a favor."

Must have been some favor. From what Dex had learned in his short time at the THIRDS, these guys covered their asses, and they were especially wary of the HPF. The relationship between the two organizations was strained at best. Whenever politics were involved, it didn't come down to who could do the most good, but who could stomp their foot the loudest before storming off and taking their toys with them. "Okay. I don't understand what's going on here." Ever since Dex had gotten recruited, Pearce had been warning him about Sloane. The whole thing was starting to unsettle him.

"There was always something off about him, and I had to know what it was. Especially since…." Pearce closed his eyes tight for a moment before seeming to compose himself.

"Since what?" What could possibly be so hard to say? "Pearce—"

"Since he was sleeping with my brother."

Dex's heart plummeted. "What?"

"Sloane Brodie and Gabe were sleeping together. A year before Gabe died, it had gotten pretty serious. They'd been together four years."

Dex was so stunned, all he could do was sit there, attempting to process what he'd heard.

"You didn't know? No, of course you didn't. Did you really think he was running off all those other agents because his work partner had died? It would have been rough, but he would have pushed through. Brodie was out of commission for six months. The THIRDS made up some bullshit about him being on special assignment or some such nonsense, like they always do when one of their agents is down for the count. They don't like to admit those guys are as vulnerable as the rest of us."

"Did they know?" Dex's voice cracked, and he cleared his throat. "The team, I mean. Did they know about Sloane and Gabe?"

Pearce shook his head. "It's against the rules. At the first hint of anything more than bromance, one of them would have been reassigned. They gave Brodie that much time for a reason, and I wanted to know what that reason was, but when I got access to his file, I couldn't find anything."

"Wait, you didn't find anything?" So what had Pearce gotten himself so worked up over?

"That's the problem. When my brother was alive, I saw his file. He wasn't supposed to show it to me, but when he got recruited, he was so excited that he took me on a tour of the place, including his office. What I saw was frightening. It had everything, from his height to where our parents took us on vacation when we were kids. The thing was a complete map of his life from when he was born. Yet in Sloane's file, the only information there is of his time with the THIRDS. There's nothing about where he came from, who his parents were, and nothing pertaining to medical records. My brother had to pass a quarterly examination that included a physical. All the results were in his file. Why aren't Sloane's?"

"I don't know. Maybe it's different the higher up the food chain you get?" At the moment Pearce seemed to know a lot more than Dex did, if what he was saying was true, though the guy had no reason to lie, especially since Dex could go back to HQ at any time and debunk his story. The desperate plea in Pearce's eyes was hard to ignore. This was obviously important to him; the least Dex could do was hear him out. "You look like you have a theory. Theories can be dangerous."

"I'm sure it has something to do with him being one of the first."

Dex frowned. "First what?"

"Jesus, Dex." Pearce scooted his chair closer and leaned in, his hazel eyes intense. "This guy is what's

keeping you from ending up like my brother, and you
have no idea who he is or what he's capable of."

Actually, he did. Sloane Brodie was his partner
and team leader; he was high-strung and emotionally
unstable, but now Dex understood why. Sloane had
been in love with Gabe Pearce. From the moment Dex
had come crashing into Sloane's life, the guy had been
waging war with himself. He liked Dex, and his heart
was giving him hell for it. He wasn't supposed to like
anyone who tried to take Gabe's place. Were the roles
reversed, Dex probably would have done the same.
He sure wouldn't have welcomed some jerk from an
outside department with open arms, watching as the
new guy waltzed in and took the place of someone
he'd loved. Sure, it wasn't the guy's fault, but his heart
wouldn't care about that. He'd have been hurting and
angry.

Dex's thoughts went to the parking garage and
the expression on Sloane's face after what happened.
Jesus, the guilt was probably eating the poor guy
alive. Sloane was attracted to him, and that probably
made everything ten times worse. Sloane wasn't on
the rebound; he was still mourning. Damn it. Dex had
fucked up. Badly.

"All I know is that the very first THIRDS agents
recruited were First Generation Therians. Sloane Brodie is one of them. He was recruited when he was sixteen, trained, and worked part-time for the THIRDS
while attending college. It was all arranged by the
THIRDS. But it's like the guy appeared one day out of
nowhere. I did some digging, and I can't find any trace
of him before then. The only way that could happen is
if the government was covering it up."

"But wouldn't that just arouse more suspicion than if they made up some bullshit?"

"Considering no one outside the THIRDS has access to the file, who's going to question it? And if someone did, you think the government's going to give them a straight answer?"

"You got a point. Jesus Christ, Pearce. How long have you been looking into this?"

"From the moment I knew it was getting serious between him and my brother." Pearce swallowed hard, his expression grim. "Of course, it doesn't matter now."

"I understand your concern, and I appreciate it," Dex stated sincerely. "But my family's been working with the guy for years, and believe me, if they thought anything suspicious was going on, they would have told me. Sloane's intense, sure, and maybe there is something there the THIRDS don't want getting out, but I don't believe it's anything sinister."

Pearce let out a resigned sigh. "You're right. I'm sorry. Guess I'm having trouble letting go."

"And that's perfectly reasonable, Pearce." He patted the guy's arm, wishing there was something he could say or do that would help. "If you need someone to talk to, ring me anytime."

Pearce smiled at him. "Thank you, Dex." His smile faded as he looked down at his fingers. "I think it's the guilt eating away at me. If I'd left him alone, maybe he'd still be alive."

"What do you mean? You had nothing to do with what happened to your brother, Pearce. He was having a meet with an informant. We all know how ugly those things can get sometimes."

The anguish in Pearce's eyes was heartbreaking. "I know, but my last words to him were unpleasant, and after he'd been so happy. Brodie had surprised him with cruise tickets. They were going to go on their first vacation together that week. I felt like I was losing him. I barely saw him because he spent all his free time with Brodie. From the moment he joined the THIRDS, it seemed like all we did was argue. We argued that night, said things we didn't mean. Next thing I know… he's dead. If I'd walked away…."

"Don't do that to yourself. You can't blame yourself for what happened to your brother. You were looking out for him, and that's what brothers do, right? What happened to Gabe was tragic, but he was an experienced agent whose job was to take those kinds of risks." He gave Pearce's arm a squeeze. "From what I've heard, your brother was a great guy. He would have wanted you to go on living."

Pearce took a long swig of his beer, a sad smile on his face. "Sorry. I didn't invite you here to listen to my sob story."

"Consider it making up for lost time," Dex replied with a big grin, holding up his beer and tapping it against Pearce's. "I don't get a lot of time to socialize outside of work these days, so it's nice. Thanks for inviting me." He noticed the black string around Pearce's neck with some kind of metal Greek-style pendant with an image of some goddess's face. "That's pretty cool."

"Thanks." Pearce flushed, looking embarrassed. "I made it."

"No shit?" Dex sat forward, taking in the intricate piece of metalwork. "Wow. I'm lucky I can use a pen. That's amazing."

"I do metalwork. I have a workshop in Brooklyn. You should drop by sometime. I'll show you around."

"I'd like that."

Dex was relieved when Pearce started talking about his metal shop and the work he did on his downtime. It was nice to forget about the HumaniTherians case for a while. Come tomorrow, he'd have to go back to staring at his board and praying they got a lead before they ended up with another victim.

Chapter 8

THIS CASE was driving him nuts.

Dex wasn't used to getting his information fed to him. When he was on homicide, he'd been responsible for investigating and gathering information. Not now. As a Defense agent, he provided backup and aided the investigation, but Recon agents carried out the investigative work. While Cael and Rosa were making phone calls and chasing leads, he was stuck at his desk, training, or staring at the same damn screen with the same damn information.

"You'll get used to it."

Dex swiveled his chair around so he could look at Sloane without having to move his head. "This sucks. Three weeks, man. It's been three weeks."

"Believe me, Rookie, after a few months, you'll be basking in these moments."

"Maybe," Dex muttered, turning back to the screen. The HPF had finally given Intel access to their reports on threats called in against HumaniTherians. It had been a dead end. Forensics reports on the first two victims were clean, too clean. No fibers, hairs, fur, blood, skin, nothing that wasn't the victim's. They were still waiting on lab results from Ortiz, though as of yet, nothing flagged as being suspicious or out of the ordinary. There were no connections between the three victims. None of them had ever been in contact with one another. The only lead they had was Lloyd Everton, an Unregistered Therian who was in the wind.

"They'll find him," Sloane said, as if reading his thoughts. He made a strange half groan, half moan noise that caught Dex's attention. He swiveled his chair around in time to catch Sloane stretching, his arms high above his head, his chest expanding and his neck exposed. He scrunched up his nose like maybe he was going to sneeze, then lowered his arms, his gaze landing on Dex when he finished. They both sat there looking at each other until Dex snapped out of it. He cleared his throat, sat up, and tapped his desk's surface to wake it up.

"Have you given table hockey any more thought?" Dex winced at his piss-poor attempt not to draw attention to whatever the hell had just happened.

"Yep."

Dex looked up hopefully. "And?"

"Nope."

"Damn. You're no fun," Dex grumbled, ignoring Sloane's chuckling.

"Work's not supposed to be fun. It's work."

Dex let out a snort. "Tell that to Ash, who gets a kick out of scaring the shit out of little old ladies."

"That only happened once. And if I recall, you laughed your ass off for hours afterward. You were still laughing days later."

Dex couldn't stop from laughing now. They'd been called out to a building over in Hell's Kitchen on another wild goose chase for Lloyd Everton. They'd breached the apartment building when a little old lady came out of her apartment and ran right into Ash. The poor granny nearly had a heart attack. When she recovered, she started attacking Ash with her huge purse, smacking him upside the head several times. "That was the funniest shit I have ever seen. I think I actually wet myself, I was laughing so hard."

"TMI, Daley, TMI."

They were both snickering about the incident when Cael and Rosa came running into their office.

"We've got a location on Lloyd Everton, the *real* Everton," Cael exclaimed, going to Dex's desk and pulling up street maps.

Sloane and Dex answered simultaneously. "Where?"

Rosa chuckled at them before motioning down to the digital map zoomed in on Dex's desk, her smile quickly fading. "Greenpoint."

"Shit." Sloane ran a hand through his hair as he paced the area next to Dex's desk. "I hate Greenpoint. It's a goddamn tactical nightmare."

"That bad?" Dex noticed everyone's concerned expression.

Rosa gave a solemn nod. "Every THIRDS team that's ever gone in has had to fight their way out. The last time we went in, it didn't go so well."

"Sounds like fun," Dex replied dryly.

Sloane grabbed Dex by the arm, pulled him out of his chair and to one side, his voice a low growl. "We're going into a war zone with an undisclosed number of threats for a suspect who may or may not be our guy. I've got enough to worry about without you running off, getting yourself wounded or killed. This is your first Threat Level Red assignment. You damn well better survive it."

"I got it, man. Don't get dead. Believe me, I want it less than you do."

"Let's go." Sloane tapped his earpiece. "Destructive Delta, gear up. We're heading out."

They all rushed from the office, Ash and Letty coming in from the right to fall in behind them, while Calvin and Hobbs fell in line from the left. By now, Dex had picked up on the formation and everyone's position in the team lineup. There was a reason behind everything the THIRDS did, even something as simple as heading to the armory.

Wherever they went, it was the same. Sloane was always at the head of the line, with Dex close behind since he was Sloane's partner and backup. They were responsible for directing the team. Behind Dex were Letty and Ash—the weapons expert and close-quarter combat expert. The four of them made up the first line of defense, protecting their Recon agents, Cael and Rosa. If somehow some bastard got past the first four agents, behind Cael and Rosa were Calvin and Hobbs—their sniper and demolitions expert. If all else failed, there was his dad, who took up the rear. Eventually Dex would be trained to fill in for Sloane should his partner be incapacitated or separated from the team. The thought scared the ever-living fuck out of Dex.

Geared up with an arsenal of weapons both lethal and nonlethal, they packed into the BearCat and headed for Greenpoint. The ride over was filled with tension, and no one uttered a word, not even Dex. He was fully aware he was a smartass, but even he knew when to shut his mouth. The large flat-screen over the console showed their location as they drove. Hobbs took the I-495 east toward the Pulaski Bridge, and Tony tapped his earpiece. "Hobbs, park on the corner of Franklin and Cayler. We're going in from behind."

Minutes later, the BearCat rumbled to a stop, and Hobbs and Calvin joined them.

Tony motioned toward the console. "Cael, bring up the map."

Cael did as instructed, and Tony leaned over him to trace a rectangle on the screen. He tapped the center, and everything within the rectangle went red. "That's our radius. Between Greenpoint Avenue and Oak Street, and Manhattan Avenue to the East River. Intel says it's where Everton will be hiding."

"How do we know he's going to stick to that zone?" Dex watched as his dad tapped the surrounding areas. Small screens popped up with scrolling information.

"Anything north of Greenpoint Avenue and west of the bridge is Canidae territory. South of Meserole Avenue and west of McGuinness Boulevard until Nassau is Bear Therian Country. Any areas not in those two territories are where you'll usually find the Felids. This here," he said, tapping the rectangle once more, "is the only area that's neutral. Intel informs us Everton's Therian form is a jaguar, which means you're our main guy on this, Sloane. Ash, you're going in as backup. Cael, you scout ahead of them. Calvin, Dex, Hobbs, Letty, and Rosa, you're on reconnaissance down West Street and everything up to the river. Sloane, Ash, and Cael, everything east of West Street. I want Everton conscious. I'll man the truck, and if you need backup, shout. All right, let's get going."

The team acknowledged their orders and quickly went about preparing. Dex stood to one side, checking Sloane's PSTC kit, when he caught Ash's quiet growl at Tony. "You're sending him out there to scout?"

They didn't bother to look up from his tablet as he spoke. "You seem to be more concerned about Cael than your new teammate."

"Hey, he signed up for Defense. If he can't hack it, he shouldn't be here. Cael is Recon. Plus this is Greenpoint, not Central Park."

"Cael can handle himself."

Ash let out a frustrated grunt. "That's not the point."

"What is the point?" Tony finally looked up at Ash, one eyebrow raised. "Do you not trust in your team's abilities, Agent Keeler?"

"You know that's not it," Ash emphasized quietly. "Remember the last time we went in there?"

"I do. That's why he has to go in again. He needs to learn from his mistakes."

Ash looked like he wanted to argue, but instead turned and shoved past Dex to get to the back of the truck. Dex would have flipped him off if he weren't so concerned about what he'd heard. He made sure his brother was busy at the end of the truck before approaching his dad.

"What happened the last time they went in?"

"You shouldn't eavesdrop," his dad grumbled.

"You've been telling me that since I was a kid. I think we both know that lesson never took. What happened to Cael the last time they went in?" he asked again, doing his best to keep a level head and not think about his family keeping secrets from him.

Tony hesitated before finally giving in.

"It's not easy for him being on a team of big cats. He has this stupid notion he has to prove himself every time they go feral. His psych evals last quarter after the incident revealed how he sees himself in regard to the rest of his Felid teammates. How he's inadequate for being the smallest, his inability to roar, the fact he runs fast but in short bursts, his hunting by vision rather than scent, and his trouble with adapting to new environments." Tony put his tablet away, his eyes filled with concern. "The last case that brought us out here, Cael got in over his head. He didn't think he needed to wait for backup and found himself up against a jaguar Therian coalition. Came out of it pretty banged up."

Dex frowned, trying to recall when that was. He surely would remember losing his shit. When Tony looked away, Dex's jaw dropped. "You told me he was undercover!" Dex recalled what Pearce said to him about the THIRDS not wanting to admit their agents were vulnerable. Dex hadn't wanted to believe it, but now he knew the truth. What else had Pearce been telling the truth about?

"Keep your voice down," Tony ordered. "You think I wanted to keep it from you? He made me promise not to tell you."

"Why would you agree to such a stupid request?"

"Because you would have expected me to do the same," Tony replied quietly. "Look, I know how protective you boys are of each other, but you need to get your heads out of your asses. You should have outgrown this phase by now."

Dex folded his arms over his chest stubbornly. "You know I'm never going to stop looking out for him."

"And he's never going to stop looking up to you. That doesn't mean you can't turn to each other for help. It's not weakness. I wish you would both get that into your thick skulls before you give me any more gray hair."

As much as he hated to admit it, his dad was right. "How'd he get out of it?"

"Ash. He got in there and beat the tar out of them. He's a Grade-A son of a bitch, but he cares about Cael. Looks after him."

"Damn. I really want to hate him."

Tony gave Dex a pat on the back. "The feeling's probably mutual."

Dex let out a noncommittal grunt. At least now he understood why Ash was putting up with him. If it weren't for Cael, the bastard would probably be making his life miserable. Not that he wasn't making a good go of it.

The sound of the heavy screen hitting the floor at the back of the truck interrupted his thoughts, and he saw Rosa standing to one side, PSTC kit strapped next to her backpack as she neatly put away Cael's gear and hung up his uniform. His brother was up first.

All these years later, and Dex still cringed when he heard his brother's painful cry as his mass shifted. Proteins, fats, and cells rearranged to bring out his Therian form. When they were kids, Dex had asked Cael what it was like to be a Therian, and he'd never forgotten his little brother's answer or his sadness when he'd given it.

"It's like half of me is missing, but it's not, it's inside me. But no matter what form I'm in, I'll never be able to get the two halves together. I'll never be whole, like you. Dad says my Therian form is my soul, so I'm as whole as a Human, but it doesn't feel that way."

It had taken Cael a lot to come to terms with being a Therian, and despite knowing he was adopted, he admitted he never wondered what it could have been like with his biological parents. As far as Cael was concerned, Dex and Tony were his real family, especially knowing the hardship Tony had endured by adopting him. Like Dex, Cael had lost his family to the riots. The apartment building his parents lived in had been primarily Therian. A group of evil bastards set it on fire in the middle of the night, not caring that it was filled with families and small children. Cael had been six months old and the only survivor.

Tony had been on the scene, a detective with the HPF at the time, and he'd been the one to find Cael. His dad always told Cael how the moment he held him in his arms, he knew he wouldn't be able to let go. It was during a time when interspecies adoption hadn't existed, and Tony faced a world of anger and prejudice from both sides. But their dad was a hardass and a good man. He fought for Cael, sacrificing his job at the HPF when he was subtly warned that having a

Therian son would be damaging to his career. Flipping them off, Tony completed the adoption process, pretty much making it up as he went along, and Cael Maddock joined their family. Tony lost his job, but his resolve and heart gained him a position at the newly opened THIRDS.

Dex took a seat on the bench, Sloane's PSTC kit on the floor by his feet. The screen lifted and Cael shuddered from nose to spotty tail, his ears twitching and his mouth opening wide in a yawn to reveal sharp fangs. He stretched his long legs one at a time, wobbling momentarily until he got his bearings. Then he trotted over to Dex and put his head on his lap while Ash stepped into the large square, the screen coming down once again.

"Hey, little brother." Dex scratched Cael behind the ears and smiled when Cael closed his eyes and purred. A low growl came from behind the screen, soon followed by a roar that shook the whole damn truck.

"Fuck." Dex swallowed hard when the screen went up. And here he thought Ash couldn't get any scarier. How wrong he was. Ash sneezed and shook his massive head, his dark lion's mane swishing with the movement. He lifted his head and looked at Dex, releasing a huff.

"Well, look at you," Dex gasped, a hand going to his chest. "So majestic."

Ash let out an angry hiss, his bared fangs bigger and sharper than Cael's. He crept closer, a low rumbling growl coming from him. Dex told himself he wasn't intimidated. It was still Ash in there. It was no surprise he was as big a dick in his Therian form as he was in his Human form. A fierce roar had Dex scrambling up onto the bench, his heart pounding against his chest and his tranq gun at the ready. Ash rushed forward, and Dex aimed his rifle.

"I swear I will send your hairy ass back to Narnia if you don't back the fuck up," Dex warned him, releasing the safety on his rifle.

"Ash!" Sloane's reprimand went unheeded as Ash swiped at Dex. Lucky for Dex, Ash's paw never made contact. Cael batted Ash's paw away and hissed sharply, his ears flattened back as he swiped at Ash, catching him on the side of his big furry head. No blood was drawn, but Cael got his point across. Claws off his big brother.

Ash gave a start, letting out a mewl as he backed up. With a huff he sat down, and Dex watched as Cael approached him and bumped his head under Ash's chin, then proceeded to lick him, which Ash seemed to enjoy, judging by his purring.

Dex jumped down and put the safety back on his gun, his glare on Ash before he shifted his gaze to his brother. "Cael, come on. Stop licking the dude. That's gross."

Letty let out a snort. "Please, like you don't lick dudes."

"That's different," Dex explained with a grimace. "None of those dudes were Ash. Besides, last time I checked, Ash was allergic to nuts."

The rest of the team laughed before Tony clapped his hands and shooed the two Felids as if they were a couple of house cats. "Out, you two. It's getting too damn crowded in here."

Letty opened the back doors for the two Felids, who scrambled from the truck and leaped out, Rosa

close behind, laughing at her partner. Outside, Dex
could see Cael and Ash play fighting, pouncing on
each other, rolling around, and nipping at each other.
It was kind of sweet. Calvin closed the BearCat's back
doors again and stood to one side.

"All right, let's go, Hobbs." Tony resumed his
seat, and Dex watched as Hobbs stepped into the large
square in nothing but a towel. He gave a solemn nod
and the screen came down. Beside the screen, Calvin
waited patiently. Dex noticed him wince when Hobbs
cried out. It was low and rough, the only sound he'd
heard from the guy in ages. He still hadn't heard him
speak.

Seconds later, there was a series of ferocious
growls and the screen came up. Dex had to admit, he
was impressed. Hobbs's Therian form was very rare, a
golden tabby tiger larger than the usual tiger Therian,
with stripes and fur paler in color. His coloring made
him more remarkable. Unlike his teammates, Hobbs
silently padded to Calvin and rubbed his head against
Calvin's leg. With a warm smile, Calvin scratched
Hobbs on the side of his head, and the two quietly
joined their teammates outside.

Well, only one left. Dex frowned at the butterflies
in his stomach. This was silly. He didn't get nervous
when the rest of his team was shifting; why should
he feel nervous now? Therians maintained their Humanity while in their Therian form, providing they
had any Humanity to begin with, which was why psy-
chopaths were more feral than the average Therian. It
was also confirmed that in their Therian form, Human
characteristics remained. An unhealthy Therian would
be unhealthy both in Human and Therian form. Many

Therians didn't see it that way. They believed their animal form mirrored the soul of the Human side. Dex
had never been very spiritual, but then he couldn't explain why he was so nervous waiting to see his partner
in his Therian form.

Sloane stood and cleared his throat, addressing
Tony. "You mind giving us a minute?"

"Sure." Tony gave Dex's arm a pat before exiting
the truck and joining the rest of the team.

"What's up?" Dex studied his partner. "You're
not getting shy on me now, are you?"

"No, I need you to understand the severity of
what's going on here. This is going to be dangerous.
You need to stick close to the team. Keep your eyes
open, don't make any sudden movements, and call for
backup if you need it. Ash, Cael, and I will be busy
tracking down Everton, so I won't be able to save your
ass. The last thing I need is for you—"

Dex held a hand up and cut him off. "You know
what? Stop."

"What?"

"I'm a rookie, I get it, but I don't appreciate this
Jekyll and Hyde thing you've got going on. One minute you're good, the next minute you're ready to take
a swing at me. It's your job to show me the ropes, not
rip me a new one for doing something I haven't even
done yet. I'm your partner. You don't have to like me,
but you sure as hell have to respect me."

Sloane blinked at him. "I… I had no idea I was
coming off that way." He pressed his lips together and
gave him a nod. "You're right. I haven't been treating
you with the respect you deserve. You're a capable

agent, and I've been letting my own insecurities cloud my judgment."

"What are you talking about?" Insecurities? Dex couldn't imagine Sloane Brodie being insecure about anything.

"After what happened to Gabe…." Sloane shook his head, and that's when it hit Dex.

"That's why you've been acting like such a jerk every time we hit the streets? Because you're worried about something happening to me?" Now that he thought about it, about what Gabe had actually meant to Sloane, it all made perfect sense, and after that media confrontation, Dex cursed himself for not being more attentive to his partner. He was quickly picking up on all Sloane's quirks and behaviors. It was true that his partner suffered from disturbing mood swings, but Dex was learning there was always a reason behind them. That pop about his partners not lasting certainly hadn't helped.

"Not just you. I worry about everyone on my team."

"I understand, but it's not your job to babysit me and kiss my ouchies. You need to trust me. I might be a pain in the ass, but I know what I'm doing." He watched Sloane carefully as his partner considered his words, his gaze somewhere off to the side. Dex didn't know what was going through Sloane's head at the moment, but he was relieved when Sloane met his gaze and held his hand out.

"Okay, but promise me you'll stick to the formation and be careful. No acting like this is a *Die Hard* flick, okay? If I hear the words *yippee ki-yay* come out of your mouth, we're going to have a serious problem."

It was kind of scary how well Sloane was getting to know him. Dex took his hand and gave him a cheeky grin. "Deal. Seal it with a kiss?"

"Get out," Sloane groaned. "You couldn't help yourself, could you?"

"Don't know what you're missing." With a wink, Dex stood back, his arms folded over his chest.

"What?" Sloane eyed him warily as he started removing his clothes. "Stop looking at me like that. This isn't a strip joint."

Dex wriggled his eyebrows. "You're right. It's better. I don't have to pay."

Sloane stopped in the middle of pulling off his shirt and glowered at him.

"All right," Dex said with a sigh. He reached into his back pocket and pulled a ten-dollar bill out of his wallet, waving it at Sloane as he walked over. "Just so you have an idea what this partnership means to me. This would have gotten me at least a lap dance at Papi Chulo's." Sloane arched an eyebrow at him, and Dex grinned broadly as he stuck his finger in the waistband of Sloane's pants and gave it a tug. Sloane let out a low grunt, and Dex very neatly slipped the bill in partway.

"You're an idiot."

Dex stepped back and waited. "Well, come on. I expect to get my money's worth."

Sloane plucked the bill from his pants, removed his wallet from his back pocket, stuck it in, returned it to his pants, and then went for his belt.

"Now we're talking." Dex could see Sloane was trying his hardest not to smile. He was biting down on his bottom lip as he removed his belt and unzipped. "Do you need music? I can provide music." He broke off into a throaty rendition of "Hit Me with Your Best Shot," and Sloane burst into laughter.

"What the fuck are you singing?"

"You're right," Dex chastised himself. "'Black Velvet' is more appropriate for this moment. I should've gone with that first." He snickered as Sloane doubled over laughing. The sound was rich and deep, and Dex found it infectious. He liked it when Sloane laughed. It made his amber eyes light up and little creases form at the sides, lines that proved Sloane used to laugh a lot more than he did, though the guy wasn't doing too badly these days.

"What in the hell is going on in here?"

They both spun to Tony, who was gaping at them. "We're in the middle of a hunt and you two are... I don't even know what you're doing, but it sure as hell isn't what you're supposed to be doing."

Dex opened his mouth when Sloane held up a hand. "It's my fault, sir."

"I don't care whose fault it is, get your asses in gear. Dex, get down here and let your partner shift, *now*."

"Yes, sir." Dex quickly snatched his ballistic shield off the wall, along with his helmet, and made his way to the end of the truck. He waited for Tony to turn around before looking over his shoulder at Sloane, who was watching him in amusement. He gave him a thumbs-up and whispered hoarsely, "I'll make you a playlist." When he jumped down, he could hear Sloane snickering from inside the truck. Dex put his helmet on and secured the straps under his chin as he joined Letty, Rosa, and Calvin.

"What were you two doing?" Calvin's voice was low so Tony wouldn't hear.

"Paying Sloane to strip for me." Dex grinned, lowering his visor. "Best ten bucks I ever spent."

Something huge and black leapt out of the back of the truck, and Dex nearly fell over his own feet from the surprise. When he found his balance, he found himself gawking at the huge black jaguar. "Sloane…."

Sloane turned his head, his amber eyes glowing bright before he darted off down the street, Ash and Cael taking off after him. Dex stood there for a moment, his heart racing. Sloane was a Therian, but finally seeing the animal inside him come out was a strange experience. He wished he'd had more time to really *see* him. He'd been impressive, that was for sure. His black coat glossy, with the faintest hints of rosettes visible on his fur. He wasn't as big as Hobbs, and Ash's mane made him appear bigger, but Sloane was all bulk and sleek muscle, and his black fur made him stand out among his fair-haired teammates.

"Okay, team. Good luck and be careful." With that said, Tony climbed into the back of the BearCat. The boom of the doors when they shut echoed around them. Well, this was it. Calvin moved first, with Hobbs moving silently beside him, the rest of them following down Cayler Street. They stuck close to each other, shields in hand and rifles at the ready. When they got to the end and made a right, things got a whole lot rougher.

"You see a black jaguar running that isn't Sloane, you shoot," Rosa told him.

Crap. He seriously hoped he didn't end up tranqing his partner. That would *really* piss Sloane off. Speaking of, his partner had been right when he said they'd be going into battle. The place looked like a war zone.

He couldn't say he'd been here more than a handful of times, maybe fewer, and that had been many years ago when he'd been a kid, before the place had turned into the desolate ruins it was. It had once been filled with families, homes, and businesses. Cars and business vans once lined the streets. Now the streets were empty and the buildings around them were all abandoned and dilapidated, their exposed ironwork rusting away.

When they got to Noble Street, things got worse. With little imagination, Dex could see himself in some foreign territory waiting to fall under heavy fire. Around them was nothing but dirt, rock, dead shrubs, and weeds growing through the cracks in the asphalt. The buildings were crumbling around them, those still standing tagged with graffiti. Piles of debris littered the streets, and the only sounds were the ones coming from the crushed gravel and pieces of broken glass underneath their boots as they moved steadily onward.

Although Dex couldn't see anything through the windowless, darkened spaces of the many buildings, he could feel eyes on him. They were being watched. As long as the Therians didn't come out to play, Dex was cool with anyone watching.

Hobbs stopped in his tracks, and everyone else did the same, watching the tiger Therian as he lifted his head and sniffed the air. He trotted ahead, and they all quickly trailed after him. When Hobbs picked up speed, so did they, until they were jogging after him. Something lunged at Hobbs from the darkness, knocking him over. Hobbs rolled, landing on his feet and hissing, his jaws opening wide and baring huge fangs. He clawed at the large cougar, catching it in the side of the neck, drawing blood and a painful hiss.

Another Therian leaped out from the shadows onto Hobbs's back, attempting to bite his neck, but again Hobbs rolled, crushing the smaller Felid under him. It was two against one, and Dex cursed under his breath when another Felid appeared and lunged at Hobbs, this time snapping his jaws around Hobbs's back leg. Hobbs let out a fierce cry, twisting his body to snap at the just-out-of-reach leopard.

"Hobbs!" Calvin bolted after his partner. Shit, it was exactly what Dex had feared. So much for tight formation.

The wounded cougar set his sights on Calvin, and Dex took aim, following the cougar as he charged. When he lunged, Dex fired, and Calvin ducked out of the way. The dart from Dex's tranq rifle plunged itself into the Felid's neck, sending it scrambling away.

Movement from Dex's left caught his eye, and he swallowed hard when several Therians emerged slowly from the shadows, their teeth bared as they hissed or growled. It was a mixture of wolf and Felid Therians. Dex breathed in deeply, telling himself to calm down, to steady his heart rate. His gloved fingers tightened on his rifle as more Therians materialized. If any of them made a move toward him, Dex was ready to take them down. He heard shots fired and saw Calvin taking on a small pack of wolf Therians. Two of them lunged at Calvin from behind, knocking him down, and his helmet hit the ground hard. Calvin didn't get up.

"Calvin!" Dex, Letty, and Rosa shot at everything moving that wasn't Hobbs, who was busy keeping his unconscious partner safe. "He's in trouble," Dex said, hitting another Therian in the neck. Shit, he was going to have to reload soon.

"So are we," Rosa pointed out.

Dex quickly scanned the terrain and spotted a three-story with a fire escape that didn't look like it was a strong breeze away from turning to dust. "There!" He motioned toward the building. "Better vantage point. If we stay here, we're sitting ducks."

"Let 'em come," Letty snarled, cocking her rifle.

"Okay, Ripley, and when you run out of tranqs and ammo, then what? Let's move. Cover the rear." He gave Rosa a small shove toward the building.

"Rookie's giving orders now?" Rosa asked, annoyed.

"Sloane's not here, so yeah, I am." They ran toward the fire escape's hanging ladder, and when they reached it, he grabbed Rosa's vest and hauled her under it. He laid his shield on the ground at his feet and let his rifle hang from its straps so he could lace his fingers together in front of Rosa, boosting her up. "Come on. Letty, move your ass."

Letty fired off another shot before hauling ass to join him, following Rosa's lead. Dex was going to tell the girls to lower the ladder when Hobbs roared. Hobbs was taking on half a dozen Therians, all in the hopes of keeping Calvin safe. Dex knew protocol was to fall back and let Hobbs deal with the threat, but screw it. His teammate was lying there like a slab of beef waiting to be served. The ladder came rumbling down in a cacophony of shrilly squeals and rattling, but Dex had other ideas.

"Dex, what are you waiting for!" Rosa called down. "Get your ass up here! I'll call the sarge."

"I got this." Dex reached behind him, unzipping the side compartment of his backpack, pulled out a couple of flash-bangs, and stuck one in his pocket. "Let's see how you like these babies." Ignoring Rosa's and Letty's curses, he snatched up his shield and hurried down the street, a flash-bang in his free hand as he concentrated on controlling his breathing. Something darted out from his right and sped toward him.

"Fuck!" He picked up the pace, pulling the pin from the flash-bang with his teeth before hurling it high and long. "Hobbs! Incoming!"

Hobbs dropped to the ground and rolled, his back paws kicking up dirt as he darted out of the way. The flash-bang exploded in a cloud of white smoke and blinding light. Something jumped out at Dex from his left, and he flailed, skidding and hitting the dirt like he was trying to steal home plate, his shield tucked against him. He slid under the wolf Therian as it leaped over him and then wasted no time in scrambling to his feet and taking off again with the wolf on his heels.

Okay, so now he understood why Sloane wanted him to cut back on the Cheesy Doodles. Running would be a whole lot easier without his damn shield, but he'd be stupid to leave it behind. He removed the other flash-bang from his pocket and pulled the pin. "Hobbs!"

The Therians snapping at Hobbs pulled back, and Hobbs seized the opportunity, leaping to Calvin and lying over him, shielding him with his body. He tucked his massive head under his big paws. A heavy mass crashed into Dex, knocking the wind out of him and sending him sprawling on the ground, his shield landing behind him. Thankfully he'd managed to keep

a tight grip on his flash-bang. With his free hand, he
snatched up his shield and covered his body, his legs
tucked up behind it as the first bite came down, the
weight crushing him between the asphalt and the ballistic armor.

"Son of a bitch!" They were surrounding Hobbs.
"Fuck this shit." Dex thrust his shield forward, receiving a shrill yelp from the Therian on the other side,
giving him enough time to pull back his arm and hurl
the flash-bang. "Incoming!"

Hobbs let out a roar from the noise, but Dex saw
him gently bite down on Calvin's vest on his shoulder before he started dragging his partner through the
dirt. A second wolf Therian materialized out of nowhere, snapping at Dex's face. Reacting on instinct,
Dex pulled back, the wolf Therian's teeth miraculous-
ly grazing only his jaw, leaving nothing but a sharp
sting behind. Unsuccessful at ripping Dex's face off,
it clamped its jaws down on the protective padding
around his upper arm. Thank God for small miracles.
It tugged and shook its head in an attempt to do some
damage. Despite the body armor protecting his arm,
the fierce jerking motion was jarring and painful. If he
didn't do something quick, the bastard was going to
dislocate something.

"Damn it!" Using his knees to balance his shield,
he pulled one of the tranqs from his vest and stabbed
it into the wolf Therian's neck. It shrieked and jumped
back, flailing and craning its neck in an attempt to remove the impaled object. The wolf pushing against his
shield scurried off, clearly unwilling to get shanked.
Pushing to his feet, Dex hurried to Hobbs and grabbed
Calvin's vest on the other side, helping Hobbs drag

their teammate into the abandoned building behind them.

"Dex!" Letty's worried cry came over his earpiece.

Dex dragged Calvin up to the cinder block wall, sitting him up before checking his pulse. He was okay. He tapped his earpiece, his breath coming out heavy.

"We're okay. Calvin's out, but he's breathing. Hobbs is with us."

"Any sign of Everton?"

Dex activated the lights on his shield, scanning the area around them. "Negative." Not that he expected to find Everton. At the moment he was more concerned with what else might be in here with them.

"Okay, we're coming to get you—holy shit."

"Letty?"

Dex edged up to the end of the wall and took a quick peek. "Oh fuck." They were all coming out of the woodwork. What the hell was he supposed to do now? He looked over at the roof of the building across, where Rosa and Letty were shooting at everything that moved. At Dex's feet, Calvin was out. Ahead of him in the darkness, he heard movement. Hobbs growled, and Dex aimed his rifle, until the growls of other Therians echoed around them. They were surrounded. What the hell had he signed up for? He needed to call Sloane, Cael, hell, even Ash.

Around them, dozens of glowing eyes became visible, and Dex swallowed hard. "Oh my God." Even with Hobbs, they wouldn't be able to take on this many Therians. What the hell had made him think he was cut out for this? He was a detective, not Special Forces. They were surrounded, like tiny insects in a roach motel. Hobbs hissed and Dex turned his head, watching him nudge Calvin's cheek with his nose. A huff escaped and a loud purring sound started rumbling out of him. Seriously? They were about to be turned into kibble and Hobbs was purring? Dex reached out, only to have Hobbs hiss at him, his snarl revealing those razor-sharp fangs. He snatched his hand back and held it up at his side.

"Sorry, sorry."

With a groan, Hobbs nudged Calvin's head again until they heard a faint groan, this time coming from Calvin.

"Calvin?" Dex crouched down next to him, gently shaking his shoulder. "Come on, buddy, I really need you to wake up."

Another nudge from Hobbs to the temple and a lick to his cheek had Calvin letting out a chuckle. He groggily stirred and opened his eyes to swat at Hobbs, who returned the favor with an added tiger kiss to the cheek. Despite the circumstances, Dex couldn't help his dopey grin, especially when Calvin grabbed hold of Hobbs's ears and tugged his head down so they could rest their heads together.

"I'm okay, buddy. I promise," Calvin assured his partner quietly.

Suddenly Hobbs's ears perked up and he pulled back, his gaze landing on Dex at the same time Calvin's did.

Dex's grin widened. "You two are so adorable."

"I won't let Hobbs turn you into kitty chow for saying that because you saved my ass."

"That's okay, because I don't think he'll have the time." Dex helped Calvin to his feet. He knew things were rough, and he wasn't too proud to admit he was a little scared, but he could do this. His family believed in him enough to want him on their team. He wasn't about to let them down, no matter what. He'd go down fighting.

"Thanks." Calvin smiled weakly, his eyes widening when he saw Dex's jaw. "Shit, are you okay?"

"Yeah, just a scratch. Don't worry about it."

"I'm sorry," Calvin replied with a wretched expression.

Dex cursed under his breath. Screw this. He grabbed Calvin's arm and put it around his neck before tapping his earpiece again. "Sarge?"

"I'm on my way. Had to shake a few off the truck. Be ready to make a run for it."

"Copy that. Letty, Rosa, I need one of you to clear the way for me."

Letty's breathy voice came over the earpiece. "I'll cover you."

Dex grabbed another one of his flash-bangs and readied himself. He took a deep breath and looked down at Calvin. "Ready?"

Calvin nodded.

Tony's gruff voice shouted at him. "BearCat's in position. Go, go, go!"

Dex pulled the pin on his flash-bang and hurled it into the darkness, leaving behind a cacophony of roars and pained cries. He swiped up his shield with his free hand and moved as quickly as he could while taking most of Calvin's weight. Lucky for him, Calvin was slightly smaller and less heavy. If he'd had to move Sloane or Ash, he would have been royally screwed. He was definitely going to take his bench presses more seriously from here on out. They ran out into the middle of the road where the BearCat was parked, the machine gun on the roof firing warning rounds all around them. Letty covered Dex's back as he helped Calvin to the back of the truck.

Rosa and Letty soon flanked him, and Rosa banged the back doors. They opened automatically, and Rosa helped Dex lift Calvin up. "Hurry up, Dex!" Letty insisted, jumping up into the back of the truck and pulling Calvin in the rest of the way. She motioned behind him, and he cursed under his breath. In the distance, Sloane, Ash, and Cael were heading right for them. Among them they had Everton corralled, and he wasn't happy about it, snapping at their teammates' paws and necks as he ran.

Dex helped Rosa up into the truck before climbing in along with Hobbs. They all hurried to the front of the truck, and Rosa banged against the steel door of the front cabin. "Get the cage ready, Sarge!"

"I'm on it."

The cage wall closest to them rose from the truck's base with a series of clangs and finally a booming sound, followed by a click—and not too soon. Everton leaped in with a roar, hitting the steel bars and throwing a paw out between them, his sharp claws ineptly trying to reach them. The remaining walls of the cage rose, the loud bang resonating through the truck. This time when Everton tried to claw at the bars, he received an electric shock that sent him reeling back. His ears flattened and he hissed, but he sat his ass down in the middle of the cage and stopped trying to get out.

Sloane, Ash, and Cael were already inside the truck, and again Rosa banged the steel door. On her signal, Tony closed the back doors and revved the engine. They each grabbed hold of one of the ceiling straps as the truck hightailed it out of Greenpoint. Everyone remained on high alert, their eyes on Everton as the truck made its way back to HQ. Once there, Dex knew the truck would drive through the tunnel at the rear of the building, but instead of making a right toward the parking garage, it would make a left, heading toward the underground detention center, where further backup would be available with the press of one button. It was also where the holding cells were, as well as areas for Post Shift Trauma Care.

When the truck came to a stop, Tony opened the back doors. Across from them was a series of curtained-off areas for shifting. Sloane, Ash, Cael, and Hobbs jumped down from the truck, each making their way into a curtained room. Shifting was an intimate, vulnerable process and not something most Therians took lightly. Rosa, Letty, Calvin, and Dex exited the truck, their PSTC kits in hand while Tony stayed with the secured Everton.

They each took a post outside their respective partner's curtain and waited. When Dex heard his name called gruffly, he removed Sloane's disposable clothes from the kit and handed them back through the curtain. They were immediately swiped up. A few minutes later, his name was grunted again. Dex slipped through the curtain, unsurprised to find Sloane sitting on the edge of a cot, his head in his hands. It would take a few minutes before the dizziness cleared. Dex reached into the backpack and pulled out a large bottle of Gatorade. Silently he handed it to Sloane, who took it with a trembling hand. It slipped from his fingers, and Dex caught it.

"It's okay, buddy. Let me help you."

Sloane let out an unintelligible slur of words, his brows drawn together in obvious displeasure as Dex put his hand to the back of his head.

"Come on, lean back." When Sloane resisted, Dex crouched down in front of him, cupping his face. "I know, you're the big bad alpha, but I'm your partner. I'm here to help you, okay? You did your job; now let me do mine." He hoped the sincerity in his voice would prove to Sloane he meant every word. It was his first time providing Post Shift Trauma Care to his partner, and he wanted to make sure Sloane had everything he needed to recover properly.

With a grunt, Sloane nodded slowly. Trying again, Dex gently cupped the back of Sloane's head, waiting for his partner to lean back. After a moment of hesitation, Sloane did, and Dex carefully put the uncapped bottle of Gatorade to Sloane's lips, administering small sips at a time until the whole bottle was gone. He waited for Sloane to lean forward again before releasing his head; then he chucked the bottle into the nearby trash can. From inside the kit, he fetched a couple of hefty high-carb, high-protein energy bars. He tore the foil off both and handed them to Sloane.

Finished eating, Sloane pushed to his feet. He faltered, and Dex threw an arm around his waist to steady him. "Whoa, easy there, big guy." He flattened his hand against Sloane's stomach, pretending he wasn't affected when Sloane's hand clamped down over it, his other arm wrapping around Dex and pulling him up against his side, squeezing him weakly. Sloane closed his eyes and breathed in deeply, releasing his breath slowly as he waited for the dizziness washing over him to pass. It wouldn't be too long before Sloane was back to his usual grumpy self.

"Thanks," Sloane said with a small smile, releasing Dex. His smile suddenly vanished, and he grabbed Dex's face with both hands. His right thumb gently brushed Dex's cheek, sending a chill down his spine. "What happened to your face?"

"Nothing, just a scratch," Dex murmured.

"You broke formation, didn't you?"

Dex pressed his lips together as Sloane cursed under his breath, releasing him. Sloane ran his fingers through his hair in frustration. "What the hell did you think you were doing?"

"My job," Dex replied calmly, walking out from behind the curtained-off area. Sloane caught up to him, gripped his arm, and turned him. "We talked about this, remember?"

"Yeah, I remember you promising you were going to be careful. Goddamn it, Dex, you had specific orders. I told you to stick to the rest of the team, to remain in formation! You almost got your fucking face torn off!"

"Sloane."

Sloane turned to Calvin and snapped. "What?"

Calvin rounded his shoulders and met Sloane's gaze. "Dex broke formation to save my ass. I was the one who broke formation first."

"What?" Sloane stared at Calvin before he looked to the rest of their team. No one said a word, but their silence was confirmation enough.

"Hobbs was in trouble…."

Sloane marched up to Calvin and grabbed him by the vest. "What the fuck were you thinking? You abandoned a rookie member of your team. He could have been killed!"

"I fucked up, I know, but—"

"Damn right you fucked up." Sloane gave him a shove toward Hobbs, ignoring Hobbs's deep frown. "I want to see you two upstairs in Maddock's office after this."

Calvin murmured his acknowledgment while Hobbs simply nodded. They stepped aside as Sloane snatched his tac vest from Letty and slipped into it, fastening the straps as he thundered to the BearCat, calling out over his shoulder. "Rosa, sort his face out." As soon as he was inside the truck, Calvin stepped up to Dex, the guilt on his face making it difficult for Dex to be pissed off at him.

"I'm so sorry, Dex. I really fucked up."

"You did." Dex watched Calvin hang his head in defeat. With a smile, Dex put his hand to Calvin's cheek and gave it a pat. "But I understand. He's your partner. I can't say that I wouldn't have done the same had I been in your shoes, but next time we go in as a team, okay?" Calvin nodded, giving him a thankful smile before he headed toward the truck with Hobbs in tow. Dex turned to Rosa, who was removing a first aid kit from her backpack. "Mind if we do it in the truck? I'd like to hear what Mr. Everton has to say."

"Sure thing."

As he walked beside her, he lowered his voice. "This isn't the first time it's happened." The way the team had busied itself looking elsewhere and not at Sloane had told Dex all he needed to know. They were worried but refused to rat out their teammates.

Rosa shook her head, stopping to pull Dex to one side as the rest of the team made their way to the truck. She handed him the first aid kit, opened it, and tore one of the industrial-sized Therian disinfecting pads open. They had a few minutes while the team got Everton to shift and administered Post Shift Trauma Care. With a nod, he braced himself as she put the pad to his face.

"Sweet Jesus, that stings." Dex ignored her chuckle as she proceeded to clean the scrapes. Her gaze darted to the truck before she continued.

"I know what you're thinking, but they're not normally that reckless. Hobbs was off his game. No one ever gets the drop on him. I don't know what's going on, but things have been tense between them lately. Calvin's not usually this quiet. And Hobbs, well, he's always been quiet, but he's usually more playful. They've not been acting like themselves. Sloane hasn't noticed because he's been busy with you." Rosa arched an eyebrow at him, her lips spreading into a sly smile. "Word is you're keeping him on his toes."

"I don't like to brag," Dex replied with a wink. "You think we need to worry about them?"

"Not after Sloane tears them a new one." She sounded certain, which helped ease Dex's mind a little. He still wasn't sure what was going on with Calvin and Hobbs, but at least he wasn't the only one to have noticed. He'd have to keep an eye on them. The last thing they needed was a repeat performance of today.

Sloane's growl interrupted his thoughts. "Rosa, you done?"

"Yep." She took the kit from Dex and snapped it shut before returning it to her backpack.

"Good. Both of you get over here."

"Coming." Dex thanked Rosa and accompanied her to the truck. They climbed in and took their seats on the bench. Everton was sitting in Maddock's seat, wearing one of the many disposable sets of clothes from the truck's small supply closet. He had a blanket around his shoulders, and there were empty energy bar wrappers on the floor. Despite no longer being in the cage, he was surrounded. Sloane stood in front of the trembling Therian, his arms folded over his broad chest, his stance imposing.

Lloyd Everton looked like any other guy. He was tall, somewhat on the lanky side, with a scruffy beard and dark hair in disarray. He was in his mid- to late fortieo, but his weary expression, the hard lines of his face, and the gray strands interspersed in his hair made him look much older. He was hunched over, his legs crossed at the ankles, and his expression that of a guy who was exhausted but resolute. More resolute, however, was the THIRDS agent before him.

Dex watched his partner carefully, curious how he was going to get Everton to cooperate. Right now the two were glaring, sizing each other up. Everton hadn't made it this far as an Unregistered without being a tough SOB. Every Unregistered Therian had his or her own reasons for not registering, everything from a belief Therians were superior to Humans and therefore above Human law, to believing it was all a government conspiracy hiding a far more sinister plot. At this moment, however, whatever Lloyd Everton's reason, being Unregistered was the least of his problems.

Chapter 9

"MR. EVERTON, I'm Agent Sloane Brodie, and I promise you, I only want to talk."

Sloane relaxed his stance, his assessment of the Therian before him completed. He didn't believe Everton posed a threat, but he wouldn't take any chances with his team in the truck. At the first hint of trouble, Sloane would take Everton down.

"You have a lot of guns for someone who only wants to talk," Everton replied somberly, his gaze never leaving Sloane's.

"Those are a precaution."

"Right. And the cage?"

"An unfortunate necessity."

Everton cocked his head to one side, his fallen expression unexpected. "You put your own kind in a cage."

Sloane had those words thrown at him countless times in various degrees of animosity. Yet Everton's soft words stung more than any hostile accusation. He schooled his reaction, something he'd learned to do when he'd first been recruited. Being anything other than a THIRDS agent was something he couldn't afford. It was his job to remain neutral, to seek justice, and keep the peace within his species. "I have to protect my team, Mr. Everton. They're my family. Wouldn't you do what you had to do to protect your family?"

There was a moment of quiet before Everton released a sigh. "Okay. Well, this clearly isn't a routine registration issue, so what is it?"

"Come on, Mr. Everton. Let's be honest with each other here. It'll make this a lot easier for both of us." Sloan took the tablet Cael handed to him and showed it to Everton. "Mr. Ortiz. You were at his house for a charity brunch with Ms. Thalia's catering company the day he was murdered, correct?" He studied Everton, who merely glanced at the image of a once-living Hector Ortiz and nodded.

"That's right."

"Did you approach Mr. Ortiz at any time?" He handed the tablet back to Cael. Rosa would be recording everything for review later.

"No. I was busy working."

"Tell me about the waiter who approached you. What did he say to you?"

Everton shifted in his seat. "That he knew what I was. How dare I pretend to be a civilized member of society? If I didn't vacate the premises, he would phone the authorities."

Sloan pursed his lips. That sounded awfully polite for the waiter who'd all but spat in their faces. "Are you paraphrasing?"

"Yes. I'm not comfortable with the language he used," Everton replied, once again fidgeting awkwardly in his seat.

"Please, Lloyd. It's important you tell me what he said, exactly as you remember it."

"Okay. He said, 'I know what you are, you Unregistered piece of shit. If you don't get the fuck out of this house right now, I'm going to report your cocksucking ass and have them lock you up in a cage like the motherfucking animal you are.'"

Sloane cleared his throat. Well, that certainly sounded more like it. At times, he wondered who the real animals were. "And despite his threat, you continued to work? Why?"

"I needed the money. Work is hard to find when you're Unregistered. They try to rip you off, not pay you after the job is done because there's nothing you can do about it. Ms. Thalia didn't do that. She always paid and on time." He gave a sniff, lowering his gaze to his fingers. "I have a wife and kids to feed."

Sloane crouched down in front of Everton, his voice gentle and sympathetic. "Then why not register. For them?"

Everton met his gaze, anger flashing through his amber eyes, eyes that reminded Sloane of what could have been. It was like looking into a warped mirror, one that showed Sloane what his life would have been like without the good fortune of having a family such as Everton had. If he would have even made it to Everton's age. Quickly he pushed those thoughts aside and concentrated on the task at hand.

When Everton next spoke, his voice was low. "I won't let the government mark me like I'm some criminal. They say we're citizens like everyone else, but they keep us under surveillance, watch our every move, and treat us like animals. Our existence makes us guilty until proven otherwise. My grandfather had been marked once, back in Germany. I won't let them do that to me or my family."

"It's not the same thing, Lloyd," Sloane said gently.

Everton pulled back, his eyes filled with sadness. "It's all got to start somewhere, Agent Brodie."

There was no point in arguing with Everton. He clearly wasn't going to budge on the matter, and who was Sloane to try to change his mind? The guy felt strongly about what he was doing, enough so that he was prepared to face the consequences of his decisions. Sloane stood with a sigh and continued with his interview. "Okay. What time did you leave?"

"Around noon. I put it off as long as I could. I was at my station from 8:00 a.m. serving vodka and orange juice and didn't move from there until I left. Guests can confirm that."

"Did you see anything or anyone suspicious? Anyone who maybe shouldn't have been there? Did you hear anything?" When Everton looked up at him, Sloane knew they were back to square one. How was it possible for a Therian to murder a Human with so many other Therians under the same roof and have them not sense anything?

"I'm really sorry, Agent Brodie, I was only there to work. I wasn't paying much attention to anything else."

"Why were you hiding?"

Everton stared at him as if the answer was obvious. "I saw the news. The moment they said they were looking for an Unregistered Felid, I knew what was going on. Even if I was innocent, I couldn't show up here and say so. Not that it made a difference in the end."

"Why Greenpoint?"

"I live there," Everton replied, his head hanging in shame.

"With your family?" Sloane asked, not surprised that a family would be living in a hostile place like Greenpoint, but that Everton would have his there. The guy was already risking so much for them. The thought saddened him. Everton was simply another Therian child the world had never wanted, discarded, and forced to fend for himself whatever way he knew how while he tried to understand what he could possibly have done wrong to deserve such a fate.

"God, no." Everton shook his head, looking horrified by the suggestion. "Everything I earn goes to my family to keep them somewhere safe, with food, clothes, and education for my kids. I'd die before I let them end up at Greenpoint. It's filled with Therians who refuse to acknowledge their Human side. Sometimes I wonder if they have any Humanity left in them."

"Thank you, Lloyd." Now that the interview was over came the even shittier part. Sloane mulled it over in his head, his gaze falling on Everton. He knew what Everton's reply would be, but he made the effort regardless. "I don't suppose it'll do much to give you an extended period to register?"

Everton gave him a sad smile. "Thank you, but no."

"Okay." Sloane turned to Ash. "Hand me the TIK." He took the black band from Ash and stepped up to Everton with an apologetic smile. "I need a sample

of your DNA and confirmation of your classification.
You'll need to be held until the lab confirms the blood
found on Mr. Ortiz isn't yours." Sloane slipped the
cuff around Everton's arm, tapped in his thumbprint
passcode, and started the scanning procedure. "If
you're cleared of all charges, you'll be released and
given a week to register. I can't guarantee there will
be a next time, Lloyd."

"Thank you." Everton put his hand over Sloane's
and smiled warmly at him. "You're a good guy."

Sloane couldn't bring himself to say anything. He
nodded and finished the analysis before removing the
TIK with Everton's full details and handing it to Ash.
When he spoke, his voice was rougher than intended.
"Agents Keeler and Guerrera will escort you to the
holding cell."

Ash and Letty took their positions on either side of
Everton, and with a final nod of thanks from Everton,
they silently escorted him from the truck. Sloane hoped
spending some time in the holding cell might make
Everton change his mind. Maybe if he got a glimpse
of what his future could be, he'd think about his family
and decide they were more important. Sacrifices had
to be made by everyone, Sloane was fully aware. He'd
made plenty of his own throughout his life. There was
no point bemoaning what could have been.

Sloane had been given a second chance, and if he
had to play the game in order to make the most of that
chance, then so be it.

"What now?" Cael asked softly.

"Now we wait for the lab results on Ortiz and
pray something comes up. We have to solve this case.
There's something we're missing."

"Well, in the meantime, why don't you all take the rest of the night off," Maddock said, heading for the end of the truck. "I'll let you know about the DNA results as soon as we've got them, as well as anything new. Lieutenant Sparks is trying to get the Chief of Therian Defense to prioritize all our lab work. He wants this case solved as quickly as we do, so I suspect we'll be granted approval. Calvin, Hobbs, my office. Sloane, park the BearCat and lock up, then hit the showers with everyone else."

"Yes, sir." Sloane stepped to one side as Calvin and Hobbs wordlessly followed their sergeant. It looked like Maddock was going to deal with their teammates himself. Sloane didn't know what had prompted Calvin to break formation like that. It wasn't like him to be so reckless.

Sloane addressed Rosa and Cael. "You two go ahead and brief Intel and then hit the showers. We'll take care of the truck." Sloane closed the doors after Rosa and Cael, securing them before making his way to the front cabin and addressing Dex. "You can unload your equipment into one of the cages and stick your vest in your locker."

"Okay, thanks."

Sloane climbed into the driver's side while Dex put away his rifles, backpacks, and most of his other equipment, leaving his thigh rig and tac vest on. Sloane had Dex bolt the door behind him when he walked into the cabin. As soon as Dex was in the passenger seat and buckled up, Sloane got them moving.

"They gonna be okay?" Dex asked solemnly.

"Who? Calvin and Hobbs?"

"Yeah."

"You know your dad. He'll scare the shit out of them and make sure they know they fucked up, especially since they put his kid in danger."

"Maybe I should have a word with him," Dex said with a frown, slouching in his seat as Sloane drove the BearCat up the ramp that led to the parking garage.

"Not a good idea, Rookie."

"I don't want him giving me special treatment because we're family," Dex replied irritably.

"First of all, he's not giving you special treatment. No one thinks that. Maddock treats you the same as everyone else. But if someone stupidly puts your life at risk, he's going to pull a combo move of pissed-off sergeant and enraged dad. There's no way around that. He's the same with Cael. You think your dad goes easy on Cael? If anything, he's harder on him, but he does it because he wants his boys safe. You're lucky, Rookie. Most of us never had that."

Dex was quiet for a moment, his gaze somewhere outside his window. "I take it your parents aren't around?"

Sloane pulled the BearCat into its space. He turned off the engine and sat there, aware of Dex watching him. Taking a deep, calming breath, Sloane faced Dex. "Okay, listen up, because I'm only going to say this once. I don't talk about my past, so don't ask me about my parents, where I came from, or what I did before the THIRDS. It's nobody's business. I don't talk to anyone about it. Not Maddock, not the team, no one."

"Did you talk to Gabe about it?" Dex studied him closely, and Sloane looked away, a sharp pain twisting his gut.

"That's not up for discussion either. Lock the door behind you." He climbed out of the truck, slamming the door behind him, the sound resonating through the cavernous underground garage. Dex caught up to him, keeping up with his long strides on the way to the elevator. He was quiet, which Sloane had come to learn was not a good thing. It also never lasted long.

"I respect that, but you're sure there's nothing I should know, as your partner?"

"Saying you respect my decision and then following it up with a question that challenges it voids your so-called claim of respect, Daley."

Dex held his hands up in surrender. "You're calling me Daley, which means you're pissed off with me. I get it. I'm sorry."

"I'm not pissed off," Sloane grunted, stepping inside the elevator and placing his hand on the display pad. "Drop it. If there was something relevant, I would tell you."

"Okay."

They were both silent on the ride up to Sparta and through the lounge to the locker rooms, where Sloane's guilt started getting the better of him. He took Dex's arm and pulled him into one of the empty training rooms. The lights were off, but there was enough illumination coming through the atrium that they could see each other. Dex stood close enough for Sloane to catch his scent, a concoction of something citrusy plus Dex's own male scent, with the addition of dirt and sweat. It took a lot for Sloane not to lean into him. It certainly knocked the wind out of his sails; his anger from moments ago completely subsided. Not since Gabe had he felt this strong a pull toward someone, and the worst part was he didn't know what to do about it. The longer he spent in Dex's company, the more messed up he felt inside.

"I'm sorry. I'm not trying to be a dick about it. I… I'm not ready to talk about that part of my life with anyone. I don't know if I'll ever be ready." He put his hand to Dex's cheek with the pretense of checking his injury. When his gaze met Dex's, he found himself mesmerized by those eyes. He'd seen plenty of Therians with eyes that pale, but not many Humans. There was also something about them that drew him in. When those pools of blue lowered to Sloane's lips, he knew he was in trouble.

"If you ever feel like you're ready, know you can trust me."

Sloane nodded, his thumb brushing over Dex's soft lips, the feel of a hint of stubble under his hand making his body react in the most inappropriate way. He needed to walk away right now. Dex stayed where he was, his breath as unsteady as Sloane's. Their bodies had gravitated toward each other when the sounds of boisterous laughter from somewhere out in the hall gave them both a start, and Sloane jerked back, his heart threatening to pound through his chest.

"We should go," he said, motioning for Dex to go first. "Thank you for earlier. For the PSTC."

Dex smiled at him. "Just doing my job."

"Well, you did good."

By the time they got to the locker rooms, Calvin, Hobbs, Ash, and Cael were already inside. Calvin and Hobbs were moping as expected, but Sloane knew it wouldn't last too long. Maybe they all needed something to lighten the mood.

Sloane walked to his locker and started to remove his vest. "Hey, why don't we all head to Bar Dekatria for a couple of drinks?"

Dex smiled widely at him. "Yeah?"

"Why not? I'll let Maddock know in case there's a callout. We deserve a little repose."

"Woo! Booze!" Cael did a little happy dance, making the team laugh, though Sloane's gaze was on Dex. The guy had an amazing smile and genuine too, the kind that reached his eyes. He liked that Dex was open about everything, and whatever he did, he put his all into it. He was a hard worker, and Sloane was growing to appreciate Dex's sense of humor, even if it drove him crazy at times. Sloane went back to getting undressed, removing his vest and shoving it at the bottom of his locker.

Dex's cell phone went off, and Sloane glanced over in time to catch him pushing his pants down over his ass. To Sloane's horror, he left them there while answering his phone. The stark white of his boxer briefs was a sharp contrast to the charcoal tac pants, and it seemed to accentuate his deliciously rounded ass. Despite the voice in Sloane's head telling him to look away, he couldn't bring himself to do it. He'd managed to resist the temptation of eyeing it until now. Dex pinned his phone against his ear with his shoulder while removing his vest, one side first, then swapping his phone to the other side to extract his other arm.

"I left it in your desk. Top right-hand drawer."

Sloane stole a quick glance to make sure no one had caught on to him before returning to his ogling. Dex was oblivious to his striptease as he continued to chat on his phone. Shirt now off, Dex stood in his snug black undershirt, the curve of his spine nearly as tan-talizing as his ass. Sloane's thoughts went to that night in the parking garage. He hadn't been able to stop thinking about what they'd done, or what had gotten into him. A day didn't go by that he didn't recall with exceptional clarity how good Dex's body felt against his, Dex's hard erection, the look of sheer pleasure on his flushed face as he came into Sloane's hand.

"Your other right," Dex said with a snicker. "I'm sorry. I'm messing with you. It's in the left."

The slam of a locker to Sloane's right startled the hell out of him, and he turned to glare at Ash. His friend leaned against his closed locker, an eyebrow arched. With a heavy sigh, Sloane went back to put-ting his clothes away.

"Enjoying the show?"

Sloane gritted his teeth, refusing to take the bait. Just his luck. Out of everyone in the locker room, Ash had to be the one to catch him eyeballing his partner.

"What?" Ash asked innocently. "Just an observa-tion. Much like the one you were making of some-one's ass." With a chuckle, Ash walked off.

"Hey, think fast." Dex tossed something at Sloane, and he caught it. It was a set of keys. "Hold on to those. You can drive us."

Behind Dex, Cael let out a loud whine. "Aw, come on, man. You're letting him drive it?"

Dex smiled broadly at his brother. "I trust him."

"You saying you don't trust *me*?"

"I do," Dex replied with a wide grin. He stepped up to his brother, took hold of his chin, and planted a sloppy kiss on his cheek. "Just not with my car." With a laugh, Dex walked off. Cael wiped his cheek with the back of his hand.

"You dick!" Cael turned to glare at Sloane.

Uh-oh. "What?" Sloane asked as he put the keys into the pocket of his jeans, neatly folded in his locker. "Is that a big deal?"

"Big deal?" Cael threw his arms up. "That car is like his freaking child. He doesn't let anyone drive it. Not me, not Dad, not his ex. He covers it up at night and makes you agree to a verbal affidavit before he even lets you sit in the damn thing. I'm his brother! I've known him my whole life. He's known you weeks and he gives you his keys?" Cael continued to rant on his way to the showers. "You think you know a guy and bam! He kicks you right in the feels. Why don't you kick me in the nuts, Dex! It'll hurt less!"

Sloane laughed, hearing Dex's reply from inside the showers. "Just remember, you suggested it."

They all hit the showers, the banter and jokes helping ease the day's tension. Cael continued to whine about Dex not letting him drive his car, while Dex alternated between teasing his brother and getting on Ash's nerves. Calvin and Hobbs were still quiet, but at least they were smiling. Afterward they met Letty and Rosa in the lounge, where Cael shared his automotive woes with Rosa. She pulled him in for a hug and babied him like she always did, muttering comforting words in Spanish about her poor little *gatito*. Letty shook her head in amusement, while Dex sped past Sloane with Ash on his heels, threatening him with an imminent demise. This should make for an interesting evening.

BAR DEKATRIA was less than a fifteen-minute drive from THIRDS HQ, surrounded by restaurants, and around the corner from Letty's favorite Jamba Juice. Dekatria was a retro-style bar and club with three floors—a martini lounge, dance floor, and rooftop deck. The first floor was classy, with retrofitted loungers and even a lava lamp sitting on the bar, sure to be a hit with Dex. There was a spacious dance floor that tended to get full once the alcohol kicked in, though the real dancing happened on the second floor. It was all rich woods with dark accents, such as the black tufted-leather bar and leather seating. The many candles painstakingly arranged around the room, along with the various wall sconces, gave the place a warm, intimate atmosphere. At the end of the long room were a couple of sleek pool tables, one of which Ash had already commandeered.

It always went the same. Cael and Ash would team up to play against Letty and Rosa. Most likely the boys would get their asses handed to them, and Ash would sulk until he was too drunk to remember what he was pissed off about. He'd hang on Cael, saying inappropriate things that would make Cael blush. Calvin and Hobbs would sit at a table nearby, chatting. Well, Calvin would chat, and Hobbs would listen and occasionally contribute to the conversation with a grunt or a hum.

Sloane would do what he'd been doing for the last year—sit at a table close to his team or at the bar, drink himself to a nice buzz, and then take a cab home. Why had he suggested coming here? He took a seat at the bar, about to order when his crazyass partner appeared, dropping onto the stool beside him.

"Hey, partner!" Dex threw an arm around Sloane's shoulders, a big grin on his face. "What'll it be? Wait!" He squinted and put a finger to his temple. "Cosmo? Fuzzy Navel? Martini, shaken not stirred? No? Okay, hm." Sloane braced himself as Dex put in an order. "Two Heinekens."

The tattooed bartender in a tight black T-shirt walked off with a chuckle to fetch their drinks. How did Dex manage to get everyone around him to fall for his charm? Except for Ash, of course. The guy seemed to be immune to that lopsided grin. The bartender returned with two bottles, popped the caps, and slid them over. "Thanks, man. Can you keep a tab open for me and my posse?"

An appreciative eye traveled over Dex. "Sure thing." He gave Dex a wide smile before some customers called him over.

Sloane shook his head. "How do you do it?" he asked, truly mystified.

"Do what?" Dex asked, holding his bottle to Sloane for a toast. Sloane obliged.

"How do you stay so damn happy all the time? It looks exhausting."

"I don't know. I guess I don't really have a reason not to be. I got a job I enjoy, good company," he said with a wink, "an awesome family, a beer in my hand. What's to be unhappy about?"

"You're one of those annoying glass-half-full guys, aren't you?"

"I'm more of a full-glass kind of guy. Who wants half of anything?" He took a long swig of his beer, and

Sloane's gaze fell on Dex's throat as he swallowed. He quickly looked away.

"I wanted to say you did good at Greenpoint. I'm not happy you broke formation, but when things got rough, you came through for your team."

"Wow. Two compliments in one day," Dex teased.

Sloane took a sip of his beer, ignoring the way Dex leaned an elbow on the bar, his cheek resting against his fist as he sat facing Sloane, his smile reaching his eyes.

"Yeah, well, don't let it go to your head."

Dex gave him a cheeky grin and held up his beer. "That's what these are for."

"Gonna be one of those nights, huh?"

"I intend to get thoroughly and wonderfully fucked," Dex replied proudly, taking another sip of his beer.

"Been a while?"

"Yeah. The last few months haven't exactly given me much cause for celebrating." He took a couple more gulps before sliding the empty bottle to one side. In seconds, another one appeared without him even asking for it. Sloane wouldn't be surprised if a few digits accompanied the next one.

"It must have been hard." Sloane hadn't really watched the news when the whole thing had gone down. He'd been busy with his own problems, but he'd heard about it. Maddock and Cael hadn't mentioned it either, though he figured they'd most likely been protecting Dex. The rest of the office was a different story. The THIRDS didn't get involved in HPF problems unless there was cause to, or if it became their jurisdiction, but seeing as how the THIRDS was all about the union between Human and Therian, the case had stirred up plenty of interesting conversation and opinions. The consensus being the HPF detective had done the right thing.

When Sloane had first met Dex, he hadn't been sure about him turning in his partner, despite knowing it was the right thing to do, but he'd also been looking for any excuse to hate the guy. Now he could see how hard the whole thing had been on Dex, and he admired him for coming through it relatively unscathed.

"I testified against my partner, which made me feel like shit. I got jumped in the parking garage after. Got home in time to watch my boyfriend move out, after he dumped me of course, then I got beat up at work, then I lost my job—so to speak. My first day of my new job, I got the crap beat out of me by my team leader, and then today I nearly got eaten by a pack of Therians. All in all, a pretty productive few months."

Sloane peered at him slyly. "Your team leader sounds like a real prick."

"He has his moments," Dex replied with a wink, causing Sloane's pulse to jump, at least until he caught onto what Dex had said.

"Wait, back up. You got beat up twice? How'd that happen?"

Dex shifted his gaze to his beer bottle, giving a shrug as he picked at the corner of the label. "They got the drop on me."

"Maybe your guilt got the drop on you."

"What are you talking about?" Dex mumbled, his feigned ignorance not fooling anyone.

"Come on, Dex. Unless you were up against armed thugs or a hoard of ninjas, you could have kicked their asses. I've seen you fight."

"What? Our little sparring sessions in Sparta?" Dex scoffed.

Sloane didn't like what he was hearing, though he couldn't say he was surprised. Dex was a good guy. He cared about those around him, and went out of his way to do what was right. "You held your own against me. Believe me, that says a lot. Those guys who got the drop on you, were they Human?"

"Yeah."

"Where they armed?"

"Yes." Sloane arched an eyebrow at him and Dex winced. "Sort of. They had a stick."

"Are you telling me a THIRDS agent couldn't take down a bunch of punks with a stick?" He knew those steel batons were a bitch. They could do some real damage, but nothing compared to a firearm or blade. Dex was a very capable agent.

"THIRDS *rookie*," Dex muttered pathetically. "And they weren't punks, they were cops."

"Shit." Sloane ran a hand over his face. He nodded his understanding, not that he agreed with what Dex had done. He leaned forward, jabbing a finger against the bar's sleek black surface. "That's the last time that happens, you hear me? Letting those assholes beat the shit out of you will not make the guilt go away, believe me. You feel like you need an ass-kicking, you let me know. I'll throw you in the ring with Ash. I'm sure he'll be happy to be of service."

Dex shuddered. "Point taken. How is it you two are best friends anyway? No offense, but the guy is a total douchebag."

"He's not as bad as he seems." Sloane took another sip of his beer. He wasn't much in the mood for drinking tonight, though it might be because he wasn't getting much of a chance while talking to Dex, not that he was complaining. Talking with Dex was easy. He could have a discussion that involved more than Ash's Rule of the Three *S*'s—shooting, sex, and sports.

"Really?"

It took Sloane a moment to remember what he'd been talking about. "Yeah. We've known each other since we were kids. We were both in a rough place. *I* was in a rough place, and he helped me through it. He's helped me through a few rough patches, actually. I know he can be a pain in the ass, but he would take a bullet for me. He has, quite literally." Sloane shook his head, chuckling at the memory. "It was only a flesh wound. He bitched for months, milked it for all it was worth, but he'd earned it. He's always had my back, and I've had his. We're the only family we got."

"What about the rest of the team?"

"They're family, of course, but you know, Rosa's got her girlfriend. They've been together ten years. Letty's got a boyfriend over in Brooklyn. Calvin's got his mom, and Hobbs has his parents and a couple of brothers. They've been friends since they were kids. Hobbs's mom used to babysit Calvin when his mom was at work. They grew up in the same apartment complex. That's why they're so tight. Then there's me and Ash." He shrugged, not sure what else he could really say about it that wouldn't sound pathetic even to his own ears. "So what happened with your partner?"

Dex looked like he might not be ready to give up the previous conversation, but Sloane was grateful when he took a swig of beer and nodded. "It was supposed to be routine. We didn't deal with Therian informants all that often, but they help the HPF more than the force wants to admit. Human criminals love to evade the HPF by hiding out in Therian neighborhoods, especially when they're willing to pay for protection. Anyway, we were trying to find this guy who'd killed a store clerk during a robbery, and we knew he was hiding with a Therian gang. We found a guy who had information, and when we met up with him, he was just a kid, fifteen at most.

"I started talking to him, but Walsh kept butting in, getting hands-on, accusing the guy of holding back information, so you can imagine how that went. The guy got defensive, didn't appreciate being pushed around or the shit coming out of Walsh's mouth. I tried to defuse the situation, but the guy said he wasn't going to say any more and walked off. Next thing I knew, Walsh had pulled his piece and fired. Hit the kid right between the shoulders. One bullet." Dex shook his head, his lips pressed together. "I stood there, dazed, telling myself what I saw hadn't happened. Walsh shook me out of it and started telling me the guy had asked for it, that he likely had a piece, was high, along with all this other bullshit. At first I didn't know what he was talking about. Then I realized what he was doing."

"Leading you. Trying to get you to believe his story as true."

Dex's mouth twisted wryly. "Yeah. I don't know if he was hoping I'd be in enough shock to convince me, but it didn't work. I wasn't stupid, though. The only thing standing between him and a prison sentence was me."

Sloane stared at him. "You really think he would have killed you?"

"To be honest, I don't know. I'd like to think not, but the coldblooded way he shot that kid, I wasn't going to take any chances, especially since there were no witnesses around. He had a lot to lose. I played dumb. Said exactly what I knew he wanted to hear. I felt so sick, I nearly puked. When backup came, I... did what I had to do. The look he gave me when they cuffed him and put him in the back of that cruiser, I'll never forget it. It was the look of a man who never saw it coming."

"I'm sorry." Sloane motioned the bartender to bring Dex another two bottles. His partner had earned them. He'd help Dex home if he had to. Walsh deserved what he got, not just for his actions but for putting a man like Dex through that kind of hell. And for what?

"I knew it would probably be the end of my career, one way or another," Dex continued, "but if I went up on that stand and lied, I could never look at myself in the mirror again." A look of tired sadness passed over his handsome face, and Sloane yearned to have that smile back.

"Yeah, and we both know how much you enjoy looking at yourself in the mirror."

"Dick," Dex chuckled, giving him a playful punch in the arm. "By the way, that dude over there's been staring at your ass so hard. I think he's looking to relocate."

Sloane glanced over his shoulder at one of the pool tables, where some young guy in a faded rock band T-shirt and scruffy Eagles baseball cap was eyeing him. The guy smiled before one of the other guys in his group pulled him away. Sloane turned back to Dex with a shake of his head. "Not interested."

"Why? He's—"

"A chaser. I don't do fetishes."

"Wait, what? How do you know?" Dex discreetly peeked over Sloane's shoulder.

"His neck. Chasers get tattoos to mirror Therian marks on the right side of their necks. Thank God it was illegal for Humans to get tattoos on the left side, or it would make Therian identification more frustrating. Though he knew there were hard-core chasers out there who took the risk. "I don't hook up with guys who only want to be with me for what I am. Not even for the sex."

"Been there, done that, and all you got was a lousy T-shirt?"

Sloane grimaced. "Something like that. I would have preferred the T-shirt to the restraining order."

"Shit, that bad?" Dex's eyes went wide, and he leaned into Sloane, his cheeks flushed. Looked like his partner was well on his way to getting merry. Why the hell not.

"It was in college. This guy was really into me and I admit, I fell for what he was selling. It was hard not to. Not when he looked at me the way he did."

Dex propped his head on his hand, a sweet smile spreading across his face. "What way?"

Kind of like the way Dex was looking at him now. Only when Sloane thought about it, he'd never gotten that heated, excited type of feeling he got when Dex touched him. His breath had never hitched the way it did when Dex was close. "Like he didn't see me as some freak who might go feral at any moment and kill everyone. He looked at me like I was... I don't know how to describe it. It was a nice change. Anyway, we started dating, sleeping together, and then things started to get a little weird. It was gradual. It's not like one day he asked to put a saddle on me or anything."

Dex sputtered a mouthful of beer, wheezing as he tried to speak. "Fuck, man. Don't say shit like that when I'm drinking."

"I'm sorry." Sloane laughed, leaning toward Dex to pat him on the back as he hacked and coughed. "You okay?"

Dex nodded, his voice hoarse when he spoke. "Yeah, get back to the... you know, the thing." He swiped up a napkin and wiped his mouth.

"Anyway, it started off small. He'd ask a lot of questions about my Therian form, which was fine. I was used to that. Then he'd use weird phrases when we were in bed together." Sloane could feel his face getting red. "I can't believe I'm having this conversation with you."

"We could talk about *my* sex life."

"Yeah, so he'd say things like, um...." Sloane cleared his throat and leaned over. "If you laugh, I will beat the shit out of you."

"Okay. No laughing."

"He'd ask me to mount him and paw him. Then he wanted me to mark him."

Dex stared at him. "Like, *mark him*, mark him?"

"Yeah, and it got weirder, but what pushed me over the edge was when he asked me to shift so he could jack off on me."

Dex cringed. "Ooh, I can see how that might cause a rift in the relationship."

"No shit. We broke up after that. Then he started stalking me, so I filed a restraining order."

"What happened to him?"

Sloane shrugged. He'd been so relieved to get rid of the guy, he hadn't given it much thought after that. "He disappeared one day. Probably moved on to someone else."

"Wow."

"Yep." Sloane finished his beer, noticing Dex had gone quiet. He dared to glance over and saw his partner nearly busting at the seams. "Just do it."

Dex burst into fits of laughter, his face going red as he doubled over. Every time he tried to get a hold of himself or say something, he'd end up snorting and laughing again.

"I knew you were going to laugh." Sloane pursed his lips, his eyes on his partner, who he assumed was trying to say sorry but instead ended up sounding as if someone was letting air out of a balloon. The lights dimmed, the music blared, and people started heading for the dance floor. Dex jumped from his stool, and Sloane swiveled to face him.

"Ooh, they're playing my song."

"Seriously, this is your song?" He listened to the disco-styled melody, the drums thumping away before a high-pitched male voice started singing naughty lyrics.

"Not really, I just like it," Dex said, subtly moving his body.

"Wait, your dad said you didn't know any songs after 1989."

Dex let out a bark of laughter. "Oh my God, and you believed him?"

"Right, because it's such a farfetched notion," Sloane said, rolling his eyes.

"Well, he was joking. I simply prefer songs from before 1989, but I occasionally listen to something a little modern." He puckered his lips and gave Sloane a come-hither look. "Let's dance."

"Fuck off," Sloane said with a laugh. "I'm not dancing to this. Isn't this a song about turning tricks?"

Dex shrugged and started to move his ass in time to the music, singing at Sloane in a high-pitched voice about being a ghetto princess.

"I'll bet you are." Any other drunken guy, Sloane would have walked away, but for some obscure reason he couldn't understand, he leaned back, his arms folded over his chest as he watched Dex—not to mention permitted him to—shimmy closer. His head was telling him he should rein in his partner before the guy made an ass out of both of them, but the silly grin on Dex's face was making it difficult. Besides, it had been a rough day on all of them, and after his chat with Dex, he knew this was the first time in a long time the guy was getting to have a little fun.

"Come on, Daddy."

"No, and if you ever call me Daddy again, I'm going to kick your ass."

"Fine, be that way." Dex spun on his heels and threw his arms up. "Ladies! Dance floor!"

Sloane watched Dex shimmy his way to the dance floor with half a dozen women, including Rosa and Letty, joining him.

"Shit. Rookie's got moves." Ash put in his order at the bar, leaning against it while he waited. "If I knew he could pull like that, I'd have asked Maddock to bring him on sooner."

"I doubt Dex is going to agree to be your wingman," Sloane muttered, chuckling when Ash flipped him off, grabbed his beers, and strolled off. With a smile, Sloane went back to watching Dex and the easy way he moved his body. Two women sandwiched Dex; the one behind him grabbed his hips while the one in front of him slid her hand up his chest, both grinding their bodies against him as they danced. Dex lifted his arms and kept dancing, a sexy lopsided smile on his face. He was having the time of his life, not caring what anyone else had to say on the matter, or that the women were feeling him up. By the second chorus, he had a harem of women around him, and he gave each and every one a smile, took turns dancing with them, teased them, and made them laugh.

A yuppie kid in his late twenties sidled up to Sloane, his hands shoved awkwardly in his expensive trousers. "Hey."

Sloane didn't bother looking up. "Hey."

"That your boyfriend?" the guy asked, nodding toward Dex.

"What?" The idea that someone might have caught onto his definitely-not-a-crush, but too-many-sexual-thoughts-not-to-be-something thoughts had Sloane sitting up straight.

"Your boyfriend is hot."

Sloane shook his head. "He's not my boyfriend, he's my partner. I mean, work partner. We work together." *Smooth.*

Yuppie Guy's smile nearly split his face. "Oh, so you don't mind if I dance with him?"

"Go for it."

"Awesome sauce."

Sloane glared at the back of the guy's feathery brunet head as he walked away. *Awesome sauce? What was he, a teenage girl? Fucking asshat.*

Yuppie Guy infiltrated the harem, but they didn't seem to mind, dancing with each other as the guy pressed against Dex, threw an arm around him, and started grinding. Soon both of Yuppie Guy's hands had made their way down to Dex's ass, gripping tight, his lips inches away from Dex's. The guy's hands were all over him, at one point slipping under Dex's shirt and getting far too close to his crotch.

Sloane swiveled his chair around to face the bar and ordered a Coke. What he should have ordered were another couple of beers, maybe a shot or two. Looked like he'd end up getting that taxi home on his own after all. Not that he had expected anything with Dex, though he had enjoyed shooting the breeze. Dex was single, but Sloane doubted he would stay that way for long. He was smart, good-looking, and funny. After all the shit Dex had been through, he deserved a good guy. Someone to hold him close, laugh at his stupid quirks, and dear God, someone who could sit through a session of whatever eighties song popped into his little blond pinhead. The thought made him smile.

"I wouldn't let that one get away."

Sloane's head shot up to find the bartender leaning on the bar across from him.

"He likes you. A lot. You could tell by the way he looks at you."

"Yeah, well, that's not really the problem," Sloane said, his voice gruff. Was he actually going to play his violin to the bartender?

"Oh, you got someone?"

Sloane shook his head, his throat feeling thick. "No, I lost someone a little while back."

"Hey, I'm sorry, man." The guy leaned forward, his gaze sympathetic as he cocked his head to one side. He looked like he was thinking something over before he appeared to come to a decision. "I don't mean any disrespect, but I'm sure your guy would have wanted you to be happy. Think about it. You don't want to lose a good guy to an asshat like that." The bartender walked off, leaving Sloane staring after him. Well, at least he wasn't the only one who thought Yuppie Guy was a douche.

Ash bumped into him playfully. Looked like his best friend was already well on his way to passing out in the back seat of Cael's car again. "Hey, you okay?" he asked Sloane.

"Yeah."

"Dude!" Ash clapped a hand against his back, leaving a sting. Yep, well on his way to being shit-faced. "You should have seen it. Your boy got totally cockblocked by his own brother."

"What?" He didn't know why he was so surprised. It wasn't as if he knew what the brothers were like together other than what he'd gleaned from them at work. They were like a couple of kids at times. But

Dex never gave the impression his brother interfered in his sex life.

"Pretty boy was dragging Dex to the bathroom, all over him, and Cael marched up to him and sent him packing. I tell you, the squirt don't take shit from no one. Dex is right. He looks like this cute little puppy, but he's got one hell of a bite."

"Why would Cael do that?" Wait, did Ash call Cael cute? His friend was totally wasted.

Ash shrugged. "I don't know, man. To be honest, Dex is so fucked up he didn't even notice. Dude can dance, but he can't hold his alcohol for shit."

"Is Cael taking you home?" Sloane asked, patting Ash's bulging bicep. The guy was down to his undershirt, which in Ash-speak meant it was almost time to go. "Buddy, you really gotta stop stripping when you get drunk."

"It's hot," Ash replied with a pout. He pointed off somewhere over his shoulder. "Cael's got my jacket. And yeah, he's taking me home."

"You sure you don't want Calvin or Hobbs to take you?" Sloane had no idea how Cael even managed to get Ash to his front door every time. The kid was strong, but Ash was twice his size.

"Cael does fine. He parks in front of the house, sits there with me for a while, and then he wakes me up and helps me to the door." Ash gave him a lazy shrug. "He's good at tucking in."

Sloane's eyebrows nearly reached his hairline. "He tucks you in?"

"On the couch." Ash peered at him. "What?"

"Nothing." Sloane put his hands up, holding back a smile.

"Look, he's a cool guy. I like him. Not like, in a gay way, just, you know, he's a cool dude and I like hanging with him. That is possible. I can be friends with a gay guy and not be gay." Ash balled his hands into fists on the bar, and Sloane carefully put a hand to his friend's shoulder.

"Whoa, easy there, big guy. No one's arguing with you. Are you okay?"

Ash nodded, giving him a shaky smile. "Yeah, I think I had too much to drink." He looked to the pool tables, where Cael was laughing with Calvin. "I gotta go."

"Okay." He watched his friend stride off and deposit himself in a chair next to Cael. He threw his arm around him and leaned into him. Cael smiled at him and bumped his head playfully against Ash's. Crap, Sloane didn't get his answer.

"Hey, man, there ya are." Dex appeared next to him with a wide grin, his words coming out slurred. "I was lookin' fer ya."

Sloane smiled. "You found me."

"I did!" Dex exclaimed excitedly. He flung an arm around Sloane's shoulders and pressed his body up against Sloane's, making him shift uncomfortably. The guy's scent invaded his space, a heady mix of male, sweat, and Dex's shower gel. The longer Dex stood there, leaning against him, the more the scent seemed to intensify.

"What happened to your friend?" Sloane asked.

"Who?" Dex frowned, his brows drawn together in deep concentration.

"The one with his tongue down your throat."

"Oh, Chris. Kit? Craig?" Dex squinted thoughtfully then snapped his fingers. "Dan. I don't know. He left."

"That your type?" Sloane asked, trying to sound casual.

"Who, Craig? Nah, he was cute, but too young and too clean-cut." He teasingly scratched Sloane's stubble under his chin. "I like 'em scruffy."

Sloane arched an eyebrow at him. "That so?"

"Yeah. I always went for guys who were easy, not like sex easy—though I went for those too, but no baggage, you know?"

Sloane's jaw muscles tensed, and he looked down into his now watered-down Coke. "Yeah."

"But see, that right there?" Dex pointed at Sloane's face, his index finger gently prodding Sloane's cheek. "It's beautiful."

"What?" No one had ever referred to him or anything about him as being beautiful. They were too busy running for their lives.

"That pain you try to hide, every day. It does something," Dex said, putting his hand to his heart.

"I hope you haven't got some kind of fetish or something, because that's fucked up."

Dex shook his head. "Tonight you laughed. I made you laugh. Knowing what's in here, and that I could make you feel good, for a little while…. I was wrong to dismiss guys like you. You need love."

Sloane swallowed hard, not quite understanding what Dex was babbling on about, but feeling uncomfortable with where it was heading.

"Guys like you need love," Dex repeated. "*You* need love."

"You are so wasted."

"I am." Dex leaned into him and laid his head on Sloane's shoulder with a small sigh. "You got good shoulders for leaning on, you know that?"

"Not really. No one's ever leaned on me before." Most of his life he'd found himself leaning on others, until there was no one left to lean on except Ash.

"I'm leaning on you now."

Sloane worried his bottom lip for a minute before surrendering and letting his head rest against Dex's. He allowed his eyes to drift shut.

"You're a big softie," Dex murmured.

"I can kick your ass, remember?"

"Yeah, but that's because you're scared."

Sloane straightened and turned, intent on asking him what he was talking about. The loss of his shoulder caused Dex to fall into him, and on instinct, Sloane caught him. Their faces were so close, Sloane could smell the beer on Dex's warm breath.

"You moved," Dex murmured, his hand sliding around Sloane's waist to his back.

"Sorry." Sloane held Dex up, his head telling him to move the guy away, but his body having other ideas. His arms slipped around Dex, gently squeezing his partner to him. "You okay?"

Dex's brows furrowed, his gaze landing on Sloane's lips. "I'm not sure."

"Feeling sick?"

"Nope." Dex shook his head. "Tingly."

"Tingly? You're not having a heart attack on me, are you?" Sloane teased.

"I don't think so. My heart's beating fast, though."

Sloane swallowed hard, unsure of what to say when Cael's voice startled him. "Hey."

"He fell," Sloane blurted, pushing Dex away from him. A bemused smile came onto Cael's face.

"Okay. He's always falling. Anyway, I'm going to take Ash home. You mind taking my brother? Ash sort of takes up the whole back seat, plus it's in the opposite direction."

Sloane opened his mouth when Dex started singing what sounded like another cheesy eighties song.

"Good luck with that." Cael didn't even wait for a reply, simply gave Sloane's arm a pat and darted off. *The sneaky little bastard.* Dex continued to sing, humming the melody in places where he couldn't remember the lyrics. Sloane got to his feet and helped Dex onto his.

"What in the hell are you singing?"

"Eddie Money," Dex replied with a yawn.

"Who?"

"1989."

Sloane couldn't help but laugh. "You are the biggest dork I have ever met." He put an arm around Dex, waving goodbye to the rest of the team as he maneuvered his partner out of the club, apologizing to people along the way when Dex stopped to compliment someone on their shirt or shoes, or to steal a fry. His cheeky smile and wink earned him a giggle from the woman whose plate he stole from instead of a punch to the face. Sloane managed to get Dex out the front door and onto the sidewalk into the crisp October air. The garage was only a block over, but it took twice as long with Dex stopping to say hello to everyone who walked by.

Finally, inside the packed parking garage, Sloane helped Dex into the passenger seat before closing the door behind him and running around to get in behind the wheel. He adjusted the seat and stuck the key in the ignition.

"Okay, so where—"

Sloane inhaled sharply, his gasp cut short by Dex's mouth on his. The kiss caught him completely by surprise. It was hungry, hard, and tasted of beer. Every alarm he had in his head was going crazy, but instead of pushing the guy away, he gripped Dex tight and deepened the kiss, his mouth taking everything Dex was offering. Their breaths mingled, hot and heavy as desire slammed into Sloane. Dex got onto his knees with some difficulty, and before Sloane knew what the guy was up to, Dex was straddling his lap, his erection straining through his jeans and rubbing against Sloane's raging hard-on.

God, he tasted amazing, and his lips were so soft. Sloane's hands slipped down to Dex's waist and under his shirt. All that smooth, firm muscle under his hands had Sloane letting out a deep groan, one that traveled up from his depths. Dex took hold of his face, kissing him until they were both gasping for air. Sloane swallowed hard at the sight of Dex's kiss-swollen mouth, his face flushed and his pale blue eyes filled with lust. God, Sloane couldn't remember the last time he'd felt so alive.

"You're so fucking sexy," Dex breathed, his body giving off a scorching heat. He put his lips to Sloane's neck, kissing and licking, moving his way up to Sloane's ear.

"Dex…," Sloane murmured, trying to get ahold of himself. This was wrong in so many ways. First off, Dex was drunk off his ass. Second, they were only starting to tolerate each other. Third, they were part-ners. The list of why this was a terrible idea was an extensive one that kept growing with every touch of Dex's warm lips to Sloane's skin. "Dex," Sloane tried again, feeling Dex still against him. "Dex?" He placed a hand on Dex's back, feeling the steady rise and fall. "You've got to be kidding me. Dex, you man-child, I can't believe you."

With a heavy sigh, Sloane carefully moved his sleeping partner to the passenger seat. After placing his seat belt on him, Sloane sat back and studied him for a moment, telling himself this was a good thing. It saved him the trouble of hurting Dex's feelings, although if it happened again while Dex was sober, they'd have to discuss the matter. What they were going to discuss was beyond him. Chances were Dex wouldn't even remember any of this in the morning. Question was, did he want Dex to?

After turning on the car, he pulled out of the park-ing space and drove to the end of the lot when it hit him. He had no idea where Dex lived.

"Shit." He carefully nudged Dex's shoulder. "Dex, wake up."

Nothing. The guy was out for the count.

"Damn it." Screw it. He'd take Dex home. The guy could sleep on his couch. At this time of night, his apartment was less than ten minutes away. There was no point in bothering Cael, who probably had his hands full with Ash's drunken ass. The whole drive home, Sloane ran through various scenarios in his head of how he would deal with Dex if he remem-bered what happened a few minutes ago.

Why was he making it into such a big deal? It wasn't as if it would've led anywhere. They weren't going to have sex in the car in the middle of a parking garage. Sloane chastised himself. They weren't going to be having sex anywhere, never mind the car.

In eight minutes, he'd pulled up to a parking spot next to his apartment building. It looked like Dex's car wasn't going to get tucked in tonight. Now how the hell was he going to get the guy upstairs? Sloane unfastened his seat belt and leaned over to tap Dex's cheek.

"Hey, McClane, wake up."

Dex didn't stir.

"I am not carrying your ass, so you better wake up." He took hold of Dex's face and tilted it toward him. His lips were still swollen from their kissing, and without thinking about what he was doing, he leaned in and pressed his lips to Dex's. There was a faint groan and a shuddered sigh before Dex stirred. Brushing a few strands of fallen hair away from his brow, Sloane stared into sleepy eyes. "Hey. I need you to wake up enough to walk. Can you do that for me?"

"Mm," Dex hummed, pushing himself to sit up. Quickly taking advantage of Dex's semiconscious state, Sloane got out of the car, closed the door behind him, and ran around to Dex's side to help him get his seat belt off. Dex leaned into him, inhaling deeply.

"Smell good," he murmured, his eyes drifting shut.

"No. No falling asleep yet. Come on. On your feet, Agent Daley." To his amusement, Dex nodded and grabbed on to Sloane's arm, pulling himself to stand. Sloane locked up the car behind them and led Dex up the two sets of metal stairs, an arm wrapped around his waist. Arriving at the elevator, Sloane propped Dex against his hip as he pressed the button. A couple of near misses later—where Dex almost slipped out of his grip—they finally reached the seventh floor. He fished his keys from his pocket, unlocked his apartment, and got Dex inside. The guy was like a zombie, dead to the world but somehow still walking. At least he wasn't drooling.

With the front door secure, he dropped his keys into the little bowl on the table beside it and helped Dex through the dining room to the living room, to the plush black fabric couch. Sloane sat him down, tossing Dex's leather jacket onto one of the armchairs, and then he tried to lay Dex down on his back, but Dex twisted his body and flopped down on his stomach.

"Okay, then."

With a heavy sigh, Sloane crouched down to pull off Dex's Converse sneakers and put them on the floor next to him. He shifted Dex's legs up onto the cushions and stood back, watching as Dex let out a loud groan and turned over, his shirt riding up in the process to reveal flat abs and a thin blond happy trail that disappeared underneath the band of his underwear just visible from beneath the low-riding jeans. Dex flung an arm over his closed eyes, and his shirt rode up farther. This was a test, wasn't it, to see if Sloane would give in to temptation?

Well, he was stronger than that. He didn't care that Dex's lips were slightly parted as his chest slowly rose and fell, his stomach exposed, his other hand lying dangerously close to his crotch. Sloane's gut clenched, hit by another spark of desire. He'd been hoping what happened in the car had been a one-off, a momentary slip brought about by Dex catching him off guard.

What was wrong with him? To make matters worse, Sloane knew what Dex tasted like. He'd dug his fingers into Dex's skin, held him close for a few agonizing minutes. Sloane couldn't keep his brain from conjuring up images of Dex naked, in his bed with that amazing ass in the air. He shrugged out of his jacket, hung it on the hooks on the wall beside the door, and left his boots on the shoe rack underneath. When he walked back into the living room, his gaze fell on the photo frame on the bookshelf, and he stopped cold. A photo of him and Gabe with the team had his heart sinking to his stomach.

What was he doing? Walking up to the bookshelf, he picked up the photo. Gabe's smiling face sent a flash of remorse through him. Was he a terrible person for feeling attracted to Dex? He missed Gabe, no doubt about it, and he still loved him. There were times when he woke up in the middle of the night, rolled over, and before the haze of sleep wore off, could feel Gabe there in bed beside him.

Dex let out a soft groan, capturing his attention. Did he even feel something for Dex, or was he lonely? Had he really been so out of it that having someone make him laugh had him believing he was attracted to them? He returned the photograph of Gabe to the shelf, knowing what he had to do. He had to forget about Dex. It wasn't fair to either of them. Sloane wasn't ready for a relationship, and fucking around for sex wasn't going to be conducive to their working relationship. The thought was painful, but no more painful than the thought of another broken heart.

Chapter 10

CRAP. HE felt like warmed-over crap. Maybe a few more minutes in bed would help.

Dex rolled over and his bed disappeared from under him. He hit the floor with a painful thud and through his haze of confusion managed to roll over, a deep frown coming onto his face at the sight of an unfamiliar ceiling. Bolting upright was immediately regretted. He shut his eyes tight for a moment, willing the room to stop spinning and for the pulse in his brain to go away. When it was clear neither were ready to depart, he opened his eyes.

Where the hell was he? Shit, had he gone home with someone? He looked down at himself and figured being clothed and sleeping on a couch were good indications he hadn't had sex. Damn, why couldn't he remember how he'd gotten here and with whom? Slowly standing, he scanned his surroundings. The living room was hella nice. It had exposed brick walls with black shelving units running along the wall from floor to about waist height, where they turned into several large drawers. Books, framed pictures, and knick-knacks filled the units.

The furniture fit nicely with the loft's rustic look. There was the dark three-seater Dex had fallen off of, a dark wood coffee table in the center, and a dark love seat on the other side. Next to the coffee table to one side sat two light-colored armchairs, and behind the love seat, a long wood table with two lamps. The shelves across from him housed a vast collection of movies, along with a sweet flat-screen TV. On the far wall were two large windows, and he peeked out to find the apartment building had a great view. It was right on the High Line, which meant pricey. Wherever he was, it was tidy, clean, and elegant. From the corner of his eye, he caught a framed photo of his team.

Shit, he was in Sloane's apartment? What was he doing here? *Oh my God, please tell me I didn't try to sleep with him.* Not that Sloane wasn't absolutely and totally fuckable, but that would bring on all sorts of drama neither of them needed right now. He tried to remember last night. He'd been drunk, but not amnesia-inducing drunk. Taking a moment to calm himself, he sat down on the edge of the couch, mentally retracing his steps from the moment they'd left work.

Work! Holy shit, what time was it? He looked at his watch. "Oh my God!" It was past ten in the morning. "Sloane!" Dex jumped up, took one step, and toppled face-first into the carpet. "Son of a bitch." He gave his stupid sneakers a kick. "Sloane!"

There were a series of thumps from somewhere to the right, and then Sloane came through one of the doorways, Glock drawn.

Dex sat up, his eyes wide at the sight of Sloane in nothing but snug black boxer briefs and a loose gray V-neck shirt, his hair sticking up in every direction, looking like he was ready to kick some ass despite being in his undies. Fuck. That was hot. Sloane quickly scanned the room until he found Dex on the floor.

"What are you doing down there?" He put the safety on his gun before helping Dex to his feet.

"Uh, I tripped."

"You tripped?" Sloane gaped at him. "Is that why you're screaming bloody *fucking* murder?" Sloane whacked him in the arm. "You scared the shit out of me."

"Sorry." He remembered why he'd been screaming and grabbed Sloane's arms. "He's going to tear us a new one!"

"What? Who?"

"My dad. We're, like, three hours late!"

Sloane's lips broke into a smile before he started laughing. "Don't you think I would have woken you up? Jesus, Dex, I called Maddock this morning and let him know we were going to be in late." Sloane slid his Glock up on the highest shelf out of sight before walking off, chuckling.

"Wait, we can do that?"

"*I* can do that, but not often, so don't get used to it." Sloane motioned for him to follow and Dex did, happily, his eyes glued to Sloane's ass. Sweet Aunt Jemima, what he wouldn't give to have a piece of that tasty—

"You hungry?"

"Starved," Dex muttered, clearing his throat and tearing his gaze away. At the end of the living room was the dining room, and to the right, the kitchen. Dex came to a halt inside. It was as impressive as the rest of the loft, all exposed brick with wood floors, white cabinets with dark wood accents, and stainless steel appliances. In the center of the floor was a large white island counter with a white marble surface and three round stools. It looked… homey.

"Have a seat. I'll make us some coffee and breakfast bagels. We can eat on the way in."

Dex took a seat at the island counter. "You mean you'll make us some coffee and breakfast bagels, which we can eat here. On this nice wipeable surface," he said, petting the marble counter.

Sloane paused when it seemed to dawn on him. "Right. Car. Precious child."

"You're a fast learner. I like that." Dex gave him a wink and leaned his elbows on the counter as he watched Sloane move around the kitchen. "Your apartment is awesome."

"Thanks." Sloane flipped the switch on the fancy cappuccino/espresso machine, and soon the heavenly aroma of freshly brewed java filled the kitchen. He pulled out a pan and walked to the huge stainless steel fridge.

"How long have you lived here?"

"Since college," Sloane replied, pulling out a carton of organic eggs, milk, cream, and butter that he placed on the counter beside the fridge. "You like cheddar? Real cheddar, not that radioactive powder on your Cheesy Doodles trying to disguise itself as cheddar."

"Yes," Dex said with a chuckle. "College? Wow. Must have cost you a pretty penny."

"If that's your way of asking how I can afford a place like this, I don't." Sloane moved the ingredients closer to the pan. "The THIRDS paid for it." Sloane turned away from him, his rough tone telling Dex it wasn't something he was comfortable discussing, but he continued regardless. "It was part of the initial conscription package."

"Pretty sweet. Did they do that for all First Gen recruits?"

Sloane turned to him, his brows drawn together. "How'd you know about that?"

"Pearce mentioned something about it."

"Pearce?"

Crap. Nice going Dex. Way to stick your size tens in it. "Uh, yeah, Isaac Pearce."

"When was this?" Sloane put his hands to his hips, a deep frown on his face.

"A few weeks ago," Dex muttered, busying himself with the bowl of fruit on the counter. He took an apple and studied it. Anything not to look at Sloane and his angry laser-beam stare. "We met up for a drink."

"You two are friends?"

Dex tried to act casual, rolling the apple across the counter from one hand to the other. "No. We never really talked until the day of the trial. When I got jumped in the parking garage, he showed up, scared those assholes off. He asked me if I wanted to grab a coffee sometime."

"And you talked about me."

"I take it you two aren't on friendly terms?" Dex glanced up, bracing himself when Sloane snatched up the apple midroll and put it back in the bowl.

"No, we're not. Answer the question," Sloane ground out.

"You sort of came up."

"What did he say?"

Dex swallowed hard, when Sloane slammed a fist on the counter. "Damn it, Dex. What the fuck did he say?"

What the hell? Why was he being interrogated? "I don't really see how it's any of your business." So he was expected to tell Sloane everything while the guy told him absolutely nothing in return? Trust was a two-way street, and right now Dex resented having one of those lanes blocked.

"When it concerns Isaac Pearce, it is my business."

"Why? Because you were sleeping with his brother?" Dex snapped.

Sloane jerked back like someone had struck him, and despite feeling guilty for the sucker punch, Dex refused to back down now. "Yeah, that's sort of how I felt. You know, it would have been nice to hear it from you." Snapping himself out of his trance, Sloane tried to walk off, but Dex caught his arm and pleaded. "Were you ever going to tell me?" Sloane didn't respond. He pulled away and went to lean his arms against the counter next to the stove, his back to Dex.

Was it that difficult for Sloane to trust him? Had he given the guy any reason not to? Since joining the team, he'd tried damn hard every single day to connect with Sloane, to show him he wanted their partnership to work. That he was in it for the long haul and would be there if Sloane needed him. That he could depend on him. Isn't that what partners did? "I wasn't expecting you to weave me a tapestry. Just tell me you were involved. Maybe I would have understood why you hated me so much."

"I never hated you." Sloane shook his head. He spun around, eyes blazing. "I can't believe you went to Isaac behind my back!"

"How is it going behind your back when I didn't know who the guy was to you? We're supposed to be partners. We're supposed to trust each other. It *was* my business to know, Sloane, because Gabe wasn't just your partner. You were in love with him, still are, and he was killed on the job. And now it's my job, and I'm your partner, and…." He bit down on his bottom lip. And what? Did he have a right to be upset about this? Was it about trust or something else?

Sloane scoffed. "And what? Because you replaced him at work, you thought you could replace him in my bed? The parking garage and your little half-assed attempt to seduce me in the car last night were nice tries, but not enough to land you the position."

That stung a hell of a lot more than it should have. "Wow. Okay." Dex nodded, pressing his lips together, not trusting himself to speak, his heart feeling as if it was one tap away from crumbling to dust. He was such a fuckwit, putting himself in this position. Sloane's cutting remark had blindsided him to the point he couldn't even feel embarrassed about supposedly coming on to Sloane in the car last night.

Dex strode out of the kitchen and into to the living room, hearing Sloane cursing loudly from the kitchen. Sloane pissed him off, but not nearly as much as his own reaction. *Who the fuck does he think he is?* The knowledge that Sloane would think Dex was trying to slip into Gabe's place in his life made him feel sick to his stomach. Was that all Sloane saw when he looked at Dex? Was it the only reason he'd let his guard down, kissed him, allowed Dex to get close to him?

He pulled on his sneakers and snatched up his jacket, slipping into it. His keys were in his pocket, so he headed for what he assumed was the front door.

Sloane came out of the kitchen and caught his arm. "Dex, wait a minute."

He needed to get the hell out of here. "Let go of me."

"Not until you listen—"

"No, you listen," Dex spat out, shoving Sloane away from him. "I am not Gabe, and fuck you for thinking of me as nothing more than a piss-poor substitute."

"I never thought that," Sloane argued quietly.

"Don't treat me like an asshole. I deserve a little more respect than that." Dex threw open the door, found the elevator, and made his way downstairs. He rushed down two sets of stairs in the rain. Fucking icing on the cake. When he got down to the bottom step, his day was completed.

"Fuck me," Dex grumbled. He was too hung over for this shit, and he hadn't even had coffee yet. "What the hell are you doing here?"

Ash eyed him suspiciously. "I could ask you the same thing."

"Come on, Ash. You're a big boy. What do you think I'm doing here?"

Ash marched up to him, and Dex was waiting for the guy to lay a finger on him. He was almost disappointed when Ash didn't. "What are you playing at, Daley? He doesn't need this in his life right now."

"What are you, his nanny? What would you know about what he needs? Or maybe you got a little crush going on you don't want him to know about? Is that it? You got something else you're hiding in your closet next to your AK-47 and knitted Christmas sweaters?"

"Fuck you, man. Sloane's like a brother to me. How would you feel if your brother lost the love of his life, and then some asshole walks in trying to fuck with his head?"

"You know what?" Dex threw his hands up. "I don't need your shit right now." He stepped down onto the sidewalk when something hard socked him in the head, the unexpected blow momentarily stunning him. For a split second, he thought maybe Ash had finally lost it and punched him, but when he put his fingers to his brow, he felt it sticky wet. The rain fell harder, washing the blood from Dex's fingers and down the side of his face. At his feet, a rock lay smeared with his blood.

"Shit, you okay?" Ash put a hand to his shoulder. "What is that?"

Dex's head shot up at the sound of skidding tires, and in the street was a guy wearing a hoodie and a baseball cap, sitting on a dirt bike laughing at him. The last of Dex's patience snapped. "You little shit!"

The guy took off down West Sixteenth Street, and Dex gave chase, careful not to get hit by a car as he ran across Tenth, sticking to the sidewalk since he was running up incoming traffic. He'd had about enough of being pushed around, of being made a fool of. He sprinted after the punk as fast as he could, swiping his hair to one side as the pouring rain plastered it down against his face. A small part of him hoped the little prick hit a pothole and ate asphalt. That'd teach him not to be such an asshole. The punk got lucky, the red light on Eleventh halting traffic. Dex sped up, following the guy onto the bike path toward the Chelsea piers. The red gate to the pier was open, and the bastard skidded as he made a sharp left onto the wooden dock. Dex didn't bother to slow down. The little shit was about to run out of dock. At the end, the guy made a right and Dex followed.

He wished he hadn't.

His eyes widened and he spun around in the hopes of running back to where he'd come from. But it was too late. This was going to hurt.

THE DOORBELL rang and Sloane finished buttoning his jeans before running over. He hoped it was Dex so he could apologize for acting like such a dick. After Dex stormed out, Sloane had paced his living room, wondering how he was going to fix this. He had to, after the shitty thing he'd done. How could he accuse Dex of trying to replace Gabe? He'd been so wrapped up in his own pain and his guilt for his attraction to Dex, he'd let his fear bubble up to the surface and then blamed Dex for it. God, he was such a shitty partner and friend, if Dex even considered him a friend. Sloane hadn't exactly done anything to deserve the title. He threw open the door, frowning when he found Ash there instead.

"Oh, it's you."

"You don't gotta sound so happy about it," Ash grumbled, stepping inside and shaking the water off his jacket onto the welcome mat.

"Sorry, I was expecting someone else."

"You mean Dex?" Ash arched an eyebrow at him and waited, but not very long. "What was he doing here?"

Sloane closed the door behind him. "Cael asked me to take Dex home, but he was out of it. I realized too late that I didn't know where he lived, so he crashed on my couch."

"And you couldn't call Cael?"

"It was late and I was tired, not to mention he was busy with you. What's the problem, Ash?" Today was turning into one hell of a clusterfuck.

"Did you sleep with him?"

"What?" Sloane stared at his friend. "What the hell, man? Is that why you came over, to ask me if I'm fucking my partner?" How long had Ash been thinking this? How could his friend think it? He was the only one who'd known about Gabe, the only one who knew everything about Sloane.

"I came over because I was worried. When Maddock said you'd called in, I knew something was wrong. You never call in. Now I know why." Ash's expression grew stern. "Well, did you?"

"No," Sloane replied through his teeth. "I did not fuck my partner."

"But you wanted to." It was more a statement and less a question, which Sloane didn't appreciate. Mostly because Ash was right, and they both knew it.

Sloane folded his arms over his chest. "You have five seconds to tell me what you want."

"Fine. I thought I should let you know your lunatic of a partner went running after some punk on a bike." Ash dug into his pocket and pulled out a rock. Sloane stiffened, his heart hammering when he saw faint blood stains. "Hit him in the head with this. He's okay. Bled some, but nothing serious."

Sloane grabbed his boots from the shoe rack. "Jesus, Ash, and you didn't think to go with him?"

"He was fine. Besides, he can handle himself. It was some little prick. If you ask me, the guy deserves to get the shit kicked out of him for being a fucking Eagles fan."

"Wait, what?" Sloane's stomach plummeted. He grabbed Ash's shoulders. "What did this guy look like?"

"About five nine, five ten, scruffy jeans, black hoodie, some lameass band T-shirt, and a stupid Eagles cap."

"Shit. That guy was at the bar last night. Call for backup!" Sloane threw his boots off and started stripping. He didn't know what the hell was going on, but it couldn't be a coincidence. Had Eagles Cap guy followed them home? Had he been watching them? How else would he know where to find Dex?

"Are you going to shift?"

"Dex is in trouble! And track him. He was wearing his com when he left." As he quickly removed all his clothes, he prayed Dex was okay. He had to be.

Oh God, what if he got there and Dex was…. He couldn't think that. He couldn't think about anything else other than getting to Dex. As he stripped down completely, hearing Ash on his cell phone behind him, Sloane closed his eyes, took a deep breath, and forced his Human side to retreat. His muscles tensed and pulled, his teeth gritted against the agonizing pain as his Therian side tore through him, clawing and twisting to come out. His vision blurred before it

became sharper, his sense of smell intensifying as his
mass shifted, his skin stretched and contracted, his fur
piercing his flesh as it surfaced.

As the pain deepened, all he could think about
was Dex. *Please let me get to him in time.*

DEX HAD taken two of the thugs down before
half a dozen more jumped him. He had enough time
to tighten his abs when the baseball bat collided with
them, knocking the wind out of him. He doubled over
and fell to his knees, hugging his abdomen. They
didn't give him a chance to get up, the bat hitting him
on his back and sending him sprawling forward. He
curled in on himself, protecting his head, the coppery
taste of blood in his mouth as they kicked him in the
ribs.

"Stay away from the HumaniTherians case, Da-
ley." It was the jerk he'd stupidly followed right into an
ambush. How the hell had the guy found him? *Smart
move, Dex.* "And stay away from Sloane Brodie."

"What?" Dex wheezed when the baseball bat collided with his arm. He let out a sharp cry, the pain in
his side almost as bad as the one in his head. His face
throbbed from where it had rubbed against the wood-
en planks of the pier when he'd hit it the first time.
He felt sick, and he knew the only reason he hadn't
thrown up was because his stomach was empty. He'd
promised Sloane he'd fight back, and he had, at first.
They didn't want to kill him, only beat the shit out of
him. He was so tired of getting beat up.

There was no point in asking questions. These
guys had been paid to hurt him, to warn him off. They
clearly didn't know him. Dex tried to move despite his

bruised and battered body, but he didn't get anywhere, a boot clamping down on his back and slamming him back into the pier. Dex sputtered rainwater, gasping as his lungs struggled to take in air. A roar shook the windows around them, and a large black body appeared in the distance. He couldn't see very clearly, but he didn't have to. He smiled through the sharp sting on his lip.

"You're all fucked now," Dex murmured as the black mass swiftly approached. He heard the thugs cursing and making a run for it, scrambling away as fast as they could in all directions. Sloane sped past, his roars and hisses echoing in Dex's ears. There were sharp cries and pleas, and although Dex knew Sloane wouldn't kill anyone, his partner wasn't against delivering a few permanent scars.

His lids grew heavy as his world filled with sirens and shouting. Defense agents with rifles flooded out of trucks; HPF officers scoured the perimeter, guns in hand. His partner hadn't just brought the cavalry out for him, but the whole fucking army. Something huffed over Dex, and he reached up, barely aware of how badly his hand was shaking. Sloane appeared before him, and despite the pain it brought to his lips, Dex couldn't keep from smiling when his partner put his muzzle to his hand, his chainsaw-like purr sending vibrations down Dex's arm.

Despite his blurred vision and the darkness that crept in around him, Dex couldn't understand how anyone could hate such a beautiful soul. He rolled slightly back, his whole body searing with pain as he shivered violently. Then all at once he was warmer. Sloane lay against him, his tail curled protectively over Dex's legs, his fur and mass emanating warmth. He laid his head gently against Dex's. A raindrop landed awkwardly in Sloane's ear, and it twitched as if he were nothing more than a big house cat. Somewhere close by, he could hear Ash calling out to him, telling him to hang on, that help was coming.

"Not the Therian! He's a THIRDS agent!" Ash shouted. "That's his partner! Round up those assholes in the truck, and don't worry about being gentle. What's that? Oh, he wants to bitch about being clawed? Bring him here. I'll give him something to really bitch about!"

Sloane's ears went flat and he bared his teeth, hissing at the paramedics as they cautiously approached. Ash ran over and crouched down in front of them. He put his hand to Sloane's head, receiving a soft mewl.

"Sloane, come on, buddy. Dex needs medical attention. You gotta let them do their thing. They're here to help him."

Sloane huffed and turned his head to Dex, nudging him, a soft growl escaping him. Dex put his hand to Sloane's nose and smiled. "'S'okay." A wide pink tongue licked at his hand, and Dex scrunched his nose. His voice was hoarse when he spoke. "Ew, that's gross, man."

Sloane closed his eyes, his muzzle wrinkling before he stood and padded to one side. Dex kept his eyes on him as the paramedics made their assessment before moving him onto a gurney, causing him to cry out at the pain when someone hit a sore spot. Sloane let out a thunderous roar, and Dex put a hand out to quiet him. The last thing he saw before he blacked out was bright amber eyes watching over him.

"THIS IS all my fault."

Despite being in a private room that resembled a bedroom more than a hospital room, Sloane still couldn't feel at ease. Normally, he wouldn't have stepped foot inside one of these places, but they'd brought Dex to the New York Presbyterian Hospital, the THIRDS' preferred medical facility. There were some perks to working for his organization, and outstanding medical treatment was one of them. It wasn't the service, however, that made Sloane anxious, but the deep-rooted anxieties it brought out in him. Still, he couldn't leave Dex. He had to know his partner was okay. He had to apologize, had to.... God, he didn't know what he had to do. He knew he'd fucked up, and now Dex was lying in a hospital bed. How was Sloane going to face Maddock and Cael knowing he'd let this happen?

"Hey, stop for a second." Ash took hold of his shoulders, stopping him from pacing a hole in the pristine carpet. "Are you okay?" He motioned around them. "In here, I mean."

Sloane breathed in deep and let it out slowly. He appreciated Ash's attentiveness. "I'm fine." He wasn't. Not by a long shot. But he couldn't leave. He deserved this for what he'd done. Dex had been nothing but supportive, making him smile, laugh, making him feel things he hadn't felt in so damn long, and what had Sloane given him in return? A lump formed in his throat at the sight of Dex under the white sheets, his tan skin covered in ugly bruises, cuts, and scrapes. The medical staff had taken X-rays, and the doctor confirmed there was nothing broken or torn. There was some swelling, and Dex would be in a lot of pain for a couple of weeks. Most surprising of all was when the doctor stated the assailants had gone easy on Dex. Like they were trying to hurt him but not cause any real damage. It was unlike any assault he'd ever come across.

"Oh my God!"

The heartbroken expression on Cael's face hit Sloane hard, and he found himself unable to do anything other than watch Cael rush to his brother's bedside. He reached for Dex's face, then hesitated. There was a nasty bump on his brow from where the rock had hit him, and despite the amount of blood it had let out, it hadn't needed any stitches. There was a small cut over his nose, nasty scratches down the right side of his face, his bottom lip was bruised at the corner, and there was another bruise on his left cheek. In the end, Cael opted for gently brushing Dex's hair away from his brow.

"What happened?" Cael asked, his voice so low it was almost a whisper.

"Dex crashed on my couch last night. I was going to take him home, but he passed out in the car, and I didn't know where he lived. Anyway, we had an argument this morning and he left. I thought he'd gone in to work when Ash showed up." He and Ash had given their statements to Recon agents as soon as they'd arrived at the hospital. That had been difficult when all Sloane had wanted was to be at Dex's side. But there wasn't much else he could do while the medical staff wheeled Dex away for emergency treatment to rule out any internal hemorrhaging, swelling, or broken bones.

Ash recounted everything that had happened while he'd stood outside with Dex, and Sloane confirmed it. "I remember the guy from the bar. Dex actually pointed him out. Thought he was interested in me. Now I know he was interested in something else. I gave Recon a description, and they're getting Intel to run it through Themis. Soon as they get a hit, they're putting an APB out. Defense agents are putting the screws on the guys who didn't get away."

Cael nodded, and Sloane stepped up to him, tentatively putting a hand on the younger Therian's shoulder. "I'm so sorry, Cael. I should have looked after him better." Cael shifted his gaze to Sloane; the anger in his eyes was expected, but when Cael spoke, Sloane had expected that anger to be directed at him.

"It's not your fault. You're his partner, not his babysitter. He's a fucking THIRDS agent, for Christ's sake. He knows better!" Cael shook his head, tears in his eyes. "He's always doing stupid shit like this. He gets hurt or pissed off, and instead of doing something about it or talking to someone, he keeps it all inside until he ends up doing something fucking stupid. Asshole."

"Hey." Sloane drew Cael into his arms and hugged him close. "It's okay. He's going to be okay. I know it looks bad, but it's mostly bruising. The doctor gave him a sedative so he could rest."

"What about the next time?" Cael replied hoarsely. "Dad's going to be so pissed at him. Good. He deserves an ass-kicking." He pulled back and wiped at his eyes with his hoodie's sleeve.

Seeing Cael like this, out of his uniform, looking so vulnerable and small, he was reminded how young

Cael was and how much responsibility Sloane now carried. He'd failed to protect Cael's big brother. The way the kid looked up to Dex, the admiration in his eyes, the way he looked out for him, boasted about him…. Sloane had forgotten that kind of love existed.

"I'm gonna go get him some coffee for when he wakes up, or he'll start bitching," Cael grumbled, leaving the room.

Sloane let out a heavy sigh and dropped down into the pale green two-seater beside Dex's bed.

"Stop it." Ash walked over and dropped down next to him, putting an arm around him.

"Ash, he was pissed off I didn't tell him about me and Gabe."

After some thought, Ash shrugged his large shoulders. "It was your decision to make."

"Yeah, but he's my partner. I should have trusted him. Instead he had to hear it from that prick, Isaac." Out of all the people who could have walked into the garage to help Dex, why did it have to be Isaac Pearce? Sloane was grateful the guy had shown up when he did, but out of all the other HPF officers who had most likely been in that courthouse, why him?

"Wait, Dex knows Isaac?"

"Kind of. He helped Dex out, then invited him for a drink."

Ash hummed. "Did Dex say what they talked about?"

"Other than him telling Dex about Gabe, I have no idea. I don't even know why he would tell Dex anyway. What does Dex have to do with it, other than he's my new partner?"

"Probably looking to stir shit up. The guy's a royal jackoff." Ash removed his arm from around Sloane and sat forward to look at him. "What's going on?"

Sloane sat back. "I'm fine."

"Really? Because this…." He motioned at Sloane in general. "This doesn't look like fine. It looks a lot like trouble. He's not Gabe."

"I know that," Sloane snapped, irritated. If he'd only acknowledged that in the beginning, none of this would have happened. "Dex is nothing like Gabe." The two were as different as night and day. Gabe with his dark eyes, his shy smile and quiet laugh, always calm and collected. He'd always known what he'd wanted and how to get it. Dex was confident, but a good deal of the time, he hid his insecurities behind his smile and jokes. He was a charmer, hot-blooded, and full of life. Vibrant, loud, and enthusiastic. Gabe had made Sloane feel secure, appreciated, loved. Dex made him feel like his body was on fire from the inside out, as if he was the only guy in the room. The way he looked at Sloane… was as if all he could see were the good things in him, as if the terrible, frightening, ugly parts didn't exist.

There was a low groan, and Sloane jumped to his feet as Dex's eyes slowly fluttered open. "Hey, you're awake." He reached out to take Dex's hand but Dex moved it away, scratching the back of it where the IV was.

"Damn this is itchy." His voice was raspy and groggy, but it was music to Sloane's ears.

Sloane couldn't help his smile. "Yeah, they're pretty annoying. I'm glad you're awake. How do you feel?" Dex arched an eyebrow at him and Sloane cringed. "Right. Dumb question." He bit his bottom lip and decided the hell with it. "I'm sorry, Dex. I'm so sorry."

"No," Dex said firmly, his mouth in a tight line.

Sloane braced himself. He would take whatever Dex threw at him. It was the least he deserved.

"Don't you dare blame yourself for this. I was stupid. I didn't use my head."

Wait, was Dex reassuring him? After everything he'd done? "Yeah, but if I hadn't been such a complete jerk, you wouldn't have left, and—"

"And they would have come after me somewhere else."

"When I saw you there on the pier, bleeding…." His heart did a little flip when Dex smiled up at him. How was it the guy always knew what to say or do where Sloane was concerned?

"Hey, one thing you'll learn about me is I have a pretty thick skull, and as you've probably noticed, I get beat up a lot. Like, more than is normal. It must be my charm. It brings all the boys to the yard. I would teach you, but I'd have to charge."

Sloane felt the back of his eyes sting, but he quickly pushed that sentiment away. "You're such an ass. I'm glad they didn't damage your cheesy sense of humor."

"Hey, Dex."

Dex shifted his gaze to Ash, his smile pleasant. "Simba."

Ash looked unimpressed. "I should pull the plug. Put you out of your misery."

"You don't need to pull the plug for that, just cover your face. I think there's a bedpan around here you could use. Probably less full of—"

"Dex!" His partner had the ever-living shit kicked out of him, yet was fine enough to continue his little feud with Ash. Amazing.

"Sorry," Dex murmured.

"Ha!"

Sloane gave Ash a sidelong glance of utter disbelief. "Really?"

"Sorry."

Casting his best friend one last warning glare, Sloane turned back to Dex. "Hey, I know you're feeling like shit right now, but what can you tell me about what happened?" Dex patted the bed, looking for the tiny remote, and Sloane slid it into his reach, waiting as the bed slowly raised Dex into a sitting position. The fact that Dex sucked in a sharp breath and winced with the bed's leisurely pace gave Sloane an idea how much pain he was in. Sloane expected the doctor would prescribe some hefty painkillers. When the bed finally reached its destination, Dex started talking.

"I didn't realize the guy was the same one from the club until it was too late. Also, I was stupidly too worked up to pay attention like I should have been. It was a warning. He told me I needed to back off the HumaniTherians case…." Dex bit his bottom lip, his gaze darting to Ash and back.

Ash held his hands up. "Fine. I'll be outside, but keep in mind, Maddock's gonna be here soon."

Sloane thanked his friend, turning his attention back to Dex. "What is it?" Dex didn't shy away from his gaze when he spoke.

"He told me to stay away from you."

"None of this makes any sense. We've been working the HumaniTherians case for months before you were recruited. Why the warning now? And why you?"

"And what does it have to do with you?" Dex shook his head with a groan. "This felt... odd."

Sloane cocked his head to one side. "What do you mean?"

"It felt like, I don't know, like the time in the garage."

"You think it was the same guys who arranged this?"

"I don't think so. That had been about the trial, this was about this case. But it had the same feeling, like it was…. This is going to sound crazy, but almost, friendly."

"You're right, that does sound crazy." Sloane recalled the doctor's words. "But now that you mention it, the doctor said something about this being one of the strangest assaults he'd ever seen. They didn't cause any real damage, as if they'd been specifically instructed not to really hurt you."

Dex's eyes widened. "Well, they did fucking hurt me, hurt me a lot if you haven't noticed."

"You know what I mean. They could have killed you, Dex, or put you in a fucking coma. Instead they banged you up, warned you to stay away. This was done by someone who knows you, maybe not personally, but they know who you are."

The air seemed to have been sucked out of the room when Sloane's words sank in. Shit, someone Dex knew had paid to warn him off.

"I think we need my dad here," Dex said.

Sloane walked to the door and poked his head out. Ash was sitting in the seat next to the door, his arm around Cael's shoulders, comforting him. "Hey, Ash."

Ash shifted to look up at him. "Yeah?"

"Can you call Maddock? We need him to get over here, now."

"Everything okay?"

"Yeah, call him up for me, will you?"

Ash looked uncertain but nodded. Sloane thanked him and went back inside to let Dex know, but in the meantime, now that he knew Dex was out of danger, he could address his frustration. He sat at the edge of the bed, glowering at him.

"I can't believe you took off after that guy. What the hell were you thinking?"

"I was thinking the fucker threw a rock at my head, it hurt, and now I'm going to kick his ass."

"And look how well that turned out," Sloane drawled, gently reaching out to inspect Dex's brow. "You scared the shit out of me, Dex." His gaze came to rest on Dex's questioning look when the door to the room burst open and Maddock stormed in.

"I was parking when Ash called. Came as soon as I could." Maddock kissed the top of Dex's head, and Sloane was reminded once again of his sergeant's other life. How did Maddock do it? Watch his kids go off into the fray every day and not worry himself shitless?

"I'm okay," Dex groaned at his dad's fussing.

"Ash told me what happened. I want to tear you a new one right now for running after that punk, but…." Maddock let out a heavy sigh. "I'm glad you're okay. I spoke to HQ. The guys we got locked up all say the same thing, that they were hired by some guy in an Eagles baseball cap just this morning and instructed

on where to be. They were told to get you on your own
and beat you, but be careful with you, which we all
agreed made no fucking sense. Themis got a hit on our
guy in the baseball cap. Ford Wallace. He's got priors.
Assault with a deadly weapon, armed robbery, theft,
among a host of other things. Themis has surveillance
of Wallace leaving the bar shortly after the both of you
last night. There's more footage of him following you
to Sloane's apartment. He was smart. Kept a good distance. Unfortunately we haven't been able to locate
any feeds close enough to Sloane's place to catch him.
It's likely he followed you both home and waited for
you. Don't know what he would have done if you'd
both left the apartment at the same time. Recon is
searching for him now. What do you remember?"

Dex looked over at Sloane, who nodded his okay.
They had to get down to the bottom of this. Just when
they thought this case couldn't get any worse.

"They warned me to stay away from the HumaniTherians case and from Sloane."

"Sloane?" Maddock's frown deepened as he
turned his attention to Sloane. "What the hell's any of
this got to do with you?"

"I don't know. We're thinking whoever warned
Dex off knows him or who he is. And for some reason
doesn't want Dex involved." Sloane heard Dex gasp.

"Isaac Pearce."

"Hold up." Maddock threw a hand up. "Gabe's
brother? What's going on, Dex?"

Sloane knew Dex wouldn't out him—so to
speak—but any time Gabe came up, Sloane feared
the truth would come out. Nothing could stay buried

forever, and often he felt as though he was biding his time until all his secrets escaped.

"Now I could be wrong, and the guy seems decent enough, but I feel I should run this past you. See what your take is. When I got jumped in the garage, out of all the garages close to the courthouse, of all the HPF officers, why was he the one to show up? I don't think he had anything to do with the attack, but what if he'd been watching me? What if he was trying to earn my trust?" Dex's brow creased with worry, and Sloane was glad to see his partner was on the same page as him. He listened intently as Dex went on. "At the time, he asked me if I wanted to grab a coffee. I told him. The guy turned me no. A few weeks later, he calls up. We meet up for a beer, and here I'm thinking he wants to shoot the shit, you know? Instead he starts asking me if I've seen Sloane's file."

Maddock and Sloane replied simultaneously. "What?"

Dex glanced from one to the other. "That was creepy."

"Just get on with it," Maddock said.

"Right. So he starts telling me that, uh…." Dex trailed off, smoothing his blanket, clearly uncertain of how he was going to proceed.

"Dex," Sloane warned quietly, leaning his arms on the bed to meet his partner's concerned gaze. "If there's a possibility Isaac Pearce has something to do with what happened to you on the docks, or God forbid, this case, we need to know about it."

"You're right," Dex sighed. "He said he's seen your file."

"How?"

"I don't know. He said he pulled in a favor. He was kind of nervous, like he wasn't sure whether he should be talking to me about it. Anyway, he kept going on about how there was nothing in there about you from before the THIRDS."

Sloane straightened, doing his best to keep his anger in check. "He told you I couldn't be trusted. That's why you asked me if there was something about my past you should know about. And why you mentioned the part about my being a First Gen. He put the idea in your head. Let me guess, he started going on about spending years looking into my file, how he couldn't come up with anything, how I was trying to hide something, how the THIRDS was trying to hide something."

Dex's jaw dropped. "How did you know?"

"Because he said the same thing to Gabe." Sloane balled his hand into a fist and wished he could punch something.

"Take it easy, son." Maddock eyed him intently.

Sloane nodded, taking a deep breath. He concentrated on controlling his breathing. It really wouldn't do anyone any good for him to lose his shit right now. "Sorry, Sarge. I'm good." That son of a bitch. The guy couldn't stop meddling in his life even with Gabe gone.

Maddock appeared to be considering everything carefully. "So he helps you out, tries to gain your trust in order to get you to distrust your partner and maybe put some distance between you two, but when that doesn't work, he pays some punks to work you over, to see if this time you'll back off? I still don't get what Sloane has to do with the HumaniTherians case. And if we're considering Pearce is somehow involved with the murders, there's nothing to back it up. Our suspect is a Therian, and there's absolutely no evidence suggesting he's working with an accomplice, much less a Human one."

Sloane took a seat, shaking his head. "Look, I know the guy's an asshole, and no one dislikes him more than me, but he's still Gabe's brother and a cop. I've known him for years. I can't imagine him doing something like this." He couldn't believe he was defending Isaac Pearce after the hell the guy had put him through. Isaac had always resented Sloane dating his brother. The two argued constantly over it. But being a Grade A asshole did not a murderer make.

"We need to tread really carefully on this," Maddock stated, walking around Dex's bed to sit beside Sloane. "If Isaac is involved, we can't do anything to send him underground, and if he's not our guy, we need to make sure we don't fuck it up. If the HPF gets wind we're accusing one of their respected detectives, a guy whose brother we lost on our watch, and he's innocent, they will rain a shitstorm down upon us the likes of which we've never seen. And with this case still unsolved, the Chief of Therian Defense will have all our nuts mounted on his wall."

"So what's our next move?" Dex asked.

Maddock and Sloane looked up at the same time. Sloane did his best not to smile, not if he didn't want to get his ass kicked by both Maddock and Dex. He was so glad he wasn't about to be on the receiving end of whatever was about to come out of Dex's mouth.

"Our?" Maddock rose to his feet, his stance imposing. Oh boy. This was going to be good. "*My* next move is to tactfully look into Isaac Pearce's where-abouts during the murders and either bring him in or rule him out as a suspect. I'll also be getting the rest of the team to bring in that bastard who assaulted you. *Your* next move is to go home until you can get your-self to the toilet without losing a spleen."

Sloane braced himself.

"*What?* You've got to be fucking kidding me!" Dex squawked. "You're going to bench me? Right in the middle of the fucking game? You can't do that!" He tried to sit up and winced. "Ow." Gritting his teeth, he glared at his dad.

"You bet your ass I'm benching you, Daley. Your body got used for batting practice. You need to recuperate."

Dex let out a loud frustrated groan. "Fuck me in the aaaass!"

"Keep your sex life out of this."

Sloane tried his damn hardest not to laugh. At times he wondered if Dex really was adopted because the two were so alike, it was scary. Well, Maddock was a lot grumpier than Dex, and his delivery was al-ways deadpan, but watching them together was some-thing else.

"Ha, ha." Dex frowned. "See this?" Dex pointed to his face. "This is my not amused face. Actually, this is my *I can't believe my own dad is benching me* face! You… you…."

Maddock lifted a brow. "If you think you're too old for me to give you a good butt-whooping, I will be more than happy to remind you that's not the case."

"Argh! Forget it. Fine." Dex pouted like a petu-lant child. "This freakin' sucks."

"Sloane's going to stay with you."

Oh crap.

"You're giving me a nanny?" Dex turned his glare on Sloane.

"Boy, please. Who do you think you're talking to? I raised you." Maddock faced Sloane, his face grim. "You know how many times I caught him climbing out his window when he was a kid?"

Nope, but Sloane was pretty sure he was about to find out.

"Enough times for me to get burglar bars installed on his *and* his brother's bedroom windows. You keep an eye on him, you hear me. He is one slippery little bastard. The minute your back is turned, he will be halfway across town or ass up in your neighbor's rosebushes."

"Oh my God, one time and you're branded for life," Dex moaned, letting his head fall back against the pillow. "Ow."

"I don't want to hear another word about it."

"Fine," Dex grumbled. "How long?"

"Until I say so."

Dex held up a finger. "I have a request."

"Denied."

"You don't know what it is. Hear me out. It hurts." Dex sat up again, his pout in full effect, and his shoulders slumped. He tilted his head to one side, eyes slightly wide. Oh he was good. Sloane would give him that. Not even Maddock was immune to that face.

"Lord, give me strength. Fine. What is it?"

"I'd like Sloane to wear one of those sexy male nurses' uniforms, the white latex ones with the assless chaps."

"Sweet little baby Jesus." Maddock turned to Sloane and cringed, most likely due to the terrified look on Sloane's face. "I'm sorry. I'll make it up to you, I promise. I'll get you some extra vacation time or something."

"I don't think there are enough days in the year," Sloane muttered, ignoring Dex's wide grin.

"The doctor should be along shortly to release him. If you need anything, give us a ring. I'll make sure you're kept up to speed. I'm also going to put a couple of agents outside the house, just in case. I don't care if you need to zip-tie him to the bed, you make sure he takes it easy." Maddock headed for the door, calling out over his shoulder. "Dex, you behave yourself or I'm docking your pay."

"You can't do that!" Dex looked to Sloane. "Can he do that?"

When the door closed, Dex let out a sigh of relief. "Don't worry, I'll tell him you're doing a great job. He'll never know."

With a sly smile, Sloane made himself comfortable on the two-seater. "Nope. I'm going to take you home and make you something to eat, and you're going to lie down, take painkillers, sleep, and then eat some more. And so help me, you're going to let me take care of you and like it."

"Let me guess, or you'll kick my ass?"

Sloane shrugged. "Seeing as how that's already happened, I'm going to go with annoy the living bejesus out of you." If he had to suffer through this, so did Dex. Just because he'd agreed to take care of his partner, didn't mean he was going to allow Dex to wrap him around his little finger with those pouty lips and big blue eyes.

"Like you're doing now?"

"I learned from the best."

Dex narrowed his eyes. "The force is strong with this one."

Sloane laughed. "All right there, Yoda."

"Please," Dex scoffed. "We both know I'd be Han. You can be Luke."

"Okay, Han."

"Ash would be Vader. Ew, Ash would be your dad." Dex chortled at his own joke, then sucked in another sharp breath. "Ow."

Oh God, Sloane let his head fall back against the love seat. Why did he get the feeling he was going to be the one in pain?

Chapter 11

SLOANE DIDN'T know who was going to end up in traction by the end of this, him or Dex. The doctor had all but kicked Dex out of the hospital after he'd attempted to instruct Dex on how best to recuperate only to have Dex interrupt every other word with a question about whether doing or not doing whatever random thing popped into his mind would impede the healing process. That included playing video games, going to the toilet, showering, sleeping, sleeping on his side, on his back, on his stomach, going up stairs, going down stairs, driving, sitting, drinking alcohol, doing laundry, taking off his shoes, getting dressed, fooling around, having sex. And that had been within five minutes of the doctor's arrival. Giving up, the doctor addressed Sloane. Silly man attempted to ignore Dex. Dex was not one to be ignored.

In the end, Sloane told Dex to get some rest, or in other words shut up, and asked the doctor to step outside with him. The look of pure relief on the man's face had made Sloane chuckle. He understood the feeling. The doctor gave Sloane instructions for Dex's painkillers, including the maximum amount Sloane could give him. After a sympathetic smile, the doctor released Dex into Sloane's care. It took him three hours to get Dex home. Mostly because the second he'd turned his back, Dex was maneuvering his wheelchair down the hospital corridor, nearly causing a pileup. Maddock was going to owe him a hell of a lot more than vacation time for this.

Finally he had Dex settled on his couch with plenty of pillows and blankets from the hall closet. Sloane didn't know what he'd expected Dex's place to look like, maybe something resembling an M.C. Escher piece, but certainly not the sleek, modern, sophisticated décor he found around him. To the left of the entry hall was the living room, dark wood floors with white walls and furniture in chocolate hues. Across from the long brown couch was a white fireplace with a large flat-screen TV positioned above it. To each side of the fireplace, the walls were set back and lined with wood shelves filled with movies, books, games, and CDs. There were side tables with lamps and framed photos of him and his family, including him with his biological parents.

"Nice place," Sloane said, looking around.

"Should have seen it after Lou moved out. Looked like I'd been robbed. I didn't realize how much shit was his until he'd taken it with him." Dex shrugged. "I unpacked a load of stuff I'd stored in the basement and went on a massive online shopping spree. They assigned me my own UPS guy and everything."

Sloane couldn't tell if Dex was making up that last part. With his partner, anything was possible. He wouldn't be surprised if the guy had charmed his way to getting his personal delivery man.

The kitchen was behind the living room, sectioned off by a large marble counter. It was all black, with white marble countertops, including the large island counter in the center. Across from the kitchen to one side was the dining room, and to the right of that the stairs, leading to, he assumed, the bedrooms.

"This sucks," Dex complained for the hundredth time.

Sloane went back to tending to Dex, removing Dex's shoes and placing them behind the couch this time so he wouldn't trip over them. "The sooner you get better, the sooner Maddock will bring you back in, so suck it up. Do you have enough pillows?"

"Yes."

"Blankets?"

"Yes."

"Painkillers?"

"Yep."

"Hungry?"

"Oh my God!"

"I'm sorry." Sloane held his hands up. "I'm trying to help."

Dex lolled his head toward Sloane, his eyes narrowed. "Don't do that. Don't do the face thing."

"What face thing?" Painkillers should be kicking in soon. Of course, Sloane had no idea if that was a good thing or not. He took a seat on the hardwood coffee table beside Dex.

"That pouty bottom lip thing," Dex replied, reaching his arm out and poking a finger at Sloane's bottom lip. On instinct, Sloane smacked his hand away, and Dex let out a painful yelp.

"Shit, I'm so sorry!" Sloane crouched down beside him. He attempted to take hold of Dex's arm, but his partner shrank away from him, his arm cradled against his chest. Dex's whole face had gone red, and Sloane cringed.

"What the fuck, man? You're a horrible nurse!"

"I forgot, I'm sorry. It was a reflex. You went and was sticking your finger in my face. You grew up around a Felid. If you wave shit in our faces, it's bound to get swatted. What can I do to make it up to you?" He knew he was asking for trouble, but he really did feel bad about hitting Dex. "You sure you have enough painkillers?"

"Not nearly enough."

Sloane's phone rang, and he silently thanked God. Getting to his feet, he was actually happy to hear from Maddock.

"Hey. Any news?"

"We did some quiet reconnaissance on Isaac Pearce's whereabouts. He's not our guy. Apparently, when he's not in his workshop in Brooklyn, he's with his church group. Several members confirm Isaac was with them during the time of the murders. There are also a couple of café owners who confirm Isaac was in their shop during our windows of opportunity. There are receipts to back this up. I ran him through Themis as well and got nothing. Good news, we should be getting the lab results back on Ortiz any day now."

"Okay. Thanks. Keep us posted."

"Will do. How's the patient?"

Sloane cast a glance at Dex who was glowering at him. "Not feeling very patient."

"I'll let you get back to it, then."

"Thanks," Sloane grumbled. He put away his phone and informed Dex about Isaac. His partner's expression remained unmoved. Sloane smiled at Dex. "So, what will it take to get you to stop looking at me like that?"

Dex perked up. "Can you plug my iPod in?"

Sloane eyed him warily. "That depends. What hellish sounds are you going to violate my ears with?"

Dex wrinkled his nose and gave a haughty sniff. "I find your lack of melodic finesse disturbing."

"Yeah?" Sloane plugged the iPod into the dock on the mantel and pressed Play. Another electro-pop, disco-sounding melody started thumping through the speaker system. He turned, arching an eyebrow at Dex. "ABBA?"

"What kind of gay man are you?" Dex thrust a finger toward the door. "Out of my house. Your kind isn't welcome here."

Sloane chuckled and took a seat on the armchair, propping his sock-covered feet on the coffee table. "Okay, fine. ABBA's acceptable. I'll give you that."

"No, ABBA is awesome." Dex subtly moved his shoulders to the beat, the only movement he could get away with without wincing before he broke off into a husky version of "Gimme! Gimme! Gimme!"

"No singing," Sloane groaned.

"You seem to be forgetting where you are. You're in Casa de Dex, and in Casa de Dex, there is much singing." Dex continued to sing, and Sloane let his head fall back, his eyes closed. In truth, he didn't mind Dex singing. He had a rather nice singing voice. It was more the principle of the thing. He didn't like Dex getting his way. He liked Dex being right even less.

Once Dex's medication started doing its thing, Sloane was pleasantly surprised to find his partner became more subdued. Not being able to get up and wreak havoc was painful for Dex, which in turn became painful for Sloane, but with his meds and his annoying pop music, Dex spent a good deal of his time napping and zoning out. This allowed Sloane to catch up on his paperwork on his tablet connected to Themis. He even did some reading and managed to catch a nap himself. Maddock had authorized him to have the time off providing nothing urgent came up. Sloane could do most of his work from his tablet, and if he needed to check in at the office in person, Cael or one of their other teammates would stay with Dex. Sloane glanced over at his slumbering partner. Dex was still a rookie. He'd only had a taste of what it was like to be a THIRDS agent. Sloane had been part of the THIRDS since he was sixteen, though he'd been with the government longer. After all these years with the THIRDS, a guy got to enjoy his downtime whenever he could.

"What're you thinking about?"

Dex's voice was quiet, his drowsy gaze on Sloane as he sat back against a garrison of fluffy pillows. He'd been asleep for the last four hours and looked sweeter than Sloane wanted to admit. His hair was sticking up in all directions, his blanket was wrapped around one leg, a sock had somehow come off while he slept, and he had a hand clutching on to the corner of the blanket over his chest. He really was such a man-child. Sloane cleared his throat and turned his attention back to his tablet.

"Just thinking about how long I've been doing this."

"How long?"

"Twenty-one years."

"Wow. You love it that much?"

Sloane shrugged. "Not so much love it as never done anything else. It's what I was trained to do. As far as government organizations, if I had to choose, I'd still go with the THIRDS."

"Why?" Dex watched him intently, and Sloane mulled over his answer. He didn't want to get into his history with the organization, but Dex was his partner, and he deserved as much of the truth as Sloane could bring himself to part with.

"Because I promised myself a long time ago that I would do what I could to help those like me. It's not about catching the bad guys. It's about helping Therians who are scared and lost, who've made mistakes or haven't had anyone to guide them, and giving them the chance to find a better path, showing them they have the chance to lead better lives."

Dex was quiet for a moment, his pale blue gaze turning sympathetic. "It must have been rough."

"Yeah." Sloane instinctively scratched along long-healed wrist scars, only realizing too late what he'd done. Dex's eyes went wide, tears pooling in them.

"I'm sorry," he said with a humorless laugh. "I'm such an idiot."

"Hey, no." Sloane got up and gently nudged Dex so he could sit on the large couch beside him. "What's this?" he asked, his thumb gently wiping away the wetness under Dex's left eye.

"Nothing," Dex replied, closing his eyes and letting out a shuddering breath. "It's the meds."

"Dex," Sloane prompted, receiving a sigh.

"You said you didn't want to talk about it."

Sloane averted his gaze, his jaw muscles tightening. "I don't. And I won't either. I'm saying you don't need to feel bad about it. I don't. It was a long time ago. I was young, on my own, and scared. It's all I had left. At least I thought so. I know now how wrong I was." Dex took his hand and turned it over, his thumb stroking Sloane's wrist and the barely visible line. The THIRDS had done a hell of a job stitching him back together. Then again, Sloane had been naïve and cut in the wrong direction. The doctors had told him he'd been lucky. Biting down on his bottom lip, Dex took Sloane's other hand and turned it over, cursing under his breath. Sloane pulled it away.

"Like I said. It was a long time ago. Things were different. I was different. Don't get sentimental on me now, Daley," he teased, wondering why he hadn't pulled his left hand away. Dex tenderly took his wrist and put it to his lips, delivering a soft kiss and leaving Sloane with his heart in his throat.

Sloane leaned in and hesitantly put his lips to Dex's. His mouth was warm, his lips parting, inviting Sloane in. Despite knowing he shouldn't, Sloane slipped his tongue inside Dex's mouth, their tongues exploring and tasting. It wasn't hurried or intense like the first time they'd kissed in the garage. Sloane's hand slipped behind Dex's head, gingerly pulling him closer, his fingers in Dex's hair. He couldn't say how long the kiss went on, only that it felt good.

He pulled back enough to rest his head against Dex's. Why did he keep doing this? He had to stop. It wasn't fair to either of them, especially Dex. He stood and went to the kitchen for a bottle of water, aware of Dex watching him. To Sloane's surprise and relief, Dex didn't say anything. He didn't bring it up later either. In fact, he carried on as if nothing had happened. Any other guy would have demanded to know what was going on or would have told Sloane to go to hell ages ago. Not Dex. Why?

The rest of the day went far better than Sloane expected. He'd anticipated things to be awkward between them, but Dex wouldn't allow it. His meds still had him feeling groggy, but he seemed determined to be upbeat about everything, though there was plenty of bitching and moaning in between. They watched TV and DVDs together. Dex had Sloane in tears of laughter during certain scenes where Dex provided colorful commentary. During the good parts, Dex was engrossed. Sloane alternated between cooking and ordering in food. He'd called Ash while Dex was asleep and had him bring over extra clothes and supplies.

By the end of the week, Dex was feeling better, and he'd stopped bitching. He was finding it easier to move around, though he was still sore as hell. Cael had come by as often as he could to check up on his big brother, bringing him the junk food Dex would request through text, junk food Sloane would refuse to buy. Like gummy bears and those damn Cheesy Doodles.

Cael would stick around for a while, and Sloane admitted he enjoyed hanging around the brothers, listening to all the funny stories from their childhood. He loved hearing their stories. He didn't miss his childhood. It was hard to miss something he'd never had.

Sloane crashed on the couch every day that week. Although the temperature was steadily dropping as they got into November, the heating in Dex's apartment kept him comfortably warm. Dex had argued it was stupid when there was a king-size bed upstairs, but Sloane remained unmoved on the matter. There was no damn way he was going to share a bed with Dex. He didn't trust either of them not to do something they'd regret, especially since Sloane was finding it difficult to resist temptation, and it was getting worse by the day.

It had started with little things. A hand to the shoulder or upper arm, sitting next to Dex on the couch when Dex was well enough to sit up, letting Dex lean against him, his head on Sloane's shoulder. He'd pat Dex's knee, then leave his hand there while they watched TV. Over the weekend, he'd placed a hand to Dex's lower back as Dex washed their dishes after dinner. At the beginning of the second week, Dex had shivered after coming downstairs from his shower, and when he sat on the couch next to Sloane, he'd put his arm around Dex and rubbed his arm to get him warm. Dex never initiated any contact between them. He waited for Sloane to make a move, then followed up on it, as if he knew Sloane would balk otherwise. It was scary how well Dex was coming to know him.

More frightening was how much comfort he felt being around Dex.

Today they'd ordered an extra-nice dinner to celebrate Maddock giving Dex the all clear that morning. Dex would be back at work the next day. He was still sore, and Maddock made Dex promise he would take things slow, though Sloane was sure Dex would have agreed to almost anything to get back to work. They were moving around the kitchen, clearing up the counter and placing the dishes in the sink, when Dex turned to say something and ran into Sloane.

"Oh damn. I'm sorry."

"No, it was my fault," Sloane replied, reaching around Dex to drop the last of the cutlery in the sink. "Wasn't looking where I was going."

"Too busy staring at my ass, huh?"

Sloane gave a snort. "Yeah, it's kind of hard to miss."

"Please. You know you want it," Dex teased.

Sloane should have followed up the comment with a smartass remark; instead, his face went beet red, and he let out a nervous laugh. Dex tilted his head to one side, smiling at him.

"Are you blushing?"

"No." Sloane wiped down the counter, trying to keep out the invading images of Dex's bare ass. Shit. "I need to go."

"Oh, okay."

Sloane faced Dex, feeling like an asshole for putting that disappointed look on his face. "I'm sorry. I'm not trying to be rude. The food was great and spending time with you… I really liked it. I just…."

"Don't want to do something you'll regret? I understand."

Sloane blinked at him, surprised by Dex's intuitiveness.

"Despite the way I act sometimes, I'm not really an ass. I don't want to do anything that would make things uncomfortable between us. I kind of like having you around."

"Yeah?"

"Yeah." Dex absently ran a hand through his hair. The gesture coupled with the bashful smile on his face pulled at Sloane's heartstrings. It was the first time he was seeing this side of Dex, and he found it absolutely endearing. Then Dex bit down on his bottom lip, and it stirred something else in Sloane. He grabbed the back of Dex's neck and pulled him against him, bringing their mouths and bodies together. After Dex's surprise wore off, he threw his arms around Sloane's neck, pressing his body up against Sloane's, his evident erection digging into Sloane's leg as a deep rumble rose through his chest and came out as a long groan. He kissed Dex hungrily, one hand sliding down between them to cup Dex's erection and rub him through his jeans, his other hand slipping into the back of Dex's waistband to grip one plump, round asscheek.

"Oh God," Dex moaned, moving his hips and thrusting into Sloane's hand. "Fuck, I want you so bad."

With the last of his resolve snapping, Sloane pulled his hands free to take Dex's shirt and pull it up over his head, dropping it to the kitchen floor before unbuttoning Dex's fly, his lips kissing, licking, and nipping along Dex's neck down to his shoulder where he bit down gently, causing Dex to shiver in the sweetest way. With a low growl, Sloane grabbed Dex and lifted him, chuckling at the surprised yelp Dex let out. His arms locked around Sloane's neck as he carried Dex to the counter and set him down.

"Dude, we eat on here."

"Shut up." Sloane returned his mouth to Dex's, kissing him as he tugged Dex's jeans down his legs, followed by his boxer briefs. He stopped long enough to look down at Dex's gorgeous cock.

"I can get you a framed painting if you like. Or you could suck it."

Sloane's gaze traveled up that beautifully flushed body, sporting a rainbow of healing bruises, to Dex's cheeky smile, his pale blue eyes filled with mischief. The bruising on his face had mostly subsided, and once again, Sloane could feel the full effect of Dex's charm. How had Sloane not noticed the little lines that formed at the corners of his eyes when he smiled? Dex arched an eyebrow at him before he winked down at his dick.

"Don't worry, fella. He needs a minute to take in all the awesome."

"How about I show you what *you* need." Sloane pushed Dex onto his back. He ran a hand down Dex's smooth chest, down his abs, until he got his hand wrapped around Dex's cock and swallowed him down until the tip touched the back of his throat.

"Fuck!" Dex closed his eyes and let his head fall back, his hands flattened against the counter's smooth surface while Sloane sucked him off. He moved slowly, his eyes open and on Dex. Sloane relished the taste of him in his mouth, the sounds coming from him, the way he arched his back up off the counter. Sloane pulled back, his tongue circling the tip, then pressing down into the slit, making Dex gasp. Watching the need wash over Dex's face, hearing his heavy breaths and soft cursing, made Sloane want to torture Dex even more, to make him writhe with need until he was begging. He lapped up the precome before picking up his pace, his tongue pressing against the base.

"Come on, man," Dex pleaded breathlessly.

Sloane grabbed Dex's hips, tugged him forward, and slung his smaller partner over his shoulder, laughing at the surprised yelp he let out. After a moment of flailing, Dex stilled. "This is messed up."

"Be quiet." Sloane slapped Dex's bare ass, the sound delicious.

"Ooh, kinky."

Sloane hurried up the stairs, careful not to run Dex into any walls. He made it to the bedroom and dropped Dex onto the king-size bed. He'd been in Dex's bedroom several times when Dex had needed help getting upstairs. The bedroom was spacious, tastefully decorated like the rest of the house, with a thick carpet in a chocolaty hue matching the curtains of the two large windows on the right side of the room and the tall headboard of the large bed, a stark contrast against white walls. There were dark nightstands to each side of the bed, each with a lamp, and also a matching dresser. Across from the bed was a long closet and to the right of that, the bathroom. But the room's best feature, in his opinion, was the naked guy in the center of the bed trembling with need for him. Sloane crawled over Dex and finished removing his pants and underwear, kissing and nipping as he went along.

"Supplies?" Sloane asked, hitting the mute button on the warning bells in his head. He was too lost in Dex, the sight of him, his scent, his body.

"Nightstand."

Sloane finished removing all Dex's clothes before rummaging through the nightstand to toss a bottle of lube and a condom on the bed. He walked around to the foot of the bed, and with a wicked smile on his face, he pulled his shirt off and tossed it to one side. Dex propped on his elbows and licked his bottom lip as he watched Sloane undress. The socks came next, followed by his jeans and boxer briefs. He put his hands on his hips. "Like what you see?"

Dex nodded. "Though the question you should be asking is top or bottom?"

A fierce heat spread up from his toes through his whole body. Damn, just when he thought he couldn't get any harder. "Top or bottom?"

Dex considered it then rolled onto his stomach. He looked at Sloane over his shoulder. "Fuck me."

"Shit." Sloane crawled over him and gently took hold of Dex's face to capture his lips with his own, his tongue forcing Dex's lips open. He kissed him hungrily before sitting back on his heels, his hands on Dex's asscheeks, kneading them, spreading them apart. Fuck, he was hot. Sloane got off the bed, grabbed Dex's ankles, and pulled him until his ass was hanging off the edge. Dex let out a grunt, his fingers grabbing the edges of the duvet underneath him, his head pressing into the mattress as Sloane got on his knees. He spread Dex and let out a groan when Dex gasped at the feel of Sloane's tongue in him.

"Oh fuck," Dex moaned, his fingers curling and uncurling. He slipped a hand underneath himself, his ass coming up slightly as he stroked himself. Sloane nipped at Dex with teeth and Dex let out a long shuddering breath, his entire body shivering. Sloane's fingernails dug into Dex's asscheeks as he licked, laved, and tongued Dex's hole.

"Sloane…."

Answering Dex's soft plea, Sloane got up and gave him a tap on his flank so he'd move up. Dex silently shifted onto the bed, getting on his hands and knees, his gaze on Sloane as Sloane tore the condom packet open and passed it to him.

"Put it on me."

Dex made a choking noise before sitting up and doing a cute shimmy over to him. He rolled the condom onto Sloane, his hand squeezing Sloane's cock on the way down and drawing a deep groan from him. Sloane nodded toward the lube, and Dex snatched up the bottle, squirted some onto his hand, and palmed Sloane's cock again, his lustful gaze on Sloane as he stroked him. When it was getting to be too much, Sloane grabbed his wrist and turned him, pushing him gently back onto his hands and knees. Sloane stroked his achingly hard dick a couple of times before taking the lube and squirting some between Dex's asscheeks, then stretched him with his fingers for a few agonizing moments. When Sloane couldn't take Dex's moaning or the way he pushed back onto Sloane's fingers any longer, he pressed the head of his cock against Dex's hole. He moved in slowly, reminding himself of Dex's injuries. It was torture, but he refused to hurt Dex.

"Come on, Sloane. You're not going to break me." Dex pulled away and impaled himself the rest of the way in, making them both cry out. Sloane doubled over Dex's back, their heads pressed together.

"For fuck's sake, Dex. I don't want to hurt you." Sloane shut his eyes for a moment to steady himself.

"Just fuck me already."

"Okay." Sloane adjusted his position, kneeling behind Dex and grabbing his hips. He slammed Dex back against him as he thrust forward. Dex let out a surprised yelp, fueling Sloane's desire to make Dex cry out again and again. He pounded into Dex in earnest, the bed moving beneath them. He couldn't deny how goddamn amazing it was to be inside Dex, how much he was enjoying fucking him senseless.

He stopped and pulled out to flip Dex onto his back. After shoving a pillow under Dex's lower back, Sloane bent to kiss him, one hand wrapping around Dex's cock while he lined himself up with the other and pushed into him, drawing another surprised gasp. Sloane pulled his mouth away from Dex's as he fucked him and jerked him off.

"Fuck, I love hearing you make those noises."

Dex shivered beneath him, and Sloane grinned. Now that he had managed to shut Dex up, all he wanted was to hear him, hear those little moans of pleasure, his gasps, his cursing as Sloane slowed down, then sped up. He slowly pulled out before snapping his hips, thrusting as deep as he could each time. Shifting his position slightly, he pulled nearly all the way out before thrusting in deep. Dex cried out when Sloane hit the right spot.

"Oh fuck!"

"That's it," Sloane purred, leaning forward. He released his hold on Dex's cock and moved Dex's hand so he could take over. "Jesus." The sight of Dex jacking off was almost enough to send him over the edge. He pulled back enough to drape Dex's legs over his shoulders and wrapped his arms around them, his groin slapping against Dex's ass as he rotated his hips and did his best to keep hitting Dex's prostate. Dex's scrunched-up brow was beaded with sweat, his mouth open, with the most delicious sounds coming out of it. Sloane leaned in, his weight forcing him deep inside Dex. He gritted his teeth as he moved faster, his thrusts short but hard. "Oh fuck. Dex...."

Dex nodded frantically. "Yes."

Sloane's hips lost all their rhythm, his breath coming out ragged and the sweat dripping down his back as he lost control. His release built up and slammed into him, a feral growl rising through him as he spilled inside the condom. Dex cried out, his release causing his body to tighten around Sloane and draw out Sloane's orgasm. His whole body shook, and then he lay down on top of Dex, careful not to crush him under his weight. He knew he should move, but the overwhelming peace that washed over him, along with the haze of what they'd done, had Sloane pulling Dex close against him instead.

He knew he was leaving himself vulnerable, but right now he needed to feel Dex in his arms, and when Dex returned his embrace with nothing but a soft sigh, Sloane was relieved. He didn't know how long it would last. Probably about as long as it took morning to come around, but for now he was happy. After a few minutes, he reluctantly pulled out, rolling over to remove the condom, tie it off, and chuck it in the wastebasket beside the nightstand.

Bracing himself, he turned, watching as Dex grabbed a wet wipe from a packet inside the other nightstand and cleaned his stomach off. When he finished, he moved to get up, but Sloane reached over. "Give it here."

Dex smiled at him and handed it over. Sloane tossed it into the wastebasket before heading into the bathroom. He splashed some water over his face before he caught sight of his disheveled and flushed skin in the mirror. Hands braced on the sink, he tried hard not to panic. They had complicated the fuck out of everything. *He* had complicated the fuck out of everything. Sloane liked Dex, a lot, which was what was making this so much worse.

"Hey, come to bed."

Sloane gave a start, finding Dex leaning against the doorframe, his hand held out to him and a sweet smile on his face. How long had Dex been standing there? Sloane waited for signs of hurt feelings or disappointment, but Dex continued to smile tenderly at him.

"I could use a good night's sleep because come morning, I am going to be *so* sore." He leaned in to whisper, "This hot guy fucked me into the mattress, and he was, like, *huge*."

Sloane chuckled, some of his tension slipping away. "Sounds intense."

"It was. Which is why I could use a cuddle."

"You want to cuddle?"

"Fuck yeah, I want to cuddle. You don't get to have this fine piece of ass and then not cuddle, so I suggest you get in that bed right now, mister."

"Yes, sir!" Sloane saluted and headed back into the bedroom with Dex on his heels. He climbed in under the warm duvet and lay on his back, smiling as Dex climbed in and snuggled up close. He turned Sloane's face toward him and kissed him gently on his lips before releasing him. Then he wrapped an arm around Sloane's chest, wrapped a leg around Sloane's, and settled in. He held Dex against him, planting a kiss on the top of his head, waiting for the steady rise and fall of his chest, along with the feel of his warm breath against Sloane's skin that signaled Dex was asleep, before he whispered, "Thank you."

DEX LET out a low groan and rolled onto his back, his hand falling to the empty side of the bed. Sloane must have left early in hopes of avoiding any awkwardness, though there certainly wouldn't be any from Dex's end. He'd seen the guilt on the guy's face the night before in the bathroom, and he didn't want to push things. As much as he wanted to explore whatever was between them, he knew Sloane wasn't ready to do the same. For now Dex would enjoy these moments while they lasted and whatever the outcome, he'd worry about it then.

He forced himself out of bed, smiling when he thought about the night before. God, he couldn't remember the last time he'd wanted someone so bad. Just the thought of Sloane fucking him had him getting hard. Nothing a nice cool shower and a hand job wouldn't cure. He finished brushing his teeth and turned to the shower with thoughts of a tall, gruff alpha with amber eyes, a sweet ass, and a thick hard cock. This was going to be the shortest handy-J in history.

"Mind if I join you?"

"Holy fuck!" Dex spun around, nearly falling over his feet when Sloane caught him, pulling him against his chest, his rich laughter invading every inch of Dex.

Sloane held him close and delivered a kiss to his lips. "Morning. Sorry. I didn't mean to scare you."

"You gotta stop doing that!"

"Doing what?"

"That popping-up-outta-nowhere thing you do."

Sloane's brows rose in amusement. "I use doors like everyone else."

"Yeah, but you don't make sounds like everyone else. You and your Felid silent stalkery thing. Scares the crap out of me."

"I'm sorry," Sloane said with a chuckle. "I'll try to announce myself the next time I walk into a room."

"You do that," Dex grumbled.

"Aw, someone needs his coffee," Sloane purred, his hand roaming down Dex's naked body. Dex jutted his bottom lip out tragically.

"I do."

"I made coffee and breakfast. That's why I left you in bed."

Dex stared at him. "You made me breakfast?"

"Yeah. Your ex never made you breakfast?"

Dex scoffed. "Lou might know good food, but that doesn't mean he can cook it. I did all the cooking. He brought home leftovers. Not that I'm knocking the leftovers, 'cause they were pretty damn tasty, but if there weren't any, it was up to me. He also slept in, and I got up early, so, you know. Passing boats in the night and all that crap."

"Well, there's breakfast for you." He pressed his lips to Dex's neck, sending a shiver through him. "You know what else you need?"

"Hm?" Dex melted into him, at this point not caring about anything other than Sloane's large hands squeezing his asscheeks.

"I think you need to undress me, get me in the shower, and show me how much you appreciate my making you breakfast."

Dex's face went up in flames, and he nodded fervently. "I can do that." His heart jolted and his pulse pounded at the sight of Sloane's pupils dilating, the lust in them making Dex ache. Licking his bottom lip, Dex snapped out of it. He grabbed the hem of Sloane's T-shirt and pulled it up over his head, tossing it to one side before moving on to his belt and fumbling to unbuckle it. There was no time or patience for finesse. He wanted Sloane naked as quickly as possible. Dex's muscles still ached, his body was still in need of recovery, but his brain pushed all that aside at the idea of doing all manner of naughty things in the shower. It was amazing what a guy could endure when sex was on offer.

As soon as he had Sloane naked in front of him, he grabbed his hand and pulled him into the shower, turning on the water to a nice warm temperature. He turned and met Sloane's gaze.

"What'll it be?"

A sinful look came onto Sloane's face, and Sloane backed up against the wall. "I want to see you on your knees with my dick in your mouth."

Holy fuck. "Okay" was all that managed to find its way out of Dex's mouth. Frankly, he was surprised his brain was still functioning enough to say that much. He got down on his knees, Sloane's hard erection in front of him. With a shaky hand, he guided it into his mouth and started sucking and licking. He kept his eyes open, the water hitting his ass and the backs of his legs as he popped off Sloane to trail his tongue up the side of his cock, up to the top, and over the slit. Sloane let out a low moan, his bottom lip between his teeth as he slipped one hand into Dex's hair, fingers curling tight around his damp locks. Sloane tentatively thrust forward, and Dex opened his mouth.

"Oh God. Yeah," Sloane moaned, slowly fucking Dex's mouth, his dick moving slow at first, drawing nearly all the way out and then just as slowly, all the way in. Dex pressed his lips tight against Sloane's hard cock, his fingers digging into Sloane's ass and his free hand palming his own cock. "Fuck. That's it, Dex. Oh God, like that." Sloane's other hand found its way into Dex's hair, but he didn't mind the pull. Seeing the look of pleasure on Sloane's face made the discomfort worth it. Sloane started pumping into Dex's mouth in earnest until he lost his rhythm, one hand behind Dex's head, holding it as he fucked his mouth. "Dex…."

Dex hummed, and Sloane let out a strangled cry as he shot his load. Dex swallowed around his partner's cock, doing his best to take all of it, and another shudder went through Sloane. He doubled over, his arms wrapped around Dex's head as he emptied down Dex's throat. A few heartbeats later, Dex came hard. Sloane slowly pulled out of Dex's mouth, leaning back against the tiny brown-and-white shower titles. Dex stood, ignoring the pain in his knees and back. He kissed Sloane, loving the low groan Sloane released at tasting himself on Dex's lips. They kissed until the water started cooling, and then Dex pulled Sloane under it, lathering him up and washing him, relishing in the feel of Sloane's firm body. They finished up and dried each other off before getting dressed. In companionable silence, they headed downstairs, where Sloane popped the tasty breakfast bagel he'd made for Dex in the toaster-oven to warm up before making Dex a great cup of coffee.

They took Sloane's sleek black Chevy Impala to work since Sloane had driven him home from the hospital in it. For some reason, Dex had expected Sloane to drive an SUV or something similar, but seeing him sitting comfortably behind the wheel surrounded by the classy jet-black interior, Dex decided it was a good look for him. It fit with Sloane's smooth looks and mysterious appeal. They didn't discuss what had happened that morning or the night before, and as Dex suspected, when Sloane recognized Dex wasn't going to bring it up, he relaxed. There was no need for the "we need to keep this quiet" conversation. Dex was fully aware what was at stake, and he had no intention of screwing everything up. He might have a big mouth, but not when it came to what mattered.

Once at HQ, they changed into their uniforms and headed up to Unit Alpha. Dex had even caught Sloane smiling on more than one occasion. Knowing he had

been the one to put that smile on his face had Dex
grinning like a dope. When they reached the Defense
Department, Dex was surprised by all the warm greetings he received. Everyone was genuinely happy to
see him, a nice change from how he'd been greeted at
the Sixth Precinct after his ex-partner's arrest. Sloane
patted Dex's back.

"Welcome home, Dex."

Coming from Sloane, Dex couldn't have soared
any higher. Seconds after booting up their desks, Destructive Delta was ordered to meet in briefing room
A. His team—with the exception of Ash—all greeted
him with hugs or pats on the backs. It was amazing
how quickly he was growing attached to these guys.
He took a seat at the table between Sloane and Rosa,
grinning at Ash, who sat across from them beside Cael
with his usual grumpy frown on his face. Well, it was
time to get to work. While Hudson and Nina were
talking to Tony at the front of the room, Dex opened
his backpack, stuck his hand inside, and pulled out his
new puppet pal.

Ash's eyes went huge. "What the fuck is that?"

Dex grinned. "Sloane got it for me at the hospital
gift shop on our way out." It was a hand puppet of a
lion with a big brown nose and a fluffy brown mane
sticking up every which way. Dex lowered his voice,
growling as his fingers moved the puppet's little paws.
"Hi, I'm Ash. My hobbies include shooting things,
shooting things, and uh, shooting things. Oh, and I
like fish."

Everyone around the table burst into laughter except for Ash, who turned his stunned gaze on Sloane.
"Are you serious?"

Sloane shrugged. "It was the only way I could distract him long enough to get him to the car. Besides, he was hurt and he liked it. I couldn't say no."

"Yes you could have," Ash ground out through his teeth. "That's just wrong."

"No, *that's* wrong," Rosa said, pointing at Dex, who was sliding his fist in and out of the puppet, making moaning noises.

"Ooh, yeah, you like that, don't you."

"Son of a bitch!" Ash lunged for the puppet and Dex gasped, holding his puppet Ash against his chest.

"Don't you dare lay a finger on him! We're in love. Nothing you can say or do will change what we have between us." He petted puppet Ash's mane, speaking quietly. "It's okay. I'm here now. He can't hurt you." He placed a kiss to its nose.

"You have problems," Ash said, jutting a finger at Dex.

Rosa laughed and hugged Dex. "I missed you."

"Okay, listen up." Tony stood at the podium. "The lab results for Ortiz have come in, and Hudson's going to fill you in on what they've found. It took slightly longer than anticipated because there was some research to be done first in order to confirm what the examiners suspected."

Hudson took the podium, tapping the display and bringing up an image of some tropical beach with black sand. "This is Punalu'u Beach in Hawaii. As you can see, it consists of black sand, traces of which were found on Ortiz, who we can confirm has never been to Punalu'u Beach in his lifetime, much less around the time of his murder, nor had his wife or any of their brunch guests. However, we submitted the sample to Themis, and we immediately got a hit. There is one establishment that imports this exact sand from Punalu'u." Hudson cleared his throat and stepped to one side, his expression troubled. Something was going on.

"Well?" Ash asked. "You guys gonna fill us in, or are we supposed to guess?"

Tony resumed his place behind the podium, and Dex braced himself. He knew that look. Whatever his dad was about to say, wouldn't be good.

"We've confirmed the sand found on Ortiz is from the Styx."

An unwelcome tension stretched over the room like a heavy fog. Whatever it was, it was serious. Dex held up a hand. "I'm sorry. I don't know what that means." No one answered, and Dex couldn't understand why until Sloane met Dex's gaze, his heart squeezing at the sorrow in his partner's eyes.

"That's where Gabe was killed. In the small alley behind it."

Dex closed his eyes, cursing softly under his breath. It seemed no matter where they were, what they were doing, the ghost of Gabe Pearce followed them. It wasn't that he wanted Sloane to forget Gabe. He could never be that selfish. The more time he spent with Sloane, the more difficult it was to see the guy's heart breaking over and over. Every time Dex thought Sloane might be reaching a point where he could start healing, something in this case popped up to drag his partner back down. Sloane needed to put Gabe to rest, but it was clear that wasn't going to happen until they got to the bottom of whatever was happening. For

Sloane's peace of mind—and his own—Dex needed
to see this through to the end.

Tony finally spoke up, his voice rougher than usual. "There's more. I've asked Hudson and Nina to reopen Agent Pearce's case. They'll be going back over
the reports and running everything through Themis."

"You think the cases may be connected?" Dex
asked when Sloane rose from his seat.

"Gabe wasn't a HumaniTherian activist. Plus it
was an open-and-shut case."

"I know," Tony replied quietly.

"Then why dredge it all up again? They have
nothing to do with each other."

"We don't know that. I have to consider all possibilities. Gabe was killed at the Styx. Our last victim
had traces of the very same sand imported by that bar,
yet Ortiz had never set foot in there. If there's anything in Gabe's file that might have been overlooked
at the time, we need to know about it. There are too
many factors not adding up in this, and we're running
out of time. I'm sorry, team. Cael, Rosa, get down to
the Styx and speak with the owner. Ash, you and Letty
go in as backup."

Sloane shook his head, his gaze intense. "No. Dex
and I will go in as backup like we always do."

Tony let out a heavy sigh. "Sloane—"

"If this *is* connected to Gabe's death, then I want
to know. You can't bench me on this. Not this time."

"You're too close."

"We're *all* too close. I can remain objective this
time, and Dex will be there to make sure of it. If at any
point he thinks I need to be pulled from the case, I'll
concede, willingly."

Everyone stared at Sloane, but naturally Ash was the first to speak up. "You're going to leave the decision to Dex?"

"Yes. My ability to perform without compromising my team and my partner is priority. I trust his decision." Sloane turned his gaze to Tony. "Well?"

Tony took a moment to think it over. "Okay. Dex, if at any point you feel your partner is putting the investigation in jeopardy, you have him pulled. Understood?"

"Yes, sir." Dex prayed Sloane didn't give him a reason to.

"All right, then. If you run into any problems, you call for backup. Get going."

The team dispersed, and Dex followed Sloane out of the briefing room. They were silent all the way to the elevator and down to the armory, where they loaded only their basic equipment. This wasn't an emergency, so they'd make do with their backup weapon and the secured rifles in the back of the black unmarked Suburban they'd be driving instead of the BearCat. Sloane needed some time to think, and Dex would make sure to give him however long he needed. When his partner was ready to talk, he'd talk.

Once inside the garage, Cael and Rosa stopped long enough to murmur they'd meet at the Styx, and Dex gave a thumbs-up to signal his acknowledgment. It's as if the whole team was walking on eggshells. Since he was the rookie, Dex climbed into the passenger seat of the decked out Suburban and buckled up. They exited the garage and drove down to East Thirty-Seventh Street, where they made a right before making a left onto Second Avenue.

"You're quiet." Sloane tapped his fingers against the steering wheel as they stopped at a red light.

"Just giving you some space." Dex focused on the bare trees surrounding the Vincent F. Albano Jr. Playground. Winter was settling nicely, and the team had started wearing their thermal knit underclothes. He was not looking forward to frolicking through snowstorms with his gear.

"You don't need to do that. I'm fine. But thank you."

Dex was surprised but didn't express it. If Sloane didn't want to make a big deal out of it, neither would he. "So where is this place?" The light turned green, and they continued down Second Avenue.

"Meatpacking District. It's a bar and a restaurant. Gabe loved it because it has this great rustic look. High ceilings, exposed brick, iron work. Good food, friendly people. The garden turns into a cocktail lounge in the evenings, and it has this cool retractable roof."

"Sounds nice." Dex smiled despite feeling as if his insides were twisting. With traffic, it took them roughly twenty minutes to get to the Styx. They parked the Suburban a few feet away from the place, and Dex turned in his seat to look at Sloane. "It's cool if you want to stay in the car."

"I'm fine. Let's get this over with."

The Styx was situated a block from the High Line—a mile-long public park filled with plants, viewing platforms, restaurants, and gathering areas for exhibitions, all of it hovering over the Meatpacking District on an elevated rail. The Styx building itself was charmingly rough, like so many others in a city offering variety and deliciously urban décor, situated on a street lined with exclusive clubs, trendy restaurants, and pricey boutiques. One side of the brick façade was crawling with that expensive artificial ivy intertwined with wisteria used often by businesses occupying old buildings, and to each side of the central scuffed wooden doors were two sets of large rectangular wooden pots filled with plants and painted green to match the entrance and exit doors. Next door was a large nightclub, which at this time of day was blissfully serene.

As they walked inside, Dex could see why Gabe had liked the place so much. It had a cozy feel to it. Trendy yet not ostentatious. Inside it was all rustic beams and brick walls containing more wisteria, especially around the medium-sized marble-top bar. It was lined with black high-back stools, and on the glass shelving unit behind the bar, a host of alcoholic spirits were on display.

To the left of the bar, Dex could see the garden Sloane had mentioned, the walls crawling with dense ivy and the floor scattered with small potted plants and trees. About a dozen white-clothed tables were spread across the tiled floor. Dex imagined the place got pretty packed in the evenings, with folks grabbing a bite to eat before heading to the club next door. His gaze dropped to the glittering stone floor, and there were traces of black sand everywhere. He'd be amazed if someone left here without getting the stuff on them. In the dining area, he found the surfaces decorated with spikes of striking purplish-blue flowers in black Greek-style vases. Strolling to one, he found each vase had black sand in it.

"Beautiful, aren't they?" Dex looked up at Rosa, who tenderly touched one of the flower's petals.

"They're hyacinths. There's a Greek myth that goes with it. A tragic love story."

Dex grimaced. "Weren't they all tragic love stories?"

Rosa chuckled just as Cael called them over. They followed a waiter into the back end, past the kitchen and into a medium-sized office where a slender man in his midfifties sporting jeans, a faded T-shirt, and trendy jacket came around the desk to greet them.

"Hey, what can I do for you agents? Please tell me it's not another murder involving my place. Frankly, I'm still recovering from the last."

Dex watched Sloane's lips press in a thin line, but his partner remained silent. Cael removed his tablet from his padded vest pocket, tapping away. "I'm sorry to say this, Mr. Danak, but our lab has confirmed the traces of black sand found on our last victim came from your establishment." He showed Mr. Danak the tablet with an image of Ortiz.

"I remember. Your agents asked if he'd ever been here. I'm afraid the answer hasn't changed. I never saw him, neither has the staff, and we would've remembered. Surely there must be another way the sand got onto Mr. Ortiz."

"That's what we're here to find out. I phoned earlier, and you stated you keep up to a year's worth of security footage?"

"That's correct." Mr. Danak motioned to the small room off to the right of his office. "Equipment's in there. Help yourself."

"Is it digital?" Cael asked.

"Yes."

With a nod of thanks, Cael headed for the room, the rest of the team following. They stood at the door as Cael hooked his tablet up to the fancy desktop. After a few taps to his tablet, Cael typed away on the desktop's keyboard, accessing its server and the stored video files. "The Styx only has a few cameras inside and one toward the front entrance. Nothing out the back, since patrons aren't supposed to exit that way. I'm going to run the last three months through Themis. Shouldn't take more than a few minutes."

Themis played the video at high speed, tiny white squares popping up over every face it came across, while a narrow screen on the right side scrolled information, names, details, dates, times, addresses, anything related to the individuals who popped up on the screen. The screen stilled on an image, the white rectangle flashing over a man's face.

"We've got something."

Dex leaned in, recognizing the guy. "Wait a second. That's…."

"Isaac Pearce," Sloane pitched in from over Dex's shoulder.

Cael nodded. "Well, Tony did tell us to keep his information in Themis just in case. It's bound to come across him again, especially since he's connected to Gabe, and Gabe's name has been reactivated in the system."

"Yeah, but what's he doing here?" Dex watched Cael play the video. Pearce sat at the bar, nursing a beer.

"Maybe he came here for the same reason I avoided it. It was Gabe's favorite place."

As they watched the video, someone in a hoodie and cap appeared in the doorway on the left. When he saw Pearce, and Pearce clocked onto him, the guy bolted. Pearce took off after him, nearly knocking over a couple as they entered the bar. "What was that? Play it back," Dex said, watching carefully.

"Who is that?" Sloane asked.

Cael shook his head, swiping his finger across the screen. "I don't know. His face was away from the camera. The second camera was pointing toward the garden at the time, and the third at the back of the indoor dining area, so Themis can't put together a 3-D map. Whoever he is, looks like he's scared of Isaac."

"When was this?" Dex asked.

"Three days ago."

Rosa turned to Sloane, her expression sympathetic. "I'm sorry, but we need to talk to Isaac."

"Then we go." Sloane left the office, and after a worried glance exchanged between Cael and Rosa, they followed Sloane out. Dex trailed behind, using the opportunity to call Calvin.

"Hey, Dex. What's up?"

"Do me a favor. Can you get Intel to cross-reference Gabe Pearce's name with the victims? This is all too much of a coincidence for my liking. This is priority."

"Sure thing. I'll let you know if they get anything."

"Great. Thanks." Dex tapped his earpiece again. "Dispatch, can you connect me to the HPF's Sixth Precinct? Thanks." He thanked the bar owner on the way out, promised he'd be back in an unofficial capacity soon, and headed for the Suburban. He climbed into the passenger seat, Sloane looking at him questioningly. He held a finger up and pointed to his ear. "Hey, Anna Banana, Dex here. Just wanted to know if Detective Pearce is in." The dispatcher's cheerful voice came over the line.

"Hi, Detec—I mean *Agent* Daley. I'm afraid today's his day off."

"Thank you, Anna. Take care."

"You too."

Dex tapped his earpiece and turned to Sloane. "Pearce is off today."

"Let's try his workshop. There's no phone there, and I'd rather not give his cell phone a ring."

"Tunnel or bridge?" Dex asked, not that it would make a huge difference traffic-wise. They were looking at a half hour minimum, even at this time of day, to get from here to Brooklyn.

"Tunnel." He tapped his earpiece. "Rosa, Cael, when we get there, I want Dex to go in and do the talking."

Dex stared at him. "What?"

Sloane tapped his earpiece and addressed Dex. "It'll soften the blow of seeing me there. He's also not fond of the team, but he trusts you. He'll talk to you. We're not dealing with some street punk. We're dealing with a cop who knows the law inside and out. He doesn't like the sound of something, he'll tell us to go fuck ourselves."

"What happened between you two? It's cool if you don't want to talk about it. I—"

Sloane let out a heavy sigh, his frown deepening. "It's fine. He never liked me. Not because I was his brother's boyfriend. He never had a problem with Gabe being gay. He had a problem with me because I'm a Therian. You know, one of those 'I don't have a problem with Therians as long as they don't date my brother' sort of deals."

"Ah, I see."

"Gabe and Isaac used to fight constantly over our relationship, and it hurt to see Gabe so unhappy. I tried to break things off once because I knew how much he loved his brother, and I didn't want to come between them. Isaac was the only family he had. But Gabe was furious, said he wasn't going to give up on us, on someone who made him happy, because his brother was too stubborn to see how much I meant to him."

They drove into the Hugh L. Carey Tunnel, and Sloane took a deep breath before releasing it slowly. "Gabe laid it all out for Isaac. Said he wasn't going to choose, that he loved us both, and he wasn't going to leave me. The only reason Isaac didn't cut us was because it would have hurt his brother's career. Being with Gabe…. For the first time in my life, I was happy. When he died, Isaac took everything. And I'm not talking about Gabe's money. I didn't give a rat's ass about that. The guy showed up at my apartment with a van and some paperwork he got from God knows where. He took everything that belonged to Gabe. It was his way of punishing me. On top of that, he cleaned out Gabe's place."

"What the hell?" Dex couldn't believe it. Isaac came off as such a sweet guy. A little twitchy at times, but he didn't seem like the kind to pull such a dick move. It must have torn Sloane apart.

"Gabe was my boyfriend, not my husband. I had no say in the matter. It was… like Isaac was trying to wipe away any trace that we'd ever been together. Isaac told me the only reason he wasn't outing me then was because he didn't want his brother's name tainted. If it wasn't for Gabe being given a THIRDS funeral, I know Isaac would have made sure I stayed away."

"Jesus. I had no idea. What's going to happen when he sees you?" No wonder Isaac kept trying to warn him about Sloane. The guy was holding on to one hell of a grudge against his partner—one he couldn't seem to let go.

"I don't know what's going to happen, but with you there, he's going to hold back. He's not stupid."

As they exited the tunnel, Dex tried to convince himself everything would be okay. All he had to do was chat with Pearce, ask him a few questions, and do what he'd done countless times while on homicide. To get the most information out of Pearce, Dex would have to make sure to stay on the guy's good side. "This is fucked up."

"I know." Sloane reached over to pat his leg. He left his hand there longer than necessary, and it helped calm Dex. "For what it's worth, I'm glad you'll be there to back me up."

Dex looked over at his partner, his heart swelling in his chest. "Likewise."

Chapter 12

THEY STOOD outside the dirty steel-and-glass double doors of a red and green four-story brick building situated across from a shipping warehouse. On one side of the building was the Cabinet Depot and on the other, under the Metro line, was a large self-storage lot with several aluminum units in various sizes, and next to that, a section selling wholesale kitchen countertops and garden supplies. Isaac's building had four windows on the fourth floor only, no fire escape, and a couple of the storage units underneath. There was a hell of a lot of mess and construction going on around the enormous black steel girders, too many places for someone to make a quick getaway. After a quick risk assessment of the surroundings, Dex went in with Cael, Rosa, and Sloane on his heels.

Inside, the large interior double doors were open. There was a grimy foyer with another set of doors ahead of them and an open single door on the right-hand side that appeared to lead out into a narrow hall-way with nothing but a set of stairs. Sloane opened one of the doors, and Dex stepped into an expansive workshop, the shrill noise of machinery resonating throughout. It resembled something out of a horror movie, with walls containing all types of metals hooks, clamps, chains, hammers in all sizes and shapes, and several other blacksmithing tools.

Heavy, thick chains and pulleys, which Dex imag-ined were used to hold up the heavier pieces Pearce worked on, hung from the ceiling in various spots around the workshop. There was a table with a sander, a vise, and some polishing tools. Lined up against the rusting paneled walls were several gas tanks, and on the left side of the space was a huge furnace that near-ly stretched to the ceiling. It looked as if it belonged in the Dark Ages. It also looked as if it hadn't been used in a long time. Not far from it was a medium-sized coal forge that was in use, and around it were stacks of several different craft metals in a variety of shapes and sizes. The pounding of a hammer against metal rang through his ears, and he headed toward the sound. It was damn hot, the air around them stifling, but the closer they got to huge open windows at the far end, the slightly cooler it became.

Pearce, sweat dripping down his face and gog-gles over his eyes, was hammering away at a piece of steel over an anvil. He was dressed in a pair of greasy, dirty overalls rolled down to his waist, heavy work boots, a short-sleeved T-shirt Dex assumed had once been white, and heavy gloves. Dex had to admit, when Pearce said he did metal work, he'd been thinking more along the lines of small items such as the pendant he'd made for himself, not blacksmithing. Dex waited for Pearce to pause before calling over to him.

"Pearce!"

Pearce looked up, surprised to see him. "Dex, hey!" His smile was wide until he saw the rest of the team, and when his gaze landed on Sloane, his expression hardened. The animosity in Pearce's face was unmistakable. "What's he doing here?"

"I'm sorry, Pearce. We're here on official THIRDS business. We need to ask you a few questions."

"I'll talk to you. Your team can take a seat." Pearce pointed toward a beat-up old couch against the wall under the windows and next to a fridge from the Cold War days. The rest of the team started heading that way, when Pearce continued. "Not your partner, though. He can wait outside."

"Pearce, Agent Brodie is—"

Pearce held a hand up and shook his head. "I'm not talking with him in the room."

Dex rubbed a hand over his jaw before walking to Sloane, pulling him to one side and speaking quietly. "How do you want to handle this?"

"You're asking me?" Sloane looked surprised.

"You're my partner, so I'm asking you. How do you want to handle this? I could lean on him."

Sloane thought it over. "No. I'll wait outside. This is too important."

"Okay." Dex watched Sloane square his shoulders and walk out of the workshop. When the thud of the heavy metal doors reverberated through the room, Dex joined Pearce, who motioned him over to a small table with a couple of mismatched chairs.

Dex sat down across from him, letting him start the conversation.

"I'm sorry. I know I've upset you by excluding your partner, but seeing him brings back a lot of unpleasant memories."

I'll bet it does. "Of course," Dex replied, sounding sincere. "I understand. We've had a breakthrough in the case. Are you familiar with a bar called the Styx? It's over in the Meatpacking District."

"Yes. I go there a lot." Pearce nodded somberly. "It's where Gabe was killed. Well, behind it anyway. I know it probably seems a little morbid, going back there, but it was his favorite." A sad smile came onto his face. "I guess I'm not ready to let it go yet."

"So were you there recently?"

Pearce nodded, removing his gloves and placing them on the table. "Three days ago. I stopped by for a drink after work."

"I'd like to show you surveillance video from that night." Dex removed his tablet from his padded front vest pocket and placed it on the table between them, bringing up the footage. "That's you, correct?"

"Yes."

"Twenty minutes in, a man in a dark hoodie enters the establishment, takes one look at you, and runs off. You run after him. Can you tell me what happened?"

Pearce's jaw muscles clenched, his fingers curling into a fist on the table. Whatever it was, the guy wasn't happy about it. "I didn't know who the guy was at the time. When he bolted, I knew something was up, so I went after him. I don't know if he made me as a cop—I'm a regular at the bar, and most of the other regulars and the staff know I work for the HPF.

Anyway, innocent guys don't run, right? I chased him all the way to Gansvoort, where I lost him in the construction area. My guess is he shifted somewhere."

"He was a Therian?"

"Yeah, I managed to get a look at his classification. He was a jaguar Therian."

Shit. Could Isaac have found their guy without knowing it? If the Therian had been there before, it was possible he could have transferred the sand onto Ortiz. "What happened next?"

"You know us cops," Isaac said with a grin. "I couldn't let it go, so I started doing some digging around." The grin faded from his face, and his expression went hard once again. "I found out the guy was a cousin of the Therian informant who killed Gabe."

Dex's eyes widened. Shit. Everything kept coming back to Gabe. It was all connected; it had to be. The case would make a lot more sense. Though there were still so many pieces of the puzzle missing.

"I don't know if he ran because he thought I somehow knew who he was and figured I'd be out for his blood, or if there was something else behind his behavior, but he was spooked."

"Have you heard from or seen him since?"

"No. He's gone underground."

"Do you have a name?"

"Tory Murphy." Pearce put his hand on Dex's, giving it a squeeze. "If there's anything I can do to help, you let me know. Please."

Oookay. Dex gave Pearce a reassuring smile. "I will. I appreciate you taking the time to talk to us." Dex went to get up when Pearce caught his arm.

"Could I speak with you a moment? It's not related to your case."

Dex searched Pearce's face, but the guy was a hard read. With a nod, he tapped his earpiece. "Rosa, Cael, I have all the information I need. It's online. We'll meet you back at HQ and fill you in. Sloane, I'll be out in a minute."

Sloane's gruff voice came over his earpiece. "Copy that."

Pearce waited for Rosa and Cael to leave the workshop before turning his attention back to Dex. What did Pearce have to say about Sloane now? He could understand Pearce's anguish. Having a younger brother of his own, he couldn't even think about something happening to him, despite knowing the risks involved in their line of work, but blaming the organization he worked for or the team members who worked alongside him was not only an unhealthy route to take, but an unbecoming one.

"You and your partner have gotten close."

Dex shrugged. "We got off to a rough start, but we're getting along better these days. I wouldn't say we're close."

Pearce gave a nod, his lips pursed together. What was the guy not telling him? He couldn't know about him and Sloane, and neither of them had given the slightest indication they were more than work partners, especially since Dex didn't even know what was going on between them.

"This all must be very hard for him."

"It's difficult for the whole team." Dex sat back, waiting. Pearce was working his way up to something;

Dex could feel it in his gut. He just didn't know what it was.

"Yes, but more for him. He really loved Gabe. I know I was an asshole to him, and I regret a lot of the things I said and did. I realize now how stupid I was. Brodie was good to my brother, made him happy. Those two…." Pearce smiled. "They probably would have been married by now. I can't imagine being that in love with someone. Can you?"

Dex gave a noncommittal hum, his gaze wandering around the workshop and finally landing back on the table in front of him, where he pushed his gloved finger into a tiny mound of silver dust. Isaac caught him doing it.

"You don't want to do that. Sorry, I should've cleaned it up. That shit will get everywhere. Gets in your lungs if you're not careful." He got up and walked off to a small stainless steel cabinet. He came back with a small dustpan, brush, and box of antibacterial wipes. He cleared the tiny dust pile away.

Dex grimaced. "Sorry."

"It's okay." Pearce popped open a box of wipes and plucked one out before he took Dex's gloved hand. He wiped Dex's finger and chucked the towelette in the trash bin behind him. "There we go."

"Thanks."

Pearce gave him a wink and patted him on the vest. "Uniform looks good on you, by the way."

Dex shifted uncomfortably. "Um, thank you. Still getting used to it. Weighs a fuckton."

"You going shy on me, Daley?"

"Me? Shy? *Pfft.*" Dex waved a hand in dismissal. Pearce moved his chair closer to Dex as he sat and leaned in. Looked like they were finally getting somewhere.

"Okay. Listen, I know Sloane thinks I hate him, but I don't. Yes, at the time I didn't agree with his relationship with my brother, and I said a lot of terrible things, but after Gabe died, I knew I had to put it behind me. The guilt ate at me for a long time. I don't want Sloane around because he reminds me of how happy my brother was. Gabe was a different person around Sloane." Pearce stopped, his head cocking to one side. "Am I making you uncomfortable talking about them?"

Dex frowned. "Why would I be uncomfortable?"

"Come on, Dex. You care about him, and I don't blame you. There's clearly something about him that attracts all these nice guys. But Sloane is still in love with Gabe. I'd hate to see you get hurt. Have you considered the possibility that he might be looking at you as a replacement for Gabe?"

Dex met Pearce's gaze dead on. "My relationship with Agent Brodie is strictly professional. There's affection there, I won't lie. He's a good guy, and I enjoy working with him. He's a good partner, but you're wrong if you think I'm a replacement for your brother." He recalled Sloane's words to Ash in the hospital when he'd woken up, how Dex was nothing like Gabe. Sloane had even accused him of it, and although he'd apologized and insisted he hadn't meant it, there was still a part of him that wondered if it was true. Maybe Sloane wasn't aware of it. Regardless, it was none of Pearce's business, and Dex wasn't about to show his hand to anyone, much less Pearce, who was studying him like a hawk.

"Is that what you wanted to talk to me about? I appreciate your concern, I do, but it's not necessary. There's nothing between Sloane and me. What he had with your brother was clearly very special. I hope you both find the strength to heal and move on."

Something flashed in Pearce's eyes, and Dex gave him a sympathetic smile. He reached over and patted Pearce's hand. "If you need someone to talk to, you call. I'm always ready to listen."

Pearce's expression softened, and he nodded. Dex thanked Pearce once again and headed for the exit, Pearce's stare boring into the back of him as he walked. As he headed for the parked Suburban, Dex's earpiece beeped. He tapped it to answer the call.

"Daley here."

"Hey, it's Calvin. I got Intel to run Gabe's name through Themis and cross-reference it with our victims like you asked."

Dex was surprised. He hadn't expected the results so quickly. Looked like his dad had gotten tired of waiting and busted a few balls. "And?"

"The first two victims have connections to Gabe."

"What?"

"When we ran Isaac through Themis, we got nothing but Maddock's initial entry, and then the video from the Styx. When we ran Gabe, we hit the mother lode. Victim number one, Bennett? He went to the same college as Gabe. They took several HumaniTherian courses together throughout the four years. Victim number two, Chambers, ran the Brooklyn Therian Youth Center. It was Gabe's first job after college."

Shit. "What about Ortiz?"

"No hits there."

"Thanks." Dex hurried toward the car and quickly climbed into the passenger side.

Sloane gave him a questioning look, and Dex filled him in. He sat silently as Sloane soaked up the new information. He'd been expecting Sloane to get pissed off at him for putting in the request without telling him about it, but he'd wanted to be sure his hunch had merit before bringing it up with Sloane. Instead of getting annoyed, Sloane gave him a nod.

"Good work."

"Thanks." Dex buckled up. "Did you get the notes from my interview with him?"

"Yep. So what are we thinking?"

Dex gave it some thought. "I don't get it. Let's say Murphy's out for some payback for his cousin. He finds two HumaniTherians connected to Gabe. He's been to the Styx on more than one occasion. Only this time, he transfers some of the sand onto Ortiz when he kills him. He visits his favorite bar again, but this time he runs into Gabe's brother, recognizes him, and makes a run for it. Aside from the fact we don't know why he would kill the first two victims, at least we know they're connected to Gabe, but what about Ortiz?" Dex pulled out his tablet and brought up Tory Murphy's police record. "This guy's an informant, or was. How does he murder three Humans without leaving any evidence behind, without being spotted, without a trace he'd been in the vicinity? And if Murphy wanted revenge, why not someone closer to Gabe? Why not the team? Why not you? According to Themis, Gabe hadn't spoken to Bennett or Chambers in years."

"Goddamn it!" Sloane slammed his hand on the steering wheel. "None of this makes any fucking

sense. We need to find Murphy. He saw Isaac and bolted, and we need to know why. Right now all we got
is theories."

The communication system in the car beeped,
and Sloane hit the speaker button. "Agent Brodie
speaking."

"It's Maddock. We've put an APB out for Tory
Murphy. We can confirm he's a jaguar Therian, which
puts him in the right classification. He's got motive
and means. We need to bring him in. Themis is getting us a list of known locations for him as well as
cross-referencing him with our victims. Also, Hudson
confirms there was black sand found on Gabe at the
time of his death, but that doesn't tell us anything we
don't already know—that he'd been inside the Styx
before ending up outside in the alley. Head back to
HQ. We're sending out all of Unit Alpha's Recon and
part of the Defense Department to find this guy. Unit
Beta's going to take our lower-risk cases off our hands
until this thing is solved."

"Yes, sir." Sloane sat back and started the engine,
and Dex couldn't help but notice how worn-out his
partner looked. He reached over and put a hand on
Sloane's arm.

"Hey, we're going to get to the bottom of this."

Sloane gave him a weary smile. "Thanks."

They headed back to HQ with Dex mulling
over his predicament. He was eager to get this case
solved. Having other agents do the legwork for him
was something he wasn't accustomed to. It would take
time. He knew as much. Still, he wished he could do
more. He'd been tempted on more than one occasion
to go off on his own, but he quickly stamped down

the urge. This wasn't the HPF. He was part of a team now. They all had their part to play, and any agent who failed to do his part would let down the rest of his team. Dex didn't want to let his team down. What's more, he didn't want to let Sloane down.

They spent the rest of the day divvying up the city among their unit's agents and transferring their low-risk cases to Unit Beta. At a unit briefing held in a small auditorium on the tenth floor, Dex got to see Lieutenant Sonya Sparks for the first time. Dex had been so busy getting used to his new position, he hadn't given any thought to the lieutenant who had hired him. Until now she'd been in Washington, fighting to get their unit the priority and clearance levels needed to get this case solved. It was the toughest one the THIRDS had faced in a long time. The bigwigs wanted it solved ASAP, but like any other government organization, they balked when the words "additional funding" made an appearance.

Lieutenant Sparks resembled a classic Hollywood pinup. In her refined white pantsuit, her curves were impressive. She was tall and intimidating, with bright red locks, big green eyes, and scarlet red lips. She had perfectly manicured nails painted in a similar shade to her lipstick, and according to Tony, half the Defense Department in DC was scared shitless of her. The interesting thing was, she never raised her voice, and she smiled. Her eyes marked her as being Therian, her classification a cougar. Any agent who was stupid enough to make a joke about it would end up wishing he'd never been born. Dex liked her already.

The briefing ran for hours. There were several occasions when some of the Intel guys were yammering on about algorithms, forcing Sloane to nudge Dex awake. Cael, on the other hand, seemed enthralled. Nerd. By the end, Dex couldn't wait to get out of there. In the showers while the rest of their team was washing away, Dex sneaked a few glances at Sloane. His partner had been pensive since their return from Pearce's workshop. Dex lingered, washing up slowly while the rest of the team finished up and headed out into the locker room to dress, leaving Dex and Sloane. He leaned over the thick frosted-glass partition.

"You okay?" The longer this case remained unsolved, the more Sloane seemed to retreat into himself.

Sloane blinked and looked up at him. "What?"

"Are you okay?" Dex put his hand to Sloane's arm. This case was taking its toll on everyone, especially his partner, whose shaky smile pulled at Dex's heart.

"No, but what can we do but move forward, right?"

"Listen, why don't you come over to my place tonight? We'll chill, have a couple of cold ones, and watch dumb people doing dumb things on TV. How about it?"

Sloane turned off his shower and nodded. "Okay. But I need to go home first, grab a few things. Haven't had a chance to do laundry yet."

"Sounds good."

They stepped out of the showers, towels wrapped around them, when Dex felt Sloane's hand on his ass. He leaned in to whisper in Dex's ear from behind.

"Maybe we'll find an even better way to relax."

Dex felt his face go up in flames. He turned his head, his lips inches away from Sloane's. "I'm sure we could come up with something." If Sloane's quiet words hadn't been enough to get Dex squirming in his towel, Sloane's quick kiss to his lips sealed the deal. Oh God, he was about to get a hard-on at work, and the bastard that was the cause of it was loving every moment of it.

Think unsexy thoughts. Think unsexy thoughts.

Ash's growl echoed through the showers. "What are you two gay boys doing in there?"

Aaand done.

Sloane rolled his eyes as he headed toward the locker room with Dex. When they got outside, Dex smiled pleasantly at Ash. "We were talking about opening a strip club together. We're going to call it Destructive Divas. You can't be in it, on account of your allergy to nuts, but we're willing to take you on as our mascot. How do you feel about leather chaps?"

Ash snarled at him.

"No? Latex?"

"Fuck you, Daley." Ash slammed his locker shut and stormed off. With a satisfied grin, Dex turned to Sloane, who was chuckling as he got dressed.

"I think he's coming around."

"Coming around to give you a beating," Sloane replied, slipping into his coat and zipping up. "I'll see you later." He gave Dex a pat on the back, and with Dex facing the rest of the team, his teammates couldn't see the way Sloane's fingers grazed down Dex's spine, falling away only when they reached his lower back. Dex clenched his teeth, watching Sloane stroll out of the locker room. Cocky bastard. Dex was going to have to make him suffer tonight.

"I'm glad you two are getting along."

Dex smiled at his brother as he got dressed. "Yeah. I was worried at first, but we worked it out."

"You mean you wore him down," Cael teased.

Dex couldn't help but laugh. "That too."

"What are you up to tonight?"

Hopefully lots of sweaty, grunting, sexy man sex. "I invited Sloane over for a couple of beers, see if I can't get his mind off this case for a while. It's really doing a number on him."

Cael's smile faded, a heavy sigh escaping him as he leaned into the locker. "Yeah, it sucks."

"You okay?" Dex closed his locker and studied his brother. There were dark circles under his eyes, and his face was paler than usual. As much as he wanted sexy time with Sloane, if his brother needed him, he'd be there. "You want to come? You look like you could use a little distraction."

"Nah, I'm fine, just haven't had much sleep trying to find something to go on. Thanks for the invite, but I'm going to catch a movie with Ash."

"Ash? I didn't know you guys hung out." Not that he had anything against it, but it was weird. Ash was so unlike Cael in every way, and Cael had an aversion to douchebags, yet he didn't seem to have a problem with Ash.

Cael shrugged. "Yeah, since I first joined. He's cool."

That made Dex snort. "You and I have very different definitions of what cool is."

"No, really, he is. I know he comes off as a jerk sometimes—don't make that face at me—but that's just what he's like at work. I mean, he's got to be tough. He's a First Gen Alpha. A lot of agents look up to him, have expectations, but he's always been nice to me."

Ash was capable of making friends. Who knew?

"Okay, you crazy kids have fun. Call me if you need me." He gave Cael's cheek a pat and walked off, pretending he wasn't at all excited about Sloane coming over tonight. Man, he was in trouble if he was excited this early in the game.

SLOANE FOUND himself tapping his fingers against his steering wheel in rhythm to some cheesy pop song on the drive home. He hadn't even realized he'd been doing it. What the hell was he listening to anyway? At the red light, he checked the station, wondering how it had gotten on *Retro Radio*. That ass. Sloane couldn't help but chuckle. Dex must have switched the station before getting out of the car that morning, because they certainly hadn't listened to it on the way to work. He reached to switch it off but decided to leave it. God help him, he must be losing his mind, but he felt oddly comforted by it.

He pulled up to a space across from his apartment building, smiling. There was also a strange fluttering in his stomach at the thought of getting to spend the night with Dex in bed. He knew he shouldn't get used to it, but if Dex was willing—and offering—to fool around without the strings attached or drama, why should Sloane refuse? Especially knowing how much he wanted it, how good it felt to be with someone who made him feel happy again. As he crossed the street, he wondered how Dex felt about the whole thing. There had been plenty of instances that could have been awkward, where everything could have turned into a disaster, but Dex had diffused any possible explosive situation with a warm smile and a tender understanding that always left Sloane breathless.

"Hey."

Sloane stopped cold at the familiar voice. "Isaac?"

Isaac stood from where he'd been seated on the ledge beside Sloane's apartment building's steps, an apologetic smile on his face. "I hope you don't mind. I wanted to talk to you about something."

"You didn't have to wait out here. You could have called."

"I thought after everything, you might tell me to get lost, and I wouldn't blame you. I've been a real prick. I brought you a peace offering." Isaac waved a brown-and-pink paper bag at him.

"Is that…?"

"Roasted plantain empanadas from Dos Caminos."

"Wow." Sloane took the bag from Isaac, his mouth watering at the thought. It had been ages since he'd had these. In fact, he hadn't been to the restaurant since he'd last been there with Gabe and Isaac, in one of Gabe's many kindhearted attempts to get them to tolerate each other.

"Didn't think I remembered?"

More like he didn't believe the guy cared enough to pay attention. "Thanks." He wasn't sure what to make of Isaac and his peace offering. There was no lost love between them, but this case had Sloane feeling upside-down and inside out.

Isaac pointed up to the High Line. "How about a walk? You eat, I'll talk. There's a can of Coke in there too."

"Okay." Sloane led the way to the glass elevator, pressing the floor for the High Line. At this time
of night in November, there weren't a lot of people
strolling about. He made sure to stay alert as he followed Isaac and dug into the first empanada. He loved
empanadas. They were a guilty pleasure of his. "I forgot how good these were," he moaned. Roasted plan-
tains, black beans, peppers, cheese, and spices. He still
couldn't get over the fact Isaac was here. Whatever the
reason, Sloane was sure it had something to do with
Gabe, so he should at least hear the guy out.

They walked down the High Line, the vegetation
and trees bare and dry now that it was nearly winter but
still oddly beautiful in a melancholic way. "I'm sorry
I can't stay long, I'm supposed to be meeting someone," Sloane said, finishing off his last empanada.

"Dex?"

Sloane swallowed and cleared his throat. "Yeah.
We were going to hang out awhile. Unwind."

Isaac headed to the rail's edge overlooking West
Fourteenth Street. "He's the reason I'm here, to be
honest."

Sloane came to stand beside Isaac, the chilly
breeze blowing Sloane's hair into his face. He brushed
it behind his ears, reminding himself he needed a cut
before Maddock started his routine threat of taking a
pair of scissors to it. "How's that?"

"Dex is a really good guy. We didn't get to talk
much at the Sixth while he was there, but then I didn't
talk much at all at the time. But I'd seen the way he
was with everyone, the way they loved him. Well,
until the mess with his partner. He cares, where most

would tell you to get on with it. He's a little weird," Isaac said with a chuckle, "but in a good way."

Sloane found himself smiling again. "Yeah."

"Anyway, when you guys came by today, I had a chat with him, and he really got me thinking." Isaac turned to him, his expression sympathetic. "This whole feud between us…. What's the point? We hurt Gabe a lot while he was alive, and if he's up there somewhere…." Isaac turned his face up to the night sky. "He'd be royally pissed with me."

Sloane didn't say anything, mostly because he didn't know what to say. Was it too little, too late? Isaac seemed sincere. Maybe he really did want to put the past behind him. Sloane leaned against the rail, frowning.

"You okay?" Isaac's hand went to Sloane's shoulder. "You're looking a little pale."

"Hm? Yeah, sorry. It's been a long day." Long week, long month, long year, long life….

"Want to sit down?"

Sloane's vision got blurry, and he grabbed on to the railings to steady himself as a wave of dizziness and nausea washed over him. What the hell? He was sweating, a cold chill running through his body.

"I came because I was worried about Dex. Talking to him today, I could see it happening."

"I'm sorry?" Sloane blinked and tried to shake himself out of whatever the hell was happening. Was he coming down with something? It was that time of year, and there were a few agents in their department who'd come down with the flu, but he'd never had blurry vision because of it. He leaned heavier on the rail.

"He likes you. Defends you. I tried to warn him about you, but you've worked that Brodie magic on him." Isaac stepped up to him, a hand patting Sloane's cheek, and the world seemed to tilt on its axis. Sloane's legs gave out from under him, and he slid down against the rail, his blood running cold. His limbs felt heavy, his movements sluggish. *Oh God.*

"What did you do to me?"

Isaac crouched down beside him, and the sound of an elevator pinged somewhere behind him. "I added an extra ingredient to your empanadas. All those Mexican spices work wonders covering up my special little serum."

Two large figures clad in black approached them, and Sloane grabbed Isaac's sleeve, his muscles seizing up. His chest constricted, and he was finding it hard to breathe. "Please, Isaac. Don't do this."

"Maybe I couldn't save my brother from you, but I'll save Dex. I'll make him see." Isaac stood, his words sounding fuzzy and far away.

"Looks like my friend's had a little too much to drink. Help me take him home, will you?"

Sloane tried to reach for his sleeve in the hopes of getting to his communicator underneath, but his body refused to cooperate. He was dragged to his feet, a terrifying darkness encroaching in on him. Shutting his eyes tight, his last thought before the darkness swallowed him up was of his failure. First he'd failed Gabe, now he'd failed Dex.

Dex....

Please forgive me.

Chapter 13

DEX SAT in front of his TV, his stocking feet up on the coffee table as he popped another Cheesy Doo-dle in his mouth. Where the hell was Sloane? Had he actually gone home to pick up some clothes or knit some new ones? He looked at his watch for the ump-teenth time. The beers had all but soaked through the cardboard coasters. Had Sloane changed his mind? Dex bolted upright. Crap, what if Sloane wasn't com-ing? What if he'd changed his mind about everything, about Dex, about whatever was going on between them? He'd suspected it wouldn't last, but he hadn't thought it would happen so soon.

"Stop being such a prom queen." Dex pulled out his cell phone and called Sloane up. After several rings, it went to voicemail. He was not going to freak out about this. "You knew the score, Dex." He tossed his phone onto the couch cushion beside him and sulked. He'd really thought they might have had a shot at something. "Over before it's begun," he murmured. With a groan, he let his head fall into his hands. His life was officially a bad eighties movie. Without the parachute pants. Checking his watch again, he decided to cut his losses and go to bed. It was already past midnight anyway.

He headed for the stairs when his phone went off. Crap! He'd left it on the couch. Like a teenage girl, he sped across the floor to get it, leaping over the back of the couch, landing with a bounce on the cushions and snatching it up. He hadn't even checked the caller ID.

"Hello?"

"Hey, Dex, sorry to be calling this late."

Dex tried not to feel too disappointed at hearing Calvin's voice instead of Sloane's. He sat back, an arm wrapped around his drawn-up knee, suppressing a sigh. For fuck's sake, he really was turning into some giddy teenager. "It's okay. What's up?"

"We found Ford Wallace."

Dex perked up. At least there was some good news tonight. "Where?"

"In some shithole apartment building in Brownsville."

"Hold on." Dex jumped off the couch and ran to the kitchen to grab a notepad and pen. "What's the address? I want to ask the bastard a few questions."

"Unless you're gonna do it using a Ouija board, that's gonna be kind of tough."

Dex froze. "He's dead?"

"Ripped to shreds. It's like something out of a slasher movie. Blood and guts everywhere, more of that black sand mixed with some other white powdery stuff. Actually, it's more a silvery powder."

"Wait. Do you have specifics on the powder?" Dex's heart lodged itself in his throat. It couldn't be. It was probably some dirt or other debris, and he was getting worked up over nothing. "Can I talk to Hudson?"

"What can I do for you, Dex?"

"Hudson, the powder you found, can you tell what it is?"

"One moment."

Dex heard Hudson moving around, clanking things together before he came back on the line.

"I can't tell you the exact elements without getting it back to the lab, but I can confirm it's some form of alloy. Steel perhaps."

"Oh fuck. It's him." Dex walked over to the couch and slowly sank into it, unable to believe it. The guy had fooled them all, leading them on a wild goose chase. No wonder everything kept going back to Gabe. Who was more obsessed with Gabe's murder than Isaac Pearce?

"What? Who?"

"Pearce," Dex replied, as he tried to make sense of everything. Pearce had alibis, he had evidence, he wasn't even the right species as their perp, but somehow, Dex knew in his gut. "He said the guy in the surveillance video was Tory Murphy, but I'm willing to bet it was our Eagles cap guy. Ford Wallace. Something must have happened after Pearce paid him to warn me off. He went after Wallace, and when we started getting close, he killed him."

"But I thought Isaac Pearce wasn't a suspect."

"I don't know what's going on, but I know Pearce is our guy. I can feel it in my gut. That silver dust was all over his workshop. Tell Sarge to get the team geared up and come pick me up. It'll be faster. And bring my gear!" He hung up and started pacing the room. Shit, Sloane! He dialed Sloane's number again, a sick feeling washing over him.

"Come on, pal. Pick up. Please, pick up." He didn't care what Sloane was doing. After the fifth try, he left a message. "Sloane, buddy, you gotta ring me ASAP. Pearce is our guy." He hung up and called Ash. The phone rang, and Ash's pleasant growl came on the line.

"What do you want?"

"Is Sloane with you?"

"Cael said you two were having a slumber party or some shit."

"I'm too worried right now to tell you to fuck off, so some other time. Oh God." Dex tried his hardest to calm down. Ash must have sensed something was wrong because when he spoke, his voice was filled with concern.

"Please tell me Sloane is with you."

Dex swallowed hard, a surreal feeling enveloping him. It couldn't be.

"Dex!"

"Ash, I think Pearce has Sloane."

TWENTY MINUTES later, a convoy of black Suburbans with flashing blue lights and three Bear-Cats, including Destructive Delta's, infiltrated Sunnyside, Queens. They blocked both ends of the street. Dex climbed out of the BearCat with the rest of his team, waiting for Tony's instructions. He refused to give in to the sick, foreboding feeling in his gut. They'd find Sloane, and he'd be napping or drunk off his face somewhere safe and sound, and then Dex would tear him a new one, they'd have make-up sex, and the world would be as it should.

Pearce's house was a narrow brick building with concrete pathways on each side that led to the building's backyard. The pathway was closed off by a chain-link gate with a cinder block on the ground propped up against it. The top floor of the building had a fire escape on the front windows, but only the right ones. Defense agents quickly got to work surrounding the building, while snipers made their way to the rooftops of the apartment buildings across from the residential neighborhood. Tony's voice came over Dex's earpiece.

"Destructive Delta, Beta Pride and Beta Ambush have scouted the perimeter. The ground floor windows are all secured with burglar bars, as is the rear entrance. From what they can see and hear, it doesn't seem like our perp is home. You're clear to go in. Use caution. We have no idea what we're going to find in there." Tony's voice was grave, his final sentence sending a chill up his spine. Dex exchanged glances with his brother. They were thinking the same thing. *Please don't let us find Sloane dead in there.*

Dex grabbed the breaching gun, and he carefully, but quickly, crept up to the door, the rest of his team in formation behind him with rifles at the ready. The front door had burglar bars, but only over the glass. Dex stuck the barrel of the large gun up to the lock and, after taking a deep breath, pulled the trigger. A flurry of activity followed the loud *bang* as he dashed out of the way, allowing his team access to the house. He handed the breaching gun to a fellow Defense agent before removing the safety on his rifle and going in after his team. They moved from room to room, making sure everything was clear, covering each other's backs and looking out for any movement. The house was average-sized, two bedrooms, living room, small foyer, kitchen, dining room, bathroom, and office. It looked like any other home.

"Clear!" Ash declared over his earpiece.

Now that there was no immediate threat, the Recon agents flooded the place. They'd turn this place inside out, search every nook and cranny, under every piece of furniture, in every available space, all in search of evidence and any hint their teammate was in danger. Dex made his way through the living room, spotting all the framed photographs of Pearce and Gabe, from when they were kids up until Gabe joined the THIRDS. He stepped up to a photo of a smiling Gabe. He'd been about Dex's age, handsome, a bright light shining in his eyes. Dex felt his heart squeeze. It was stupid, but he glanced around him, found there was no one within hearing distance, and picked up the frame.

"I know you can't hear me, and I might be losing it, but please, help me find him. I need to find him." He swallowed hard, fighting back the fear threatening to grip him tight, statistics and facts hammering away at his heart. "I can see why you fell in love with him and why you'd want him back. He's a good guy. But maybe… maybe you can let me look after him for a while?"

Something shattered behind him, and he gave a start. In the kitchen, Cael stared down at something on the floor in pieces. He looked up at Dex and shrugged. "Sorry. I must have knocked it over when I turned around."

Shaking his head at his own silliness, Dex returned the frame to the mantle and joined his brother who was picking up pieces of what he'd broken. It was an "I heart coffee" ceramic mug that wasn't going to be hearting any coffee anytime soon. He was about to head back into the living room when he saw a small shard belonging to the mug over by the fridge. Walking over, he saw it was a small red heart. He reached down and plucked it from the floor when a breeze hit his cheek. Turning his face toward it, he saw a groove running up along the wall behind the fridge.

"Cael, get over here."

"What?" Cael stood beside him, and Dex pointed to the fridge.

"Help me move this. I think there's something behind it." They each took one side and shifted the heavy two-door refrigerator out of the way. "Fuck me, it's a door." He tapped his earpiece. "Destructive Delta, I found something in the kitchen." His team was there in seconds, standing behind him and Cael, staring at the door. There was no door handle. He put a gloved hand to the painted wood, testing it, and pushed it in. The door popped out.

Dex quickly took a step back along with the rest of the team. Motioning for them to move out of the way, he flattened against the wall to the left of the door and gradually opened it. "Hobbs," Dex whispered, motioning to the dark entryway. If there were anything fishy, any explosives, Hobbs would sniff them out. The large agent approached the door, rifle in hand. He checked the doorway before disappearing inside. A few seconds later, Hobbs came back out and nodded. Coast was clear. Dex went in first, making his way down the wooden steps to what appeared to be a basement. Why would Pearce block off his basement? It was clearly in use, seeing as how Dex spotted the small high window across the stairs that had been left slightly open. At first it looked like any other basement with stacked boxes, washing machine, dryer, shelving units, filing cabinets, old exercise equipment, anda dust-covered Christmas tree box, but when he turned the corner, it became anything but.

Making a beeline for the wall behind the stairs, Dex came to an abrupt halt in front of it, his chest constricting and a lump forming in his throat at the eight-by-ten photograph pinned to the huge corkboard. "Oh my God…." Slowly he stepped up to it, doing his best to keep his hand steady as he plucked it from the board. He stared down at the haunting scene captured through a madman's lens. Beautiful blue skies, rich green hues on manicured lawns with blooming flowers in pinks, reds, and yellows. In the center, Sloane, dressed in ceremonial uniform, was helping the rest of his team carry the coffin of his fallen lover and partner. The grief and despair in his face was so acute, it tore at Dex's heart.

He forced his gaze up, swallowing hard at all the photographs of Gabe's funeral. Each and every one had Sloane in them. Corkboards filled with photos of Sloane lined the entire wall.

"What the hell?" Ash stood stunned. He reached up and snatched another photo off the wall. His eyes became glassy and he shoved the photo at Dex. "What kind of sick fuck would do this?"

The photo in Ash's hand was yet another of Sloane, and it was even more heartbreaking than the last. Dex wouldn't be able to get the image out of his mind for a long time. No man should have his anguish displayed for the world to see. Sloane was crouched down in front of Gabe's tombstone, a hand to his mouth as he cried. There were several more like it. An intimate moment that should have been respected had been violated by a man who took pleasure in another's despair.

A call came in to Dex's earpiece, and he tapped it. "Daley."

"Have you found my little treasure trove?"

"Pearce." Dex did his best to control his voice. He wanted to lose his shit, to beat the ever-living hell out of Isaac Pearce and show him what real pain was, to make him suffer the way he'd made Sloane suffer. Instead he took a steady breath. "Where's my partner?"

"Sloane and I are reminiscing about the good old days. You're welcome to join us, but your friends will have to stay behind. If I see them, the next you'll see of your partner is a viral video of him bleeding to death after I slit his throat."

Dex refused to play into Pearce's game. He replied calmly. "Where?"

"The only love I have left. See you soon."

The line went dead, and Dex tapped his earpiece, then remembered Pearce had called him on there. Shit. He pulled out his cell phone and called his dad. "Sarge, I got a call from Pearce."

"I know. We all heard it. Our line's been compromised. Get your team out here."

Dex hung up and slipped his phone back into his pocket to address his team. "Let's go. Sarge wants us outside." They left and reported their find to the Recon agents, who took off toward the basement to collect all the evidence. Outside, Tony waited by the Bear-Cat. He climbed in when they approached, and they followed.

"Dex, do you know where he is?" Tony asked, manning the surveillance console.

"Yeah, he's at his workshop in Brooklyn. The place is a minefield." He tapped the address into the system, and a 3-D street map popped up. Dex pointed to the right of the building. "There. It's filled with self-storage units and a garden supply center. It's completely visible from the fourth-floor windows, which are the only side windows of the building."

"Ash," Tony prompted.

Ash stepped up to the 3-D map, dragging and turning it on screen as he studied it. "We can get snipers on the shipping department across the street. It'll be easy access, since all the roofs connect. The workshop building is another story. We can park the BearCat here next to the kitchen stone tile company. It leads to the Indoor Lumber Yard parking lot, but the scaffolding all around that area will conceal us. There's scaffolding here next to the building where they're working on the girders; we could put some guys—"

Dex shook his head. "No guys across the street or girders. If Pearce gets wind there's anyone remotely near him who isn't me, he'll kill Sloane."

Ash rubbed a hand over his face, and Dex could feel the guy's frustration. "You know he's going to try and kill him anyway. He's always blamed Sloane for Gabe's death."

"I know." Dex was determined to do whatever it took to get Sloane back in one piece. "But I also know he wants to talk. He's been trying to get me on his side from the beginning. If I can make him believe I'm coming around to his way of seeing things, I might be able to distract him long enough to take him down, or at the very least, get Sloane out of there."

"He's a cop, Dex. He's not stupid," Ash argued. "The second you walk in there, he's going to disarm you. Then we've got two hostages."

Dex turned to his dad. "I don't need to be armed to take him down. I can do this."

Ash shook his head. "You can't send in a rookie to take down Pearce. Best case scenario, he gets himself caught. Worst, he gets himself and Sloane killed."

"I can do this," Dex repeated adamantly, meeting his dad's gaze. "You know I can."

Tony leaned an elbow on the chair's armrest, his gaze on Dex as he mulled it over. "Okay, you're going in, but we're going to be close by. Cael, I want you to set up a second line of communication and hide the signal. Keep the first line open to the rest of Unit Alpha's Defense agents stationed on Tenth and Second. Hobbs, get us over there."

The ride over took mere minutes, though it seemed like a lifetime to Dex. As soon as the Bear-Cat pulled up to the Indoor Lumber Yard parking lot, Tony stood and put a hand to Dex's shoulder. "You get yourself killed, and I will find a way to bring you back so I can kick your ass. You understand me?"

Dex swallowed hard and threw his arms around his dad, talking in his ear. "I'll be careful." Tony gave him a squeeze before releasing him.

"Get going."

With good luck wishes from his team, Dex climbed out of the truck when Ash stepped in his way.

Seriously? They were going to do this now? The guy really needed to learn when to give it a rest. "What is it, Ash? I'm kind of in the middle of something."

Ash loomed over him, his expression guarded and his face set in grim lines. He poked Dex in the vest. "You bring him back alive, Rookie. You got me?" His brows drew together, and he avoided Dex's gaze. "And don't get dead."

Dex stood speechless. Was Ash actually worried about him? He opened his mouth, but before he could utter a word, Ash stormed off, disappearing inside the BearCat. Shaking himself out of it, Dex ran through the parking lot onto a narrow road that ran along the back of Pearce's workshop. Two lefts, and he was there. He tried to peek inside the front window, but besides all the grime, dirt, and rust, most of the window was boarded up on the inside. At least he knew Pearce was the only tenant in the building. Still, he was going in blind. His worst nightmare. Opening the front door, he held his rifle up with one hand as he made his way through the foyer when Pearce called out.

"In here."

Slowly, Dex entered the workshop, biting down on his tongue to keep quiet. Sloane stood in the middle of the workshop, arms high above his head, a couple

of thick chains hanging from the ceiling binding his
wrists, another around his neck to keep him from
shifting to his Therian form. If he shifted, he'd end
up breaking his neck. His ankles were bound by duct
tape, and he was bare-chested, his black T-shirt on the
floor. There were cuts and lacerations spread over his
torso and arms, along with small burn marks. That son
of a bitch had tortured him. Dex couldn't tell if Sloane
was breathing. His head hung low, his black hair falling in disarray.

"Sloane?"

On hearing his name, Sloane's head came up, his
eyes widening. He shook his head, his muscles straining and pushing as he tugged against the chains holding him. Dex took a step forward when Pearce stepped
out from behind one of the pillars, a steel poker with a
glowing tip in his hand.

"Hello, Dex. Thank you for coming."

"Pearce." Dex managed to say the name without
spitting it out. Normally he could be objective with his
feelings when it came to a case. That's where his sense
of humor came in, keeping him from falling into the
ugliness that was the world around them sometimes.
But now? Right now he hated Isaac Pearce, and the
worst part was that he had to act as if he didn't. "I'm
here like you asked. Can we talk? I'd like to understand what all this is about."

"All right, because you asked so nicely. But first
you can put your equipment over on the couch. That
includes weapons, vest, gloves, everything in your
pockets, and your earpiece—make sure you turn it off
first. And don't try anything or…." He put the tip of
the fiery poker near Sloane's skin, causing his partner

to cry out, his eyes shut tight. The muffled scream shook Dex down to his very core. "At this temperature, this will go through his body like butter."

"I understand." Dex released his rifle, letting it hang from its straps, and put his hands up. He walked to the couch and started removing all his equipment, including his earpiece. He'd have to find another way to communicate with his team. Pearce's eyes watched his every move.

"You're going to ask me why. This is about doing what we do best, Dex. Seeking justice."

"For Gabe's death." Dex unfastened the straps to his vest and laid it down on the cushions, followed by his thigh rig. He needed an opportunity to get closer to Pearce. From what he gathered, the guy wasn't carrying any firearms, though this place was filled with tools that could easily be fashioned into a weapon, which was exactly what Dex had hoped. Finished with taking off his gear, he turned with hands held up, and Pearce motioned him over to where he'd stood previously.

"Exactly! See, you do understand. I knew you would. He has to pay for what he did to my brother. It's his fault Gabe's dead."

Dex did his best to sound sympathetic. "Isaac. It's not Sloane's fault Gabe was there that night. We talked about that, remember?"

"You're right. It wasn't his fault Gabe was there," Pearce replied through his teeth, his hard gaze on Dex. "But it was his fault *I* was."

What? "You were there when Gabe got killed?" Dex recalled the conversation they'd had at the pub when it dawned on him. Pearce hadn't been blaming himself....

"We argued that night, said things we didn't mean. Next thing I know... he's dead. If I'd walked away.... I think it's the guilt eating away at me. If I'd left him alone, maybe he'd still be alive."

He'd been confessing.

Pearce nodded, his eyes glazed. Suddenly he let out an anguished cry. "I never wanted to hurt him. I *loved* him!" Tears sprang in his eyes, his face red and contorted with anger and pain. "I was trying to keep him safe, talk some sense into him. I thought if I kept trying, he would eventually come around, but instead he became angrier and more frustrated. The night he went to meet his informant behind the Styx was supposed to be his last night before he took off on his vacation, so I went to warn him, to tell him he deserved better than some Therian piece of shit. He told me he'd had enough. That I had to choose. Can you believe it? He told me, *me*, his own brother, that I had to either accept his relationship, or he'd walk out of my life for good." Pearce grabbed Sloane's jaw, squeezing until Dex saw Sloane wince. Dex had to do something quick before things got out of hand.

As if they weren't already.

"That must have hurt you," Dex said carefully, moving so he could be in Pearce's field of vision. "What happened then, Pearce? What did you say to Gabe?"

Pearce turned his attention back to Dex, the hand carrying the poker dropping to his side. "Well, I sure as hell wasn't going to accept it. My baby brother with a Therian? No. No way. So we argued, and the more we argued, the more he defended this bastard. I was livid. Gabe was choosing *him* over his own family. He shoved me, so I shoved back." Pearce wiped the tears from his cheeks. "It was only when he was lying on the ground with his neck broken that I realized what I'd done. When that Therian punk showed up, I knew what I had to do. Afterward, I watched the chaos. Front-page news. 'THIRDS Human agent killed by Therian informant.' The worse the news stories became, the more I saw how little it would take to start a war in this city." Pearce's lips lifted in a truly sinister smile. "It's already begun."

"So you had those HumaniTherians killed?"

"I didn't have anyone killed," Pearce stated proudly. He waited, watching Dex intently, until realization dawned on Dex. He took in the shop around him. All the materials, the tools, the means, everything was there before his very eyes.

"You did it yourself?" Dex asked, stunned.

"See"—Pearce wagged a finger at him, smiling broadly—"I knew you were one of the smart ones. The moment I saw you, I knew there was something special about you." He walked over to the large furnace, the one not in use, and stuck his hand inside, reaching high. When he removed it, he had a long metal box in his grip. He placed it on the table, carefully opened it, and slipped his hand inside. When he removed it, Dex couldn't help his sharp intake of breath.

"It's a work of art, isn't it?" Pearce held up the contraption of iron bands and rings measured to fit Pearce's right arm with complete precision. It almost resembled a mechanical arm, but with Pearce's flesh and bone inside instead of wires and electronics. The ends of the metal fingers contained four large metal claws, curved and sharp. "You see these? Each one is the exact same size, shape, and width of a jaguar Therian claw. Four exact replicas, except made of beautiful iron. I figured if I was going to pass the killings off as having come from a Therian, I would need to be inspired." He walked over to Sloane, placing a claw under his chin. "Guess who my inspiration was?"

Dex discreetly shifted to his left, in front of the drafting table. "Why those HumaniTherians?"

Pearce removed the horrid contraption and placed it back in its box, returning it to the furnace, the poker remaining in his hand. "Because they set Gabe up on the road to ruin. Bennett was the one who started Gabe on that HumaniTherians bullshit in college, encouraging him to take courses, spreading his LiberTherian lies. He got his claws into Gabe real good. And then that bitch gives him a job, starts introducing him to all these Therians, dragging him under. When Gabe asked me to help him get into the HPF, I thought he was leaving it all behind, but it was just so he could work his way up to the THIRDS."

"And Ortiz?"

"The first two were personal, but it was time to take things to the next level. Think big. Sadly, it all had to end a little sooner than I'd planned. I allowed my emotions to get the better of me. On your last day, after I dropped you off at your car, knowing you were going to be *his* partner… it was difficult. I got sloppy, went after Ortiz the same day after visiting the Styx instead of waiting. When you showed up at my door, I knew the time had come."

"For what?"

Pearce's grin sent an icy chill up Dex's spine. The guy was unstable. His grief over the loss of his brother, coupled with who knew what else, had done something to him.

"For war, Dex. The weak Humans will get picked off, but the strong Humans like me and you? We'll survive. Then the government will have no choice but to send in the military and eliminate the Therian threat. Those who aren't destroyed will be locked away in cages like the animals they are."

Dex's eyes went wide. The guy couldn't be serious. "You're talking about genocide, the murder of innocent Therians."

Rage flashed through Pearce's eyes, and he grabbed a fistful of Sloane's hair, his snarling face inches away from Sloane's. "Therians aren't innocent. They're abominations! Someone slipped Mother Nature a roofie, and a few months later, out they popped. Look at him. A filthy mutated creature underneath the beautiful façade of a Human, but his eyes, oh, they give him away. If you stare at them long enough, you can see the embers of hell itself in there."

Dex reached behind him, his fingers curling around a heavy set of iron tongs. Carefully he slid them off the table, opened them, and hooked one clamp through one of the thick heavy belt loops of his tac pants. Letting his arms hang at his sides, Dex took a step forward, and Pearce spun toward him, the poker held out in front of him.

"Easy there, Dex."

"I'm sorry." Dex held his hands up. "I'm just worried about you. What's going to happen now? You think they'll just let you get away with what you've done? You said it yourself. It's about justice. The families of those you hurt will want justice."

"Sometimes sacrifices must be made for the greater good. That's why I called you here. In fact, that's why I helped you that day in the parking garage. I wanted you to see you could trust me. Something big is about to happen to this city, Dex, and I sure would love to have you on the winning team. You're a smart guy with a good heart. A little naïve, perhaps, but we can fix that."

"We?"

"My associates."

"The ones who lied for you?"

Pearce smiled, "You call it lying, I call it supporting. They believe the same as me. Now we need to get this little show on the road. How about it? Will you join your race? Or will you die with *him*?"

"What about my brother?"

"Yes, I see how you would have been taught to have affection for him." Pearce shrugged. "Well, I'm sure we could make an exception. We'll say he's your pet."

Motherfucker. It took everything Dex had not to go for the guy right now. Instead, Dex pretended to mull it over.

"Join me, Dex, and we will set the world to rights."

"What do I have to do?"

Pearce's gaze went to Sloane, and Dex unhooked the iron tongs from his belt. "First things first." Pearce pulled back the poker, and Dex swung the tongs with all his strength, hurling them across the room and catching Pearce on his kneecap. With a howl, Pearce dropped the poker, clutching his knee as he hit the floor. Dex raced across the room, launching at Pearce as the guy pushed to his feet. They crashed to the floor, Dex landing on Pearce and throwing a fierce right hook, only to have Pearce block and catch Dex on his ribs with a left jab. They rolled on the floor, thrashing and kicking, each one trying to get the upper hand, punches flying, hoping to make contact.

Most movie fight scenes were bullshit. In a real fight, there was no choreography. Your opponent wasn't going to be some martial arts expert. He wasn't going to give you the space to pull some fancy moves. He wasn't going to pause or hesitate. He was going to fight hard and dirty. It was about striking wherever you could when you could. Absorb the strike and use it to hit back. Dex rolled and jumped to his feet, his fists held up in front of him. He studied Pearce, tried to anticipate his movements.

Pearce came at him with hooks from every angle, and Dex held his arms close to his body, shielding himself, using the opportunity when Pearce pulled back to get in his own punches. He grabbed Pearce's arm, spun on his heels so he was beside Pearce, and threw his elbow back, landing a blow on the side of Pearce's head, followed by a harsh swipe to his leg, sending Pearce sprawling face-first. Before Dex had a chance to strike, Pearce kicked out, catching Dex on the side of his knee and sending him falling. He rolled onto his back, his shirt caught in Pearce's grip as he pulled back a fist. Dex caught it, smacking it away, and brought a knee up between Pearce's legs. As a trained officer, Pearce could fight through the pain in his family jewels for roughly five seconds max. Dex seized Pearce's wrists and swiped a leg from under him. Pearce smacked the concrete floor hard, sucking in a sharp breath and coughing when he got a mouthful of dust and dirt. He held on to himself, his teeth gritted.

Dex scrambled to his feet, making a run for his rifle. It was just out of arm's reach. Something solid struck him in the back, and he gasped for air, the blow propelling him forward. *Motherfuck!* That hurt. He lay on the floor on his stomach, and the iron tongs he'd used to catch Pearce off guard lay on the floor mere feet away. He stretched his arm out when Pearce grabbed a fistful of his hair with one hand and threw his other arm around his neck, squeezing. Pearce leaned in, his voice raspy in Dex's ear.

"I'm sorry, Dex. This is for your own good. I can't leave you in his hands. He destroyed my brother. I won't let him do the same to you. I'd rather kill you myself."

Dex bit down on Pearce's arm until he tasted blood, and Pearce screamed, jerking his arm away and sitting back, giving Dex the chance he needed to roll onto his back under Pearce who, in his rage, threw a punch as Dex had expected. He caught Pearce's wrist, jerked him toward him, and remembering the move Sloane had pulled on him the first day they sparred together, he threw his arm around Pearce's neck and gave his wrist a yank, sending Pearce rolling off him.

Pearce scrambled to his feet, snatching up Dex's thigh rig but forgetting the safety mechanism. He let out a yelp when Dex tackled him into the couch, snatching up his rifle as they tumbled to the floor, but not before Dex snapped up his earpiece. Dex tossed the strap around Pearce's neck and gave it a yank. His legs tried to pin down Pearce's as he flailed and clawed at Dex. He switched on his earpiece, calling out.

"Backup! I need backup!"

Pearce managed to release the Glock from the rig, and Dex was forced to let go of his earpiece along with the strap to grab the gun in Pearce's hand, but the safety was off by then. They continued to struggle, Dex wrapping around Pearce, his fingers digging into Pearce's hands as they fought for the gun. A shot went off, ricocheting off the wall and hitting the chain above Sloane's head with a spark.

Damn it! Jaw clenched, Dex spotted the tactical knife on his thigh rig. Keeping his right hand on the Glock, he threw his left out and grabbed the rig, releasing the knife. The moment Pearce saw it, he threw a fist back, catching Dex in the nose, before he rolled off Dex and made a run for it, despite the limp he now had from where Dex had caught him with the tongs. With a curse, Dex rolled onto his side, spitting out blood-filled saliva. He aimed his Glock when Pearce ran past a row of gas tanks. Fuck, if he hit those, they were all toast. He got to his feet as Pearce ran out the door into the hall.

"Dex!"

Hearing his name, he scrambled for his earpiece and put it on. "I'm here. I'm going after Isaac. I need you to—" An explosion rocked the workshop, and he froze. It had come from down the street. He tried not to panic as he called out into his earpiece. "Sarge?"

"Son of a bitch must have planted explosives ahead of time. He blew the kitchen supply store. Fucking sink fell on the truck. It's a goddamn mess. I hear you, Dex. Agents are on the way, but there's shit blocking the road."

Dex wasn't about to wait for backup and chance Pearce getting away. He grabbed his vest, slipping into it as he ran over to Sloane, who shook his head and motioned toward the door.

"Okay. I'll take that bastard down, I swear."

Sloane nodded, and Dex bolted after Pearce, fastening the straps of his vest before reaching the hall. He carefully peeked out and with the coast clear, he swiftly made his way to the staircase as the sound of heavy footsteps pounded against the wooden stairs two floors up. Dex wasted no time, using his training to keep his boots from making noise as he followed. He controlled his breathing, his Glock raised and close to him as he hurried. His adrenaline pumped through his veins, his heart raced, and his stomach felt queasy. He had to stop this bastard.

A door slammed somewhere high above him, and Dex ran the rest of the way up, coming to a stop on the landing under the fourth floor. He could see the closed door Pearce had gone through moments ago. Scanning his surroundings, he swiftly crept along the back of the stairway and along the wall until he was flattened against the wall beside the chipped blue door. There was only the one door on the floor. Dex remembered windows, no fire escape. He had to be extra vigilant. Isaac Pearce had fooled them all. Fooled *him*. By now Tony would be devising a strategy. At least Pearce was away from Sloane.

Carefully he stretched his arm across the door and tested the doorknob. It was open. Fuck. That couldn't be good. He pushed it open with his boot, remaining on the side of the door, gun aimed and ready to shoot anything that moved. There was nothing and no one. The room was empty with only the four windows. There was no way Pearce could have gone out the window without making a sound. Cautiously he entered the room, turning to cover all his angles. There was nothing but a bunch of exposed pipes running around the room vertically and horizontally, stretching up to the ceiling.

As he turned, he was knocked to the ground, but he kept his grip on his gun, swinging his arm to aim, only to have it seized. Pearce straddled him as they struggled. Where the hell had the asshole come from, the ceiling? Dex twisted his body, using what momentum he could to deliver a left hook into Pearce's ribs, a painful growl escaping him when his fist made contact with something hard. Bastard was wearing protection.

"This is your last chance, Dex! Join me or I'll put a bullet in you. Then I'll put a bullet in that animal downstairs."

"Fuck you." Dex snapped his head forward, slamming his forehead into Pearce's nose. A fierce cry filled the air as Pearce's head jolted back. Dex aimed at Pearce's chest and fired. Pearce flew off Dex onto his back. He rolled over, gurgling and gasping as he held on to his chest, blood pouring out of his nose and down over his mouth. Dex pushed to his feet, ready to unload his magazine into the asshole, but his plan went awry when Isaac pulled something from inside his vest. Dex lunged to one side as a steel knife plunged into the wall behind him. He had to end this. Dex scrambled to his feet just as Pearce collided with him, sending them crashing through a glass pane. Dex used his arm to shield his face, the sting of the many shards slicing and cutting not nearly as painful as the thought of what lay below. As Pearce's body sent them hurtling out the shattered and splintered window, Dex braced himself.

He'd survive this.

He had to.

Chapter 14

THEIR BODIES hit the aluminum storage container below, knocking the air out of Dex's lungs. He lay on his back, gasping and shaking, his blurred gaze on the blackness of the girders above him. His chest felt as if it were in a vise, his body burning from the inside out. In the distance he could hear the wailing of sirens and chaos. The air around him was foggy and thick. Beside him, Pearce groaned and rolled over. Dex slapped a hand out, feeling for his gun. Who the hell knew where it landed? He carefully shifted; his limbs protested, but he didn't think anything was broken, just rattled around. Looking up at the window they'd fallen through, he could see it was high, but with the height of the container, not enough to put them out of commission. He should have known Pearce would have a plan.

Dex rolled onto his side, sucking in a sharp breath before breathing heavily through his nose. With a growl, he pushed to his knees, watching as Pearce rolled off the container. Dex crawled to the edge, cursing under his breath as Pearce made his way through the mound of cardboard boxes. Well wasn't that fucking convenient.

"Fucking bastard." Dex pushed off the side of the container and landed on the pile of cardboard. With a wince, he kicked and pushed the boxes out of his way as he crawled to the floor and forced himself to his feet. His right ankle burned and protested, but he pushed through the pain, running off after Pearce when another explosion went off, this one lifting him off his feet and flinging him against the storage unit he'd rolled off. He hit the floor in a painful heap. Instinct kicked in and he rolled into a ball, covering his head as burning debris rained down around him. There was a smaller explosion to his left, and he forced himself to his feet. In the distance he could hear familiar shouts. His team was close by. Regardless, he had to get Sloane out.

Heat and fire sprang up from containers where explosions had peeled back the aluminum like the lids of tuna fish cans. More containers went up in black smoke, and Dex scolded himself.

"Move your ass, Daley." The explosions were getting closer, containers bursting in a fiery mess of black smoke and burning metal. Even if his team was close, Dex knew the score. They had their priorities where loss of life was concerned, and Dex wouldn't be surprised if Pearce had known. Civilian safety came first. He could hear orders being shouted as fellow agents secured the area, clearing it and assessing the risks. Tony rambled something about a pack bot, but screw

that. Dex couldn't wait for that. He had to get Sloane
out. He ran back into the workshop, coughing when
black smoke wafted through the doors. Shit, the place
was on fire. There was no doubt in his mind Pearce
had made a contingency plan. Snatching up one of the
bolt cutters, Dex cut the chains binding Sloane's wrists
and carefully unfastened the one around his neck. He
pulled the tape off Sloane's mouth, then moved to remove the tape from around his ankles. His partner was
silent, and when Dex moved away, Sloane crumpled
to the floor.

"Sloane, buddy, look at me. I need you to get on
your feet. We need to get out of here."

"He killed Gabe." Sloane's voice was so low, Dex
had barely heard him.

"I know, I'm so sorry, but this place is filled with
all kinds of flammable shit, and it's on fire. We need to
get out of here." He grabbed Sloane's face and met his
gaze, his voice rough. "Please, Sloane. I'm not ready
to let you join him."

Sloane blinked, a tear running down his cheek.
He nodded, and with Dex's help, got to his feet. They
quickly made their way out of the building, Dex's arm
wrapped around Sloane's waist, but even with his ankle fighting him every step of the way, Dex refused
to stop, not until they'd put a hell of a lot of distance
between them and anything that could blow them up.
There might not have been explosives planted in the
workshop, but there were enough flammable chemi-
cals and gases to do the job. He could see Ash coming
up fast, an ambulance not far behind. Behind them the
smaller explosions continued, and Sloane flinched.

Ash got to them first, throwing a thermal blanket around Sloane and wrapping an arm around him.

"It's okay. We got you," Ash said as the EMTs dashed over, getting Sloane onto a gurney. As soon as he sat down on it, he sagged in exhaustion. Ash took hold of Dex's arm. Fire trucks sped past, heading for the workshop and the storage lot.

"Daley, you need to get yourself checked out."

"I'm riding with him." Dex tried to jerk his arm out of Ash's iron grip.

"He'll be fine. For fuck's sake, Dex, you're hurt. Not to mention you fell out of a fucking window!"

Dex rounded on Ash. "He's my partner. I'm going with him. So help me, if you don't let go of my arm, Ash, I will—"

"Ash, let him go," Tony ordered quietly. "They'll take care of him on the way to the hospital."

With a terse smile toward his dad, Dex climbed into the back of the ambulance. The doors shut, and they took off. Dex took hold of Sloane's hand as the team got to work cleaning his wounds and giving him oxygen. One of the medics tried to fuss with Dex's ankle, but Dex sent him away. He leaned over Sloane, reminding himself they weren't alone.

"It's going to be okay," Dex promised, his hand resting on Sloane's brow. Amber eyes stared at the roof, silent tears rolling down the sides of his face. "You can't blame yourself."

Sloane shut his eyes tight in response, and Dex knew it was what his partner was doing. His grip tightened on Sloane's hand, and he leaned in to talk quietly to him.

"Pearce was unstable. If it hadn't been you, it would have been someone else. You know that. Gabe loved you. He was willing to fight for what you had, but he had no idea what was happening to his brother. Pearce got what he deserved." There was no way the guy had survived the explosion. He'd run right into it. It was finally over. "It's time for you and Gabe to have peace." He brushed Sloane's hair away from his brow, watching as Sloane opened his eyes before shaking his head and closing his eyes again. He pulled his hand out of Dex's, laying it on his stomach.

"Okay." Dex swallowed hard and sat back, closing his eyes, his heart sinking. Whatever had been between them, whatever chance they might have had, it was falling by the wayside. As much as it hurt, Dex understood. All that pain Sloane had felt when Gabe died was most likely coming back, along with the guilt, the nightmares, and the grief. Pearce had killed his brother, and instead of living with his guilt, he'd transferred all his anger, bitterness, and blame onto Sloane.

All Dex could do now was be a good partner. He'd help Sloane through this however he could, tucking away the ache inside him. It had been good while it lasted, and maybe it was for the better. Hiding a relationship from his teammates was one thing, but from his family was another matter. As he drifted off to the sound of sirens, an image of Gabe came into his mind, the one he'd held in Pearce's house. With a silent thank-you, he gave in to his exhaustion.

TWO DAYS before Christmas, Dex was lounging in front of his TV, flipping through the channels, watching nothing in particular. After the incident with Pearce, he'd been given Christmas leave early. He should have been bouncing off the walls. He loved holidays, especially Christmas. And although he was looking forward to spending it with his family, he still couldn't get over the hurt he felt at Sloane's refusal to see him.

Sloane had been given Christmas leave early as well, to recuperate both physically and emotionally. It had hit everyone pretty rough, knowing Gabe had died at the hands of his brother, everyone believing if maybe they had just done something different, Gabe might still be alive.

Dex had tried to see Sloane at the hospital, but Ash had stopped him from going in. Normally, they would have threatened each other until Ash got so frustrated he'd let Dex have his way, but this time it was different. Ash had actually looked upset when he somberly pleaded with Dex, telling him Sloane asked him not to let Dex in. It had cut deep, but Dex simply nodded and left. For the rest of the week, he'd tried calling Sloane and even texted him. Nothing.

The doorbell rang, and with a groan Dex got to his feet and shuffled to the front door. It was probably Cael again. His brother had been worried about him, and despite Dex reassuring him a hundred times that he was fine and needed some time on his own, his brother would show up with pizza or burgers, trying to get him out of his funk. He opened the door, his greeting dying on his lips.

"Hey."

Dex blinked a few times, wondering if he was seeing what he thought he was seeing or if he was hallucinating. Sloane stood on his doorstep, wrapped up in a black winter coat, a black-and-pale-blue striped scarf around his neck and a matching wool cap on his head. His cheeks and nose were rosy from the cold, and in his hand he was holding a huge present wrapped in light blue paper with white snowflakes and a big silver bow on top. There was a large red gift bag hanging from his wrist. All Dex could get out was a pathetic "Hi."

"Can I come in?"

"Yeah, sure. Sorry." Dex stepped aside and let Sloane in, closing the door behind him. He was surprised when Sloane handed him the box and then dropped the gift bag on top.

"Merry Christmas."

"You… got me Christmas presents?"

"Sort of. It's part Christmas present, part bribe." Sloane removed his hat, scarf, and coat, hanging them on the hooks by the door. Then he removed his boots. He paused halfway. "Is it okay? I mean, I don't want to presume you want me to stay."

"It's fine." Dex looked down at the presents in his hands. "A bribe for what?"

Sloane ushered Dex into the living room and over to the couch. He took the box from Dex and put it on the floor, then took Dex's hands and pulled him down to sit beside him. His brow was creased with worry. "In the hopes you'll forgive me. I know I hurt you, not letting you come see me and not answering your many, many attempts to get in touch with me. I needed time to think."

"About what?" Dex's pulse shot up, his heart all but ready to burst through his chest. Bribery was a good thing, right? Surely Sloane wouldn't come all the way to his house with a gift the size of Cael just to give him bad news, right?

"Everything. The case. Us."

Dex's heart flipped. "Is there an 'us'?"

"You were right, what you said in the ambulance about it being time for me and Gabe to have peace. It's time I put Gabe to rest, for me to move on." Sloane licked his bottom lip, his gaze on their hands. "I know what I'm asking of you isn't fair, and I don't expect you to wait for me, but yeah, I'd like for there to be an 'us.' Maybe, if you're willing to take things as they come, see where they lead, you can help me. I know it's asking a lot, but I like you, Dex. I like who I am with you." He looked up at Dex; then a small smile crossed his face. "I've felt things I didn't think I would ever feel again."

"What about the team? My family?" Dex already knew what his answer was, but he had to ask.

"Whatever happens between us has to stay between us, or one of us will be transferred to another team. You know that."

Dex nodded. How the hell could he keep something like this from his dad? Worse, from Cael? It would break his brother's heart if he found out Dex had kept secrets from him. He felt Sloane give his hands a squeeze, and he returned his gaze to Sloane's hopeful one. Sloane needed him. "We'll just have to make sure no one finds out."

With a big smile, Sloane took hold of Dex's face and brought him in for a passionate kiss. Dex surrendered completely, melting against Sloane, relishing in the softness of his lips, the warmth of his mouth, and the taste of him. He refused to acknowledge how much he'd missed this. It would be stupid to fall for Sloane or even think about getting on that path.

Sloane wasn't making any promises, wasn't offering him a relationship, just a possibility to see what could be. If Dex wasn't careful, he could end up falling hard, and that would be bad for both of them. For now he'd return Sloane's hungry kisses, getting what he could. He climbed onto Sloane's lap, moaning at the feel of those large hands on his ass. When they came up for air, Dex pulled back, his breath coming out shaky. His gaze shifted down.

"What in the name of Frosty's snow-covered balls are you wearing?"

Sloane followed Dex's gaze, looking down at himself. "It's a sweater."

"It's got reindeer on it. And snowflakes."

"Yeah, but it's vintage Ralph Lauren, and that makes it sophisticated." Sloane wriggled his eyebrows, and Dex let out a snort.

"If you say so."

"Since Maddock invited me and Ash over for Christmas dinner with you guys, and I'll be wearing mine, I thought I'd get you one." Sloane plucked the large red gift bag up from the floor and held it out to Dex.

"You expect me to wear a sweater with reindeer on it?" He arched an eyebrow at Sloane and took the bag from him. "We're getting off to a rocky start already."

Sloane laughed. "Just check it out."

Dex rolled off Sloane's lap and reached into the bag. He pulled out a red-and-black knit sweater. *Oh*

God, here we go. He held it up, his eyes going wide. "What the—"

"You like it?" Sloane asked hesitantly.

"This is fucking *awesome*!" Dex jumped from the couch, holding his sweater up. It was red with a black collar and sleeve cuffs. It had various patterns of snowflakes and baubles repeated horizontally in black and white, but the coolest part was the two old school robots in the center. One of them had a Santa hat on and the other a striped scarf, and they were facing forward, looking like they were about to high-five.

"I thought you might like it." Sloane sat back, beaming up at him.

"How'd you know?" Dex pulled off his sweat shirt and pulled on his new sweater. It fit perfectly. This was the coolest, ugliest sweater he'd seen in a long time.

Sloane scratched the stubble on his chin. "Just a lucky guess." He pointed toward the huge box. "You can open that if you like."

Dex was so excited he thought he might hurt something. He got down on his knees and tore through the fancy wrapping paper like a cat wigging out on catnip. Once the gift was revealed, he let out a huge drawn-out gasp, his voice coming out high-pitched. "Duuude!" He wiped an imaginary tear from his eye. "You bought me guns."

Sloane smiled broadly. "It's a laser tag set."

"I am so going to kick your ass at this," Dex said, jumping to his feet. He ran to his tree and came back with a medium-sized box. He handed it to Sloane, a big dopey grin on his face.

"Are these"—Sloane peered at the wrapping paper—"stripper Santas?"

Dex wriggled his brows. "In thongs. Pole dancing."

"Sometimes I worry about you." Sloane shook his head before tearing through the paper. He opened the unmarked white box and took out a bust. He held it up in front of him, his brows drawn together in concentration. "You got me a…. What is it?"

"It's a Death Trooper!"

"A what?"

"A Stormtrooper zombie." Dex pointed out the intricately painted decay. "Hence, Death Trooper." Sloane stared at the bust with wide eyes, and Dex held back a smile. "Come on, you can be honest with me. I won't judge you."

"What the hell are you talking about?"

Dex dropped down onto the couch facing Sloane. "Please, you're totally a closet geek! You think I didn't notice the bowl you put your keys in by the door is the bottom half of the Death Star? The bookends holding up your *Star Wars* movie collection is the Mos Eisley cantina scene! Han totally shot first, by the way, and if you state otherwise, we're over."

Sloane arched an eyebrow at him, and with a sigh, Dex stood and wrapped his arms around Sloane's head, petting him. "Hush now. I'll help you come out. It'll be okay. I know it seems scary, and not everyone will accept you, but I will. Come out and spread your wings like a little red angry bird."

"Angry birds don't spread their wings," Sloane muttered.

Dex continued to pet his head, speaking softly. "You're only strengthening my case."

"You're such an ass." Sloane laughed, pushing Dex away. He held up the bust again, his bottom lip between his teeth. A slow smile crept onto his face, and he shifted his gaze to Dex. "This is pretty fucking amazing."

"Ha! I knew it!" Dex punched the air a few times while Sloane laughed at him. He'd taken a chance, but he'd seen enough of Sloane's apartment to recognize the signs. Under all the sleek sophistication lay a complete movie geek. Oh, the arguments that awaited them. The loud thundering theme of an emergency broadcast cut through Dex's happy dance, and he turned to the TV screen.

"We interrupt your scheduled programming for this breaking news update. A disturbing video has gone viral, and officials are stumped as to where it's originating. If you have small children in the room, you'll want to send them out with a loved one."

A figure shrouded completely in black stood against an aging stone wall, his voice using some form of enhancer when he spoke.

"Good evening, New York City. While you sit in your homes, sipping your eggnog, unwrapping a gadget that will be obsolete in three months while rolling your eyes at yet another commercial to replace the word 'Christmas' with 'Holiday' so as not to offend the hippies, a disease is spreading through our beloved city, a disease that can no longer be ignored. They believe themselves to be the next step in Human evolution, but they're not Human. They're animals. And what do you do with an animal that is putrid and infested with disease? You put it out of its misery. Fear not, the Order of Adrasteia is here to help you."

"What the fuck is this?" Sloane got to his feet, coming to stand beside Dex.

A sick twisting feeling gripped Dex as a symbol with the head of a Grecian goddess flashed on the screen. He'd seen that somewhere before. When it faded, Dex stared at the THIRDS agent gagged and bound, kneeling on the floor next to the cloaked figure's feet. "Who is that?" Dex asked Sloane, who shook his head, his expression as confused and stunned as Dex's.

Their cell phones rang, and Dex gave a start. They each answered, hearing Tony's voice coming over loud and clear from both phones.

"You two in the same room?"

"Yeah, Sloane came over to give me my Christmas present and catch up."

"Okay, Dex, hang up. Sloane, put me on speaker." They did as instructed.

Sloane was the first to ask. "What's going on, Sarge? What is this?"

"We don't know. What we do know is, it's legit. That's Agent Greg Morrelli. He was reported missing last night. He went home after work and disappeared. Intel has been trying to track the source of the video but having a hell of a time pinpointing the location. It's a nightmare. We've got teams all over the city trying to find Morrelli, but it's like looking for a needle in a haystack."

The voice spoke up once more, and everything went quiet. "In order to cure our city of its disease, we must dispose of its carriers, starting with the organization that promotes the sickness. We will unleash Hell upon these sinners, starting with the THIRDS." From his cloak, the figure removed a gun, aimed it at the pleading agent's head, and fired.

"Oh my God." Dex's body stiffened in shock. Had they just witnessed an execution? "How…." He shook his head, unable to believe it. A heavy silence fell over everything, as the figure faced forward. When he spoke, it felt as if he was addressing Dex.

"You had your chance. Now watch your world crumble around you. No Therian will be safe in this city, and your precious heroes will be too busy fighting for their lives to protect you. We are the embodiment of righteous anger, the antipathy roused by those who are sins against nature. We are all around you. Your neighbors, your children's teachers, your doctors. We are inescapable." He aimed the gun toward the screen. "And we will set the world to rights." A shot rang out, and the screen went black.

"…and we will set the world to rights."

Dex turned to Sloane, his partner's startled expression confirming they were thinking the same thing. Sloane took hold of Dex's arm and pulled him into his embrace, his voice almost a whisper.

"He's alive, isn't he?"

Dex nodded, his arms wrapping around Sloane, and his face buried against his chest. Isaac Pearce was alive, and he'd issued a declaration of war against them.

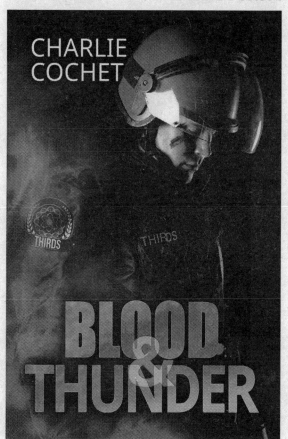

CHARLIE
COCHET

THIRDS

BLOOD
&
THUNDER

Blood & Thunder

Sequel to *Hell & High Water*
THIRDS: Book Two

When a series of bombs go off in a Therian youth center, injuring members of THIRDS Team Destructive Delta and causing a rift between agents Dexter J. Daley and Sloane Brodie, peace seems unattainable. Especially when a new and frightening group, the Order of Adrasteia, appears to always be a step ahead. With panic and intolerance spreading and streets becoming littered with the Order's propaganda, hostility between Humans and Therians grows daily. Dex and Sloane, along with the rest of the team, are determined to take down the Order and restore peace, not to mention settle a personal score. But the deeper the team investigates the bombings, the more they believe there's a more sinister motive than a desire to shed blood and spread chaos.

Discovering the frightful truth behind the Order's intent forces Sloane to confront secrets from a past he thought he'd left behind for good, a past that could not only destroy him and his career, but also the reputation of the organization that made him all he is today. Now more than ever, Dex and Sloane need each other, and, along with trust, the strength of their bond will mean the difference between justice and all-out war.

Now Available at
www.dreamspinnerpress.com

Chapter 1

"YOU SURE this is the place?"

Dex shifted his entry weapon to one side and stepped up behind his brother at the surveillance console while the rest of the team double-checked their equipment at the other end of the BearCat. Cael tapped away at the keyboard, bringing up a grid of the area, satellite mapping, and a host of surveillance feeds from local businesses he'd undoubtedly "borrowed."

"College Point, Queens, near the Canada Dry bottling plant. That's what our source tells us."

"Reliable?" Dex asked, receiving a curt nod.

"Hasn't let us down yet."

Hopefully this wouldn't be the first. The last thing they needed was to waste more time with another dead end. Four months of reconnaissance and intel gathering from Unit Alpha's Intel and Recon agents, and Defense agents finally had something useful to go on regarding the whereabouts of the Order of Adrasteia, though they still didn't know how big the group was or how spread out they were.

Despite being Human perpetrators, which should have fallen to the jurisdiction of the Human Police Force, the threat was against Therian citizens, not to mention the Order had declared war against the THIRDS by executing a THIRDS agent. The online video of Agent Morelli's death had gone viral and ended up being broadcast on television two days before Christmas. Dex could still hear the bastard's voice in his head as if he'd watched the whole thing yesterday, the spiteful words dripping with venom.

In order to cure our city of his disease, we must dispose of its carriers, starting with the organization that promotes the sickness. We will unleash Hell upon these sinners, starting with the THIRDS.

Seconds later, the THIRDS organization went to Threat Level Red. They had to stop the Order before they had any more loss of life and before any more zealots jumped on the crazy train. Since then, the already tremulous relationship between Human and Therian citizens was growing more unstable by the day, which was exactly what the Order wanted.

The THIRDS had recruited volunteers to patrol the city, removing the Order's hateful propaganda, but it was a futile endeavor. With every poster spouting "Humans 4 Dominance" or sporting the Adrasteia goddess symbol the THIRDS took down, three or four took its place. So many flyers littered the streets, they resembled the aftermath of a ticker-tape parade. Everywhere Dex looked, the Order was leaving its bloodred mark, promising hellfire and chaos, refusing to give in unless they got their way or the city burned, whichever came first. The media wasn't helping any either. Turning on the TV, one would think a presidential election was going on, what with all the ludicrous accusations and childish attempts to discredit the opposing side.

In the middle of it all were the THIRDS. Since the Order had surfaced, the organization had been accused of everything from sitting on the fence (too cowardly to pick a side), to being traitors to their species (depending on the agent being accused), to being the source of evil itself, to being the only thing keeping this city from crumbling. No matter what they did, someone accused them of something—not working hard enough or fast enough or not giving enough of a shit. It would have driven Dex out of his mind ages ago if he let it get to him, which was why he didn't. Most importantly, he wouldn't allow it to get to his team.

Sloane strode up to him, addressing Cael as he handed Dex his ballistic helmet. "What do we know about the area?"

Dex snatched the helmet from his partner with a groan. "I hate this thing."

"When a bullet hits your helmet instead of your skull, Rookie, you'll love it."

Damn. Can't argue with that.

Cael didn't bother hiding his amusement as he answered Sloane's question. "Mostly industrial estates and construction firms. Fifteenth Avenue ends at the East River, though there's a small dirt drive that heads into the sign and window factory's parking lot—if you can call it that." His expression sobered, his Therian pupils dilating in his silvery eyes. "But the immediate area surrounding it is residential, with Popps a couple of blocks away."

"What's Popps?" Dex asked. He wasn't all that familiar with the area, and after months of running around the city, the neighborhoods were all starting to blend together.

"The Poppenhusen Institute. It's a community center offering programs for kids and families."

Ash joined them with his usual cheerful growl. "Great. Bastards know what they're doing. The industrial sites offer plenty of cover, but the residential area makes it difficult to go in aggressive. Last thing we need is a stray bullet catching some poor kid."

Sloane nodded his agreement before motioning to the console's large flat-screen. "Do we have an exact location?"

"Here." Cael pointed to a small area near the edge of the river at the end of Fifteenth Avenue. The property consisted of two small buildings on a small expanse of dirt with a chain-link fence going around the front and the East River around the back. "It's listed as IGD Construction Supply Services, but it's a front. At least, now it is. I conducted a search for businesses and individuals who've had contracts with them and turned up plenty of hits, but they were all jobs completed over a year ago, with nothing in the works since. I called from one of our secure lines back at Recon, pretending to be a client, and the 'secretary' said the company was in the middle of a restructure and not taking on any new projects."

"Security?"

"A piss-poor security network, consumer-grade crap. There's a camera on the north side, another on the south, and one on this house here, which acts as the office. I can have the feed looped faster than Dex can sing the chorus to Alice Cooper's 'Poison.'"

Dex opened his mouth, and Sloane clamped a gloved hand over it. "No. Cael, don't encourage him. Ash, entry."

"I don't like this." Ash studied the screen, his beefy arms folded over his tac vest. "We're talking confined quarters. If they're in there, they've got to be prepared. The second structure is our primary target and where they'll most likely be. It has no windows, two small entrances on the side, and three vehicle entrances at the front. The good news, it's aluminum, so it'll be easy to blow that shit sky-high." Ash's frown deepened.

"Either way, 110th Street is out of the question. They'll see us coming. I say we have three teams. Team one comes up Fifteenth Avenue, past the bottling plant, to there," he said, pointing to a medium-sized, tan brick house on the screen. "They can use that entryway. The wooden fence and the house will cover them. They go around the back, cut through the chain-link fence, and end up in the back of IGD's yard. They can sneak up on them from behind, take out whoever's in this office, and then come in strong from the front, especially since the windows have burglar bars so our perps won't be able to get out that way. Anyone comes at the team, they can throw the bastards in the river, but that's just my opinion.

"Team two takes the same route, comes up behind the primary target, breaches the perimeter using this door here, giving you room to maneuver should the bastards come through the second and third entrance or the side doors. And speaking of, if they do, we'll have the third team ready across the street, having approached through the back of the sign and window factory. There's enough construction equipment and debris to conceal them."

With a curt nod, Sloane gave Ash a firm pat on the shoulder. "Good work. You heard him, team. Cael, you're our eyes. Keep us informed of all activity."

"Copy that." Cael turned back to the console while Sloane addressed the rest of the team.

"Letty, Rosa, you're team one. You take the office. Calvin, Hobbs, you're team two. Go around the back of the primary target, take out the door, and smoke 'em out."

Calvin gave him a curt nod and walked off with Hobbs close behind to prepare the necessary explosives and nonlethals.

"Ash, Dex, you're with me. We're coming in behind the sign and window factory." Sloane tapped his earpiece. "Agent Stone, Agent Taylor, this is Agent Brodie."

The team leaders' gruff voices came in over their earpieces. "Agent Stone here. What are your orders, Agent Brodie?"

"Agent Taylor here. Ditto."

Sloane rolled his eyes. "Agent Stone, I want you and your team situated at the corner of 110th Street and Fourteenth Road. Make sure no one comes in or out. Have Beta Pride on standby, and keep an eye out for civilians."

"Copy that."

"Agent Taylor, you and your team take the corner of 112th Street and Fifteenth Avenue. You know the drill. Have Beta Ambush on standby, and keep an eye out for civilians. Try not to scare any kids today."

There was a deep rumble of laughter from the other end. "And take away Keeler's fun? Perish the thought."

"Kiss my ass, Taylor."

"You just come on over here and bend over, Keeler. We'll have ourselves a gay ole time. Taylor out."

"Pussy," Ash muttered.

"That's kind of the opposite of why I'd kiss your ass," Agent Taylor said with a laugh.

Ash opened his mouth for a rebuttal—undoubtedly one laced with enough obscenity to make their ears bleed—but Sloane was too quick, tapping Ash's earpiece and jutting a finger at him. "You and Taylor can have your battle of wits some other time." Ignoring Ash's glare, Sloane turned his attention back to the team.

"All right, watch your backs, and let's show those sons of bitches what happens when they mess with our city. Letty, Rosa, give us a five-second lead."

"You got it." Rosa put on her ballistic helmet and lowered the visor; the rest of the team followed suit. Sloane's voice came in loud and clear.

"Let's move out."

Destructive Delta's BearCat was parked at the corner of 112th Street and Fifteenth Avenue, and they gave a small wave to Beta Ambush's truck as it pulled up to the sidewalk a few feet away from them. Everyone scrambled out, heading toward their respective starting points.

Dex fell into formation behind Sloane with Ash at his back, their rifles in their hands as they quickly jogged down the sidewalk and turned onto Fourteenth Road. They could see Beta Pride's BearCat parked near the corner, and they headed toward it, alert to everything around them as they passed all the two-story houses with their white picket fences. The sky was blue with some wispy clouds hovering over them, the weather in the mid-60s, and the neighborhood quiet at this time of day. No one would ever suspect anything was wrong, unless they looked out their windows and spotted the three heavily armed THIRDS agents dashing by.

Before they got to the truck, Sloane signaled for them to cross the road, where they stopped at the corner of 110th Street. Although they were a block away from IGD, Sloane wasn't taking any chances of their getting spotted. They turned the corner, and following his silent signal, they dashed behind the parked cars and waited. As soon as they received the okay, they darted across the street, down the side of one of the businesses, and around the back to its parking lot.

A man in a gray suit carrying a portfolio and an armful of papers froze on the spot, eyes going wide. Dex motioned for him to go inside, but it took three tries before the guy snapped himself out of it. He made like the wind back toward the building's exit, nearly running into the glass door in his attempt to flee. Sloane motioned forward, and Dex readied himself, inhaling deeply and releasing it. Eight months on the team, and at times he still couldn't believe he was a Defense agent for the THIRDS. His agency dog tags pressed against his skin under his uniform reminded him he was no longer a homicide detective but a soldier. He'd been awarded his tags six months in, after passing his probation with flying colors.

Despite his initial reluctance to join the THIRDS after HPF bureaucrats had all but forced him into it, Dex had never felt more content than the moment his lieutenant placed those tags around his neck, with his dad and brother looking on, nearly busting at the seams with pride. Those tags were a reminder of his new life and everyone who now depended on him. Destructive Delta had taken him in, even if it had been a shaky start, but one thing he knew for certain—he had no intention of letting them down.

They reached the wooden fence separating them from the back of the sign and window building. Sloane stepped aside and gave Dex a nod. Rookie gets to breach. Let the fun begin. Dex turned, giving Sloane access to his backpack and the Hooligan kit inside. Seconds later, Sloane handed him a small crowbar, and Dex jammed the end between two of the wooden boards before giving the iron bar a fierce jerk. The wood creaked and splintered. He grabbed the looser board with a gloved hand and tore it off. Once the second board was off, it was easier to remove a third. He turned to give the crowbar to Sloane, only to be met with a set of scowls.

"What?"

Ash motioned to the fence. "Your skinny Human ass might fit through there, Daley, but we'll be lucky if we can get a shoulder in."

Seriously? Dex turned back to the fence, grumbling under his breath as he stabbed the crowbar between two planks. It wasn't his fault his Therian teammates were built like brick shithouses. He was lucky he didn't end up having to remove half the fence. Not only was he still getting used to being on a tactical team, but on a Therian one. Being inconspicuous while armed to the gills took skill. Being inconspicuous while standing at nearly seven feet, weighing almost three hundred pounds, and armed to the gills took some kind of voodoo magic. He was still trying to figure out what manner of sorcery Hobbs had used to disappear behind a Scion iQ during their last assignment.

"Move your ass, Rookie," Ash growled.

"You'd like that wouldn't you?" Dex replied with a groan, tearing off one particularly stubborn board. "You really need to stop eyeballing it, man, or I'm gonna start getting ideas." He chuckled when Ash cursed him out under his breath. With the took vim plete, Dex handed the crowbar to Sloane, who quickly returned it to its place in Dex's backpack. He gave Dex a pat on the arm to signal he was done, and Dex stepped aside, falling into formation once again. He paused, arching an eyebrow at Ash.

"I'm not going to look at your ass, Daley. Not if you were the last fuckable thing on this planet."

Dex grinned widely. "So you're saying I'm fuckable?" God, he loved winding the guy up. It was so damn easy.

Ash gave him a shove through the fence. "I'm saying if you don't shut your trap, the next time I look at your ass will be while I'm taking aim to shoot it."

"The next time?" Dex laughed. "Oh shit. Keeler's been looking at my ass."

"Sloane," Ash grunted.

Sloane shook his head as they used the heavy machinery around the sign company's yard to conceal them. "Dex."

It wasn't quite a warning, more a friendly reminder to shut his pie hole. Regardless, Dex looked over his shoulder at Ash, who was grinning smugly. Dex mouthed the word "Narc," causing Ash's grin to fall away to a glower. That was more like it.

They scurried along the side of the building, their sights on the target across the street. A small bulldozer was parked a few feet away from the building's back entrance, and they crouched down beside it in the dirt and patches of dry weeds. He heard Sloane's quiet words come through his earpiece.

"Letty, Rosa, what's your twenty?"

"We're coming up behind the office now."

"Copy that. Calvin?"

"We're about to fix the det cord to the door. Do you want us to—"

Calvin was cut short when a shot popped through the air.

"Calvin?" Sloane edged toward the front of the bulldozer. They could hear low groans coming through their earpieces, and Dex's heart was in his throat. Sloane's curses continued as he tried to get an answer from their teammate. "Goddamn it, Calvin, talk to me. What the hell happened?"

"Shooter," Calvin wheezed, his breath ragged as he tried to talk. "I'm okay. Got hit in the vest. Fuck, shit hurts. We're under fire." Just as he said the words, more shooting erupted. It was coming from somewhere close by.

Sloane peeked around the bulldozer looking to pinpoint the location of their shooters. "I've got a visual. There's a charter bus just ahead. All the windows are smashed to shit. It's been stripped. I make two shooters inside."

"Looks like someone wasn't happy with their service," Ash muttered.

"Cael, is the area clear?" Sloane asked.

"Aside from our shooters, affirmative. No civilians."

"Agent Stone, Agent Taylor?"

"This is Agent Stone. Area's secure."

"Agent Taylor here. Area's secure."

"Copy that. Destructive Delta, we're going in aggressive. Go, go, go!" Sloane darted out from behind the bulldozer with Dex and Ash on his heels to a chorus of gunfire, bangs, and shouting across three locations. They sprinted to the stripped black-and-gold charter bus, and Sloane pitched a couple of smoke bombs through one of the smashed windows before they breached the bus through the open driver's side.

"On the ground! Get on the ground now!" Sloane yelled. The two Human shooters threw their rifles to one side just as Ash grabbed them and roughly forced them onto the floor of the bus.

"Hands behind your backs," Ash spat out, taking zip ties from his utility belt and securing their wrists.

Calvin's warning came through their earpieces. "Fire in the hole!"

"Dex, side doors!" Sloane pushed Dex to the front of the bus. They ran across the street to the aluminum structure as the third vehicle door catapulted off the building in a burst of smoke, skidding across the dirt until it launched off the side into the river. Like there wasn't enough shit down there already.

Dex and Sloane positioned themselves to either side of the smaller entrances with their backs to the aluminum structure and waited. They didn't have to wait long. The doors swung open, a rifle poking through the doorway beside Dex. He snatched it with his right hand and thrust his left elbow into the gunman's face, snapping his head back and bloodying his nose. Dex tossed the gun to the grass beside him with one hand, and with the other, pointed his rifle at the emerging Humans coughing and gasping, their eyes bloodshot and tearful from the smoke.

"On the ground! Get on the ground now!" Dex ordered. "Hands where I can see them!" One of the gunmen tried to reach under his open plaid shirt, but Dex shoved a boot down against his back, pushing him harshly onto his stomach against the dirt. "I said hands where I can see them!" He unhooked a handful of zip ties from his belt, crouched down, and lifted the hem of the guy's shirt to find a revolver. He tossed it out of their reach, then looped a tie around the man's wrists and gave it an extra tug, enough to make the guy hiss. As soon as he'd checked all three for additional weapons and secured them, he stood and tapped his earpiece. "I've got three in custody."

Rosa's breathy voice came through. "We've got four in custody."

"We got five in custody," Calvin added roughly, yelling something at one of the perps. His teammate sounded grumpy, but then who wouldn't be after taking a bullet to the vest? Dex took a step back, watching in amusement as Ash dragged over the two gunmen from the bus, both practically dangling off the ground. Unit Alpha's Therian Defense agents were all made of apex predators, large Felids, each Therian agent with the strength of two Human agents. When the teams faced Therian perpetrators, the score was pretty even, with a Therian agent's advantage depending on the shape they were in, their skill, and their smarts. When facing Humans, Therian Defense agents didn't even break a sweat. Dex liked those odds.

Sloane stepped up beside Dex and patted him on the back in approval as he gave his orders. "Beta Pride, Beta Ambush, move in. I want our perps lined up, asses to the floor. Agent Taylor, Agent Stone, see if you can get any information out of them."

As soon as their fellow agents from Beta Pride and Beta Ambush showed up, they left the perps to them, and Sloane motioned for Dex to follow. Along the way they removed their ballistic helmets and handed them to one of the agents standing by. They headed into the main structure, which was still smoky from Calvin and Hobbs's entry.

"What have we got?" Sloane asked as they took in their surroundings. The aluminum structure was supposed to be a three-car garage but instead had been set up as a base, with insulated walls, rows of metal shelving running down two of the walls, a third wall strewn with corkboards containing maps, newspaper articles, invoices, and a host of other random paperwork. In the center of the room were three large metal tables with supplies, boxes, burner phones, masonry tools, and weapons. Dex caught Hobbs's gaze and followed the silent agent's finger pointing to one of the large shelving units. Calvin joined his partner and called them over.

"Sulfuric acid, nitroglycerine, batteries, timers." Calvin picked up a box of heavy-duty nails. "From the looks of it, they weren't thinking about just taking out buildings."

Sick bastards. It was bad enough they wanted to plant bombs, but to build them with the specific purpose of killing and maiming innocent citizens? How deluded could they be to think they'd be doing good? Like crime in this city wasn't bad enough, now they had a whole new level of fucked-up to deal with.

"Any explosive devices already constructed?" Sloane asked.

Calvin shook his head. "No, just the materials, though Hobbs says they'd need more than this. He thinks maybe they were in early stages, collecting supplies, getting ready to build the bombs." He cast Hobbs a glance, and his large Therian partner nodded somberly.

"Okay, thanks, guys." Sloane let out a sigh, and Dex knew what his partner was thinking. Unless one of those bastards out there spilled, they wouldn't have much to go on. Getting these assholes off the street was a win, but until they had Isaac Pearce, the danger was nowhere near over. Who knew how many more bases just like this one were out there. How many already had devices waiting to go off?

Dex stepped up to the corkboards, hoping to glean some information, anything that might give them a clue as to where to find the Order's leader. "Everything's so neat."

"What do you mean?"

Sloane joined him, and Dex waved a hand over one of the corkboards. "All the maps are brand new, like they'd just been bought, and they're not of any specific locale. There's a street map of Brooklyn, a subway map of New York City, a bike map of Manhattan, and I'm pretty sure that one there of this area is an internet printout. The news articles are perfectly clipped, and all from the last two months. They pinned up the invoices, for Christ's sake. What bomber pins up their supply invoices? Are they planning on writing off the expenses?" He leaned in closer. "They're also all dated two months ago." Looking around the room, he strode back over to one of the shelves, where he ran a gloved finger over one of the timers. "There's a thin layer of dust on most of the supplies. Like they'd been placed on the shelves and not touched since. They could have been waiting for orders, or...."

"They could have been waiting for us," Sloane finished. He stroked his jaw. "Good job, Dex. You're right. This all seems too... easy. Let's see if anyone's cracked." He tapped his earpiece. "Cael?"

"Call in the CSAs?" Cael replied over their earpiece.

"Yeah. I want this place swept from corner to corner, and I want to be notified as soon as they get the detailed inventory attached to the case file."

"You got it."

Dex followed Sloane outside, where fifteen perps were sitting on the ground in a neat row, hands secured behind their backs, with nearly twice the number of heavily armed agents positioned around them in case someone got a stupid idea in their head. It was amazing what some criminals did when they were desperate. Just as the thought crossed his mind, one of the men jumped to his feet and started running.

Ash stared after the guy. "Where the fuck does he think he's going?"

With an agent drawing in from every angle, the guy came to a skidding halt, then stunned them all by jumping into the East River, where he proceeded to sputter, gasp, and in between drowning, call out for help.

"Seriously?" Dex had seen some pretty stupid shit in his time, but this one was right up there with the guy who tried to steal his patrol car with him in it back when he'd been an HPF rookie.

Ash let out a snort of laughter. "What an asshat."

After losing a round of rock-paper-scissors, one of Beta Ambush's Therian agents started stripping, cursing up a storm the whole way. Down to his colorful boxers and flipping off his fellow teammates whistling and throwing catcalls at him, he dove into the river, popping back out a few breaths later and dragging the wheezing man with him. The dark-haired agent pulled himself up with one hand and tossed the man up onto the dirt with the other.

The agent climbed out, snatched the towel from a teammate, and glared at their arrestees. "That's the last time I'm doing that. Someone else wants to be a moron, you're going to drown. Shit, that water's cold." He gave a sniff. "Ugh, it reeks. Am I going to be quarantined? This shit smells toxic."

His teammates laughed until Sloane held up a hand, silencing everyone. He stepped up to the line of somber-looking men, a couple looking no older than Cael. In fact, one in particular caught Dex's attention. The kid was sixteen, seventeen at most.

"Where's Isaac Pearce?" Sloane demanded. He paced slowly in front of them, his intense amber gaze studying their perps. Dex wasn't surprised to find fear creeping into some of their defiant gazes. None of them looked like hardened criminals. Standing over six and a half feet tall and weighing 240 pounds without the eighty pounds of equipment strapped to him, Sloane Brodie was imposing to most even when he wasn't in intimidation mode. Add the fact he was a Therian, with the government tattoo on his thick neck marking him as a jaguar Therian, and the twenty-odd years of field experience, and you'd have to be dumber than the guy who swan-dived into the river not to be scared shitless.

"Do you realize the severity of your situation? Do you think the THIRDS takes terrorism lightly? Your so-called leader murdered an officer of the law in front of the world. He's made threats against innocent civilians, against innocent children. He's looking at life in prison if he's lucky. This is your chance to do the right thing, to save what's left of your future."

One beer-gutted idiot spat at Sloane's feet. "We'll never talk to you, Therian freak. Your kind is a mistake. The Human race is superior. You're nothing more than a glorified pet. Your kind should be locked away in zoos with the rest of the animals or put down. Humans for dominance!" The guy started chanting, and Dex rolled his eyes. "Humans for dominance! Humans for—"

Sloane's boot against the guy's chest, knocking him over and onto his bound-up arms, put a stop to the chanting. It wasn't even a kick. A tap from Sloane was enough to send the guy tipping over and flailing like a turtle on his shell trying to right himself. Dex put a gloved fist to his mouth to keep himself from laughing. "Anyone have something useful to say?" Sloane asked.

Dex studied the silent, glaring group, his gaze landing on the teenager again. The kid swallowed hard, his eyes not moving from the ground. An older man with a strong resemblance knelt beside him. Dex tapped his earpiece. "Sloane." His partner glanced at him and without a word walked over, following Dex to one side.

"What's up?"

"I think we should try the Deceptive Dash."

Sloane arched an eyebrow at him. "You think it'll work?"

"That kid's ready to shit a brick. I'm thinking the guy next to him is his old man. Probably dragged him into this mess."

His partner rubbed his jaw, then nodded. "Okay." Sloane turned and signaled Ash over.

"What's going on?" the surly agent asked, and Dex could tell Sloane was trying hard not to smile when he spoke.

"We're going with the Deceptive Dash."

As expected, Ash let out a low groan. "Fuck me." He glared at Sloane. "I can't believe you not only allowed him to make this a thing, but you let him name it."

Sloane shrugged, his eyes lit up with amusement. "You couldn't come up with anything better."

"Because I didn't agree with the stupid idea."

"Yeah, well, it's effective, so suck it up." Sloane gave him a hearty pat on the shoulder, chuckling at their teammate's pout.

"Who's the target?" Ash grumbled.

"The kid." Dex tapped his earpiece. "Cael, drive the BearCat up."

"Copy that."

Dex headed toward the approaching BearCat and hopped into the back when his brother opened the doors.

"What's up?"

"We're doing the Deceptive Dash." Dex positioned himself to one side of the truck, hearing Ash cursing and growling as he approached.

"I can't believe you convinced Sloane to adopt that as an official strategy," Cael said with a laugh, settling in behind the surveillance console. Guess his brother was going to stick around for the show. "Ash *hates* it."

Dex wriggled his brows. "I know." Though he knew Ash's disapproval of the maneuver stemmed from it being Dex's idea and that it worked. His teammate especially didn't approve of having his name married with Dex's to form "Dash." For all his bitching, Ash couldn't deny their clashing personalities had a way of providing results when it came to interrogations. Ash was the kind of guy who made babies cry just by looking at them. The maneuver was less "bad cop/good cop," and more "holy fuck get him away from me/I'll talk to you because you're not psychotic." The best part was, there was little acting involved.

"Get the fuck in there." Ash shoved the wide-eyed teen into the back of the BearCat so roughly he stumbled. Dex caught him before he could run head-first into something and knock himself out.

"Jesus, Keeler, take it easy." Dex ducked his head to look at the kid. "You okay?"

The kid pressed his lips together, his brows furrowed. Dex motioned to the long bench where the team usually sat.

"Why don't you take a seat, um…. What's your name?"

"You gonna sing him a lullaby too, Daley?" Ash snorted.

Dex ignored Ash, his focus on the kid who'd reluctantly taken a seat on the bench. "What's your name?"

He received no reply. Ash stormed over and grabbed a fistful of the kid's shirt, hauling him off his feet with a snarl. "He asked you a fucking question. Are you going to cooperate, or am I going to have to shift and pick my teeth with your scrawny ass bones?"

Dex schooled his expression, doing his best not to laugh at Ash's cheesy lines. The kid's eyes widened, a squeak escaping him when Ash dropped him roughly onto the seat and loomed over him. "You got five seconds to state your name before I get really pissed. Five."

"Keeler," Dex sighed. "That's not going to help."

Ash rounded on him, poking him in the vest. "That's your problem, Daley. Too busy making daisy chains and cracking jokes to get your hands dirty."

"What the hell's that supposed to mean?" Dex planted his hands on his hips. Ash stepped closer, his voice a low growl, but Dex wasn't intimidated.

"It means you don't got the balls to get in there and do what you gotta do, always trying to be the good guy."

"I *am* the good guy. We're all the good guys! Screw you, man. I know how to do my job, and just because I don't go around scaring old ladies or trying to make it rain vengeance and wrath, doesn't mean I'm afraid to get my hands dirty."

Nostrils flaring, Ash stormed over to the kid and lifted him off his seat again. "Now you listen to me, you little shit. Every minute you spend not talking is another minute I gotta be in here with that gummy-bear-eating, Cheesy-Doodle-crunching, eighties-music-singing asshole, and that puts me in a bad mood. Do you want to put me in a bad mood?"

The kid shook his head fervently.

"Then answer his goddamn questions, or I swear on my momma's grave I'm gonna make you wish you were never born."

"Simon!" the kid burst out. "My name's S-Simon Russell."

Ash dropped the kid roughly onto his ass before turning to bark at Dex, "Get on with it, Daley."

Dex took a seat beside Simon, who was looking rattled and miserable, his shoulders slumped and his wary gaze going from Ash to Dex.

"I apologize for my teammate, Simon. He gets cranky when it's time for his sippy cup of OJ and a nap." Dex could have sworn he saw the end of Simon's lips twitch. "My name's Agent Daley, and despite what you might think, I'm here to help you."

Simon looked Dex over, assessing him. "Dad says all Human THIRDS agents are traitors to their race."

The words were low, but Dex could hear the uncertainty in them. Dex would bet his salary the kid never would have gotten involved in this kind of thing if his fuckwit of a father hadn't filled his head with hateful nonsense. "I'm not a traitor, Simon. I'm just a regular guy trying to do the right thing. It's my job to

protect innocent citizens and help those who are feeling lost. I believe everyone has a chance to lead a safe,
happy life, no matter their species. You know, I was
an HPF officer before I became a THIRDS agent, just
like my dad was."

Simon tilted his head and shifted slightly. Dex
knew everything he needed to know about the young
man in that instant, and he continued while he had Simon's attention.

"My dad was a homicide detective for the Sixth
precinct. He and his best friend Tony were the best
at what they did. I was so proud of him. My friends
would get sick and tired of me telling them how great
my dad was," he said with a chuckle, still feeling a
squeeze to his heart when he thought of his father. A
day didn't go by when he didn't miss his parents. "He
was my hero."

"Was?" Simon asked with a frown.

"Yeah, he was killed during the riots, along with
my mom." Dex let out a sigh and shook his head.
"He'd gone off to deal with the riots on several occasions while on the job, and then he goes out to the
movies one night with my mom, their date night"—he
swallowed hard, his gaze on his gloved hands clasped
in front of him—"and there was a shootout at the movie complex. My dad tried to get everyone out, including my mom. She… got hit in the crossfire. My dad
got shot in the chest trying to save her."

"I'm sorry," Simon mumbled, looking even more
deflated.

Dex gave a sniff and blinked back the sting in
his eyes. Twenty-eight years and it still felt as though
it were yesterday. "Yeah, I miss them, a lot. But, soon

after, Tony adopted me, and a few months later, I got me a baby brother. I wouldn't trade him in for anything. You got any brothers or sisters?" He didn't know what possessed him to share what had happened to his parents with Simon, but as soon as he started, it came tumbling out. Simon was young. He had his whole future ahead of him, if he would only stand up for what he wanted, not what his father wanted for him.

Simon nodded. "An older brother. Matthew. He lives in Boston now."

At least Matthew had gotten away. "He a good big brother?" Dex asked, noting the way Simon's eyes lit up. Dex tried not to curse. The kid was younger than he'd anticipated. Fifteen at most.

"He's awesome. He always looked out for me, played video games with me. We got into fights, but brothers do. He never thought he was too cool to hang out with me, even when his friends teased him about it. What about you?"

Dex smiled widely. "Am I a good big brother? I don't know. Let's find out." He turned his head, grinning at Cael. "What do you say? Be gentle."

"Aside being really annoying sometimes," Cael replied, his smile reaching his eyes, "yeah, you're an awesome big brother."

Dex turned back to Simon whose jaw was all but hitting the floor. When he recuperated, he sputtered. "*He's* your brother? But… but he's a Therian!"

"Tell me something, Simon. If something happened and you ended up… different, would Matthew turn you away?"

Simon opened his mouth, then seemed to think better of it. His shoulders slumped, and he shook his head. "No. He'd love me no matter what. I know he would."

"So why would I do that to my little brother? He's a regular guy, just like you." Dex shrugged. "Maybe his DNA's different, but I love him just like your big brother loves you. He's also the only guy who can kick my ass at video games. He's a total nerd."

"Pot, meet kettle," Cael snorted.

Dex put his hand on Simon's shoulder. "Something tells me Matthew doesn't share your dad's views."

"No. They fought a lot. Dad had always told us Therians were wrong. Abominations from hell trying to corrupt God's children. Matthew believed it at first."

"But then?"

"He met Jenny."

"Ah." Dex smiled knowingly. "Your brother fell in love with a Therian."

"Yeah. I was so scared for him. When Dad found out, he went nuts. Threatened Matthew, but Matthew refused to leave Jenny, so Dad kicked him out of the house, said he was dead to him. Dad told me I no longer had a brother, but I couldn't do it. I couldn't act like Matt was dead. I wanted so bad to go with him, but Matt was only sixteen, and Dad threw him out without any money, didn't even give him a chance to get some clothes." Simon's frown deepened, his voice growing angry. "How could he do that? How could he kick Matt out like that? I wanted to hurt Dad so bad, but I was small and scared. I hated him." He hung his head, tears in his eyes. "God, I'm such a pussy."

"Hey." Dex squeezed his shoulder. "Don't be so hard on yourself. There wasn't much you could do, and your dad's bad decisions are on him. It's okay to be scared, but you're not a kid anymore, Simon. You can make your own decisions. What your dad's involved in will put him away for a long time. He wants to hurt innocent Therians, Therians like Jenny, like my little brother." Simon's gaze shifted to Cael before guiltily darting away. "Is that what you want for yourself? Do you want to give up any chance of a future, at seeing Matt again, for your dad's mistakes?"

Simon bit down on his bottom lip, and after what seemed like an eternity, he shook his head. "No, I don't want to go to prison, not for that asshole. I never wanted to do this, but he told me if I was going to be a Therian fucker like my brother, then I should leave, that I'd be better off dead." A tear rolled down his reddened cheek. He met Dex's gaze. "Can you really help me?"

Dex nodded. "I promise, Simon. I will do everything in my power to get you to Matt, but I need you to help me."

"Okay." Simon gave him a curt nod, his expression determined. "What do I need to do?"

"I need you to tell me everything you know about Isaac Pearce."

CHARLIE COCHET is an author by day and artist by night. Always quick to succumb to the whispers of her wayward muse, no star is out of reach when following her passion. From adventurous agents and sexy shifters to society gentlemen and hardboiled detectives, there's bound to be plenty of mischief for her heroes to find themselves in—and plenty of romance, too!

Currently residing in Central Florida, Charlie is at the beck and call of a rascally Doxiepoo bent on world domination. When she isn't writing, she can usually be found reading, drawing, or watching movies. She runs on coffee, thrives on music, and loves to hear from readers.

Website: www.charliecochet.com
Blog: www.charliecochet.com/blog
Email: charlie@charliecochet.com
Facebook: www.facebook.com/charliecochet
Twitter: @charliecochet
Tumblr: www.charliecochet.tumblr.com
Pinterest: www.pinterest.com/charliecochet
Goodreads: www.goodreads.com/CharlieCochet
Instagram: www.instagram.com/charliecochet
THIRDS HQ: www.thirdshq.com
Would you like to receive news on Charlie Cochet's upcoming books, exclusive content, giveaways, first access to extras, and more? Sign up for Charlie's newsletter: bit.ly/CharlieCochetNews

Follow me on BookBub (www.bookbub.com/authors/charlie-cochet)!

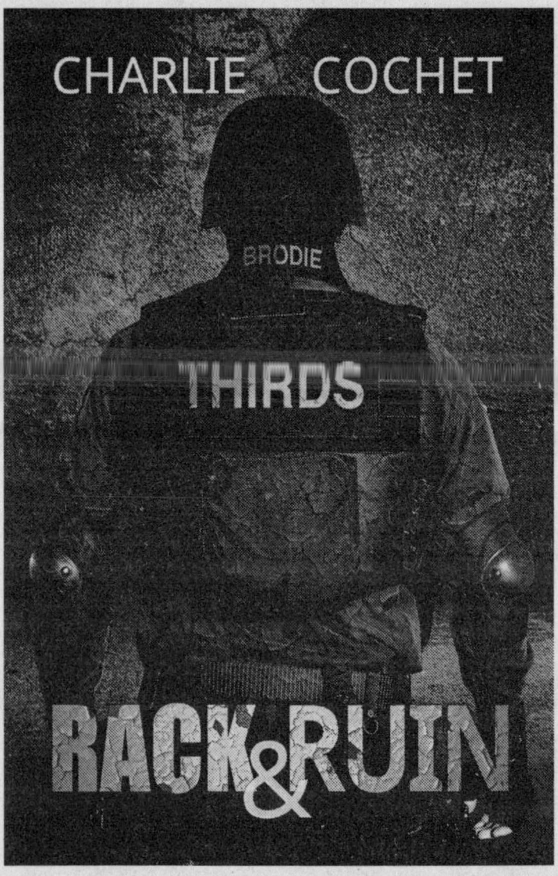
CHARLIE COCHET
BRODIE
THIRDS
RACK & RUIN

Sequel to *Blood & Thunder*
THIRDS: Book Three

New York City's streets are more dangerous than
ever with the leaderless Order of Adrasteia and the
Ikelos Coalition, a newly emerged Therian group, at
war. Innocent civilians are caught in the crossfire and
although the THIRDS round up more and more members of the Order in the hopes of keeping the volatile
group from reorganizing, the members of the Coalition continue to escape and wreak havoc in the name
of vigilante justice.

Worse yet, someone inside the THIRDS has been
feeding the Coalition information. It's up to Destructive Delta to draw out the mole and put an end to the
war before anyone else gets hurt. But to get the job
done, the team will have to work through the aftereffects of the Therian Youth Center bombing. A skir-
mish with Coalition members leads Agent Dexter J.
Daley to a shocking discovery and suddenly it be-
comes clear that the random violence isn't so random.
There's more going on than Dex and Sloane originally
believed, and their fiery partnership is put to the test.
As the case takes an explosive turn, Dex and Sloane
are in danger of losing more than their relationship.

www.dreamspinnerpress.com

Sequel to *Rack & Ruin*
THIRDS: Book Four

After an attack by the Coalition leaves THIRDS Team Leader Sloane Brodie critically injured, agent Dexter J. Daley swears to make Beck Hogan pay for what he's done. But Dex's plans for retribution are short-lived. With Ash still on leave with his own injuries, Sloane in the hospital, and Destructive Delta in the Coalition's crosshairs, Lieutenant Sparks isn't taking any chances. Dex's team is pulled from the case, with the investigation handed to Team Leader Sebastian Hobbs. Dex refuses to stand by while another team goes after Hogan, and decides to put his old HPF detective skills to work to find Hogan before Theta Destructive, no matter the cost.

With a lengthy and painful recovery ahead of him, the last thing Sloane needs is his partner out scouring the city, especially when the lies—however well-intentioned—begin to spiral out of control. Sloane is all too familiar with the desire to retaliate, but some things are more important, like the man who's pledged to stand beside him. As Dex starts down a dark path, it's up to Sloane to show him what's at stake, and finally put a name to what's in his heart.

www.dreamspinnerpress.com

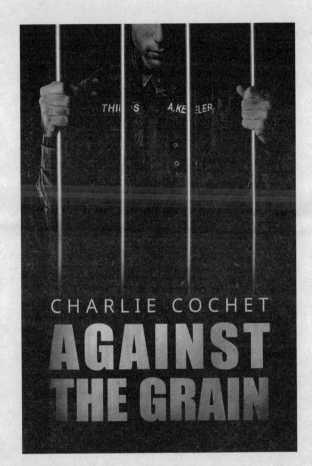

CHARLIE COCHET

AGAINST
THE GRAIN

Sequel to *Rise & Fall*
THIRDS: Book Five

As the fiercest Defense Agent at the THIRDS, Destructive Delta's Ash Keeler is foul-mouthed and foul-tempered. But his hard-lined approach always yields results, evident by his recent infiltration of the Coalition. Thanks to Ash's skills and the help of his team, they finally put an end to the murdering extremist group for good, though not before Ash takes a bullet to save teammate Cael Maddock. As a result, Ash's secrets start to surface, and he can no longer ignore what's in his heart.

Cael Maddock is no stranger to heartache. As a Recon Agent for Destructive Delta, he has successfully maneuvered through the urban jungle that is New York City, picking up his own scars along the way. Yet nothing he's ever faced has been more of a challenge than the heart of Ash Keeler, his supposedly straight teammate. Being in love isn't the only danger he and Ash face as wounds reopen and new secrets emerge, forcing them to question old loyalties.

www.dreamspinnerpress.com

Sequel to *Against the Grain*
THIRDS: Book Six

Calvin Summers and Ethan Hobbs have been best
friends since childhood, but somewhere along the line,
their friendship evolved into something more. With
the Therian Youth Center bombing, Calvin realizes
just how short life can be and no longer keeps his feelings for his best friend a secret. Unfortunately, change
is difficult for Ethan; most days he does well to deal
with his selective mutism and social anxiety. Calvin's
confession adds a new struggle for Ethan, one he fears
might cost him the friendship that's been his whole
world for as long as he can remember.

As partners and Defense Agents at the THIRDS,
being on Destructive Delta is tough at the best of
times, but between call-outs and life-threatening situations, Calvin and Ethan not only face traversing the
challenges of their job, but also working toward a future as more than friends.

www.dreamspinnerpress.com

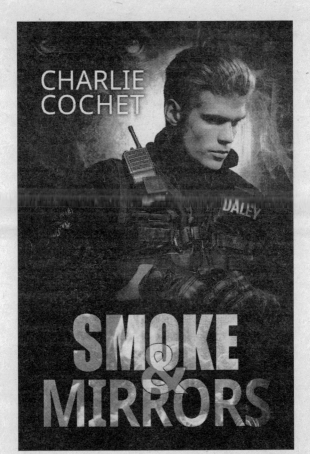

CHARLIE
COCHET

DALEY

SMOKE
&
MIRRORS

Sequel to *Catch a Tiger by the Tail*
THIRDS: Book Seven

Life for Dexter J. Daley has never been easy, but he's always found a way to pick himself back up with a smile on his face. Taken from his home and the arms of Sloane Brodie, his boyfriend and THIRDS partner, Dex finds himself in a situation as mysterious and lethal as the Therian interrogating him. Dex learns what he's secretly believed all along: his parents' death wasn't an accident.

Discovering the whole truth about John and Gina Daley's homicide sets off a series of events that will change Dex and Sloane's life forever. As buried secrets rise to the surface and new truths are revealed, Dex and Sloane's love for each other is put to the test, with more than their relationship on the line. If traversing the waters of murder and secret government agencies wasn't enough, something inexplicable has been happening to Dex—and nothing will ever be the same.

www.dreamspinnerpress.com

CHARLIE COCHET

THIRDS

DALEY

THICK & THIN

Includes
GUMMY BEARS
& GRENADES
A THIRDS Novella

Thick & Thin
Sequel to *Smoke & Mirrors*
THIRDS: Book Eight

In a matter of days, Dex has been kidnapped, tortured, killed, revived, become half-Therian, offered the chance to become a spy, and accepted a proposal to marry his jaguar Therian boyfriend, Sloane Brodie. Dex is still trying to wrap his head around everything, but he has to move forward. After the events of *Smoke & Mirrors*, Dex and Sloane find themselves in one of the most frightening situations of all: revealing the truth to their Destructive Delta family. When the dust settles, nothing will ever be the same, and it's up to Dex to prove that in the face of change, the one thing that remains the same is family.

Gummy Bears & Grenades
A THIRDS Novella

THIRDS agent Dexter J. Daley can't wait to marry his fiancé, Team Leader Sloane Brodie, but first he's looking forward to celebrating his bachelor party—which he intends to be a shenanigans-free evening of getting his groove on with family and friends.

Of course events don't work out as planned, but for Dex that's nothing new. One thing is for sure, dodging drug dealers and hired thugs amid booze, dancing—and even a bear costume—will guarantee it's a night Dex will never forget. Now he just needs to survive all the fun.

Enjoy this bonus story from the THIRDS universe. These events occur between *Darkest Hour Before Dawn* and *Tried & True* in the series timeline. While reading this story would enhance your experience of the THIRDS series, it is not essential to read before *Tried & True*.

www.dreamspinnerpress.com

Sequel to *Thick & Thin*
THIRDS: Book Nine

Life for Dexter J. Daley has never been easy, but he's always found a way to pick himself back up with a smile on his face. Taken from his home and the arms of Sloane Brodie, his boyfriend and THIRDS partner, Dex finds himself in a situation as mysterious and lethal as the Therian interrogating him. Dex learns what he's secretly believed all along: his parents' death wasn't an accident.

Discovering the whole truth about John and Gina Daley's homicide sets off a series of events that will change Dex and Sloane's life forever. As buried secrets rise to the surface and new truths are revealed, Dex and Sloane's love for each other is put to the test, with more than their relationship on the line. If traversing the waters of murder and secret government agencies wasn't enough, something inexplicable has been happening to Dex—and nothing will ever be the same.

www.dreamspinnerpress.com

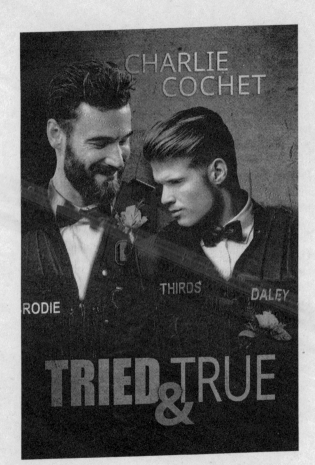

Sequel to *Darkest Hour Before Dawn*
THIRDS: Book Ten

When THIRDS agent Dexter J. Daley met Team Leader Sloane Brodie, he couldn't have imagined how slamming into his new partner—literally—would shake both their worlds. Now four years later, they've faced dangers, fought battles both personal and professional... and fallen deeply in love. Now their big moment is finally in sight, and they're ready to stand up together and make it official. Unfortunately, as the countdown to their big day begins, an enemy declares war on the THIRDS....

With their family in danger, Dex and Sloane are put to the test on how far into darkness they'll walk to save those they love. As secrets are unearthed, a deadly betrayal is revealed, and Dex and Sloane must call on their Destructive Delta family for one last hurrah to put an end to the secret organization responsible for so much devastation.

Dex and Sloane will have plenty of bullets to dodge on the way to the altar, but with happiness within their grasp, they are determined to get there come hell or high water....

www.dreamspinnerpress.com